# ANCIENT JEWISH NOVELS

# Ancient Jewish Novels

*An Anthology*

Edited and Translated by
Lawrence M. Wills

2002

OXFORD
UNIVERSITY PRESS

Oxford New York
Auckland Bangkok Buenos Aires Cape Town Chennai
Dar es Salaam Delhi Hong Kong Istanbul Karachi Kolkata
Kuala Lumpur Madrid Melbourne Mexico City Mumbai Nairobi
São Paulo Shanghai Singapore Taipei Tokyo Toronto

and an associated company in Berlin



Published by Oxford University Press, Inc.,
198 Madison Avenue, New York, New York 10016

www.oup.com



Library of Congress Cataloging-in-Publication Data
Ancient Jewish novels : an anthology / edited and translated by Lawrence M. Wills.
p. cm.
Includes bibliographical references and index.
ISBN 0-19-515141-0; ISBN 0-19-515142-9 (pbk.)
1. Greek fiction, Hellenistic—Jewish authors—Translations into English.
2. Jews—History—To 70 A.D.—Fiction. 3. Jewish fiction.
4. Apocryphal books (Old Testament)—Translations into English.
I. Wills, Lawrence M. (Lawrence Mitchell), 1954–
PA3632.A55 2002
883'.01098924—dc21 2001052049



2 4 6 8 9 7 5 3 1

Printed in the United States of America
on acid-free paper

# PREFACE

It is remarkable that the ancient Jewish novelistic tradition is so little known by modern readers. Though certain texts may be somewhat familiar, others are totally unknown, and the genre as a whole has often gone unrecognized. This situation appears to be changing, however, and with the recent increased interest in ancient Greek and Roman novels and in the social world of ancient Judaism, it seemed an appropriate time to publish new translations of these novels and related texts.

I have been working on the translations of these texts for several years, struggling with a number of intriguing problems connected with them: What texts should be included and why? What style in English best communicates the reading experience of the ancient audience? What ancient comparisons are relevant and illuminating? In this resultant attempt to introduce modern readers to the world of popular Jewish literature in the Greco-Roman period, there are still question marks hanging over many important issues, but the question marks can remain.

There are a number of people who have influenced my perceptions of the novels over the years, but a few have had a particular imprint on this collection: Richard Horsley, Gregory Nagy, and Christine Thomas. I am also indebted to the members of the Ancient Fiction Group of the Society of Biblical Literature for creating an invaluable forum for the study of ancient novels and related literature, and to the faculty and students at Episcopal

Divinity School for their encouragement and support. Cynthia Read and the editorial staff at Oxford University Press have done a marvelous job of bringing this project to fruition. Finally, my family, Shelley, Jessica, and Daniel, have been very encouraging of all my projects, but more important, they have been a source of that creative chaos that makes for inspiration. I would like to thank them as well.

# CONTENTS

# A NOTE ON TEXTS AND TRANSLATIONS

The translations of the books of the Greek Bible are based on the *Vetus Testamentum Graecum* (Göttingen: Vandenhoeck & Ruprecht). For *Greek Esther* I have translated the B-text of the Septuagint edited by Robert Hanhart (vol. 8.3, 1966); for *Susanna* and *Bel and the Dragon* I translated the Theodotionic text as found in Joseph Ziegler, *Susanna, Daniel, Bel et Draco* (vol. 16.2, 1954); for *Tobit,* the Sinaiticus version as edited by Robert Hanhart (vol. 8.5, 1983); for *Judith,* the text edited by Robert Hanhart, *Iudith* (vol. 8.4, 1979). The text of *Third Maccabees* used for the translation is that of Robert Hanhart, *Maccabaeorum liber III* (vol. 9.3, 1960).

The Greek text of *The Marriage and Conversion of Aseneth* used for this translation is the b text edited by Christoph Burchard in the *Dielheimer Blätter zum Alten Testament* 14 (1979) 2–53, with notations from the d text edited by Marc Philonenko, *Joseph et Aséneth: introduction, texte critique, traduction et notes* (Leiden: Brill, 1968). The Greek text of Artapanus is found in Carl R. Holladay, *Fragments from Hellenistic Jewish Authors. Volume 1: Historians* (Chico, Calif.: Scholars Press, 1983). The texts for *The Tobiad Romance* and *The Royal Family of Adiabene* were taken from the Loeb edition, *Josephus* (10 vols.; Cambridge: Harvard University Press/London: Heinemann, 1961). Volume 9 is edited by Ralph Marcus, and volume 10 by Louis H. Feldman. The translation of the *Testament of Joseph* is based on the text of R. H. Charles, *The Greek*

*Versions of the Testaments of the Twelve Patriarchs* (3rd ed.; Hildesheim: Olms, 1966). For the text of *Testament of Job* I used the SV text found in Robert Kraft, et al., *The Testament of Job According to the SV Text* (Missoula, Mont.: Scholars Press, 1974), with occasional emendations utilizing the P text edited by S. P. Brock, *Testamentum Iobi* (Leiden: Brill, 1967). The translation of *Testament of Abraham* was based on the longer A text edited by Francis Schmidt, *Le testament grèc d'Abraham* (Tübingen, Germany: Mohr [Paul Siebeck] 1986).

# ANCIENT JEWISH NOVELS

ONE

# INTRODUCTION

Although the Hebrew Bible is full of good storytelling, there arose among Jews in the Greco-Roman period a new genre for retelling Bible stories and for composing new stories as well: the novel. This collection brings together both well-known and little-known Jewish texts from the Greco-Roman period that all have the goal of entertaining through written prose narrative. The novels and novelistic texts in this collection use direct and emotional, even manipulative means to rouse and entertain the audience. The settings have historical and geographical sweep and the pomp of royal courts. Motifs and themes typical of novels are found here: love, danger, adventure, emotion, and virtue; piety and prayer; character and motives; interior life and psychologizing—in rudimentary form, to be sure, but all the more interesting because they represent the novel in the making. The novels illuminate the social and psychological life of Jews in an era that in some ways was strangely like our own.

In recent years there has been a significant increase in scholarly interest in popular literature in the ancient world. Five Greek and two Roman novels have been studied extensively: Chariton, *Chaereas and Callirhoe;* Xenophon of Ephesus, *An Ephesian Tale;* Achilles Tatius, *Leucippe and Clitophon;* Longus, *Daphnis and Chloe;* Heliodorus, *An Ephesian Story;* Apuleius, *The Golden Ass;* and Petronius, *Satyricon*. They have moved from a marginal position in ancient studies, where they were once looked down on as greatly inferior to the "classical" genres, to occupy a more important place in historical and literary research. In addition, lesser known ancient works, not quite full-blown novels in their own right but still partaking of some of the same entertainment values, are also being brought under the same microscope.[1] The Jewish novelistic literature of this period is also now beginning to be studied in this context. What has resulted is a long overdue attempt to bring all ancient popular literature into the same area of study. It is the goal of this collection to make the Jewish material available in one volume, as has already been done for the Greek novel.[2]

Five of the Jewish texts here can be classified as novels proper: *Greek Esther, Greek Daniel* (only part of which is included here), *Tobit, Judith,* and *The Marriage and Conversion of Aseneth* (also called *Joseph and Aseneth*). These narratives take as protagonists little-known or totally unknown figures from Jewish history, and as their main themes, Jewish piety and identity. The arena of the dramatic action can be a high court (*Greek Esther, Greek Daniel*), a middle court (*Judith*), a low court (*Susanna*), or a mix of high court and the household (*Tobit, Marriage and Conversion of Aseneth*), yet extended family and the responsibility for other Jews is never far from the center. The protagonist who experiences the threats and challenges is also more likely in these novels to be a woman. This attention to leading women characters is typical of the ancient Greek novel as well as the early modern European novel. While the Jewish novels place a female protagonist at the very

1. For instance, Xenophon of Athens, *Cyropaedia; Ninus and Semiramus; The Story of Ahikar; Sesonchosis; Petubastis; The Alexander Romance,* and *Life of Aesop.*

2. The Greek novels and most of the related novelistic literature can be found in B. P. Reardon, ed., *Collected Ancient Greek Novels* (Berkeley: University of California Press, 1989). See also William Hansen, ed., *Anthology of Ancient Popular Literature* (Bloomington: Indiana University Press, 1998), and Miriam Lichtheim, *Ancient Egyptian Literature: A Book of Readings* (3 vols.; Berkeley: University of California Press, 1973–76). Each of the Roman novels is available in separate editions.

center of the action, unlike the Greek novels, which make the woman a partner in a romantic union, the Jewish novels more often present her all alone. Other texts in this collection are the historical novels and the testaments, or last words of the patriarchs, which make use of novelistic techniques even though on the surface they appear to belong to other genres. Within this last category we also find one text, *Testament of Abraham,* which is a satirical novel; just as in the Greek and Roman world there are some novels that overturn the usual picture of a pious protagonist, so is there here one among Jewish novels.

## What Is a Novel?

For this collection, the novel can be defined as written popular narrative fiction, expanded significantly beyond a single episode, which focuses on character and virtue. Each part of this definition can be described briefly.

*Written:* For many years scholars have made a sharp distinction between written literature and oral compositions, whether oral epic or oral prose stories. Literature composed in the written medium is very different from that based ultimately on oral traditions. This observation allowed for a fruitful investigation into the oral origins of many ancient texts, such as Homer, the Bible, Indian epic, and so on. A second generation of scholars on oral traditions, however, recognized the need to divide discourse into more than the two categories of written and oral, and to observe the peculiar rules of different kinds of discourse.[3] One such new

3. See especially John Miles Foley, *The Theory of Oral Composition: History and Methodology* (Bloomington: Indiana University Press, 1988), and Heda Jason, *Ethnopoetry: Form, Content, Function* (Bonn: Linguistica Biblica, 1977). Recent study has introduced an almost infinite number of kinds of discourse as scholars note closely the rules or tendencies of composition, transmission, and consumption of different popular types, such as pamphlets, decrees, news stories, jokes, sermonettes, and so on.

subcategory is popular literature, as opposed to "high" literary works on one hand and oral narratives on the other. Although Jewish novels in many cases probably originated as oral tales and legends (see the introductions to *Tobit* and *Greek Daniel*), the editing and expanding of these stories occurred at the written stage, and they were heavily influenced at that point by new literary techniques. Further, because they developed in a written medium, they are often quite different from the oral narratives that were included in the Hebrew Bible such as Ruth or Jonah, and different as well from the oral narratives ultimately recorded as part of the later midrashic collections of rabbinic Judaism.

*Popular:* Popular literature refers to texts that are written for entertainment and not for official use. Thus "popular" is defined not by the number of readers a text has attracted, but by the function of the text to entertain outside of official or professional circles. Because literacy was not common in the ancient world among the lower classes, and writing materials were still very expensive, popular literature was generally aimed at the wealthier classes. Still, popular written texts reflect a broader swath of society than do the official histories and aristocratic literary productions, and they often reveal to us the wealthier classes in more relaxed moments. The idea of a frivolous literature may even pose a challenge for us. Some readers today may be surprised or even uncomfortable with Jewish texts that are different from the Hebrew Bible and rabbinic literature, even though they may be is quite pious.

Popular literature differs from high literature in a number of ways. One scholar points out that popular literature depends upon a straightforwardness of presentation that often lacks subtlety or indirectness.[4] It is often dependent on an alternation of

4. The characteristics of popular literature outlined in this paragraph are analyzed by a number of scholars. On straightforwardness of presentation, see Hansen, ed., *Anthology of Ancient Popular Literature,* xiv–xxi; on maximum *peripeteia,* see Frank Kermode, *The Sense of an Ending: Studies in the Theory of Fic-*

tension and release that is more extreme than the *peripeteia* or reversal of classical drama; it is so extreme, sudden, and repetitious that it can be likened to myth or apocalypticism, as "maximum *peripeteia*." Another suggests that popular art values the importance of content over form, while high art values form over content and champions a "pure" aesthetic standard. Another lists a series of techniques common to popular literature, such as a composition process that utilizes interchangeable episodes which have no necessary order in the arc of the narrative as a whole. Popular literature is usually anonymous and indifferent to concerns of plagiarism or canonization, even though it is sometimes later canonized. The text is not fixed and variant versions are readily created. Popular literature also has an ambivalent relationship with tradition. On one hand, popular literature evolves quickly and reflects constant innovation; on the other, the innovation is rarely marked as an individual's artistic creation. High art, by contrast, honors traditional genres but at the same time emphasizes the uniqueness of the individual work of art and the individual artist. Further, in high art the demands that the work places upon the audience are often taken as a measure of its artistic qualities.

At the same time, it is important not to overstate or misrep-

---

*tion* (New York: Oxford, 1967), 18–19; on content over form, see Pierre Bourdieu, *Distinction: A Social Critique of the Judgement of Taste* (Cambridge, Mass.: Harvard University Press, 1984), 32–35; on interchangeable episodes, see Dorothy Bayer, *Der triviale Familien- und Liebesroman im 20. Jahrhundert* (2nd ed.; Tü bingen, Germany: Tübinger Vereinigung für Volkskunde, 1971), 52–57; on canonization, variant versions, and ambivalence about tradition, see Jason, *Ethnopoetry*, 5–7; on the demands of high art see Hans-Robert Jauss, "Literary History as a Challenge to Literary Theory," *New Literary History* 2 (1970): 15; in general see also John G. Cawelti, *Adventure, Mystery, and Romance: Formula Stories as Art and Popular Culture* (Chicago: University of Chicago Press, 1976), 18–19; and Oswald Ducrot and Tzvetan Todorov, *Encyclopedic Dictionary of the Sciences of Language* (Baltimore: Johns Hopkins University Press, 1979), 151.

resent the differences between high art and popular art. The view that high literature is marked by a higher aesthetic standard and that it is more demanding obscures the fact that much high art began as popular art. Shakespeare and Dickens come to mind as familiar examples. When they were introduced, they were perceived as typically popular, intended as entertainment and not demanding; it was only their rediscovery by a later audience that elevated them to acceptance within the canon of high art. One can already see how popular art of the twentieth century is making its way into the university courses on art or music history, not just as the history of popular art, but in some cases, such as the films of John Ford or the music of Duke Ellington, as high art as well.

*Narrative:* The novel is narrative in that it narrates events in order; this is not just an incidental aspect of the work but its central means of communication. Other genres, such as epic poetry and history, narrate events, so the novel is not unique in this regard. However, novels do not have the beauty of poetic language or the importance of events to sweep them along; only the compelling nature of the narrative itself will motivate the reader to continue.

What is interesting for the present collection is the way that testaments, which are not a narrative genre in origin, in some cases become novels by introducing narrative. The testament was a common type of text in the Judaism of the Greco-Roman period. It used the setting of the deathbed statements of an ancient Hebrew patriarch to present teachings with a strong ethical content. These testaments had a tendency to emphasize moral psychology and also to dramatize—two important elements of novels—thereby placing events in a narrative, novelistic context. Thus in *Testament of Joseph* we see novelistic explorations in what appears to us to be a poorly edited sermonic whole. This testament retells the Joseph story in a higher dramatic register. This evolutionary tendency within testaments finds its culmination in the *Testament of Job* and the *Testament of Abraham*. They are both coherent, fully told short novels with a beginning, a middle, and an end, at the same time that they outwardly retain the form of the last will and testament of the ancient patriarch.

*Fiction:* Written prose narrative can be used to describe the past (history) or a person's life (biography), but most would agree that the essence of the novel is the use of written prose narrative to describe events that never happened—in fact, that are invented. Fiction is an implied contract between author and reader in which both parties presume that the narrative is not attempting to recount actual events in the past. But this distinction between fiction and nonfiction is not as neat as one might assume. It is fascinating to consider which of the texts collected here were self-consciously written and read as fiction.

One may begin with texts that were more likely perceived as fiction: *Susanna* has a domestic setting, *Esther* and *Judith* are patently improbable, *Tobit* is like a fairy tale, *Bel and the Serpent* is a humorous exposé—are these therefore to be taken as fiction? It is interesting in this regard that several of the texts contain clearly impossible historical conditions: Esther is a Persian queen, Joseph in *The Marriage and Conversion of Aseneth* serves temporarily as the Pharaoh of Egypt, *Judith* is set in the reign of "Nebuchadnezzar, king of the Assyrians" (Nebuchadnezzar was king of the Babylonians), Daniel serves under "Darius the Mede" (Darius was king of the Persians), and *Tobit* mentions "Xerxes, king of Media" (Xerxes was king of the Persians). These kings were all famous enough in the ancient world to render it exceedingly unlikely that accidental errors crept in. Rather, these whimsical settings indicate that the audience probably experienced these texts as fictions.

Several other texts, however, appear to be histories, even if they seem fanciful and unbelievable by modern standards: *Third Maccabees, The Tobiad Romance, The Royal Family of Adiabene,* and Artapanus's *On Moses.* It is not clear where they would fit on a scale of fiction/nonfiction, and perhaps not all would be read in the same way. The sensationalist aspects of *Third Maccabees,* for example, could be contrasted with the more restrained and rational world of *Adiabene,* but that distinction does not aid us in determining which was read as fiction. Astounding miracles are just as likely to occur in ancient histories as in the novels. Further, the varieties of sensationalist history current in the Greco-Roman world would lead one to assume that these texts might indeed have a place in the history writing of the period.

Unfortunately, we cannot look to the ancients themselves for much help. We have no clear indication as to how the Jewish novels, nor the Greek and Roman novels, were read. There is no Hebrew, Greek, or Latin word for novel, although some more general terms may have been applied to novels, such as Greek *plasma.* As impressive as they are to modern readers in size and scope, it is striking that there is almost no mention of the Greek and Roman novels by ancient authors, especially in the early centuries of the genre. In the first century the Roman satirist Persius Flaccus makes a passing and somewhat contemptuous remark about people with unrefined tastes who read "Callirhoe," perhaps referring to Chariton's *Chaereas and Callirhoe.* In the third century Philostratus criticizes a certain Chariton, presumably the author of the novel, and in the fourth century Emperor Julian condemned the reading of *plasmata,* again a likely reference to novels.[5] But such offhand and minimal references are the most we have on the topic. When the idea of "fiction" is discussed, it is treated more as a theoretical possibility than a reality. Aristotle distinguished history, which communicates "what happened" (*ta genomena*), from poetry, which communicates "what might have

5. The references are Persius Flaccus 1.134; Philostratus, *Letter* 66; and Julian, *Letter* 63. For a discussion of some of these references and others as well, see Ewen Bowie, "The Readership of Greek Novels in the Ancient World," in *The Search for the Ancient Novel,* ed. James Tatum (Baltimore: Johns Hopkins University Press, 1994), 443–47.

happened" (*hoia an genoito*).[6] Out of the latter there arose at least the potential to consider prose fiction as well. By the first century C.E. a number of philosophers and rhetoricians discussed the category that we might call fiction. They divided narrative into three types: (1) *historia,* or true accounts of events that actually occurred; (2) *plasma* or *argumentum,* accounts narrating events that did not occur but that are like real events; and (3) *mythos* or *fabula,* accounts that narrate events that are not true and not similar to real events.[7] The second class, *plasma,* is most like fiction, but the rhetoricians do not say much about it, at least not prose fiction. It is also not clear that the ancients applied the category consistently. Plato, for example, who wrote before these theorists, considered the *Cyropaedia* of Xenophon of Athens to be historical, while Cicero, who had the full benefit of their reflection, thought it was fictitious.[8]

We have little direct evidence of how the Jewish texts were regarded as well. It is interesting to note that fragments of novelistic literature found at Qumran were written on smaller scrolls, what one scholar refers to as the "paperbacks of antiquity."[9] This fact indicates a reading function different from the many other

6. Aristotle, *Poetics* 1451a37–b11, 1460b13–23. On this see Margalit Finkelberg, *The Birth of Literary Fiction in Ancient Greece* (Oxford: Clarendon, 1998) 12–15.

7. Pseudo-Cicero, *Rhetorica ad Herennium* 1.8.12–13, Quintilian 2.4.2. See David Konstan, "The Invention of Fiction," in *Ancient Fiction and Early Christian Narrative,* ed. Ronald F. Hock, J. Bradley Chance, and Judith Perkins (Atlanta: Scholars Press, 1998), 3–18, and John Marincola, *Authority and Tradition in Ancient Historiography* (Cambridge: Cambridge University Press, 1997), 118.

8. Plato, *Laws* 3.694c–698a; Cicero, *Letters to His Brother Quintus* 1.1.23.

9. "Éditions de poche' de l'antiquité": J. T. Milik, "Les modèles araméens du livre d'Esther dans la grotte 4 de Qumrân," *Revue de Qumrân* 59 (1992): 363–65. On Josephus's treatment of Esther and Daniel, see Lawrence M. Wills, *The Jewish Novel in the Ancient World* (Ithaca, N.Y.: Cornell University Press, 1995), 222, and on the use of Judith and Esther as examples in the first century, see *First Clement* 55.4–5.

kinds of texts found there. Further, although some of the Jewish novels came to be included as part of the biblical canon and were later alluded to as narratives of historical events, they may have originally been composed and read merely as pious example-stories.

At the same time that there is a confusion regarding the attitudes of the ancients, questions are also being raised about the categories themselves. There is an increasing emphasis in recent scholarship on the ways in which history fictionalizes the past by interpreting it in a selective or biased way, while fiction reveals the historical conditions under which it was composed. That is, history fictionalizes and fiction historicizes. The result is that the boundary between history and fiction is seen as much less distinct than it once was, and we may propose instead that fiction and history, and therefore novel and history, be seen on a spectrum. Readers in the ancient world, much like readers of historical fiction today, may have often been blissfully unclear about whether their reading experience was *purely* fictitious or *purely* historical. The category "entertaining and exhilarating" brought the novels and historical novels together and outweighed the importance of distinguishing what is fiction from what is nonfiction. The distinction of fiction and nonfiction is perhaps more of a problem for modern readers and scholars than it was for the ancients, and this is probably the case precisely because prose fiction is now an accepted and honored category.

*Expanded beyond a single episode:* Part of the essence of the novel is that treatment of characters and events is extended; a novel contains more than one episode, and events occur over a period of time. Literary effects that are used elsewhere, such as dialogue or description, are often extended much further in novels than they would be in histories or biographies. Techniques for extending the narrative beyond a single episode are still sometimes quite primitive in ancient novels, however. These novels are often rightly called "episodic" because the many episodes seem interchangeable. Each one presents a situation of threat or tension and release and is guaranteed to be followed by a similar episode, that is, by a new tension and a new release. Greek, Roman, Jewish, and Christian novels are generally constructed, with greater or lesser efficiency, on this building plan. There appears to have been a desire on the part of the ancient author and reader to extend the reading experience beyond the single episode even before the means to do so were fully worked out. Thus the Book of Daniel in the Hebrew Bible consists of six separate, interchangeable legends about Daniel and his three companions in the courts of the great kings (Daniel 1–6) that likely circulated as a short novel before being combined with four apocalyptic visions (Daniel 7–12). *Susanna* and *Bel and the Serpent,* included in this collection, were simply new episodes that were added on to extend the text and render it more of a novel. In *Judith,* therefore, a major innovation is seen when despite the apparent simplicity of the style, a longer narrative is created that is not composed of interchangeable episodes but has a beginning, a middle, and an end. The author managed to extend the narrative beyond the size of Daniel without resorting to the insertion of separate episodes.

To be sure, the Jewish novels have not been extended as much as the Greek and Roman novels, nor are they as long as modern novels. Other labels, however, are not quite satisfactory. The "short story," for example, is a peculiarly modern invention which came about after the novel was established. It is a specialized study of a particular moment in time or a particular emotion, and intentionally it has very little sweep. The Jewish texts could be labeled "novellas," but this term too is usually applied to short works of fiction with a restricted sweep. Also the function of these narratives in Jewish society was essentially the same as was the case for Greek novels, and the movement in the direction of an extended narrative is clear. If we term them "short novels," we will not be far off the mark.

*Character and virtue:* Character is at the center of the discussion of the modern novel, but it is usually argued that in the Greek and Roman novels the protagonists are not depicted in a three-dimensional way; and the hallmark of the modern novel, which is character development—that is, the depiction of the growth and change of characters—is never present in the Greek and Roman novel. Still, despite the fact that the Greek and Roman novels contain at best two-dimensional characters, there is still a focus on character, specifically in the fact that it is the characters' beauty *and virtue* that propel the narrative. In the Greek novels, the pure and innocent character of the protagonists, in addition to their physical beauty, creates the tensions that render the story interesting. Character, not in terms of development nor in terms of complexity, but in terms of purity and motive, is explored through this medium.[10] It is not normal human beings of mixed good and bad traits who are being threatened with degradation, but exceedingly pure young people, and the threat of degradation is greater as a result. Even where the virtue of the protagonist is questioned, it is still an issue.

The Jewish novels are similar to Greek novels in emphasizing character and purity of motive, but they differ in the *goal* of human attainment. The ideal is not the romantic couple who will marry and start a nuclear family, but rather the pious Jew, usually a woman who is faithful to her extended family and to Jewish values. In addition, it has been suggested that character *change,* a theme supposedly absent from ancient literature, is explored at some points in the Jewish texts. Even in the early stage of the *Esther* tradition, that is, the version now found in the Hebrew Bible, Esther struggles with her moral dilemma in chapter 4 and finds it within herself to rise to a new challenge. She takes orders from Mordecai at the beginning of the novel, but

10. It is also probably not coincidental that the Greek concept of *haplotes*—integrity, simplicity, generosity, or purity of motive—is developed at this time, especially in Jewish literature. In addition, the earlier Jewish and non-Jewish court legends—the story of Joseph in Genesis 37–50, the individual legends of Daniel 1–6, the Hebrew version of *Esther, The Story of Ahikar*—already reflected a strong emphasis on purity of character.

gives them to him by the end.[11] The exploration of the change in character may be rudimentary, but like a meteor, it is clearly visible in passing. One might argue that in *Greek Esther* this fascinating development is not expanded upon but rather is obscured by the more typical threat-and-adventure interests of the novel; even so, the character growth still remains in the subsequent version. In a different vein, the character of Abraham in *Testament of Abraham* runs through a number of moods which are not random; they are in a progression, and although one would hardly call it a *growth* of character, it is a change of awareness and attitude.

## Rise of the Novels

Novels are not universal to human cultures but have arisen only occasionally, where the literacy of at least a small part of society makes written novels possible. They are found in Greek and Roman culture and among the minority ethnic groups of those empires, in medieval China and Japan, in modern Europe (including Russia) and North America. It was in Europe and North America where the novel eventually became established as a "serious" art form, and by the end of the twentieth century in most other parts of the world as well. But the comparison of the novel across cultural boundaries has not been easy. Even departmental divisions in modern colleges and universities have prevented the comparison of novels from different cultures. Many classicists, for instance, who have broken down barriers to allow for the study of Greek and Roman novels in classics departments, do not venture to the study of the Jewish experiments in the novel that often predate the Greek and that may have been written and read in the same cities.

11. Michael V. Fox, *Character and Ideology in the Book of Esther* (Columbia: University of South Carolina Press, 1991), 164–70.

Jewish novelistic literature began in a Hebrew- and Aramaic-speaking environment, even though the texts were translated and expanded, and in some cases new texts were also composed in a Greek-speaking world with a much broader horizon. At the end of the fourth century B.C.E. Alexander the Great had created a vast new umbrella empire stretching from Greece to India in the east and Egypt in the south. Although Alexander himself died young, the successor states managed to bring Greek culture and administration to a new world, and the client kingdoms, including Judea, became significantly Hellenized. The Romans, who gradually took control of the collection of Greek kingdoms, continued to rule in the Greek language and hold up Greek education and letters as the standard of civilization. It is not surprising, then, that a more international worldview and a new emphasis on education and letters should give rise to wholly different literary forms.

The rise of popular literature in modern Europe is often ascribed to the rise of a middle class, higher literacy, and cheaper production of books. Something of these phenomena existed in the Greco-Roman world, but not nearly to the same extent. A new class of international trader grew up in the Hellenistic cities, one not tied to old, conservative city and clan loyalties. This new class probably did not exist in the countryside and was not large enough to be considered a separate "middle class," but it was nevertheless a wealthy subculture between the old citizens and aristocrats on the one hand and the poor and slave class on the other. Literacy in the Greco-Roman cities was certainly higher than it had been, although the extent of this increase has been debated. The increased use of letters in business and family relations and the number and variety of literary texts indicate that literacy among this urban class was significant, even if small compared to nineteenth-century Europe.[12] Many of these changes in

12. Some scholars minimize the extent of literacy and limit it to the upper classes, but the New Testament itself stands as evidence of the possibility of

Hellenistic culture applied also to the large number of Jews in the Greek and Roman cities. But while it was certainly true that some Jews, such as Philo and Josephus, could aspire to the higher levels of Greek composition, few of the Jewish popular texts reflect this attainment. They are written in a simple and less educated style, similar to that of the Christian gospels. Two of the six additions to *Esther,* however, are composed in an elegant if florid Greek, and the author of *Third Maccabees* seems to have scoured the fine print of a thesaurus looking for unusual Greek words. But other than these, the level of diction is relatively low—lower, for instance, than the Greek novels.

Two recurrent themes may be highlighted as typical of the Jewish novels. The first is the tension between the ethnic identity of the Jews and the "universal" claims of the Greeks and Romans. We note how strongly and clearly Jewish identity is defined through the threat of persecution. There is a long history of trying to read actual historical events in the narratives of *Esther* or *Judith,* but the persecutions in question may never have happened, and even if they did occur, they have been refracted through the identity-formation of popular culture. The exuberance of some of the Jewish novels communicates, rather, a sense of triumph over the more powerful empires.

The second common theme has to do with penitential renewal as viewed through the eyes of the heroine. The idea of a

---

significant literary activity outside of aristocratic circles in the first and second centuries. On the minimalist approach to literacy, see William V. Harris, *Ancient Literacy* (Cambridge, Mass.: Harvard University Press, 1989); Susan A. Stephens, "Who Read the Ancient Novels?" in Tatum, ed., *Search for the Ancient Novel,* 406–7. Higher rates of literacy are argued for the Roman period by James G. Keenan, review of Harris, *Ancient History Bulletin* 5 (1991): 101–7; Rosalind Thomas, *Literacy and Orality in Ancient Greece* (Cambridge: Cambridge University Press, 1992), 158–70; and James L. Franklin, Jr., "Literacy and the Parietal Inscriptions of Pompeii," in *Literacy in the Roman World,* ed. Mary Beard et al. (Ann Arbor, Mich.: Journal of Roman Archaeology, 1991), 77–98.

female protagonist is not new in Israel—there are many important female characters in the Hebrew Bible—but a different kind of female figure emerges in these novels. Near the middle of several of the novels, the woman must pause and pray to God for guidance or strength. It was typical in ancient Israel in times of national catastrophe for one to prepare for prayer by enacting the signs of ritual mourning—rending one's clothes, wearing sackcloth, strewing dust or ashes on one's head—but in these scenes the woman goes beyond these traditional ritual actions. The prayer scene is no superficial report of her piety, but a rending scene of penitence and self-abnegation, even self-abasement. The female protagonist condemns her beauty, takes off her beautiful clothes and puts on the clothes of mourning, debases herself, and at the end reclothes herself in her beautiful garments and proceeds to her mission in the story. The scene is not simply about repentance, nor about preparedness and heroism, but seems to tap a growing Jewish concern about the sin inherent in the body and sexuality, a concern that emerges also in asceticism in early Christianity. But if one were to assume that the Jewish novels retain a pious and religious message that is lacking in the love stories of the Greek novels, that assumption would be a distortion. Recently classicists have emphasized the quasi-religious nature of Greek novels as well. Greek popular literature in general, as William Hansen notes, is a literature of "questing and salvation," of "fulfillment in one or another kind of commitment": love, religion, philosophical life, adventure, and conquest.[13] Older theories on the hidden references to mysteries in the Greek novels are no longer entertained in this specific form, but the general religious worldview of the Greek novels is now also increasingly emphasized.[14]

13. Hansen, ed., *Anthology of Ancient Popular Literature,* xix.

14. The older theory that Greek novels contained hidden references to the mysteries is found in Karl Kerenyi, *Der antike Roman* (Darmstadt: Wissenschaftliche Buchgesellschaft, 1971), and Reinhold Merkelbach, *Roman und Mysterium*

Whether novels resulted from a steady evolutionary process or erupted full-blown in the Hellenistic and Roman world is often debated, with the pendulum swinging first toward evolution, then toward a creationist theory, and more recently, back toward evolution. The evidence of the Jewish novels would seem to argue clearly for an evolutionary approach, but the either/or of evolutionary versus creationist should probably be supplanted by an explanation that incorporates both. Because of the clearly visible stages in the Jewish literary tradition, especially in the cases of Daniel and Esther, it is possible to posit an evolution of novelistic techniques and themes, even if the full extension of the ancient novel had to wait for Chariton's creative vision. A further question about the evolution of the Jewish novels is whether the motifs arose from a free-floating narrative tradition, supplemented from cross-cultural and folkloristic influences, to create an "ocean of story," or whether some of the motifs were introduced to respond to perceived problems in the Hebrew text of the Bible.[15] This latter development, a combination of scribal and oral tradition that eventually gave rise to the rabbinic midrashim, doubtless did influence the narratives, but the two processes are by no means mutually exclusive.

Even though, as was noted earlier, some of the Jewish experiments in the novel can be dated before the Greek, for several reasons we cannot simply replace the Greek origins of the novel with the Jewish origins. First, Jewish popular literary tradition was not the font out of which Greek popular literature arose; rather, the two traditions represent parallel streams, both products of the new Hellenistic internationalism. Second, Jews were

*in der Antike* (Munich: Beck'sche, 1962). See now Tomas Hägg, *The Novel in Antiquity* (Berkeley: University of California Press, 1983), 90; and Terry Comito, "Exile and Return in the Greek Romances," *Arion* n.s. 2 (1975): 58–80.

15. The latter is argued by James L. Kugel, *In Potiphar's House: The Interpretive Life of Biblical Texts* (San Francisco: HarperCollins, 1990).

not alone in utilizing popular narrative traditions to affirm ethnic identity. The more accurate description of the origins of popular literature must include the variety of texts produced by different ethnic groups in the eastern Mediterranean, such as *The Story of Ahikar, Ninus and Semiramus, Sesonchosis, Petubastis,* and *The Alexander Romance.* These texts are early, derive from eastern kingdoms conquered by Cyrus of Persia and Alexander the Great, and interestingly, in some cases became part of an international popular literary tradition, crossing boundaries and entering into world literature.[16]

## On the Translation of the Novels

The translation of the Jewish novels is not a transparently easy process, despite the fact that the language is usually simple. Translation is an art, not a science; translating ancient texts into modern idioms is the art of studied anachronism. The main challenge here is in arriving at the best equivalent style in English, but the situation is further complicated in this collection by the ubiquitous presence of biblical style in Judaism. When the Hebrew Bible was translated into Greek, it exerted an influence on Jewish and Christian writing perhaps greater than the influence on English of the King James translation of the Bible. As a result, the Jewish novels are often translated today in a very literal "biblical"

16. On the international rather than nationalistic tone of some of these texts, see Elias Bickerman, *The Jews in the Greek Age* (Cambridge, Mass.: Harvard University Press, 1988), 51–52. The early books of the Hebrew Bible are not included in this description principally because there is no evidence that the stories within it crossed ethnic boundaries until later in the Greco-Roman period, unlike those texts mentioned above. However, one may wonder at the possible non-Jewish influences on the Book of Job, similarities between autobiography in Ezra and Nehemiah and in Greece, and so on. On this question in general, see Wills, *Jewish Novel,* esp. 1–39.

style. But were the ancient authors really mimicking biblical style, or were they simply using the typical popular idiom of Jewish and Christian literature of the day? Some of the novels, of course, were translations of Hebrew and Aramaic originals that were themselves mimicking biblical histories. The opening formula in *Judith* 1, for example, copies the biblical historical books. However, these formulas are soon forgotten and a new novelistic mode takes over in each case, and this feature is what becomes distinctive about the texts. We need only compare *First Maccabees* to see a text that truly mimics the style of the biblical historical books throughout.

The tension between literal and free translation is not unique to these texts; it arises in all fields. Note, for example, the remarks of Leonard Tancock on translating French literature: "The translator must always be faithful to his original, and he has no right whatever to take any liberties with it. He is a translator, not an editor, nor a paraphraser, nor a popularizer," and contrast them with those of Gerald N. Sanday on his translation of *The Story of Apollonius King of Tyre:* "It has also been hard to resist the temptation to correct deficiencies such as repetition, parataxis, and the failure to subordinate one idea or event to another, or even to differentiate between distinct periods of time."[17] The justification here for a freer translation is in the attempt to recreate what the reading *experience* was like. Because our novelistic tradition in English requires variations of terms and some subordination of clauses, I have played somewhat freely with the variation of words and sentence structure. It is my conviction that the reading experience of Jewish novels was marked by exuberance and experimentation; exuberance and experimentation are what I have tried to present to the reader two millennia later. I have, however, remained more literal at some points in translating the

17. Leonard Tancock, *The Princesse de Clèves* (Harmondsworth, U.K.: Penguin, 1978), 24–25, and Gerald N. Sanday in Reardon, ed., *Collected Ancient Greek Novels,* 737–38.

gender of God as masculine. God is often a character in the novels, and it is a very masculine, fatherly God who is present. God is perhaps more monochromatic here than in other contemporary genres. The masculine God is thus retained in these translations as an integral part of what the reading experience would have been like in the ancient world.

## GENERAL BIBLIOGRAPHY

Bickerman, Elias. *Four Strange Books of the Bible.* New York: Schocken, 1967.

———. *The Jews in the Greek Age.* Cambridge, Mass.: Harvard University Press, 1988.

Braun, martin. *History and Romance in Graeco-Oriental Literature.* New York: Garland, 1987.

Charlesworth, James H., ed. *The Old Testament Pseudepigrapha.* 2 vols. Garden City, N.Y.: Doubleday, 1983.

Cohen, Shaye. *Beginnings of Jewishness: Boundaries, Varieties, Uncertainties.* Berkeley: University of California Press, 1999.

Collins, John J. *Between Athens and Jerusalem: Jewish Identity in the Hellenistic Diaspora.* New York: Crossroad, 1983.

Finkelberg, Margalit. *The Birth of Literary Fiction in Ancient Greece.* Oxford: Clarendon, 1998.

Fraser, P.M. *Ptolemaic Alexandria.* 3 vols. Oxford: Oxford University Press, 1972.

Gruen, Erich S.. *Heritage and Hellenism: The Reinvention of Jewish Tradition.* Berkeley: University of California Press, 1998.

Hadas, Moses. *Hellenistic Culture: Fusion and Diffusion.* New York: Norton, 1972.

Hägg, Tomas. *The Novel in Antiquity.* Berkeley: University of California Press, 1983.

Hansen, William, ed. *Anthology of Ancient Popular Literature.* Bloomington: Indiana University Press, 1998.

Hengel, Martin. *Judaism and Hellenism: Studies in Their Encounter in Palestine During the Early Hellenistic Period.* 2 vols. Philadelphia: Fortress, 1974.

Hock, Ronald F., J. Bradley Chance, and Judith Perkins, eds. *Ancient Fiction and Early Christian Narrative.* Atlanta: Scholars Press, 1998.

Holzberg, Niklas. *The Ancient Novel: An Introduction.* London: Routledge, 1995.

Humphries, W. Lee. "A Life-Style for Diaspora: A Study of Esther and Daniel." *Journal of Biblical Literature* 92 (1973): 211–23.

Konstan, David. *Sexual Symmetry: Love in the Ancient Novel and Related Genres.* Princeton, N.J.: Princeton University Press, 1994.

Kugel, James L. *In Potiphar's House: The Interpretive Life of Biblical Texts.* San Francisco: HarperCollins, 1990.

Levine, Amy-Jill, ed. *"Women Like This": New Perspectives on Jewish Women in the Greco-Roman World.* Atlanta: Scholars Press, 1991.

Morgan, J. R. and Richard Stoneman, eds. *Greek Fiction: The Greek Novel in Context.* London: Routledge, 1994.

Nickelsburg, George W. E. *Jewish Literature Between the Bible and the Mishnah.* Philadelphia: Fortress, 1981.

Niditch, Susan. *Underdogs and Tricksters: A Prelude to Biblical Folklore.* San Francisco: Harper and Row, 1987.

Perry, B.E. *The Ancient Romances.* Berkeley: University of California Press, 1967.

Pervo, Richard I. *Profit with Delight: The Literary Genre of the Acts of the Apostles.* Philadelphia: Fortress, 1987.

Radford, Jean, ed. *The Progress of Romance: The Politics of Popular Fiction.* New York: Routledge and Kegan Paul, 1986.

Reardon, B. P., ed. *Collected Ancient Greek Novels.* Berkeley: University of California Press, 1989.

———. *The Form of the Greek Romance.* Princeton, N.J.: Princeton University Press, 1991.

Stern, David and Mark Jay Mirsky. *Rabbinic Fantasies: Imaginative Narratives from Classical Hebrew Literature.* Philadelphia: Jewish Publication Society, 1993.

Tatum, James, ed. *The Search for the Ancient Novel.* Baltimore: Johns Hopkins University Press, 1994.

Tcherikover, Viktor. *Hellenistic Civilization and the Jews.* Philadelphia: The Jewish Publication Society, 1966.

Wills, Lawrence M. *The Jew in the Court of the Foreign King: Ancient Jewish Court Legends.* Minneapolis: Fortress, 1990.

———. *The Jewish Novel in the Ancient World.* Ithaca, N.Y.: Cornell University Press, 1995.

# PART I

## *Jewish Novels*

TWO

# GREEK ESTHER

The Greek version of *Esther* that became canonical in the Eastern Orthodox Church and (in its Latin version) in the Catholic Church is longer than the Hebrew Book of Esther as found in the Jewish and Protestant Bibles. There are six additions in *Greek Esther* that transform a great short story into a true novella:

A. Mordecai's symbolic dream of what is about to occur
B. Text of Haman's decree of extermination of the Jews
C. Mordecai's and Esther's prayers
D. "Romantic" aspects of Esther's audience before the king
E. Text of the king's decree rescinding Haman's decree of extermination
F. Mordecai's interpretation of his dream and conclusion

What is especially interesting is the way that *Greek Esther*—like *Greek Daniel*—reflects the *extension* of the narrative in an evolutionary way, a novelistic expansion to create a new form. Materials of all descriptions are added into an already existing narrative to add new dimensions. Judging from the very different Greek styles, the additions were not written by the same author. Some may have been composed originally in Hebrew or Aramaic, but the edict to annihilate the Jews and the further edict to rescind it are composed in rather elegant Greek. As with *Third Maccabees,* there appears to be an intentional effort to utilize pretentious Greek to address the issue of maintaining Jewish identity within the broader Greco-Roman world.

The Hebrew Book of Esther already contained important narrative developments that we might term novelistic: the sweep of pageantry, the domestic drama within the palace, danger and the release of tension. The additions, however, all introduce new narrative elements and extend old ones that are even more typical of the ancient Greek novels. *Greek Esther* now begins with an artificial apocalypse, a prophecy of the threatening events to follow. Esther's brave decision to come before the king is now also played out in a quasi-romantic exchange between them. The texts of the two decrees regarding the Jews allow the audience to perceive themselves as viewed from the perspective of the gentiles around them. (Compare *Third Maccabees* in this regard.) Most of all, the prayer scenes of Mordecai and Esther provide two different perspectives on the inner life of the protagonists. Whereas Mordecai's prayer is full of bravery and steadfast piety, Esther's is penitent and rending and reflects her vulnerability. It is probably both an ideal of women's spirituality and a monologue of the vulnerable soul that could be read and experienced by both the male and female members of the audience. And while Hebrew Esther had two important turning points—the interchange between Mordecai and Esther in which he reminds her of her duty (Esther 4), and the beginning of the unraveling of Haman's plan when the king could not sleep (Esther 6)—*Greek Esther* has created a new center: the transformation of Esther in penitence and prayer that allows her to return purified to God's good graces and to do God's will. This is the same center that we find in the women's prayers in *Susanna, Judith,* and *Marriage of Aseneth.*

To be sure, it is difficult to be certain precisely what tone the additions to *Esther* are attempting to communicate, especially in relation to that of Hebrew Esther. Some have argued that the literary and satirical qualities of Hebrew Esther have been diluted in *Greek Esther.* The comical King Ahasuerus in Hebrew Esther becomes a poor romantic partner in *Greek Esther.* The inner thoughts of Mordecai and Esther in the Hebrew version are expressed through dialogue, while in *Greek Esther* they come flooding out in monologues. Finally, the farcical quality of Hebrew Esther, which does not include even a mention of God, is in *Greek Esther* mixed with a more earnest sentimentality and repeated references to God's providential actions. Others have argued, however, that the satirical tone of Hebrew Esther is actually continued in *Greek Esther,* and that the broad sentimentality of the new scenes is intentionally overplayed for comic effect. Certainly the pretentious style of the two edicts in *Greek Esther* may be intended to reflect the bloated self-importance of the Persian king. But the additions do not all come from the same hand, and it is equally possible that some of them are earnest expressions of a religious sentimentality, while the edicts reflect back on the Persian king in a satirical way. Either way, while the farcical qualities of Hebrew Esther have been greatly appreciated by Jews because of its association with the Purim festival, the popular genre that is found in *Greek Esther* reflects the development of this story for a new situation, one in which the audience was seeking the same kind of reading experience that the other peoples of the Mediterranean world would come to find in the Greek novels.

A postscript at the end of *Greek Esther* gives some unusually specific information on this version of the Esther story. It was translated by a certain Lysimachus in Jerusalem and was brought to Egypt in the fourth year of the reign of "Ptolemy and Cleopatra." However, it is not clear which Ptolemy and Cleopatra was meant. The two likeliest dates would be in the fourth year of the reign of Ptolemy IX Soter II and Cleopatra III, that is, 114 B.C.E., or of Ptolemy XII Auletes and Cleopatra V in 77 B.C.E. The translation would have been completed, therefore, in the second or early first century B.C.E.

The reader should be forewarned that the chapter numbers

in *Greek Esther* are out of order. When Jerome translated the Bible into Latin, he removed the additions to Esther and placed them at the end. When chapter numbers were added to the Bible in the medieval period, they were assigned according to Jerome's rearrangement of the chapters. The names of the characters also often differ in the Greek version of *Esther,* but I have in general retained the names as they appear in the Hebrew Bible because they are often more familiar. The one exception is the name of the Persian king. In the Hebrew version he is Ahasuerus, or Xerxes, who ruled from 486 to 465 B.C.E., while in most (but not all) Greek versions and in the works of Jewish historian Josephus he is Artaxerxes, who ruled from 465 to 425. I have used the latter as representing the intended historical setting of the Greek version.

## *Greek Esther*

(11) Once there was a Jew named Mordecai, who lived in the city of Susa and served as a high official in the court of the Persian king. He was of the tribe of Benjamin, descended from Jair, Shimei, and Kish, and along with Jeconiah, king of Judea, had been taken captive from Jerusalem by King Nebuchadnezzar of Babylon. During the second year of the reign of Artaxerxes, on the first of the month of Nisan, this Mordecai had a dream:

> Thunderclaps! Earthquakes! Great noises and confusion! Disturbances over all the earth! Two huge dragons appear, preparing to do battle, roaring fiercely! At the sound of their roar, every nation rises up for war, arming themselves against the nation of the righteous. Darkness and forboding, gloom and tribulation, evil and consternation loom over the earth! The entire righteous nation is troubled, afraid of the evils arrayed against them, and fearing their impending doom, they call out to God. And from this

> cry there appears, as though from a tiny spring, a mighty river, overflowing with water. Light then appears as the sun rises, and the meek are exalted and consume the mighty of the earth.

Mordecai arose from this dream, and although he realized what God intended to do, he continued to dwell upon it until nightfall, trying to understand its every detail.

(12) Once Mordecai took his rest in the courtyard with Bigthan and Teresh, the two eunuchs of the king who guarded the court. He overheard them talking, and investigating their intentions carefully, he discovered that they were conspiring against Artaxerxes the king. He informed the king against them, and when the king interrogated the two eunuchs, they confessed and were taken away. The king recorded these deeds in his records, as did Mordecai in his. The king commanded that Mordecai serve in the court and rewarded him for his actions, but Haman, son of Hammedatha, a Bougean[1] and a leading official in the king's administration, sought to harm Mordecai and his people on account of the two eunuchs.

(1) This took place during the reign of Artaxerxes, who ruled the area reaching all the way to India, a hundred and twenty-seven provinces. In the third year of his reign, while he resided in Susa his capital, he gave a banquet for his friends and nobles among the Persians and Medes and others of the client nations, and the rulers of the provinces. He exhibited the riches of his kingdom and the bounty of his table for one hundred and eighty days, after which the king then gave a drinking party for the various peoples gathered in the city. This was to take place for six days in the king's courtyard. Draped around the courtyard were curtains of linen and cotton, hung on cords of purple linen, stretched from gold and silver blocks set atop columns of marble

1. The meaning of this term is unknown. Haman is called an Agagite in Hebrew Esther, that is, descended from Agag, and is an Amalekite, ancient enemies of the Israelites. Near the end Haman will also be called a Macedonian.

and other stones. Gold and silver couches were arranged upon a mosaic floor of emerald, marble, and mother-of-pearl, the couches covered with spreads of fine, shimmering fabric, embroidered with roses arranged in a circle. Cups made of gold and silver were set out, along with a precious miniature cup made of ruby, worth thirty thousand talents. The best wines from the king's own stores were served, and flowed in abundance. The drinking, however, was not confined to the toasts, but the king had instructed the stewards to serve both him and the guests as much as they wanted. While these festivities were underway, Queen Vashti also gave a drinking party for the women in the palace where the king was.

On the seventh day, the king, feeling merry, ordered Mehuman, Biztha, Harbona, Bigtha Abagtha, Zethar, and Carkas, the seven eunuchs who served before him, to fetch the queen and bring her before him. He wanted to present her as queen, place the royal diadem upon her head, and display her beauty before all the rulers and peoples of the various nations, for she was indeed very beautiful. But Queen Vashti refused to obey his orders and appear with the eunuchs. This offended the king, who fell into a rage and said to his favored guests, "You hear what Vashti has said. What do you advise in this matter?"

Then Harkesaios, Sarsathaeus, and Malesear, the officials among the Persians and Medes who were closest to the king, approached him and declared what the law stipulated should be done to Vashti, since she had not obeyed the command of the king which the eunuchs had given her. Memucan, the one who had informed them of the queen's defiance, addressed the king and rulers: "It is not just the king whom Vashti has wronged, but all the rulers and officials of the king. Because she has defied King Artaxerxes, the wives of the other rulers of the Persians and Medes will dare to show similar disrespect to their husbands when they hear what she has done. If it please the king, let him proclaim a royal decree—written according to the laws of the Medes and Persians, so that it cannot be altered—that Vashti not be permitted to come before him again, and that her crown be given to another better than she. Let this law of the king be proclaimed throughout the kingdom, so that all of the women, from the richest to the poorest, will give honor to their husbands." The king and the rulers approved of this advice, and the king did just as Memucan had said: letters were sent throughout the kingdom, province by province, to each in its own language, that every man should receive due respect in his own home.

(2) Some time later, when the king's anger had abated, he was no longer concerned about Vashti and her actions, and what he had decreed concerning her. The servants of the king said to him, "Let beautiful and marriageable young girls be sought for your majesty. Officers should be appointed in all the provinces of the kingdom to select beautiful young virgins to be brought to the harem in the city of Susa and placed in the charge of the king's harem-keeper. Provide them with their perfumes and cosmetics, and let the king choose one of these women to reign in place of Vashti." The king agreed to this, and did just as they suggested.

There was a Jew in the city of Susa, whose name was Mordecai, of the tribe of Benjamin, who was descended from Jair, Shimei, and Kish, and was captured from Jerusalem when King Nebuchadnezzar of Babylon took the city. He had a foster-child, the daughter of Aminadab his father's brother, whose name was Esther. When her parents had died, Mordecai had brought her up, and she had grown to be a very beautiful woman. The king's decree brought many young women to the city of Susa, placed in the care of Hegai, the harem-keeper. Among them was Esther, who quickly became Hegai's favorite. He provided cosmetics for her, extra portions of food, and seven maids assigned to her alone from the king's palace; in every way she and her maids received favored treatment within the harem. Esther, however, did not reveal to him her people or country, as Mordecai had commanded, but each day he walked about in the courtyard of the harem, inquiring how Esther was doing.

Now the women did not enter into the king until they had spent twelve months in preparation, six months with anointments of oil of myrrh, and six with perfumes and cosmetics. After this, each maiden would take a turn entering into the king. Placed in charge of the person appointed, she was escorted by him from the harem to the palace. She would then enter in before the king at night, and leave again in the morning to the second harem, under the watch of Hegai the harem-keeper, not to come again before the king unless summoned by name. When the time came for Esther, daughter of Aminadab, the uncle of Mordecai, to come before the king, she overlooked nothing of the harem-keeper's instructions, for Esther had won the charms of everyone who had cast eyes upon her. And when she entered in to Artaxerxes the king in the seventh year of his reign, in the twelfth month (that is, Adar) the king immediately fell in love with her. He preferred her to all the other virgins, and placed the queen's diadem upon her head. For seven days the king gave a banquet for all his friends and noblemen to celebrate his marriage to Esther, granting at the same time a release from taxation for all his subjects.

Mordecai was at that time serving in the courtyard, but Esther had not disclosed her people, for Mordecai had thus taught her to fear God and to keep his laws. This was how she had conducted herself when she was in his care, and she continued in this way. But two of the king's courtiers, his own bodyguards, burned with resentment because Mordecai had advanced in the court, and sought to kill Artaxerxes the king. When Mordecai heard of the plot, he sent word to Esther, who in turn informed the king. The two courtiers were interrogated by the king, and then hanged, and the king commanded that a notation in praise of Mordecai's loyalty be placed in the royal chronicles.

(3) After this, King Artaxerxes also honored Haman, son of Hammedatha, the Bougean, promoting him above all of the other officials in the king's administration. Everyone in the court bowed down to him, just as the king had ordered; Mordecai,

however, would not. The other courtiers asked him, "Why do you disobey the king's command?" And though they pressed him each day, he would not answer them. As a result, they informed Haman that Mordecai was disobeying the king's command. Now Mordecai had also told them that he was a Jew, and so when Haman found out that Mordecai was not bowing down to him, he became enraged and plotted to exterminate the entire nation of Jews who resided in Artaxerxes' empire.

So during the twelfth year of Artaxerxes' rule, Haman cast lots for each month, one by one, and for each day of the month, to determine on which day he should destroy the people of Mordecai. The lot fell on the thirteenth of Adar. He then went to speak to King Artaxerxes: "There is a people scattered among the nations throughout your kingdom, whose laws are different from all other peoples, and who disobey the laws of your majesty. It is not expedient for your majesty to tolerate them. Therefore, if it please the king, publish a decree that they should be destroyed, and I shall deposit ten thousand talents of silver into the royal treasury."

The king took his royal signet-ring and gave it to Haman to seal this declaration against the Jews, adding, "You may keep the money, and this people you may deal with as you wish."

In the first month, on the thirteenth day, the king's scribes were summoned, and wrote under the king's authority what Haman commanded to the generals and rulers in the one hundred and twenty-seven provinces from India to Ethiopia, addressing the officials in each province in their own language. Couriers were dispatched throughout the kingdom of Artaxerxes with orders to exterminate the Jewish people on one day in the twelfth month, which is Adar, and to seize all their property. (13) The letter read as follows:

> From the great king Artaxerxes to the governors and appointed officials of the one hundred and twenty-seven provinces from India to Ethiopia.
>
> Since I have come to rule over many nations and subdued the

entire world, I have resolved—not invoking the full power of my authority, but exhibiting throughout a kinder and gentler spirit—to ensure that my subjects can lead their lives in every way untroubled by cares and hardships, to promote harmonious social relations throughout the kingdom, to guarantee freedom of travel to the edges of its borders, and to restore the peace that is the hope of all people.

When I inquired of my counselors how this end might be accomplished, it was pointed out to me by Haman, a man who excels among us for his sound judgment, and known as much for his steadfast loyalty as for his unshakable good will, ascending now to the second rank in the royal court, that interspersed among all the nations of the world there is a certain hostile people, constituted by their laws to be opposed to every nation, and who continually transgress the ordinances of the kings, with the result that our program for the unification of the kingdom, which has been blamelessly administered, cannot be brought to completion.

Since we understand that this nation alone stands in constant opposition to all people, rejecting established laws in favor of a strange and foreign way of life, and is contemptuous of our administration, to the extent that they have committed the worst evils in order to keep the harmony of our kingdom from becoming a reality, we have decreed that those so indicated to you in the letters of Haman, who has been appointed prime minister and is our second father, shall be totally destroyed, along with their wives and children, by the swords of their enemies, without any mercy or pity, on the thirteenth day of the twelfth month, that is Adar, in the present year, so that all those who have been or are now hostile, may be eliminated with extreme violence and consigned to Hades, and allow our administration to be henceforth stable and untroubled.

Copies of this letter were posted in every province, and every principality was notified to be ready for the approach of that day. The citizens of Susa were also notified of the decree, but while Haman joined the king in drinking and revelry, the city was in turmoil.

(4) When Mordecai learned what was happening, he tore his clothes, put on sackcloth, and covered himself with ashes, then rushed out to the middle of the city and cried out, "An innocent people is about to be destroyed!" He ran as far as the king's gate, but there he stopped, for it was not permitted for anyone to enter the courtyard clothed in sackcloth and ashes. And throughout every province, wherever the letters were posted, there was among the Jews weeping, moaning, and loud lamentations, as they too put on sackcloth and ashes. The maids and eunuchs who waited on the queen entered and informed her of what had happened; she too was wrought up and sent word to Mordecai to take off his sackcloth and dress in his normal attire, but he would not. Esther then summoned her eunuch Hatach and sent him out to inquire of Mordecai what was happening. Mordecai then explained to him what had occurred and told him how Haman had promised to pay ten thousand talents into the king's treasury in return for the annihilation of the Jews. Mordecai then gave to Hatach a copy of the decree that had been posted in Susa commanding the destruction of the Jews to show to Esther, and sent word through him that Esther should enter into the king's presence to entreat him and beg for clemency for her people. "Do not forget," he said, "those days when you were under my care, and not so exalted as you are now. Now Haman, the king's prime minister, has condemned us to death. Go, call upon the Lord, then speak to the king concerning us; by this you can deliver us from death."

Hatach then returned to Esther and gave her Mordecai's message. "Return to Mordecai," she said, "and tell him, 'All the people of the kingdom know that for any man or woman who enters the inner court of the king without being summoned there is no hope of escape, unless the king extends his golden sceptre. And it has been thirty days since I was last summoned.'"

Hatach delivered Esther's message to Mordecai, to which Mordecai replied, "Go then and say to her, 'Esther, do not say to yourself that you alone of all the Jews in the entire kingdom will be saved. For if you keep silent at a time such as this, aid and deliverance for the Jews will come from elsewhere, but you and your father's house will be destroyed. And what is more, who knows whether it was for this purpose that you have become queen?'"

Esther then returned this message to Mordecai: "Go now and gather the Jews in Susa and fast on my behalf. Neither eat nor drink for three days, both night and day, and I and my maids shall do the same. Afterward I shall enter into the king, though it is contrary to the law and I may be killed."

Mordecai then departed and did what Esther had instructed. (13) He prayed to the Lord, recalling the Lord's great works: "O Lord, Lord, you rule as king over all things, the entire universe is under your authority, and if you decide to deliver Israel, no one can stand up to your might. You created heaven and earth and every wonder under heaven. You are Lord of all, and no one can oppose you. You know all things. You know, O Lord, that in refusing to bow down to the arrogant Haman, I was not acting out of haughty pride or a desire for status, for indeed I would have gladly kissed the soles of his feet to save Israel. But I did this because I could not give greater honor to a person than I do to God; I could never bow down to anyone but you, my Lord. I do not do these things out of pride, but now, O Lord, God and King, God of Abraham, spare your people, for we are being stalked for destruction by those who are trying to annihilate the people that has been your inheritance from the beginning. Do not now discard your own people, whose very freedom you ransomed from the Egyptians, but heed my prayer and have mercy on your inheritance. Change our mourning into celebration, so that we may live and praise your name, O Lord. Do not silence the voices of those who praise you."

All of Israel cried out in a loud lamentation, as they beheld the specter of death before their eyes. (14) Esther the queen, gripped by the fear of impending death, turned to the Lord for refuge. She stripped herself of her rich garments and robed herself in clothes of mourning and tribulation, daubing her head with ashes and dung in place of her expensive perfumes. She debased herself, covering her entire body, which she had earlier adorned with such delight, with her fallen tresses. Then she called upon the Lord God of Israel and said, "My Lord, you alone are our king. Help me who am alone and have no helper but you. Now I am taking my life into my hands. I have always heard, from the time of my upbringing in the tribe of my family, that you, Lord, chose Israel out of all the nations, and our forebears out of the forebears of the other nations to become an eternal inheritance, and you did for them what you promised. But now we have sinned before you, and you have therefore handed us over into the hands of our enemies, because we have heaped great honors upon their gods. But you are righteous, O Lord. Now, however, they are not merely content to confine us to bitter servitude; they have made a covenant with their gods to annul the promise which came forth from your mouth and annihilate your inheritance, to stop the mouths of those who praise you, to extinguish the divine presence in the altar of your temple. At the same time, they would cause the mouths of the nations to sing hymns of praise to the virtues of their vain and empty idols, and from this day forth to express awe and devotion for a mortal king. Do not surrender your scepter, O Lord, to that which does not even exist, to let them mock and jeer at us in our calamity, but entrap them now in their own plot, singling out for special punishment the one who is responsible.

"Remember me, O Lord; let me know you are with us in the hour of our affliction. Grant me courage, O King of the gods and Ruler over every dominion, and let my speech be eloquent before the lion. Let the heart of the king seethe with hatred for this man who is at war with us, so that he and all who have joined forces with him may perish. Deliver us by your hand, and help me who am alone and have no one except you, O Lord. You know all things. You know that I despised the veneration I received from the lawless and loathed the bed of the uncircumcised or of any foreigner. You know that I am forced to act as I do, and that I despise the symbol of my high estate, which I wear on my head when I appear in public. I despise it like a menstruous rag, and do not wear it when I am alone in my quarters. Your servant has also refused to eat at the table of Haman; neither have I attended the king's banquet nor drunk the wine of his libations. Your servant has had no happiness from the day of her selection as queen until now, except in you, O Lord, God of Abraham. O God who conquers all, hear the plea of those in despair; deliver us from the clutches of those who would do us evil and deliver me also from my fear."

(15) On the third day she ceased praying, and taking off the clothes in which she had worshipped, put on once again her beautiful attire. Thus clothed in splendor, she called upon the all-seeing God and savior, and chose two maids to accompany her. On one she leaned gracefully for support, while the other trailed behind her, carrying her train. Blushing and in the full bloom of her beauty, her face seemed bright and cheerful, as though she were basking in her love's affection; within, however, her heart was frozen with fear. Making her way through each of the doors, she came before the presence of the king, as he sat upon his royal throne, dressed in the awesome radiance of his majesty and covered with gold and precious jewels—a formidable sight! He lifted his face, flushed with the power of his bearing, and glared at her in anger. The queen suddenly swooned, turned pale and faint, and collapsed upon the maid at her side. God then changed the spirit of the king to gentleness, and in alarm he leapt from his throne and took her in his arms until she came to. In a gentle voice he comforted her and asked, "What is it Esther? I am your brother.[2] Take heart, you shall not die, for

2. The warm relationship of husband and wife is also invoked by the words "brother" and "sister" in *Tobit* and *The Marriage and Conversion of Aseneth,* and these terms can even be erotic as in Song of Songs 4:9.

the law applies to others, not to you. You may come to me." Lifting the golden scepter and touching it to her neck, he then embraced her and said, "Speak to me."

"You appeared to me, lord," she said, "like an angel of God, and my heart was stricken with fear at your glory. Your countenance is resplendent with grace, and I was awestruck." But while she was speaking, she swooned and fainted once again. The king was alarmed, as all his attendants tried to comfort her.

(5) "What do you wish, Esther?" asked the king. "Do you have a request? I shall grant it to you, up to half of my kingdom."

"This is a very special day for me," said Esther. "If it please the king, let him come with Haman to the banquet which I shall give tomorrow."

"Hurry and inform Haman," said the king, "so that we may do as Esther says."

Thus the king and Haman both arrived at the banquet which Esther gave for them. Over the wine the king said to Esther, "What is it, Queen Esther? Only ask, and it is yours."

"My request is this," she said. "If I have pleased you, let the king and Haman come again tomorrow to a banquet which I shall give for them, and tomorrow I shall do for you as I have done today."

Haman was lighthearted and happy as he left the king, but when he saw Mordecai the Jew in the courtyard, he clouded over with anger. He returned home and called in his friends and Zeresh his wife, and recounted to them his wealth and all the honors that the king had bestowed upon him, and told them how he had been named prime minister of the entire kingdom. "And," he added, "did the queen not invite me alone to join her in the banquet for the king? Tomorrow I am also invited once again. But all these things give me no pleasure, so long as I see Mordecai the Jew in the courtyard."

His wife Zeresh and his friends responded, "Have a gallows erected eighty feet high, and in the morning speak to the king to have Mordecai hanged upon it. Then you can proceed to your banquet with the king and celebrate." Haman was very pleased with this suggestion and had the gallows prepared.

(6) That night the Lord held back sleep from the king, and so the court scribe was summoned to bring the books of chronicles to read before him. There he found written the account of Mordecai's deeds, how he had informed the king of the two royal eunuchs who had planned to kill him while on their watch. The king then asked, "What honor or reward have we bestowed upon Mordecai?"

"None has been bestowed," said the king's servants.

And just as the king was hearing of Mordecai's loyalty, Haman entered the court. "Who is in the court?" asked the king.

"It is Haman," responded the king's servants. Haman had just entered to ask the king to hang Mordecai upon the gallows he had prepared.

"Admit him," said the king, and when Haman came before him, he asked him, "What shall I do for the man whom I wish to honor?"

"Whom would the king wish to honor more than me?" thought Haman, so he said to the king, "For the man whom the king wishes to honor, let the king's servants bring the linen robe that the king wears, and the horse on which the king rides, and let one of the king's highest nobles place the robe upon the man whose service the king cherishes, and let him mount him upon the horse and proclaim throughout the city, 'Thus shall it be done for the man whom the king honors.'"

"You have spoken well!" said the king to Haman. "Now go and summon Mordecai the Jew, serving in the courtyard, and do for him as you have said; do not omit a single thing."

Haman took the robe and horse and wrapped Mordecai in the robe and mounted him upon the horse, proceeding through the city proclaiming, "Thus shall it be done for any man whom the king wishes to honor."

Afterward Mordecai returned to the courtyard, but Haman now scurried home, covering his head in grief. When Haman described to Zeresh his wife and his friends everything that had befallen him, they said, "If Mordecai is one of the Jewish people, and you are now humiliated before him, you will surely suffer a fall. You will never prevail over him; the living God is with him."

As they were speaking, eunuchs arrived to escort Haman to the banquet that Esther had prepared. (7) The king and Haman thus entered together into the queen's banquet, and on the second day during the wine course the king said to Esther, "Queen Esther, what is your request? It shall be yours, up to half of my kingdom."

"If I have pleased you, my request is that you spare my life and the life of my people, for I have now heard that I and my people have been marked for destruction and to be sold into slavery—we and our children—all to become servants. And the one who has denounced us is not worthy of his position in the king's court."

"Who is he?" asked the king. "Who would dare to attempt such a thing?"

"This evil man Haman is our nemesis!" replied Esther.

Haman stood dumbfounded before them, as the king rose to his feet and walked into the garden. Realizing now that he was in grave danger, Haman turned to beg the queen for mercy. Throwing himself upon the queen's settee, he implored her to save him, but at that point the king returned from the garden.

"What?" said the king. "Would he even accost my wife in my own home?" At this, Haman could only cover his face in shame.

Just then Harbona, one of the eunuchs, said to the king, "Haman, indeed, has constructed a gallows for Mordecai, the one who gave information that saved the king. He had it erected in his own courtyard, and it stands there now, eighty feet high."

"Hang him on it!" commanded the king, and Haman was executed upon the gallows which he had prepared for Mordecai. After this, the king's anger began to subside.

(8) On that day, King Artaxerxes handed over to Esther all that belonged to their accuser, Haman, and since she had now informed him that Mordecai was her close relative, the king

summoned Mordecai to come before him. The king then took off his signet-ring, which he had taken from Haman, and gave it to Mordecai, while Esther set Mordecai over all that Haman had possessed.

Once again, however, Esther spoke to the king, falling at his feet, begging him to avert the evil plan that Haman had concocted to destroy the Jews. The king reached out with the golden scepter and touched Esther, whereupon she arose and stood before him. "If it pleases you," she said, "and I have found favor in your sight, send immediately and recall the letters sent by Haman ordering the destruction of the Jews who reside in your kingdom. For how could I stand by and witness the destruction of my people, or be spared myself while my nation is wiped out?"

"Already," said the king, "I have handed over to you all of Haman's property and hanged him upon the gallows, because he threatened the Jews. What further do you seek? You two may write a decree in my name, saying whatever you think best. Seal it with my signet-ring, for whatever is written under my authority and sealed with my signet-ring cannot be rescinded."

On the twenty-third day of the first month, that is, Nisan, in the same year, the scribes were summoned and word was dispatched to the Jews, informing them of what had been commanded to the officials and governors of the one hundred and twenty-seven provinces from India to Ethiopia, to each province in its own language. The edict came under the king's authority, sealed with his signet-ring and sent by mounted couriers, ordering that in every city the Jews were to observe their own laws, and that they were to defend themselves and to repay their enemies as they wished, all this to occur on the same day throughout the kingdom of Artaxerxes, the thirteenth of the twelfth month, that is, Adar.

(16) The contents of the letter read as follows:

> From the great king Artaxerxes to the governors of the one hundred and twenty-seven provinces from India to Ethiopia, and to those who are concerned for our commonwealth, greetings.

Many among us who have been cloaked with honors from the unstinting generosity of their benefactors have responded by becoming proud and arrogant, seeking not only to commit evil against our subjects, but have even been prompted by the great gifts they have received to plot against the very people who bestowed them. Not only do they cheapen the very notion of gratitude for others, but swept away by the vaunting of their flatterers, they suppose that they will escape the terrible justice of the God who witnesses all things. In addition, Gentle Persuasion, after first helping to establish in high office many presumed friends, entrusted with the management of affairs of state, often extends the guilt to others, making them partners in the shedding of innocent blood, and embroiling them in unrelieved disasters, as these "friends" manage to manipulate the guileless hearts of their rulers with the lying deceptions lurking in their wicked natures. You can see for yourselves from our present experiences, as well as from the historical records which we cherish and pass on, what horrible deeds have resulted from the evil sickness that lies within those who hold office unworthily.

In the future, however, we shall endeavor to hold the kingdom to a more peaceful course for all people, making whatever changes are necessary to ensure that in the issues that come before us, we render a fair and equitable judgment. For Haman, son of Hammedatha, and a Macedonian[3]—in truth a foreigner, with no Persian blood, and quite alien as well to our purity of heart—was well received by us, benefiting from the same good measure of gifts that we bestow on every people, to the extent that we even proclaimed him our father, and everyone continually bowed down to him as a man second only to the royal throne. But unable to con-

3. Alexander the Great was a Macedonian ruler who defeated the Persians a century after the events of this story, and thus, with the hindsight of history, Macedonians would have been viewed as enemies of the Persians. In addition, however, the Seleucids, whom the Jewish Maccabees had more recently ousted, were also successors to the Macedonians, and so at the time of the writing of this story there would have been a double association of the term "Macedonian."

tain his arrogance, he attempted to deprive us both of our kingdom and our life, by asking, with lies and duplicitous deceits, for the destruction of our own savior and benefactor, Mordecai, and our blameless partner on the throne, Esther, together with all of their people. In this way he hoped to catch us defenseless, and transfer the rule of the Persians over to the Macedonians. Now we find, however, that the Jews, who were consigned to total destruction by this thoroughly scurrilous villain, are guilty of no crime whatsoever, but being children of the mighty, living God Most High, who has maintained our kingdom in its perfect harmony, both for our ancestors and for ourselves, they conduct their lives in accord with the most just of laws.

It would be well for you then to ignore the decree circulated by Haman, son of Hammedatha, for as the perpetrator of all this villainy, he has been hanged at the gate of Susa, together with his household, for the God who rules over all things has summarily handed down the punishment he justly deserved. A copy of this letter is therefore to be conspicuously posted in every city, and the Jews are to be allowed to observe their own laws. Further, give to them the reinforcements they need so that on the thirteenth day of the twelfth month, that is, Adar, on that very day they may exact vengeance on those who were arrayed against them in the hour of their affliction. For now the God who rules all things has made this day a day of joy instead of destruction for his chosen people. Therefore, you must also celebrate this joyfully as a special holiday among your appointed festivals, so that both now and hereafter it will be a symbol of deliverance for us and for loyal Persians, but for those who plot against us, a reminder of destruction. Any city or province that does not obey this pronouncement shall feel our intense anger and be destroyed and burned. Not only shall it remain forsaken by human beings, but shunned for all time by bird and beast. (8) Now let copies of this decree be posted conspicuously throughout the kingdom, so that all the Jews may be prepared on that day to take up arms against their enemies.

Mounted couriers then rode out swiftly to enact the king's order, even as the decree was being posted in Susa.

Mordecai went forth from the king's presence wearing the royal robe, with a golden crown and a turban of purple linen on his head. The residents of Susa rejoiced when they saw him, and the Jews celebrated with lighthearted festivities. In every city and province where the decree was posted, the Jews enjoyed celebrations and revelry, and many of the gentiles were circumcised and became Jews out of fear of them. The chief governors of the provinces, the princes, and the king's scribes all held the Jews in highest esteem, for they feared Mordecai. According to the decree of the king, his name was to be honored throughout the kingdom.

(9) On the thirteenth day of the twelfth month, that is, Adar, the decree of the king was posted. On that day the enemies of the Jews were destroyed; indeed, no one opposed them out of fear. In the city of Susa, the Jews killed five hundred men, including Parshandatha, Dalphon, Aspatha, Poratha, Adalia, Aridatha, Parmashta, Arisai, Aridai, and Vaizatha, the ten sons of Haman, son of Hammedatha the Bougean, and the enemy of the Jews, and they seized all their property.

When the number of those killed in Susa was reported to the king, he said to Esther, "The Jews have killed five hundred men in the city of Susa. How do you suppose they have fared in the countryside? Now what is your request? Ask and it shall be yours."

Esther said to the king, "Let it be granted to the Jews to do tomorrow as they have done today; also hang the bodies of the ten sons of Haman from the gallows." The king granted her request and handed over the bodies of the sons of Haman to the Jews of the city to be hung upon the gallows. The Jews in Susa then gathered on the fourteenth day of Adar and killed another three hundred men, but this time did not seize their property. The other Jews in the kingdom also gathered together in self-defense and were thus delivered from their enemies, killing fifteen thousand of them on the thirteenth of Adar, but seized no property. On the fourteenth day of the same month they rested, spending that day in joy and revelry. The Jews in the city of Susa gathered again on the fourteenth day but did not rest; instead they spent the fifteenth day in revelry. For this reason, then, the Jews who were dispersed in every province spent the fourteenth day of Adar as a holiday with many festivities, exchanging gifts of food with one another, while those residing in the principal cities also celebrate the fifteenth of Adar as a festive holiday, with the exchange of gifts.

Mordecai then wrote down everything that happened in a book, sending it to all the Jews in the kingdom of Artaxerxes, both near and far, with the instruction that they establish the fourteenth and fifteenth days of Adar as holidays, because on these days the Jews were delivered from their enemies, and to spend in celebration the entire month in which this reversal from sorrow to joy and from mourning to festivity occurred. There would be feasting and merrymaking, the giving of gifts to one another and to the poor. The Jews then ratified Mordecai's account of the events: how Haman, son of Hammedatha, the Macedonian, plotted to make war upon them and wipe them out on a day determined by the casting of lots, and how he had approached the king to arrange for the hanging of Mordecai; but as it happened, all of the wicked things that he had devised against the Jews had come back on his own head, and he and his sons were hanged instead. It is for this reason that these days are designated "Purim," because in their language lots are called *purim,* and it stands as a reminder of all that was contained in the letter, and everything that had befallen the Jews. Mordecai established this observance, and the Jews ratified it for themselves and their progeny and all who joined their nation, never to be broken or altered. These days should stand forever as a memorial from generation to generation, in every city, family, and province, to be kept for all time, that future generations never forget what happened here.

Esther the queen and daughter of Aminadab, and Mordecai the Jew then confirmed and established this letter of Purim, and

Mordecai and Esther the queen then swore by their life and health to establish this plan. In this way Esther confirmed it forever, and it was recorded for posterity.

(10) The king then levied a tax upon his kingdom, both land and sea. As for his power and courage, and the wealth and splendor of his empire—are they not recorded in the chronicles of the kings of the Persians and Medes? Mordecai was second only to King Artaxerxes, a powerful man in the kingdom, and greatly honored among the Jews. Because of his virtue, he was admired by all his people.

"All this has come from God," said Mordecai, "for I now remember my dream which foretold all of this; not a single detail was lacking. First there was the little spring that grew to become a river, and there was light and sun and overflowing water. Esther is the river, whom the king made a queen when he married her. The two dragons are Haman and myself, while the nations are those who gathered together to destroy the name of the Jews. My nation, however, is Israel, who cried out to God and was saved. The Lord saved his people, delivering us from all these threats of treachery, and performed signs and wonders which have never been wrought among the other nations. For this reason, he made two lots, one for the people of God and one for the nations. These two lots came at an hour and moment and day of decision before God and among all the nations, and God remembered his people and judged in favor of his inheritance. The fourteenth and fifteenth days of the month of Adar shall be set aside for them as days for gathering to share in joy and feasting before God, from generation to generation among the people of Israel forever.

(11) In the fourth year of the reign of Ptolemy and Cleopatra, Dositheus, who said that he was a priest and Levite, and Ptolemy his son brought to Egypt the foregoing letter of Purim, which, according to them, was genuine, having been translated by Lysimachus, son of Ptolemy, a resident of Jerusalem.

## SUGGESTIONS FOR FURTHER READING

Berlin, Adele. "The Book of Esther and Ancient Storytelling." *Journal of Biblical Literature* 120 (2001) 3–14.

Collins, John J. *Between Athens and Jerusalem: Jewish Identity in the Hellenistic Diaspora,* pp. 87–89. New York: Crossroad, 1983.

Fox, Michael V. *Character and Ideology in the Book of Esther.* Columbia: University of South Carolina Press, 1991.

Gruen, Erich. *Heritage and Hellenism: The Reinvention of Jewish Tradition,* pp. 177–86. Berkeley: University of California Press, 1998.

Moore, Carey A. *Daniel, Esther, and Jeremiah: The Additions.* Garden City, N.Y.: Doubleday, 1977.

Nickelsburg, George W. E. *Jewish Literature Between the Bible and the Mishnah,* pp. 172–75. Philadelphia: Fortress, 1981.

Wills, Lawrence M. *The Jewish Novel in the Ancient World,* pp. 93–131. Ithaca, N.Y.: Cornell University Press, 1995.

THREE

# SUSANNA AND BEL AND THE SERPENT (GREEK DANIEL)

In the Eastern Orthodox and Roman Catholic Bibles the Book of Daniel contains several significant additions, among them *Susanna* and *Bel and the Serpent*. Like the narratives found in Daniel 1–6, *Susanna* and *Bel and the Serpent* probably arose as separate episodes in a cycle of Daniel legends similar to those in Daniel 1–6. Similar narratives have also been found among the Dead Sea Scrolls. Although they were likely written in Hebrew or Aramaic, these additions are now known from the ancient Greek translations of the Bible, and so they are sometimes referred to as *Greek Daniel*. *Susanna* and *Bel and the Serpent* are not novels in themselves, but their inclusion in the growing Daniel corpus illustrates clearly the novelistic tendency to expand narratives by incorporating more episodes. The author and audience come to explore more fully the themes of threat and release, virtue and motive, repentance and psychological introspection. Many of the novelistic works of this period, both Jewish and non-Jewish, grow in this piecemeal manner; they are "novels by addition."

*Susanna* is set in the Jewish Diaspora of Babylon. One cannot detect any suffering of the exiled community, but more striking, there is no tension with other ethnic groups. This situation is unusual in the texts collected here, but not unknown. (This theme is also absent from *Testament of Abraham*.) The action centers around Susanna, the beautiful young wife of a wealthy Jew. When she takes her daily bath, two wicked elders linger in the garden to watch her, and when they discover each other's presence, they connive to force her to have sex with them. She refuses, and as a result they convene a court and accuse her of having committed adultery with a young man who has run away. She is saved by the young Daniel, who, through clever cross-examination of the two elders, uncovers their treachery. The story depicts Daniel in his early years, just discovering his unusual gifts in discerning the wisdom of God. It would thus work well at the beginning of the Book of Daniel and is indeed placed there in some ancient manuscripts; however, it is also placed at other positions in the different versions of Daniel, and so it is not clear what its original location was.

In plot structure *Susanna* is like the story of Joseph in Genesis 37–50, Esther, Daniel 3 and 6, and the non-Jewish *Story of Ahikar.* They are court legends in which the protagonist is falsely accused, imprisoned or sentenced to death, yet remains steadfast in maintaining his innocence and is finally vindicated. The Jewish examples advocate in narrative form a pious lifestyle for Jews in the Diaspora. Two important differences in *Susanna,* however, reflect new, more novelistic interests: the court is no longer the king's court but rather the local court before hometown Jewish leaders, and the accused protagonist is now a woman. Both of these changes create a more domestic scenario, and not since the Book of Ruth had Judaism had such an "everywoman" protagonist. Later artists also took up the depiction of the beautiful and innocent Susanna bathing before the two wicked elders. Despite the sin of the elders, the opportunity of observing Susanna nude was too much of a temptation (see especially Rembrandt's version). This combination of eroticism and innocence was a fundamental ingredient of the ancient novel, as of the modern.

*Bel and the Serpent* consists of two episodes involving Daniel and a sympathetic foreign monarch, Cyrus of Persia. It is traditionally called in English *Bel and the Dragon,* but the Greek word *drakon* can actually mean snake, serpent, or dragon. The story plays on the ambiguity of whether the beast is divine or mundane, dragon or snake; thus "serpent" is used to connote both possibilities. As in many of the Jewish novels, the conflict arises from the tensions between Jews and the other ethnic groups. In the presence of the king, Daniel exposes the corruption of the Babylonian priests of Bel and also proves that the serpent they worship is not a "living god." The Babylonians, who under Cyrus would have also been a ruled minority, react by conspiring against Daniel and forcing the king to execute him in the lions' den. This section of *Bel and the Serpent* is obviously related to the lions' den punishment in Daniel 6, but it may not be a mere copy of it. It is possible that both narratives arose from a common oral legend of Daniel in the lions' den.

Dorothy Sayers suggested that *Susanna* and *Bel and the Serpent* constituted the earliest known examples of detective stories, and this idea reflects part of their appeal and inventiveness. The threat to innocent protagonists and the use of cleverness and wisdom to uncover injustice make these stories minor gems of adventure and virtue. A further value of these short stories, however, lies not in their qualities considered separately, but in their role in filling out the Book of Daniel, in lengthening it toward the page range of the genre of Jewish novels, and in developing further the typical themes of the novel. The Daniel tradition is thus an important laboratory example of how the popular novel in the ancient world could come into being.

Because the apocalyptic visions of Daniel 7–12 can confidently be dated to the crisis of the Maccabean Revolt of 168–65 B.C.E., and *Susanna* and *Bel and the Serpent* were added to the Book of Daniel after Daniel 7–12 had been incorporated, *Susanna* and *Bel* can probably be dated to about the second to first century B.C.E., although an earlier origin for the two stories is not impossible. The date for *Greek Daniel* as a whole, however, is probably first century B.C.E.

## *Susanna*

There once lived in Babylon a man named Joakim, who was married to Susanna, the daughter of Hilkiah. She was very beautiful and revered the Lord. Her parents were also righteous and had instructed their daughter according to the law of Moses. Joakim, who was very rich, had a beautiful garden adjoining his house, and all the Jews would come to visit him, because he was the most honored of them all. In the year they were married, two elders of the people were appointed as judges, concerning whom the Lord had said, "Iniquity came forth out of Babylon, from elders who were judges but only seemed to govern the people." These men also frequented the house of Joakim, where they heard the cases of those who had brought suit.

Now when the people departed at noon, Susanna would retire to her husband's garden for a walk. The two elders watched her every day as she entered and strolled about, and they became consumed with desire for her. Their thoughts became perverted, and no longer fixing their minds on heaven, they ceased rendering righteous judgments. Both of them were stricken by her but did not intimate to each other their distress; they were too ashamed to admit that they wanted to lie with her. Each day, however, they waited anxiously for a chance to see her. One day they said to each other, "Let us return home, for it is now time for lunch," and turned to take their leave of each other. But both turned back again, and when they met, they pressed each other for the reason, and confessed their longing. Then together they arranged for a time when they both might find her alone.

As they were watching and waiting for an opportune moment, she came one day with only two maids, as was her custom, and since it was very hot, desired to bathe in the garden. No one was present except the two elders, hiding in the bushes and watching her. Susanna said to her maids, "Bring me some oil and ointment, and close the doors of the garden so that I may bathe." They did as she instructed, and closed the garden gates. They then left by the side gates to fetch what they had been commanded, unaware that the elders were there hiding.

When the maids had left, the two elders leapt out, ran over to her, and said, "The garden gates are now shut tight! There is no one here to see us, and we both burn with desire for you! Give in to our demands and lie with us! If you refuse, we shall accuse you of having a young man here with you, and say that it was for this reason that you sent the maids away."

Susanna groaned aloud and said, "I am trapped either way! If I do what you ask, it would mean death for me, yet if I do not, I shall never escape your clutches! Yet it is better for me to refuse and fall into your hands than to sin against the Lord."

Susanna cried out loudly, but the elders yelled even louder, drowning out her voice. One of them quickly ran and opened the garden gates. When the household servants heard the shouts from the garden, they rushed in through the side doors to see what was happening. The elders told their story, and the servants were very ashamed, for never had such a thing been uttered about Susanna.

When the people gathered the next day at Joakim's house, the two elders came with their evil plot to put Susanna to death. They stood before the people and said, "Send for Susanna, the daughter of Hilkiah, and wife of Joakim." So they summoned her, and she came with her parents, her children, and all her relatives. Susanna was a refined woman, and very beautiful, but as she was veiled, the wicked elders commanded that she be uncovered, so that they might take their fill of her beauty. Her family and all who saw her began to weep.

The two elders stood before the people and placed their hands upon her head, but she gazed up through her tears into heaven, because she remained faithful to the Lord. The elders said, "As we were strolling in the garden alone, this woman entered with two maids. She then closed the garden gates and dismissed the maids. Then a young man, who had been hidden, came to her, and lay with her. We were in the corner of the garden when we saw their wicked deed and ran out to where they were. We found them lying together, but were not able to apprehend the young man, since he was stronger than we. He then opened the gates and escaped. As for her, we held her and questioned her as to who this young man was, but she would not tell us. This is our testimony."

Since they were elders of the people and judges, the assembly believed them and condemned her to death. Susanna cried out in a loud voice, "O eternal God who perceives all hidden things and knows all events before they come to pass, you know also that they have brought false witness against me. Now I am about to die, even though I have not done any of the wicked things they have charged against me!"

The Lord heard her cry. As she was being led away to die, God aroused the holy spirit of a young boy named Daniel, and he called out, "I am innocent of this woman's blood!"

All the crowd turned to him and said, "Why are you saying this?"

He stood in the middle of them and said, "How foolish you are, O Israelites! Although you have not examined the case closely nor investigated the facts, are you ready to condemn a woman of Israel? Return once more to the court, for these men are falsely accusing her."

The people quickly reassembled, and the gathered elders said to him, "Here, sit before us and address us, for God has bestowed upon you the status of an elder."

"Separate the two elders from each other," Daniel said to them, "and I shall examine them." When they had been separated, he called in the first of them and said, "You have spent many years in wickedness, but now your sins have caught up to you. You have rendered unjust judgments; the innocent you have condemned and the guilty you have set free, even though the Lord says, 'You shall not put the innocent and the righteous to death.' Now then, if you really saw her, tell me, under what tree were they lying together?"

And he answered, "Under a clove tree."

"You have condemned yourself with your lies," said Daniel. "Already an angel has received from God the sentence to cleave[1] you in two!" Then dismissing him he called in the other. "You seed of Canaan, and not of Judah! Beauty has led you astray, and desire has perverted your heart. You have been acting in this way with the daughters of Israel, and they were lying with you through fear, but no daughter of Judah would consent to this wickedness![2] Tell me, then, under what tree did you find them lying together?"

He replied, "Under a yew tree."

"Very well, your lie has condemned you as well!" said Daniel. "The angel of God stands waiting, sword in hand, to hew you in two and destroy you both!"

The whole crowd then cheered, and blessed the God who saves those who place their faith in him. They took the two elders, whom Daniel had convicted by their own testimony, and

1. The Greek word for cleave, *schizein,* is very similar to the Greek word for mastic tree, *schinon;* this is a humorous play on words, in that by lying, the elder names his own punishment. The same is true in the next interrogation, where Greek *prinon* (evergreen oak) and *prizein* (hew) are used. I have followed a common practice of choosing English names for the trees that also sound like the verbs. The Greek word play was taken in the ancient world to be evidence that the stories were composed in Greek and thus could not be authentic, but the word play can be produced in Aramaic as well, just as it is in English.

2. The author is distinguishing between residents of Judah, where Jerusalem is located, and those of Israel, or the northern part of David's kingdom. Reflected here is the continuing animosity between these two regions.

did to them what they had plotted to do to their neighbor, and executed them according to the law of Moses.

On that day, innocent blood was spared. Hilkiah and his wife praised God for their daughter, as did her husband Joakim and all her relatives, because no wickedness was found in her. And from that day forward Daniel was reckoned a great man among his people.

## *Bel and the Serpent*

When King Astyages was laid to rest with his ancestors, he was succeeded on the throne by Cyrus of Persia. Daniel was a confidant of the king, and the most honored of all his friends. The Babylonians at this time had an idol named Bel, to which they offered each day twelve bushels of fine flour, forty sheep, and fifty gallons of wine. The king revered the idol as well, going daily to worship him, but Daniel continued to worship his God. So the king said to Daniel, "Why do you not worship Bel?"

"Because," replied Daniel, "I do not revere idols made with hands, but the living God who created heaven and earth and rules over all living things."

"But do you not think," asked the king, "that Bel is such a living god? Do you not see how much he eats and drinks each day?"

But Daniel answered him, laughing, "Do not be deceived, O King. This creature is only clay on the inside, and bronze on the outside, and has never tasted a thing."

The king became furious and, summoning his priests, he said to them, "If you cannot show me who it is who consumes all of these provisions, you shall die. But if you can prove that Bel is the one who eats them, then Daniel shall die, because he has blasphemed against Bel."

And Daniel replied, "Let it be done as you have said."

Now there were seventy priests of Bel, not counting their wives and children. The king came with Daniel to the temple of

Bel, and the priests of Bel said, "Now we shall step outside of the temple, while you, O king, set out the food and mix the wine. Then you yourself close the door and seal it with your signet-ring. When you return early tomorrow morning, if you do not find that all these things have been eaten by Bel, we shall die; but if, on the other hand, Daniel has wrongly accused us, let him die." They were not concerned about this test, since they had constructed a trapdoor beneath the table, through which they had regularly been entering the temple and eating the food.

So as they had arranged, they left the temple, and the king set out the food for Bel. But Daniel, in the presence of the king alone, ordered his servants to bring ashes and sprinkle them over the whole temple. After they had all withdrawn, they closed the door and sealed it with the king's signet-ring, and departed. During the night the priests, with their wives and children, came as usual and consumed all of the food and wine that had been laid out for Bel.

Early the next morning the king, with Daniel beside him, arrived at the temple. "Are the seals still intact?" he asked Daniel.

"Yes, they are, your majesty," Daniel replied.

The king then opened the doors and looked in at the table, and immediately cried out, "Great are you, O Bel, and in thee there is truly no deceit!"

But Daniel laughed, and restraining the king from going in, said, "Look at the floor, and note whose footprints these are."

"Why," said the king, "I see the prints of men, women, and children!"

Furious, the king arrested the priests, their wives, and their children. They showed the king the trapdoor through which they entered the temple to consume the food and wine. Then the king executed them all and handed Bel over to Daniel, which he in turn destroyed, along with the temple.

There was also there a great serpent that the Babylonians worshipped, and the king said to Daniel, "Surely you must agree that this is a living god. Bow down, then, and worship him."

But Daniel responded, "I shall worship only the Lord my God, because he is a living God. And if you give me permission, your majesty, I shall kill the serpent, without using a sword or staff."

"I give you permission," said the king.

So Daniel took pitch, fat, and hair, and boiling them together, formed them into cakes, and fed them to the serpent. When the serpent swallowed them, it burst open.[3] "Look what you have been worshipping!" said Daniel.

But when the Babylonians heard about this, they became very angry and rose up against the king. "The king has become a Jew!" they charged. "He has destroyed Bel, slain the serpent, and executed the priests!" So coming together before the king, they shouted, "Hand Daniel over to us! If you do not, we will kill you and your family!"

The king realized that they had forced his hand, and so against his will, he was compelled to turn Daniel over to them. They threw Daniel into the lions' den, and he remained there for six days. In the den were seven lions, which each day were fed two human bodies and two sheep. But on this occasion they were not given any food, so that they would devour Daniel.

Now the prophet Habbakuk was in Judea,[4] making a stew and breaking bread into a bowl to take to the reapers in the field, when an angel of the Lord said to him, "Take this meal that you have prepared and go to Babylon, where Daniel is sitting in a lion's den."

"But my lord," responded Habbakuk, "I have never been to Babylon, and do not know anything about a lion's den."

But the angel of the Lord grabbed him by the top of the head

3. These items are evidently not magical but swell up in the serpent's stomach from their natural properties. There are other Jewish stories from this period (in addition to the first part of *Bel*) that focus on the naturalistic exposé of the fallacy of idols.

4. An interlude concerning the prophet Habbakuk has evidently been inserted here. The original narrative resumes later.

and, lifting him by his hair, placed him in Babylon beside the lions' den with the force of his breath. Habbakuk called out, "Daniel, Daniel, take this meal that God has sent to you."

And Daniel replied, "You have remembered me, O God, and have not forsaken those who love you." So Daniel got up and ate, as the angel of God immediately returned Habbakuk to where he had been.

On the seventh day the king came to mourn for Daniel, but when he approached the lions' den and looked in, there was Daniel, sitting before him! He let out a cry and said, "Great are you, O Lord God of Daniel! There is no God but you!" He then pulled Daniel up out of the pit, but those who were responsible for his punishment he threw into the den, where they were immediately devoured before his eyes.

## SUGGESTIONS FOR FURTHER READING

Gruen, Erich. *Heritage and Hellenism: The Reinvention of Jewish Tradition,* pp. 167–77. Berkeley: University of California Press, 1998.

Levine, Amy-Jill. "'Hemmed In on Every Side': Jews and Women in the Book of Susanna." In *Reading from this Place.* Ed. Fernando F. Segovia and Mary Anne Tolbert, pp. 1.175–90. 2 vols. Minneapolis: Fortress, 1995.

Moore, Carey A. *Daniel, Esther, and Jeremiah: The Additions.* Garden City, N.Y.: Doubleday, 1977.

Nickelsburg, George W. E. *Jewish Literature Between the Bible and the Mishnah,* pp. 19–30. Philadelphia: Fortress, 1981.

Steussy, Marti J. *Gardens in Babylon: Narrative and Faith in the Greek Legends of Daniel.* Atlanta: Scholars Press, 1993.

Wills, Lawrence M. *The Jew in the Court of the Foreign King: Ancient Jewish Court Legends,* pp. 75–152. Minneapolis: Fortress, 1990.

———. *The Jewish Novel in the Ancient World,* pp. 40– 67. Ithaca, N.Y., and London: Cornell University Press, 1995.

FOUR

# TOBIT

The *Book of Tobit,* found in the Eastern Orthodox and Catholic versions of the Bible but not in the Jewish or Protestant, contains both piety and humor, and it is not clear which—if either—is intended to predominate. The story is set in the eighth century B.C.E., when the ten northern tribes were captured by the Assyrians and part of the populace were exiled to Nineveh, the Assyrian capital. The details of the narrative, however, are much more appropriate to the time of the exile and the beginning of the diaspora after the destruction of the Temple in 587 B.C.E. The work must therefore have been written after the exile, but since it does not make any reference to the Maccabean Revolt in 168–165 B.C.E., it was likely written before that event. A date sometime in the fourth to early second century B.C.E. is therefore likely, and there are other similar Jewish writings from this period as well. Like the *Tobiad Romance,* this book may have been a family romance of the Tobiads, a family of wealthy entrepreneurial Jews who, like the figures in this story, traded between east and west.

*The Book of Tobit* falls into three parts. In the first part Tobit is a righteous Jew who maintains his piety in the face of repressive laws—a common theme in the Jewish novels. Specifically, he persists in burying the bodies of dead Jews even though the Assyrian king has outlawed the practice. Tobit is forced to go into hiding and his property is confiscated, but when that king dies, Tobit is reinstated by the successor. All this serves as the backdrop to the main body of the writing, which introduces the parallel problems of Tobit and his distant kinswoman, Sarah. Tobit, though pious, has been blinded, and Sarah's seven husbands have been killed in succession on their wedding nights by the evil demon Asmodaeus. Tobit and Sarah simultaneously pray for death as a release from their sufferings, but the angel Raphael is sent to resolve both of their problems. In human guise he accompanies Tobit's son Tobias on his journey to recover money that has been left on deposit; it is this central quest that gives Raphael the opportunity to work his magic, bringing all the mortals' problems to a happy resolution. Raphael shows Tobias how to chase away the evil demon Asmodaeus, and also convinces him to marry Sarah, who is now freed from the curse. Tobias, Sarah, and the angel Raphael now return to Tobit's city, where the angel shows Tobias how to restore his father's sight. The angel then reveals his identity to the gathered family and leaves.

Following this main body is an addendum (chapter 14) in which Tobit gives his last testament to Tobias and his grandchildren, predicting the end of Nineveh, the fall and rebuilding of the Temple in Jerusalem, and the eventual conversion of the gentiles and return of the Jews of the Diaspora to Jerusalem. It has a strikingly different tone and may have been added. It is introduced in a repetitive and awkward way, and many motifs of the first two parts of Tobit are treated differently here. For example, the figure of Nadab, Tobit's cousin, who is presented in a positive light in chapters 2–13, is here depicted as evil (as he is also in the non-Jewish *Story of Ahikar*), and the eschatological boundaries of Jew and non-Jew are sharply drawn.

It is the first two sections that attract most of the literary interest. They address the problem of suffering and God's justice but at the same time interweave irony and humor. The irascible Tobit, for example, subjects Raphael to a rigorous job interview, interrogating him about his family pedigree, and later the parents of Sarah must scurry about to cover up the grave they have dug for their son-in law Tobias when, to their surprise, he survives his wedding night. Even though Tobit at one point cries out like Job, his fall is not tragic; he has a divine safety net of which the audience is constantly made aware.

The core narrative of the first two sections is similar to folk narratives involving supernatural heroes and villains. The common folktales of "The Grateful Dead Man" and "The Dangerous Bride," as told in a number of cultures around the world, provide many parallels to this text. In the former folktale, for example, a traveler buries the body of a man who has been killed by robbers, and he is later joined on his journey by a mysterious stranger who helps him ward off the demon that has tormented a rich young woman. The traveler is now able to marry the woman and live happily ever after. Tobit is a novelized folktale, however; the focus has shifted somewhat to the human characters. The domestic drama has moved onto center stage, and the moral character of the protagonists is presented in some detail. This in itself is perhaps enough to indicate that the narrative is more novelistic than the folktale versions, but it is not novelistic in a way that we are used to. Despite the presence of trials, demons, magic, and danger, there is never any real suspense built up in the narrative—we are told near the beginning that all will end happily. Such a disclosure, however, is not uncommon in ancient novels—the Greek novel *Ephesian Tale* by Xenophon of Ephesus anticipates a happy ending as well (1.6)—and it does not detract from the novel's ability to entertain. The entertainment does not come from building and resolving tension, but rather from seeing how the story will unfold and how all the threads will be tied together at the end.

The reader should also note four motifs that permeate chapters 1–13 and become increasingly interrelated. The first is kinship: every named human character in this section, other than the Assyrian kings, is related, and even the angel Raphael poses as a distant relative. The words "brother" and "sister" are ubiquitous, sometimes used for spouses and sometimes for extended family (compare their use for spouses in *Greek Esther* and *The Marriage and Conversion of Aseneth*). The second is burial: one of the obligations of kinship for Tobias is to give an honorable burial to his parents, and this issue is mentioned constantly, along with the comical burial scene already mentioned. The third and fourth motifs are blessing and marriage: the culmination of the story contains a long series of blessings, especially surrounding the marriage of Sarah and Tobias and the acceptance of these two romantic figures by their respective in-laws. It is quite possible that this book was a reading for a wedding festival. This is an especially attractive theory if, as seems likely, the book was first composed and read as a Tobiad family romance.

*Tobit,* like some of the other novels, combines narrative prose with other literary forms. The story pauses early on for Tobit to bestow his best wisdom upon his son in the form of a series of proverbs; near the end we find a hymn of praise for all God's gracious actions. These passages are not distractions from the main narrative, much as they might seem to be for modern readers, but rather serve to emphasize aspects of the overall story. The proverbs are an ironic counterpoint to the events surrounding them: Tobit assures his son that God will reward piety, when his own experience has just called that possibility into question, and he himself in his despair has prayed for death. The hymn of praise at the end is not ironic but gives full voice to the happy ending of the story, a sort of Greek chorus of acclamation. The combination of narrative with other forms, especially songs, is common in the Bible, and we can especially note its use in *Judith, The Marriage and Conversion of Aseneth,* and *The Prayer of Azariah and the Song of the Three Jews* (not included in this volume).

*Tobit*

(1) This is the story of Tobit, a member of the tribe of Naphtali and the family of Asiel, descended in order from Tobiel, Hananiel, Aduel, Gabael, Raphael, and Raguel. While Shalmaneser was king of the Assyrians, Tobit was taken captive from the village of Thisbe, which is south of Kedesh Naphtali in Upper Galilee, and northwest of Hazor, and north of Pe`or.

I, Tobit, walked in the ways of truth and righteousness all my life, performing many acts of charity for my kinfolk and my people who were taken with me as captives into Nineveh of Assyria. When I was still a young man in my native country of Israel, the whole tribe of Naphtali my forefather broke away from the house of David and from Jerusalem, the city chosen from all the land of Israel as the place of sacrifice for Israel's tribes. This temple of God's presence had thus been sanctified as an eternal house for each generation, but my kinfolk—the entire tribe of Naphtali my forefather—sacrificed instead on the mountains of Galilee to the calf which Jeroboam, king of Israel, made in Dan. All alone, however, I continually made my way back to Jerusalem for each of the festivals, as it is prescribed in the eternal commandment for all Israel. For the offerings of the first fruits and the firstborn, for the tithes of the cattle and the first shearings of sheep, I hurried off to Jerusalem to deposit these with the priests, the sons of Aaron, for the altar. The tithe of wheat, wine, oil, pomegranates, figs, and the other fruits I would also present to the Levites who were ministering in Jerusalem. In addition, for six years I exchanged the second tithe for money and gave it each year to the orphans, widows, and proselytes who had joined the people of Israel. Every third year I brought this gift, as we ate together according to the commandment laid down in the law of Moses and in keeping with the injunctions of Deborah, the mother of my father Tobiel (for my own father had died and left me an orphan). And so when I grew up, I married a woman from my own family, and we had a son whom we named Tobias.

Having thus been taken away captive to Assyria, I settled in Nineveh, and although my kinfolk and my people now all ate gentile food, I myself was resolved against it. As I remained faithful to God with my whole heart, the Most High granted that I should become a favored member of Shalmaneser's court; I was appointed chief purchasing agent for the king. Until the time that he died, I traveled to Media as his agent, and while there deposited bags of silver, amounting to ten talents, with Gabael, brother of Gabri. When Shalmaneser died, however, and his son Sennacherib succeeded him, the roads to Media were closed to travel, and I was no longer able to journey there. During the whole of Shalmaneser's reign, I performed many acts of charity for my kinfolk and all my relations. I gave bread to the hungry and clothed the naked, and if ever I saw that one of my people had died and the body had been thrown outside the walls of Nineveh, that person I buried. During the days of judgment, when the King of Heaven punished Sennacherib for all his blasphemies and he fled Judea, I buried the Israelites whom he killed, for in his fury he had indeed killed many, leaving their corpses lying unburied. Later, when Sennacherib sought them and could not find them, a resident of Nineveh informed him that I was the one who had buried them. I then went into hiding, but when I learned that he was not only aware of what I had done, but also sought me for execution, I became even more frightened and ran away. All of my property was confiscated by the king; all that was left were my wife Anna and son Tobias. Forty days did not pass, however, before Sennacherib was murdered by his two sons, who then fled into the mountains of Ararat, leaving Sennacherib's other son, Esarhaddon, to succeed him. He appointed Ahikar, son of my brother Anael—and thus my nephew and a close relative—over all the king's accounts, and he came to have control over the king's entire administration. He had been cupbearer, keeper of the seal, and prime minister under Sennacherib, and Esarhaddon had reappointed him to these offices. As a result he was able to intercede on my behalf and allow me to return to Nineveh.

(2) Under Esarhaddon I thus returned to my home, and my wife Anna and my son Tobias were restored to me. During our Festival of Weeks, a great banquet was prepared for me and I sat down to enjoy it. The table was already richly laid, but I said to my son Tobias, "Go, my son, and if you find someone from among our kinfolk, a captive here in Nineveh, who is poor but wholeheartedly devoted to God, bring that person here to join me in my feast. I shall wait for you, my son, until you return."

Tobias went out to search for a poor person from among our kin, but when he returned, he shouted, "Father!"

"What is it, my son?" I replied.

"One of our people has been murdered! He was strangled and thrown into the marketplace and is lying there now!"

Without tasting my dinner, I sprang up and went out to retrieve the body from the street. I placed it in one of the outbuildings until sunset to bury him.[1] Returning then to my dinner, I washed and ate my meal with a heavy heart. I recalled what the prophet Amos said about Bethel: "Your feasts will be turned into mourning, and all your songs into lamentation," and I began to weep. When the sun had set, I went out to dig a grave for the man, but all of my neighbors jeered at me and said, "Is he still not afraid? It was not long ago that he was being sought for execution for this very practice, and ran away. But he is at it again, burying the dead!"

That night I washed and went into the courtyard and fell asleep by the courtyard wall. I left my face uncovered on account of the heat, little realizing that sparrows were on the wall above my head. Their droppings fell upon my eyes, and from the warm droppings, white patches formed. I went to doctor after doctor to be healed, but no matter what ointments they rubbed on my eyes, they only became increasingly worse, until I was totally blind. For four years, I remained blind, and my entire family

1. Tobit waits until sunset either to observe the feast day (on which burial is prohibited), or possibly to conceal his purposes.

grieved for me. Ahikar came to take care of me for two years, until he went away to Elymais.

During this time my wife Anna earned extra money at women's work; she would return her finished work to her employers and receive from them her wages. On the seventh of Dystrus, when she had cut a piece she was weaving from the loom and delivered it to her employers, they paid her the regular fee, but in addition to that gave her a kid from the flock. Upon her return, the kid began to bleat, and I called out to her, "Where did the kid come from? Have you stolen it? Return it to its rightful owners, for how could we eat stolen food?"

"But this was given to me as a gift," she assured me, "in addition to my wages!"

I did not believe her, however, and although I was ashamed to admit her actions, I ordered her to return it. She, however, retorted, "Now where are all your acts of charity? Where are all your righteous deeds? Everyone can see what has happened to you!"

(3) Grief welled up within me at the sound of these words. I moaned and wailed and began to pray: "O Lord, you are righteous, and all your deeds are just. Your ways are kind and true. You are always a righteous judge. Now, O Lord, remember me and look upon me. Do not punish me for my sins, nor for my transgressions, nor for those of my forebears. They committed sins against you and broke your commandments, and now you have given us over to plunder and captivity and death, and we have become a laughing-stock in all the nations where we are scattered. Your many judgments are true in exacting the penalty from me for my sins, because we did not keep your commandments and did not live honestly in your presence. Do with me, then, according to your will and command that my spirit be released; allow me to return to the earth and become earth. It is better for me now to die than to live, for I have been subjected to unjust reproaches, and my grief will consume me. O Lord, lift this burden from me; release me to the eternal abode! Do not turn away from me, O Lord. It is now better for me to die than to live with such grief and suffer such reproaches!"

It so happened that on that same day Sarah the daughter of Raguel, who lived in Ecbatana of Media, was also forced to bear the reproaches of one of her father's maids. Although Sarah had been given in marriage to seven men, Asmodaeus the evil demon had killed them all before the unions could be consummated. Her maid had railed at her, "It is you who have killed your husbands! Now you have been given to seven men, but you have not taken the name of one of them! Why do you beat us on account of your husbands' deaths? Join them! May we never see a child of yours!"

And so on that day Sarah was also tormented. Retiring to her upper room, she wept and resolved to hang herself. She paused, however, to consider what might happen: "They would slander my father and say, 'You had but a single beloved daughter, and she hanged herself from all her woes!' That would bring my poor aged father down to his grave with sorrow. Indeed, it would be better not to hang myself, but to beg the Lord instead to let me die, and no longer hear unjust reproaches." She then spread her hands toward the window and prayed: "Blessed are you, O merciful God. Blessed be your name forever; may all your creation bless you forever. Now I raise my face and eyes to you. Allow me to be released from this earth so that I may no longer hear unkind reproaches. You know, O Master, that I have never been defiled by any man and have never brought any disgrace on my father's name in the land of our sojourn. I am my father's only child. There is no other to inherit his estate, nor a brother or close kinsman for whom I might preserve myself. Seven husbands of mine have already perished—why should I yet live? If it does not please you to kill me, then spare me, O Lord, these shameful insults."

At one and the same moment, the prayers of Sarah and Tobit were heard in the glorious presence of God, and Raphael was sent to heal them both: he was to remove the scales from Tobit's eyes so that he might see with his own eyes the light of day, and release Sarah from the spell of the evil Asmodaeus and give her to Tobias the son of Tobit as wife, for Tobias, alone of all her suitors, was entitled to marry her.[2] And at the same moment, Tobit returned from the courtyard into his house and Sarah the daughter of Raguel descended from her upper room.

(4) It was also on that day that Tobit recalled the deposited money which he had left with Gabael in Rages of Media, and he thought to himself, "Indeed, now I have prayed for death, but should I not first call for Tobias, my son, and tell him of this money before I die?" He called Tobias, and when he came he said to him, "Give me a decent burial. Honor your mother and take care of her all the days of her life. Do her bidding; do not cause her grief in any way. Be mindful of her, my son, because she took many risks for you while you were still in the womb. When she dies, bury her next to me in the same tomb. Heed the Lord all your days, my son, and do not be tempted to sin or transgress his commandments. Perform good deeds for as long as you live, and never walk in the paths of iniquity, for those who practice truthfulness will be rewarded in all their endeavors, and to all who practice righteousness, the Lord will return a good reward.[3] But whomever he wills, the Lord humbles to the grave

2. As will be seen, Tobias is the closest male relative of Sarah, and it is presumed that as a result he has the strongest claim to marry her. This is similar, but not identical to the law of levirate marriage in Deuteronomy 25:5–10 and the custom recounted in Ruth 4. Alternatively, it is possible that the author is suggesting that Tobias was destined by heaven to marry Sarah, but compare chapter 6, where both views are presented.

3. Other ancient versions of *Tobit* contain more maxims at this point, and some scholars argue that they are original to the story and were accidentally dropped from the Sinaiticus text by scribal error (as in the similar case in chapter 13). However, the maxims in the Sinaiticus text are more pointedly ironic, since they are at variance with the righteous Tobit's apparent punishment by God, while the block of maxims in the other versions introduce new motifs which, while admirable, lack any ironic counterpoint to the narrative. They may have been added for pious purposes only. Further, the summary statement at the end of chapter 4 refers back to the maxims printed here but not to those from the other versions.

below. My son, remember these commandments, and never let them fade from your heart.

"Now, my son, I want you to know that I placed ten talents of silver on deposit with Gabael, son of Gabri, at Rages in Media. Therefore do not be afraid, my son, because we have become poor. You will be blessed with good fortune, if you but fear God and flee all sin, and do good before the Lord your God."

(5) "Father," answered Tobias, "I shall do whatever you command. But how can I go to claim money left on deposit with a man who does not know me, nor I him? What proof shall I give him that he may recognize me and trust me and return the money? What is more, I do not even know the way to Media."

Tobit then answered Tobias, "The man with whom I deposited the money gave me a written contract, as I did him. I tore his contract in two parts, and we each kept half. His half was placed in the bag with the money. It has been twenty years now since I deposited the money with him. Go, my son, and seek a trustworthy man to accompany you, and upon your return we shall pay him his wage, and in this way you can retrieve the money."

Tobias then departed to find someone to guide him over the roads to Media. Standing before him he found the angel Raphael, but not realizing that he was an angel of God, said to him, "Where are you from, young man?"

"From your kinfolk, the Israelites," answered Raphael. "I have come here to find work."

"Do you know well the way to Media?" asked Tobias.

"Yes, indeed," he replied. "Many times have I been there, and I know all the roads well. I have traveled to Media often, lodging with Gabael our kinsman, who lives in Rages of Media. It is a two days' journey from Ecbatana to Rages, for Rages is situated in the hills, while Ecbatana lies in the plain."

"Well then, young man," said Tobias, "wait here until I tell my father. I need someone such as yourself to accompany me to Media and shall pay you your wages."

"I shall wait here then," said Raphael, "but do not tarry."

Tobias returned to his father and said, "I have just found a kinsman, one of the Israelites."

"Go, my son," said Tobit, "and bring him to me. I want to find out from what tribe he comes, and whether he can be trusted to accompany you."

Tobias went and called him, saying, "My father would like to see you."

When Raphael arrived, Tobit greeted him.

"Good tidings to you!" said Raphael.

"How can anything good come my way?" Tobit replied. "I am now totally blind, and cannot see the light of heaven. Instead I sit in darkness, like the dead. I am living, yet like the dead I can only hear people's voices, and not see them."

"Have courage!" said Raphael. "God's healing is close at hand."

Tobit said to him, "Tobias, my son, wants to go to Media. Can you accompany him and guide him on his way? If so, brother, I shall pay you your wage."

"I can take him there," replied Raphael. "I know all the roads and have been to Media often. I have traveled all its plains, its mountains, and highways."

"Brother, please tell me," asked Tobit, "what is your family, and which tribe are you from?"

"Why do you need to know my tribe?" asked Raphael.

"Indeed, my brother, I would like very much for you to tell me honestly whose son you are, and what your name is."

"I am Azariah, son of Hananiah the elder, your kinsman."

"Enter then in good health, brother!" said Tobit, "And please do not be angry with me because I wanted to know your tribe and family. Indeed, as it happens, you are a kinsman, and from a fine family. I knew Hananiah and Nathan, the two sons of the elder Semelias. They used to go with me to Jerusalem and worship with me there, and they were always faithful. Your kinfolk are good men. You are obviously from good stock yourself, and I am happy to welcome you. I shall give you the wage of a drachma a day, and you will have the same provisions for the trip as my son. Keep him company on his journey, and I shall also add a bonus."

"I shall be his companion," said Raphael, "and do not worry; we shall leave in good health and return to you the same. It is not a perilous journey."

"God bless you, my brother!" declared Tobit, and he called in his son. "My son, make all the preparations for the journey, and set out with your kinsman here. May the God in heaven safeguard you there and bring you back to me unharmed, and may his angel accompany you, my son, and ensure your safety."

As Tobias prepared to take his leave, he kissed his father and mother. "Have a safe journey," said Tobit.

His mother, however, began to cry, and turning to her husband said, "Why have you sent my son away? Is he not our rod and support? Does he not do our every bidding? Do not throw good money after bad, but consider it a loss for the sake of our son. The Lord has granted us life—let this be enough!"

"Do not be concerned for his safety," Tobit replied to her. "He leaves in good health and will return safely. You will see the day when he returns to you unharmed. Do not fear for them, for a good angel will accompany him and prosper their way, and bring him back unharmed." (6) Then Anna stopped her crying.

Tobias set off on his journey, accompanied by the angel; his dog also went at his side. Thus the two of them traveled together, and when the first night came, they camped by the side of the Tigris River. The young man went down to the river bank to bathe his feet, when suddenly a great fish leapt out of the water to snap at his toe. Tobias cried out, and the angel shouted to him, "Seize the fish and hold it!" Tobias caught hold of the fish and hauled it on to the bank. The angel then instructed Tobias, "Split the fish open and take out its gall, its heart, and its liver, and set them aside; throw away the rest of the entrails. The gall, the heart, and the liver will make very useful medicine." So the young man split the fish open and retrieved the gall, the heart, and the liver. Then roasting some of the fish, he ate it, and set the rest aside to be salted.

Afterward, as they proceeded on their journey to Media, Tobias asked the angel, "Brother Azariah, what medicine is to be found in the gall, the heart, and the liver of a fish?"

"The heart and the liver of a fish," replied Raphael "can be used to make smoke in the presence of a man or woman who is under the spell of a demon or evil spirit. The demon will flee, never to return again. The gall can be used as an ointment for a person whose eyes are covered with white scales. Once the eyes are anointed and one blows over them, they will become well."

As they entered Media and approached Ecbatana, Raphael turned to his companion and said, "Brother Tobias!"

"What is it?" answered Tobias.

"We should lodge tonight in the house of Raguel, for he is a kinsman of yours. He also has a daughter, whose name is Sarah. No other child does he have except this Sarah, and since you are a closer kinsman than any other man, it is right for you to marry her and inherit her estate. Furthermore, the young woman is prudent, upright, and very beautiful, and her father is noble. Take my advice to heart; I shall speak to her father tonight, and thus we can arrange a marriage for you. When we return from Rages, we shall celebrate the wedding. I am certain that Raguel would never deny you permission to marry her or betroth her to another, for that would merit death according to the commandment of the book of Moses. Indeed, he knows it is only right for you, of all men, to receive his daughter's inheritance. So now, my brother, heed my advice, and tonight we shall discuss the marriage and betroth her to you. She can then accompany us when we return home."

"But Brother Azariah," Tobias replied, "I have heard that she has already been betrothed to seven men, and they died on their wedding night when they entered into the marriage chamber. People say she is possessed by a demon who kills these young men, and yet the demon, so it is said, does not harm her, only those who dare come near her! I am afraid that I may perish, bringing my father and mother down to their graves from grief, since they have no other child left to bury them."

"Do you not remember your father's injunctions?" asked Raphael. "He ordered you to take a wife from your father's house. Do what I say, brother, and do not be concerned about the demon, but marry this young woman. I know that tonight you will take her as wife. When you enter the marriage chamber, simply take the liver and the heart of the fish, and place them in the incense burner. The odor will rise up, and the demon will smell it and flee, never again to torment her. But when you are about to join her in the marriage bed, both of you must first arise and pray to the Lord of Heaven that you obtain mercy and deliverance. Now do not fear, for she was destined to be yours from the beginning. You will indeed save her, she will remain with you, and you will likely have many children who will become like brothers and sisters to you. So do not be afraid." When Tobias heard these words of Raphael and considered that Sarah was a kinswoman from his father's house, he loved her deeply, and his heart longed for her.

(7) When they arrived in Ecbatana, Tobias said to his companion, "Brother Azariah, lead me directly to Raguel our kinsman."

He led him to the house of Raguel, and they found him sitting beside the doorway to the courtyard. They greeted him first, and he replied, "Many greetings to you; I hope you are well." He then led them to his house, but pulling his wife Edna aside, he remarked, "How closely this young man resembles Tobit, my kinsman!"

Edna then asked them, "Where are you from, brothers?"

"We are of the tribe of Naphtali, from among the captives in Nineveh," they answered.

"Well, then, do you know Tobit, our kinsman?"

"Yes, indeed, we do."

"Is he well?"

"Yes, he is alive, and in good health."

"He is my father," added Tobias.

Raguel leapt up and with tears in his eyes embraced him and said, "God bless you, my boy, you are indeed the son of a noble man! But oh, what a terrible misfortune, that such a righteous and generous man should become blind!" He embraced Tobias his kinsman and began to cry again. Edna his wife and Sarah their daughter also wept for Tobit. Afterward, Raguel slaughtered a ram from the flock and welcomed them graciously.

After they had bathed and washed their hands, Tobias and Raphael reclined at dinner. "Brother Azariah," said Tobias, "speak to Raguel, and ask on my behalf that he grant me Sarah, my kinswoman, as wife."

But when Raguel heard this request, he answered, "Eat, drink, and be merry tonight, my brother, for it would not be proper for any man but you to receive her hand in marriage. I do not have the right to betroth her to another, since you are my closest of kin. But, my son, I must tell you the truth: I have given her in marriage to seven men, all of them kinsmen, and all of them died on their wedding night when they went in to her. But for now, my son, eat and drink, and may the Lord be kind to you both."

"I will neither eat nor drink," replied Tobias, "until this matter is settled."

"Then I grant your request," Raguel answered. "She is yours according to the commandment of the book of Moses. It has been decreed by Heaven that she be yours; receive your sister. From now on and from this day forth, you will be her brother and she your sister, and may the Lord of Heaven keep both of you safe through the night, granting you mercy and peace."

Raguel then called Sarah, his daughter, and when she entered, took her hand and presented her to Tobias. "Take her according to the law and commandment which is written in the book of Moses concerning the betrothal of women. Take her and go in health to the house of your father. May the God of heaven grant you peace and good fortune."

He then called in her mother and instructed her to bring a scroll, upon which he wrote a marriage contract to grant Sarah to Tobias as wife, according to the commandment in the law of Moses. With the contract completed, they proceeded to eat and drink their feast. Raguel then said to Edna privately, "Sister, prepare the spare room, and take Sarah there." Edna did as he had told her and led Sarah to the room. At first she began to cry for her, but wiped away her tears and said, "Do not lose hope, my child. May the Lord of heaven grant you joy in place of your grief. Have courage, my daughter!" Then she left.

(8) When they finished eating and drinking, they decided to retire. They led the young man into the bedroom, and Tobias recalled Raphael's instructions; producing the liver and heart of the fish from his pouch, he placed them in the incense burner. The odor of the fish repelled the demon, who immediately fled to Upper Egypt, where Raphael pursued him and bound him securely. When the others had left and the door was shut, Tobias arose from the bed and said to Sarah, "Come, Sister, let us pray to our Lord that he grant us mercy and save us." She arose with him, and they began to pray for deliverance. "Blessed are you, God of our fathers," prayed Tobias. "May your name be blessed forever for all generations. May the heavens bless you and all creation, forever and ever. You created Adam and made Eve as a helpmate and support. From the two of them came all of the generations on Earth. You said, 'It is not good for man to be alone. Let us make for him a helpmate like himself.' And now I take this, my sister, not in illicit lust, but in true marriage. Grant us mercy and allow us to grow old together." They then said together, "Amen," and slept the night.

Meanwhile, Raguel arose and summoned his servants, and together they went out and dug a grave, "lest," he said, "the young man die and we become a laughing-stock, scorned by all." When they had finished digging the grave, Raguel came back in the house and called his wife. "Send one of the maidservants to go into the bedchamber to see if he is still alive. If he is dead, we shall bury him before anyone finds out."

She sent a maidservant, who proceeded to the bedchamber and, with lamp in hand, opened the door and went in. There she found them lying in bed asleep. The maidservant came out and informed them that he was still alive and that no harm had come to him. They blessed the God of heaven and said, "Blessed are you, God, with every pure and holy blessing! May you be blessed forever! May all your angels and your chosen ones bless you forever! Blessed are you, for you have gladdened my heart; indeed, it has not happened as I feared it would. You have dealt with us according to your great mercy. Blessed are you, for you have dealt mercifully with two people who are only children. Grant to them mercy and deliverance, and make their lives prosper in happiness and mercy." Then he instructed his servants to fill up the grave before morning came.

Raguel then bid his wife to begin baking many loaves of bread, while he went to the herd and selected two oxen and four rams. He ordered that they be slaughtered and began the other preparations that would be necessary. He said to Tobias, "For fourteen days you shall not leave us but shall stay to gladden the heart of my daughter, who has been so afflicted. Of all that I own, you may take half and go in good health to your father. When my wife and I die the other half will also be yours, my son. Take comfort in this, my son, for I am now your father and Edna your mother. We will be with you and your wife from this day forth. Take heart, my son."

(9) Tobias then called Raphael and said to him, "Azariah, my brother, take four servants and two camels, set out for Rages, and when you arrive at the home of Gabael, give him the contract and collect the money; then let him accompany you here for the wedding celebration. For you know that my father will be counting the days, and every day I delay will grieve him. You have seen what Raguel has vowed for our celebration. I cannot

violate his oath." So Raphael departed with the servants and camels for Rages of Media and lodged with Gabael. Presenting Gabael with half of the contract for the deposited money, he recounted to him the travels of Tobias, son of Tobit, how he had found a wife and had invited him to the celebration. Gabael arose and counted out to him the bags of money, their seals still intact.

Early the next morning, the two of them arose and proceeded to the wedding. When they arrived at the home of Raguel, they found Tobias reclining at the feast, but he immediately jumped up and greeted them. Gabael began to cry, and blessed him, saying, "Good and noble youth, son of a good and noble father, who is both pious and kind! May the Lord bestow upon you the blessings of heaven, and upon your wife and your wife's father and mother. Blessed be God, for I have seen Tobias, the son of my kinsman, and his very spit and image!"

(10) Meanwhile Tobit was sitting in Nineveh, counting each day that passed, calculating how many his son would require to travel to Rages, and how many to return. When the number of days was completed and his son had still not returned, he said, "Has he perhaps been delayed? Perhaps Gabael has died, and there is no one to give him the money."

He grieved deeply, and Anna his wife said to him, "My son has died and is no longer among the living!" She began to weep, grieving also for her son, and said, "O, my child, my child, I allowed you, the light of my eye, to depart from us!"

"Stop crying now, sister!" said Tobit. "Do not be anxious. I am sure he is well. There has most likely been some delay, but the man who accompanied him is very trustworthy and a kinsman of ours. Do not grieve for him, sister. He will return soon."

"You are the one who should be quiet!" she responded. "Do not lie to me! My son is dead!"

So each day when she arose, she watched and waited at the side of the road; no one could move her from her post. And when the sun set each evening, she would come back in the house and wail and moan the whole night long, not even pausing to sleep.

When the fourteen days of the wedding were over which Raguel had sworn to provide for his daughter, Tobias took Raguel aside and said to him, "Allow me now to depart for home, for I know that my father and mother believe they will never see me again. I must ask you now, father, to give me leave to return to my father's house, for I have told you how he was when I left him."

"No, my son," said Raguel, "stay instead here with me, and I shall send messengers to Tobit your father who will explain to him your good fortune."

"No, I cannot," said Tobias. "I beg of you, let me return to my father."

So Raguel arose and presented Sarah to Tobias as wife, and one-half of all his possessions, including male and female slaves, cattle and sheep, asses and camels, clothing, silver, and utensils. He bade them farewell, embraced Tobias, and said, "Be well, my son, and have a safe journey. May the Lord of heaven guide your steps and those of Sarah, your wife. May I see your children before I die." Then turning to Sarah, his daughter, he said, "Go now to your new parents-in-law, for from this day forth they shall be your parents, as surely as if they had borne you. So go in peace, daughter. May I hear a good report of you as long as I live." Bidding his last farewell, he turned to let them go.

Then Edna said to Tobias, "My son and beloved brother, may the Lord bring you back our way, and may I live long enough to see children for you and my daughter Sarah. In the presence of the Lord, I entrust my daughter to you; do not bring her to any grief all the days of your life. Go in peace, my son. From now on I am your mother and Sarah is your sister. May this union bring us happiness all the days of our lives." She kissed them both and bade them farewell.

Tobias was joyful and in good spirits as he left Raguel, and he blessed the Lord of heaven and earth, King of all, who had prospered his way. And Tobias blessed them and said, "It has been commanded me by the Lord to honor you both all the days of my life."

(11) And as they approached Kaserin, which is near Nineveh, Raphael said, "You know how we left your father. Let us go on ahead of your wife and prepare your household for the news while the others are still coming." And as they proceeded ahead, Raphael added, "Now take the gall in your hands." The dog accompanied them also, following along behind Raphael and Tobias.

Anna was sitting at the side of the road, waiting for her son, and when she saw the dog now running along ahead of them, she ran and called to Tobit, "Look, your son is coming, along with the man who journeyed with him!"

But before they reached them, Raphael said to Tobias, "I assure you that your father's sight can be restored. Smear the gall of the fish on his eyes, and its healing power will shrink the white patches and allow you to peel them away. Your father will once again behold the light of day."

Anna ran to them and threw her arms around her son, saying to him, "I see you, my son! Now I can die in peace!" Then she wept.

Tobit arose and stumbled to the door of the courtyard. Tobias walked over beside him and, taking the fish gall in his hand, blew the vapors into his eyes. He held his father and said, "Have courage, Father!" He then took the medicine and applied it to his father's eyes, and with both hands, peeled the scales away from the corners of his eyes.

Tobit clutched his son and, weeping, said to him, "I see you, my son, light of my eyes! Blessed be God! Blessed be his great name! And blessed be all of his holy angels! May his great name abide with us. And blessed be all of his angels for all time. He afflicted me, but now I see Tobias my son."

Tobias then rejoiced and blessed God with all his heart. He recounted to his father how his journey had prospered, how he had recovered the silver, and had taken Sarah, the daughter of Raguel, as wife. "Indeed," he said, "she is also here, at the very gate of Nineveh."

Tobit went joyfully out to the gate of Nineveh to meet his daughter-in-law, blessing God as he went. When the people of Nineveh saw him marching forth, striding briskly with no one at his side to guide him, they were astounded. Tobit declared before them all how God had shown mercy upon him, and how he restored his sight. As Tobit approached Sarah, the wife of Tobias his son, he blessed her and said, "Welcome, daughter! Blessed be God who brought you to us, my daughter! Blessed be your father, blessed be Tobias my son, and blessed be you, my daughter! Welcome, daughter! Welcome to your new home! Enter in joy and blessing!"

There was great joy on that day among all the Jews of Nineveh; Ahikar and Nadab, Tobit's kinsmen, joined in the celebration. (12) And when these festivities came to an end, Tobit called Tobias and said, "My son, make sure that you pay the man who accompanied you, and give him also an extra sum over and above his wages."

"How much shall I pay him, Father?" asked Tobias. "It would not be too much to give him half of the money that we brought back with us. He conducted me safely, healed my wife, retrieved the money for me, and restored your sight. What then should be his wage?"

"It is right, my son," replied Tobit, "for him to receive half of the sum of money that he retrieved."

So Tobias called Raphael and said, "Take as your payment half of all the money that you retrieved, and go in peace."

But Raphael asked to speak to the two of them privately and said, "Bless God, and before all living creatures confess the good things he has done for you so that they can bless and sing praises to his name. Declare the deeds of God to all people openly; never cease confessing him. It is good to conceal the king's secrets, but acts of God should be proclaimed openly. If you do good, evil will never find you. A prayer with a pure heart is good, and charity with righteousness is better than riches obtained through guile. It is better to give alms than to store up gold, for alms-giving delivers from death and cleanses away all sin. Those who give alms reap a long life, but those who commit sin and unrighteousness are at war with their own souls.

"I shall now tell you the whole truth, holding nothing back. As I have just said, 'It is good to conceal a king's secrets, but acts of God should be declared openly.' When you and Sarah prayed, it was I who brought your prayer before the glory of the Lord, and likewise when you, Tobit, buried the dead. And when you did not hesitate to rise up and leave your dinner, but went and buried the dead, it was also I who was sent to test you, and again God sent me at the same time to heal both you and Sarah, your daughter-in-law. I am Raphael, one of the seven angels who stand before the glory of God and enter in to him."

Awestruck and frightened, the two of them fell down on their faces. But Raphael said to them, "Do not fear. Peace be with you. Bless God forever, for when I was with you, it was not through my design, but by the will of God. So bless him all your days, and give him praise. Surely you noticed that I ate nothing; indeed I am simply a vision that has appeared before you. Now bless and confess the Lord on earth, and I shall ascend to him who sent me. Write down everything that has happened to you." Then he ascended. They stood up but could not see him. They blessed and praised God, confessing all the great things he had done, and rejoiced that an angel of God had appeared to them.

(13) Then Tobit composed a prayer of joy and praise:

"Blessed be the living God and his kingdom forever.
He chastises, and grants mercy.
He leads down to Hades, below the earth,
And leads up out of the destruction.
There is nothing that can escape his hand.
Confess him before the nations, O children of Israel,
For he has scattered you among them,
But even there he has also shown you his glory.
Exalt him before every living creature,
Because he is our Lord, he is our God,

He is our Father, he is God forever.
He will chastise you for your sins,
But shall have mercy on all of you
And gather you from all the nations,
Wherever you are scattered among them.
If you return to him with all your heart and soul,
And are truthful before him,
He will turn to you
And will no longer hide his face from you.
Behold now what marvelous things he accomplished through you.
Give thanks to him with all your heart.
Bless the Lord of righteousness
And exalt the everlasting king.
From the land of my captivity I give him thanks
And declare his strength and majesty among a nation of sinners.
Turn, sinners, and do what is righteous before him,
For who knows whether he may yet have mercy upon you?
I shall exalt my God,
And my soul rejoices in the king of heaven;
It shall proclaim his majesty.
Let all people declare him
And give thanks to him in Jerusalem.
O, Jerusalem, holy city!
He scourges you for your children's deeds,
But will have mercy on the children of the righteous.
Give thanks to the Lord with a pure heart,
And bless the everlasting king,
So that his tabernacle may be joyfully rebuilt.
He will cause the captives among you to rejoice;
The downcast among you he will love for all generations.
A bright light will shine in every corner of the earth.
Many nations will come from afar to you.
Inhabitants from every corner of the earth will come to your holy name,
Bearing gifts in their hands for the King of heaven.
Generation after generation will sing your praises;
The name of the elect city shall endure forever.

Cursed shall be all who speak a harsh word against you;
Cursed shall be all who destroy you and cast down your walls,
And all who overturn your towers and burn your homes,
But blessed shall be those who revere you.
Come, therefore, rejoice for the children of the righteous,
For they shall be gathered together
And will bless the eternal Lord.
Happy are those who love you,
And happy are those who will rejoice in your peace.
Happy are all who grieve with you over all your afflictions,
For they shall rejoice with you and see your jubilation forever.
O my soul, bless the Lord, the great King,
For Jerusalem shall be built up again as his house forever,
And I shall be happy if a remnant of my offspring beholds your glory
And gives thanks to the King of heaven.
The gates of Jerusalem shall be built with sapphires and emeralds,
And all of your walls with precious jewels.
The towers of Jerusalem shall be built with gold,
Their battlements with finest gold.
The streets of Jerusalem shall be paved with garnets and stone of Ophir.
The gates of Jerusalem will sing out with hymns of joy;
All its houses shall shout 'Hallelujah!'
Blessed is the God of Israel!
The blessed shall bless his holy name forever and ever."

(14) So ended the words of Tobit's confession. He died peacefully at the age of one hundred and twelve years and was buried with honor in Nineveh. He was sixty-two years old when he lost his eyesight, and after regaining it, lived contentedly and gave alms, continually blessing God and giving thanks for his majesty.

As he was dying, Tobit sent for his son Tobias and gave him these instructions:

"My son, take your children and go away to Media, because I believe the word that God spoke through Nahum against Nineveh. Everything pronounced against Assyria and Nineveh by the prophets of Israel whom God sent will come true. Not one word will fall short; all things will be fulfilled in their appointed times. Deliverance, however, will come in Media, not in Assyria or Babylon. I am convinced, indeed I know that everything that God said will come to pass; not one word will prove false. All of our kin who reside in Israel will be scattered and deported as prisoners from that good land, and the land of Israel will become wasteland. Samaria and Jerusalem will become desert, and for a time the house of God will lie in mourning, burnt to the ground.

"But God will once again have mercy on them and return them to the land of Israel, where they will rebuild the house of God, but not as before, until the time when all is fulfilled. Then everyone will return from captivity and rebuild Jerusalem gloriously, and there the house of God will be rebuilt just as the prophets of Israel had predicted. All the nations of the world will have a change of heart and come to fear God in sincere worship, forsaking all the idols that had led them astray into falsehood, and they will bless the God of eternity in righteousness. All of the Israelites who are saved at that time and who are truly mindful of God will be gathered together and will come to Jerusalem to reside there forever, secure in their possession of the land of Abraham. Those who truly love God will rejoice, but those who are sinful and wicked will disappear from the earth. And now, my children, this I command you: serve God sincerely and do what is pleasing to him. Let your children be instructed to be righteous and give alms, to be mindful of God and to bless his name sincerely and with all their strength at every opportunity.

"And now, my child, you must leave Nineveh; do not remain here. On the very day you bury your mother beside me, you should go and not spend another night within these city walls. I see committed here much wickedness and shameless acts of treachery. Consider, my son, what things Nadab did to Ahikar, even though he had raised him. Did he not bury Ahikar alive? But God repaid this sin right before his eyes. Ahikar emerged once again into the light of day, but Nadab entered into the eternal darkness because he had tried to kill Ahikar. But because he gave alms, Ahikar escaped from the trap set for him just as Nadab fell into it, and it took his life. Now, my children, see what alms-giving can do, and what wickedness brings—death! But now I am fading."

They laid him upon his bed, and he died and was buried with great honor. When his mother also died, Tobias buried her beside his father. He and his wife went to Media and lived with his father-in-law Raguel in Ecbatana. Tobias cared well for his wife's parents in their old age, and buried them in Ecbatana of Media. He inherited both the estate of Raguel and that of his father Tobit, and he died at the age of one hundred and seventeen, much honored by all. Before he died, however, he heard about the destruction of Nineveh by Cyaxares[4] king of Media. He blessed God for all he had done to the people of Nineveh and Assyria. Before he died he rejoiced over Nineveh and blessed the Lord God who lives forever and ever.

## SUGGESTIONS FOR FURTHER READING

Levine, Amy-Jill. "Diaspora as Metaphor: Bodies and Boundaries in the Book of Tobit." In *Diaspora Jews and Judaism.* Ed. J. Andrew Overman and Robert S. MacLennan, pp. 105–17. Atlanta: Scholars Press, 1992.

Moore, Carey A. *Tobit.* New York: Doubleday, 1996.

Nickelsburg, George W. E. *Jewish Literature Between the Bible and the Mishnah,* pp. 30–35. Philadelphia: Fortress, 1981.

Wills, Lawrence M. *The Jewish Novel in the Ancient World,* pp. 68–92. Ithaca, N.Y.: Cornell University Press, 1995.

Zimmermann, Frank. *The Book of Tobit.* New York: Harper and Brothers, 1958.

4. The text reads "Ahikar," but this is surely an accidental substitution from above. Cyaxares is the correct Median ruler and is supplied here, but as was noted in the main introduction, the novels are notoriously inaccurate in matching famous kings and historical events.

FIVE

# JUDITH

The *Book of Judith,* more than most of the other Jewish writings, has long been considered a "romance," largely because of the strength of the woman character and the erotic suggestiveness of the central episode, the near-seduction and beheading of the enemy general Holofernes. This story was probably composed in Hebrew or Aramaic in the second century B.C.E. It falls naturally into two parts: the appearance on the horizon of Nebuchadnezzar's general Holofernes and his great army (chapters 1–7), and the heroic rescue of the Jewish village Bethulia (which means "virgin") by the pious and beautiful Jewish widow Judith (which means "Jewess"; chapters 8–16). The initial impression upon reading the text is often that the first half develops too slowly, especially in contrast to the high spirits and brisk denouement of the second half. However, the first half introduces many important motifs and themes and is a marvelous backdrop for the climactic decapitation scene in the second half. The might and worldwide success of the Assyrian king Nebuchadnezzar and his general Holofernes are depicted, along with the terror of the peoples round about, the initial fear of the Jewish partisans, and the important connecting character Achior, who both interprets the Jews to Holofernes and later converts himself to the religion that he has described so positively.

In addition, there are a series of parallels and contrasts within each of the two sections that very strongly develop the theme of the omnipotence of the God of the Jews, and the affirmation that God can empower a faithful woman to overcome a mighty general by using his own sword. The parallels and contrasts are in a "chiastic" pattern, that is, they resemble a Greek *chi* or X in that elements from the first part of each section are repeated in the second, but in reverse order (adapted from Craven, *Artistry and Faith,* pp. 60–63):

*First half*

A. Campaign against disobedient nations; the people surrender
  B. Israel is "greatly terrified"
    C. Joakim prepares for war
      D. Holofernes talks with Achior
        E. Achior is expelled
        E′. Achior is received in the village of Bethulia
      D′. Achior talks with the people
    C′. Holofernes prepares for war
  B′. Israel is "greatly terrified"
A′. Campaign against Bethulia; the people want to surrender

*Second half*

A. Introduction of Judith
  B. Judith plans to save Israel
    C. Judith and her maid leave Bethulia
      D. Judith beheads Holofernes
    C′. Judith and her maid return to Bethulia
  B′. Judith plans the destruction of Israel's enemy
A′. Conclusion about Judith

Although this division into the structured halves and episodes may suggest that *Judith,* like *Greek Daniel, Greek Esther,* and *Tobit,* is composed of a narrative frame expanded by the addition of episodes, that is probably not the case. The sections of *Judith* are more properly considered chapters, with occasional reflective pauses in the action, all composed to fit into a clearly constructed plot from beginning to end. There is one narrative thread of rising action, denouement, and falling action, even though it is developed by means of individual scenes. The *Book of Judith* achieves the length of a Jewish novel through a unitary conception of what a novel should look like, not by mere insertion of episodes. Thus in terms of the development of the *written* novel, it may be considered an advance beyond *Greek Daniel* and *Greek Esther,* and it is less episodic than some of the Greek novels.

Behind this complex arrangement is a single artistic vision that takes its structure from the cross-cultural paradigm of the warrior-hero. This figure is often withdrawn from society, comes to the fore when the community is threatened by a beast of huge proportions, and slays it. Even the prayer and dressing scene in *Judith* is an adaptation of the dressing of the hero in his armor. Just as *Susanna* brings the older royal court legend down to a more realistic level in the local court, Judith "novelizes" the hero legend by transferring it to the struggle between a pious woman and an arrogant, overblown general.

In addition to these large strokes, the story also exhibits considerable artistry in its humorous and ironic touches. First to be noted are the many ironic statements in the dialogues. Judith's double entendres allow this pious Jewish woman to step dangerously close to sexual license. This feature was doubtless an element of the excitement for the original audience. Second, the action of the story is carefully controlled. As has been indicated, the plot is slowed down to allow for dialogue and thematic development in the first half, and accelerated as it approaches the denouement. The decapitation scene, which all readers ancient and modern would have associated with Judith, is told quickly and almost bloodlessly in just a few verses. Third, although Sigmund Freud criticized the character of Judith as a woman out of control, he would have recognized the use of sexual symbols. When Holofernes lies drunk and impotent on his bed, Judith takes his own sword and beheads him in a symbolic castration. Further, it is also clear in the way the author describes Holofernes' tent, with an inner and outer chamber, that it is a vagina symbol, and Judith, from the village of "Virgin," is penetrating Holofernes' "vagina." Judith "violates" Holofernes and takes the curtain from the inner chamber—Holofernes' "hymen"—with her as she escapes and brings it as a spoils-offering for the Temple in Jerusalem. The interest in Judith, in the ancient period as now, lies partly in its extreme reversal of gender roles.

Interestingly, the character of Judith was apparently not considered a threatening female presence in the ancient world, either to Jewish or to Christian authors. She was a symbol of the victory of the pious over the ungodly, or even allegorically as virtue over vice. After about 1600, however, a new sense of realism in reading biblical texts led to a reinterpretation of Judith in literature and in visual art. She now took on a Medusa-like aspect (compare the reaction of Freud mentioned earlier) and was often viewed negatively up to the twentieth century, when she was finally reevaluated by feminist commentators.

## *Judith*

(1) In the twelfth year of the reign of Nebuchadnezzar, who ruled the Assyrians from his capital in Nineveh, Arphaxad was reigning over the Medes from Ecbatana. He had erected a great wall around Ecbatana, made of hewn stones, each five feet thick and nine feet long. The wall constructed from them was a hundred feet high and seventy-five feet thick, and the towers, placed at the city gates, each stood a hundred and fifty feet high and were ninety feet thick at the base. The gates of the city were a

hundred feet high and sixty feet wide, so that his battalions could march forth with his infantry in full formation.

It was during that time that King Nebuchadnezzar made war against King Arphaxad in the great plain along the border of Ragau. All those who lived in the hill country opposed Nebuchadnezzar, as did those who lived along the Euphrates, the Tigris, and the Hydaspes, and they were joined by Arioch, king of the Elymeans in the plain, and by many of the Cheleoudites. Nebuchadnezzar, king of the Assyrians, therefore summoned to war all the residents of Persia and all those living to the west: the residents of Cilicia, Damascus, Lebanon, and Antilebanon, all those living along the coast, the peoples of Carmel and Gilead, Upper Galilee, and the great plain of Esdraelon, all the residents of Samaria and its cities, the region beyond the Jordan River, as far as Jerusalem, Bethany, Chelous, Kadesh, the Nile River, Tahpanhes, Raamses, and the whole land of Goshen as far as Tanis and Memphis, and all those who lived in Egypt as far as the border of Ethiopia. Everyone in these areas, however, responded by making light of the declaration of Nebuchadnezzar, king of the Assyrians, and refused to send troops to join him in battle. They were not afraid of him; rather, they considered him an ordinary man, and they sent his messengers away shamefaced and empty-handed. Nebuchadnezzar, as a result, became so incensed with the entire region that he swore by his throne and kingdom that he would take vengeance on the whole territory of Cilicia, Damascus, and Syria, cutting them to pieces by the edge of the sword, as well as those residing in Moab, the Ammonites, all of Judea, and all of Egypt as far as the coasts of the two seas.

In the seventeenth year, he took to the field in a campaign against King Arphaxad and was victorious, overthrowing Arphaxad's entire army, including cavalry and chariots. He conquered all of his cities, advancing as far as Ecbatana, where he seized the towers and plundered the city's markets, bringing its former glory into disgrace. When Nebuchadnezzar overtook Arphaxad in the mountains of Ragau, he ran him through with his spear, on that day bringing his dynasty to an end. He and the mixed armies arrayed with him—a mighty host of warriors!—then returned, and began a period of rest and celebration which lasted a hundred and twenty days.

(2) And in the eighteenth year, on the twenty-second day of the first month, plans were laid in the palace of Nebuchadnezzar, king of the Assyrians, to exact revenge on the entire region, just as he had promised. Summoning all his ministers and nobles, he placed before them his secret plan and declared his resolve to lay waste the whole countryside. This plan, to destroy everyone who had not obeyed his command, was then ratified by those present.

As soon as his plans were complete, Nebuchadnezzar, king of the Assyrians, called in Holofernes, the commander-in-chief of his army and his right-hand man, and said to him, "Thus says the Great King, lord of all the earth: 'I want you to go out from my presence and, taking an army of tested and seasoned troops, consisting of 120,000 infantry and twelve thousand cavalry, proceed against the entire country to the west, since they have disobeyed my command. Proclaim to them that they are to prepare an offering of earth and water, for I am about to descend upon them in my anger. My army will cover the entire face of the earth, and I will hand these people over to my soldiers as plunder. Their wounded shall fill the hollows; every stream and river shall swell to overflowing, choked with their corpses. I will lead them away into captivity, exiling them to every corner of the earth. But I want you to go before me, to seize every territory for me in advance. If they surrender themselves to you, you shall hold them for me until I arrive to punish them. But if any resist, show them no mercy; give them over to slaughter and pillage throughout the land. For as I live, I swear by all my power that what I have promised I will do with my own hand. As for you—make sure that you do not transgress any of your lord's commands, but execute these orders with all due speed.'"

Taking his leave of Nebuchadnezzar, Holofernes assembled all the commanders, generals, and officers of Assyria's armies, and mustered his army of seasoned troops, 120,000 infantry and twelve thousand mounted archers, as his lord had commanded, arraying them in battle formation. He commandeered in addition a vast quantity of camels, asses, and mules to carry supplies, as well as innumerable sheep, oxen, and goats for provisions. A plentiful supply of food was provided for each man, and from the king's palace he brought along a large amount of gold and silver. Thus prepared, he set out with his whole army to march out ahead of King Nebuchadnezzar and descend upon the western regions, covering the entire face of the earth with his chariots, cavalry, and seasoned troops. Accompanying them also was a motley throng of people, too large to number, like locusts or a cloud of dust. They marched from Nineveh three days to the plain of Bectileth, making camp near there at the mountain north of Upper Cilicia. Holofernes then proceeded into the hill country with his entire army of infantry, cavalry, and chariots and totally destroyed Put and Lud, plundering the people of Rassis and the Ishmaelites on the border of the desert, south of the land of the Cheleans. Following the Euphrates and proceeding through Mesopotamia, he laid waste all the fortified towns along the Wadi Abron as far as the sea, and from there marched to Cilicia and occupied that region, destroying all those who resisted him. Next he came to the southern border of Japheth, facing Arabia, and surrounded all the Midianites, burned their tents, and plundered their sheep. He crossed the plain of Damascus during the wheat harvest and burned their crops, then proceeded further to slaughter their flocks and herds, sack their towns, strip their fields, and strike down their young men with a sword.

A deathly fear of Holofernes fell upon all those who lived along the coast at Tyre and Sidon, and on the residents of Sur, Ocina, Jamnia, Azotus, and Ashkelon. (3) Envoys were sent to him begging for peace, saying, "We, servants of Nebuchadnezzar the great king, lie prostrate before you to do with as you please. All our buildings, our land, every wheat field, our flocks and herds, all the sheepfolds of our encampments are yours as well; do with them as you wish. Our cities and their inhabitants are your slaves; come and deal with them as you please."

The envoys came to Holofernes and entreated him in this manner, whereupon he and his army came down to the coast and garrisoned all of the fortified cities, taking from them a few chosen men as allies. They and the surrounding areas welcomed him with garlands, dancing, and tambourines. He demolished all their shrines and cut down their sacred groves, for he had been commissioned to destroy all of the gods of the land, so that every nation should worship Nebuchadnezzar alone, and every tongue and every tribe should invoke him as god.[1] He then advanced toward Esdraelon, near Dothan, not far from the great ridge of Judea, and pitched camp between Geba and Scythopolis. There the Assyrians remained for one month, gathering together all of the supplies for his army.

(4) When the Israelites living in Judea heard what Holofernes, the commander-in-chief of Nebuchadnezzar, had done to all the nations, and how he had plundered and destroyed all their temples, they were terrified at his approach and feared both for the fate of Jerusalem and for the Temple of the Lord their God. They themselves had indeed just returned from captivity; only recently had the people of Judea been gathered together again. Their sacred vessels, altar, and Temple had just been reconsecrated after the profanation.[2] So they sent into every region of Samaria, Kona,

1. The language is ironic, for it is used also of religious reforms in the name of the Israelite God, for example, Second Kings 23:14–15. It is also reminiscent of Nebuchadnezzar of Babylon's confession of God in a contemporary novelistic work: Daniel 2:46–47; 3:28–29; and 4:1–3, 34–37.

2. The text here is anachronistic in that it recounts Jewish history that occurs after both Nebuchadnezzar and Assyria were destroyed—part of the unreal atmosphere of this novel that begins in the very first line and continues throughout. *Judith* was probably written after the rededication of the Temple by the Maccabees in 165 B.C.E. that is celebrated in Hanukkah; therefore, the description here would have also conjured patriotic feelings for the Maccabean restoration.

Beth-horon, Belmain, Jericho, Choba, Aesora, and the valley of Salem and took command of all the high hilltops, erecting fortifications around every village on them. The food just harvested from the fields they stored away as a preparation for war.

Joakim, the high priest, who was at that time in Jerusalem, wrote to the residents of Bethulia and Betomesthaim, which lies opposite Esdraelon toward the plain near Dothan, and told them to take control of the passes into the hill country. The best entry into Judea was through them, and it would be easy to prevent the Assyrians from passing through, since there was room for no more than two men to pass at a time. The Israelites did as Joakim the high priest and the Council of the Israelites in Jerusalem had commanded.

All of the Israelites then called upon God from the depths of their heart and earnestly humbled their souls. All then put on sackcloth: the men, their wives, their children, their cattle, and every alien, hired worker, and slave. All of the Israelites residing in Jerusalem—every man, woman, and child—prostrated themselves before the Temple and placed ashes on their heads and draped their sackcloth before the Lord. Even the altar was draped in sackcloth, as they all cried out fervently to the Lord not to give their babies over to capture nor their wives as plunder, nor to allow their ancestral cities to be destroyed and the sanctuary profaned, to become a laughing-stock for the gentiles.

When the Lord heard their voice, he had compassion on their affliction, as the people continued fasting for many days over all of Judea, and also in Jerusalem before the Temple of the Lord Almighty. Joakim the high priest and all the priests who stood before the Lord and served him dressed in sackcloth and offered the continual burnt offerings, votive offerings, and freewill offerings of the people. They placed ashes on their headdresses and cried out to the Lord with all their might to look kindly on the whole house of Israel.

(5) And so it was reported to Holofernes, commander-in-chief of the Assyrian army, that the Israelites had laid their prep-

arations for war by closing the passes through the hill country and fortifying the top of every mountain, and also by laying traps in the plains. Enraged, Holofernes summoned all of the leaders of Moab, the Ammonite commanders, and the governors from along the coast, and said to them, "You Canaanites, tell me, who is this people situated in the hill country, and in what cities do they dwell? How big is their army? What is the source of their power, and what king has arisen to lead their armies? And why is it that they alone of all those residing in the west have not capitulated before me?"

Then Achior, leader of the Ammonites, answered him, "Let my lord hear the advice of his slave, and I shall tell you the truth concerning this people who resides in the hill country near here; no lie shall I speak. Descendants of the Chaldaeans, they migrated first to Mesopotamia because they resolved not to worship the gods of their ancestors from the land of the Chaldaeans. Departing from the ways of their forebears, they began to worship the God of heaven, a god whom they had by then come to know. They were driven out from before the gods and fled into Mesopotamia, where they sojourned for many years. Their god commanded them to leave the land of their sojourn and proceed to Canaan. There they dwelt and acquired great wealth in gold, silver, and livestock.

"When a famine covered the land of Canaan, they went down into Egypt where there was food and sojourned there. There they multiplied until they became a great people, beyond number. The king of Egypt, however, turned on them and forced them into hard labor, where they worked as slaves to make bricks. They called upon their god, however, who struck the entire country of Egypt with plagues from which there was no cure. The Egyptians then expelled them from their midst, but God dried up the Red Sea before them and led them on to Sinai and Kadesh-barnea. They in turn cast out all those who lived in the desert and, after utterly destroying all the Heshbonites, inhabited the land of the Amorites. Crossing over the Jordan River, they took possession of the hill country and drove out before them as they went the Canaanites, the Perizzites, the Jebusites, the Shechemites, and all the Girgashites. They dwelt in that land for many years. And as long as they did not sin in the eyes of their god, things went well for them, because the god who hates iniquity was with them. But when they strayed from the path in which he had directed them, they were destroyed by many wars, taken prisoner, and deported into foreign lands. The temple of their god was also leveled to the ground, and their cities were captured by their enemies. But now turning again to their god, they have gathered again from their dispersion and have once more occupied Jerusalem, where their sanctuary is located, and settled in the hill county, because it was uninhabited. So now, my lord and master, if this people has committed any sin or misdeed against their god, and we discover that they are guilty of such an offense, we should immediately proceed to wage war against them. But if they have not sinned, let my lord pass them by, lest their lord and god protect them with his shield, and we become a laughingstock the world over."

When Achior finished saying these things, all of the people standing around the tent began to object. Holofernes' officers and all of the inhabitants of the seacoast and Moab called for Achior to be cut to pieces. "We have no fear of the Israelites!" they said. "Indeed, they are a people with no power or military strength. Let us then proceed, lord Holofernes, and your great army will swallow them whole!"

(6) When the disturbance of the people outside the council had subsided, Holofernes, commander-in-chief of the Assyrians, said to Achior in the presence of the Moabites and all the gathered peoples: "Who are you, Achior, and the mercenaries of Ephraim, to prophesy among us as you have today, and tell us that we should not make war against the people of Israel because their god will defend them? For who is god except Nebuchadnezzar? He will send his army to wipe them off the face of the earth, and their god will not be able to save them. But we, the

servants of the king, will destroy them as we would if they were one man, for they will never resist the power of our cavalry. We will toss them in a heap; their mountains will become drunk with their blood, and their fields will be stacked high with their dead. No trace of them will remain in the wake of our attack, but they will be totally destroyed. Thus says King Nebuchadnezzar, lord of the entire world. Once he has spoken, not a single word will go unfulfilled.

"As for you, Achior, you are nothing more than an Ammonite mercenary, uttering these words in treachery. I assure you, you shall not see my face again from this day forth until the day when I take my vengeance on this people from Egypt. And upon my return, the sword of my army and the spear of my servants shall run you through as well, and you shall fall among their dead. My slaves will now take you into the hill country and place you in one of the towns in the high passes, and you will not perish until you are wiped out along with the others. And if indeed you still entertain the hope that they will not be taken, you will have nothing to fear. But I have spoken, and not one of my words will fail to come true."

Holofernes commanded the slaves who were serving him in his tent to take Achior to Bethulia and hand him over to the Israelites. They took him and led him out of the camp to the plain, and from there up into the hill country to the springs below Bethulia. When the men of the town saw them approaching, they seized their weapons and ran out of the town to the crest of the hill, where their slingers forced them to halt their ascent by pelting them with stones. Finding shelter below the hill, they bound Achior and left him lying there at the bottom, and returned to their lord.

When the Israelites came down from their town and found him, they untied him and brought him up to Bethulia; there they presented him to the town's magistrates, who were at that time Uzziah, son of Micah of the tribe of Simeon; Chabris, son of Gothoniel; and Charmis, son of Melchiel. They then summoned the elders of the town, as well as all the young men and women, who hurried to the assembly, and they placed Achior in the middle of the gathering. Uzziah began to question him concerning everything that had happened, and Achior informed them of the council of Holofernes and what they had discussed there with the Assyrian leaders, and how Holofernes had boasted about what he would do to the house of Israel. The people fell down when they heard this, prostrating themselves before God, and cried out, "Lord God of heaven, behold their arrogance, and have mercy upon our people on account of our humiliation. Look down upon the face of those set aside for your service." They then reassured Achior, praising him warmly, as Uzziah took him from the assembly to his home, and there prepared a feast for the elders. Throughout that night they called upon the God of Israel for help.

(7) On the next day Holofernes commanded his entire army and all of the people who had joined forces with him to break camp and set out for Bethulia to capture the passes into the hill country and to wage war against the Israelites. Every able-bodied soldier thus set out that day, the army of seasoned troops numbering 170,000 infantry and 12,000 cavalry, not counting the retinue of the supply train and their guard—a very great army altogether. They set up camp beside a spring in the valley near Bethulia. The encampment spread in the direction of Dothan all the way to Belbaim, and in the other direction from Bethulia to Cyamon, near Esdraelon. When the Israelites beheld the size of the army, they said to each other in the grip of fear, "These men will certainly devour the whole countryside. Neither the mountains nor the valleys nor the hills can withstand them." Then each man took up his arms, lit the beacon-fires, and stood guard on the towers throughout the night.

The following day Holofernes led out his entire cavalry before the Israelites in Bethulia. He reconnoitered the passes that led to their town, and surveyed the springs and secured them with armed troops. Then he returned to the camp. All of the leaders of the Edomites and all of the rulers of the Moabites and the generals from the coastal areas approached Holofernes and said, "Let our master heed our advice, and his armies will suffer no losses. These Israelites do not place their trust in their spears, but in the height of the mountains on which they dwell, for it is no easy task to make a way through the crests of these hills. So, my lord, it is best not to make war against them in full formation, as it is normally done. If this advice is followed, not a single man from your people will fall. Remain in your camp with your entire army, but allow your servants to take control of the spring that flows from the base of the mountain, for all those who live in Bethulia draw their water from this source. They will soon be overcome by thirst and will hand over their town willingly. We and our people shall ascend to the mountaintops near their town and set up camp there; from there we shall stand guard to ensure that not a single person leaves their town. They, their wives, and their children will waste away from famine, and before the sword ever strikes them, they will be strewn about the streets of their town. In this way you shall indeed exact a severe vengeance upon them for rebelling against you and not coming out to meet you in peace."

Holofernes and all his ministers thought well of this counsel and gave orders to carry out their plan. The army of the Ammonites set out with five thousand Assyrians and pitched camp in the valley; from there they seized the springs and wells belonging to the Israelites. Then the Edomites and the Ammonites went up and pitched camp in the hill country opposite Dothan, and sent some of their troops to the southeast in the direction of Egrebeh, near Chusi on the Wadi Mochmur. The rest of the Assyrian army encamped in the plain, covering the face of the earth. Their tents and supply train were spread out about them in one vast encampment, for the size of the army was huge.

The Israelites, now fainthearted, cried out to the Lord their God when they saw that they were surrounded by their bitter enemies and there was no means of escape. The Assyrian army—

infantry, chariots, and cavalry—was arrayed on all sides, and it laid siege for thirty-four days. The jars of water that the residents of Bethulia possessed gave out, their cisterns were going dry, and even though they rationed water each day, there was never enough to drink. Their babies grew weaker, the women and young men fainted from thirst and were collapsing in the streets and gates of the town, sapped of their strength. All the people—young men, women, and children—rose up against Uzziah and the leaders of the town and cried out to them, "May God judge between us, for you have committed a grave injustice by not seeking peace with the Assyrians. Now there is no hope, for God has sold us into their hands to die from thirst. Therefore, call upon them and offer to hand over the entire town as spoils to Holofernes and his army; it would be better to be plundered by them and become their slaves, for at least our lives would be spared, and we would not witness the deaths of our babies before our eyes, nor our wives and children drawing their last breath. We call heaven and earth to witness against you, and the Lord the God of our forebears who punishes us for our sins and the sins of those who came before us: do this day the things that we have asked!"

Thus they lamented loudly, raising a mighty cry to the Lord God, but Uzziah responded, "Brothers and sisters, take courage! Let us hold out for just five days more, and our God will have mercy on us and not forsake us. And if indeed these days pass with no help in sight, then I shall do as you say." He then dismissed the people, sending the men back to their posts on the walls and towers and the women and children to their homes. The entire town, however, remained in despair.

(8) Now at this time there was also a certain woman named Judith, daughter of Merari, son of Ox, son of Joseph, son of Oziel, son of Helkiah, son of Hananiah, son of Gideon, son of Rephaim, son of Ahitub, son of Elijah, son of Hilkiah, son of Eliab, son of Nathaniel, son of Salamiel, son of Sarasadai, son of Israel. Her husband, Manasseh, of her own tribe and family, had died during one of the barley harvests; he was overseeing those binding

sheaves in the fields, and after standing in the blazing sun, collapsed upon his bed and died later in Bethulia, his town. He was buried with his ancestors in the field between Dothan and Balamon. Judith remained in her house as a widow for three years and four months.[3] On the roof of her house she erected a tent, and she wore only sackcloth and widow's garments. Everyday she fasted, except for the Sabbath and the day of preparation, the day of the new moon and the day before, and the days of feasting and joy at the Temple in Israel. Exceedingly beautiful, she was left by her husband Manasseh gold and silver, male and female slaves, livestock and fields. She continued in charge of his estate, yet no one spoke ill of her, because she was very reverent toward God.

When Judith heard the harsh words that the people had spoken against the magistrate—the result of faintheartedness brought on by thirst—and that Uzziah had in response sworn to them that he would surrender the town to the Assyrians after five days, she sent her favorite maid, who was in charge of all her possessions, to summon Uzziah, Chabris, and Charmis, the elders of the town. When they arrived, she said to them, "Hear my words, magistrates of all the citizens of Bethulia, because you had no right to speak to the people as you did today. You have made a vow between God and yourselves and have promised to hand over the town to our enemies unless the Lord comes to our assistance in five days. But who are you to test God today and put yourself in God's place among the people? You are trying to test the Lord Almighty, but you will never understand anything! Indeed, you cannot even search out the depths of the human

3. Judith's period of mourning is far beyond what was prescribed in Jewish law. The mourning customs become for her a sort of ascetic spirituality, perhaps a theological precursor to later Christian asceticism; see Wills, *Jewish Novel,* 15, 123, 139, 228–44. In chapter 9 Judith uncovers the sackcloth that she was presumably wearing under her clothes to make a more visible show of her preparation.

heart, nor comprehend a person's innermost thoughts. How then could you possibly search out God, who created these things, and understand his mind or follow his reasoning? My brothers, do not provoke the Lord our God! If he does not choose to aid us in these five days, he possesses the power—in whatever number of days he wishes—to come to our defense, or to destroy us in the very presence of our enemies. Do not attempt to extract a pledge on the designs of the Lord our God, for God is not like a man, to be threatened, or to be bargained and cajoled on human terms. Therefore, while waiting patiently for his deliverance, let us pray to him for aid. He will listen to our voice, if it pleases him.

"Indeed, there has not arisen in our memory, nor is there today, either a tribe or family or district or town among our people who worships gods made with hands, as was done in the past. And it was for this reason that our forebears were given over to sword and plunder, suffering terrible defeats before our enemies. We, however, do not recognize any God but him, and thus we hope that he will not spurn us or any of our people. For if we fall, so will all of Judea. The sanctuary will be ransacked, and God will exact from us the penalty for its desecration. The murder of our brothers and sisters, the captivity of the land, and the desolation of our inheritance he will bring upon our heads wherever we are enslaved among the nations, and we shall become an object of derision and reproach among those who possess us. Our slavery will never be replaced by gladness, but our Lord God will reckon it to our shame.

"So now, my brothers, let all our other brothers and sisters watch our example. Their fate depends on us; the sanctuary—both the Temple and the altar—they are in our hands. Let us give thanks for all these things to our Lord God, for he tests us just as he did our forebears. Remember all he did for Abraham, and how he tested Isaac, and what happened to Jacob in Mesopotamia of Syria as he was herding the sheep of Laban, his uncle. For he is not putting us to the test by fire as he did them, nor has he taken his revenge upon us, but the Lord scourges us who would approach him in order to admonish us."

Uzziah replied to her, "Everything that you have said was spoken with an upright heart. No one can contradict your words. Your wisdom has not sprung up in a day, but from your youth all our people have recognized your understanding, and it must surely derive from a good heart. But the people are now wracked by thirst; they have forced us to do what we have done, and take upon ourselves an oath which we cannot violate. Pray for us, therefore, for you are a pious woman, and the Lord will send enough rain to fill our cisterns, and we can regain our strength."

"Listen to me now," said Judith, "for I am about to do something that will live in the memory of our people for many generations to come. Stand by the gate tonight, and I shall come with my maidservant, and during that period after which you vowed to surrender the town to our enemies, the Lord will save Israel by my hand. Do not ask me anything further about it—I shall say nothing more about what I am about to do until it is accomplished."

"Go in peace," replied Uzziah and the town magistrates, "and may the Lord God go before you to take vengeance on our enemies." And leaving her tent, they returned once more to their posts.

(9) Falling upon her face, Judith smeared ashes over her head and uncovered the sackcloth she was wearing. At the same moment that the evening's incense offering was being brought into the house of God in Jerusalem, she uttered a loud cry to the Lord and said, "O Lord, God of my forefather Simeon, to whom you gave a sword to use for vengeance upon foreigners who stripped a virgin's garments to defile her.[4] They uncovered her thighs to

4. Judith refers here to the revenge by Simeon, one of the twelve sons of Jacob, on Shechem, a non-Israelite, for his rape of Simeon's sister Dinah (Genesis 34). Simeon's revenge is also treated positively in the *The Marriage and Conversion of Aseneth,* but in Genesis 34:30 and 49:5–7 it is condemned by Jacob.

shame her, and disgraced her by polluting her womb, and even though you had said, 'This shall not be done,' yet they did it. For this reason you handed over their leaders for slaughter, and their bed, which blushed for their treachery, you allowed to be stained with blood. You struck dead the slaves with their princes, and the princes upon their thrones. Their wives became plunder, and their daughters were led away to captivity; all their spoils were divided by the sons whom you loved, who were zealously devoted to you and abhorred the pollution of their blood, and called upon you for help. O my God, listen now also to the plea of a widow! For you are the one who is responsible for everything that happens—all that happened then, but also what happened before and after, down to the present day, and everything that is to come. Everything has come about exactly as you have planned. All the things that you have willed to be have stood forth and said, 'Here we are!' All your ways have already been prepared; you have passed judgment knowing all things in advance.

"The Assyrians have grown into a huge army, priding themselves in their horses and riders, and glorying in the might of their infantry. They have placed their faith in the shield and the javelin, the bow and the sling, but they refuse to recognize that you are a Lord who crushes wars—the Lord is your name! Break through their battle lines and bring low their might in your wrath. They intended to pollute your sanctuary, defiling the tabernacle in which the name of your glory finds its rest, and sever the horns of your altar with a sword. Look upon their arrogance! Send forth your wrath against them, and give into my hand—the hand of a widow!—the strength that my plan requires. By the guile of my lips strike the slave with his ruler and the ruler with his slave! Crush their arrogance by the hand of a woman! For your power lies not in numbers, nor does your strength dwell among the strong, but you are a God of the humble, a helper of the poor, protector of the weak, guardian of those in despair, deliverer of those bereft of hope. Listen, O God of my ancestors and God of the inheritance of Israel, ruler of heaven and earth, creator of all the waters, king of your whole creation! Listen to my plea! Grant, I pray, that my deceitful speech wound and maim those who have plotted evil against your covenant, your sacred house, Mount Zion, and the house of your children's possession. Let every nation and tribe know that you are God—the God of all power and might!—and that none but you will shield the people Israel."

(10) When Judith had ceased crying out to the God of Israel and had concluded her prayer, she arose from where she had lain and, summoning her maid, went down into her house where she spent Sabbaths and feast days. Removing her sackcloth and her widow's garments, she bathed and anointed herself with costly ointment, braided her hair, placed a tiara on her head, and dressed in her most beautiful garments, those that she had worn in earlier days when her husband was alive. She then put sandals on her feet, which she also adorned with anklets, and put on her bracelets, rings, and earrings, in addition to all her other cosmetic finery, so that she was now beautifully adorned from head to toe, able to bewitch the eyes of as many men as might see her. She gave her maid a small wineskin full of wine and a flask of oil, and she filled a pouch with a barley loaf, a cake of figs, and fine bread, and wrapping her dishes, she placed them also in her maid's pouch. They then went out to the town gate and found waiting there Uzziah and the elders of the town, Chabris and Charmis. When they beheld her, now transformed before their eyes, they were amazed at her beauty. "May the God of our ancestors be with you," they said to her, "so that your plans may be successful and redound to the greater glory of Jerusalem and the Israelites." And she bowed to God.

"Now command that the town gates be opened," she said to them, "and I shall go accomplish all the things about which we spoke." They ordered the gatekeepers to open the gates as she requested. Judith and her maid went out, and as they proceeded, the men of the town watched her closely until she had descended the mountain and crossed the valley, where they lost sight of her.

As Judith and her maid were passing through the valley, they were met by an Assyrian patrol. Placing her under guard, they began to question her: "To what people do you belong? Where do you come from and where are you going?"

"I am a Hebrew, but I am fleeing from them because you will soon devour them. I am now on my way to meet Holofernes, commander-in-chief of your army, to give him reliable information. I shall show him a path by which he can take control of all the hill country without losing a single life."

As they listened to her they took note of her remarkable beauty and said to her, "By coming down now to meet our lord, you have saved your own life. Now you may go to his tent; some of our men will escort you and present you to him. When you are brought before him, do not be afraid, but tell him exactly what you have told us and he will treat you well." A hundred men were then chosen to escort her and her maid to the tent of Holofernes.

A hubbub followed them as they proceeded through the encampment. News of her arrival spread from tent to tent, and soldiers came and gathered round her as she stood outside Holofernes' tent waiting to be admitted. The soldiers marveled at her beauty, but marveled at the Israelites as well on her account, saying to one another, "Who could despise a people who has a woman such as this among them? We cannot allow a single man of them to live; those left standing would surely be able to beguile the whole world."

All of those who sat in council with Holofernes and all of his servants came out to meet her, and they escorted her into the tent. There Holofernes was reclining on his bed behind a curtain interwoven with purple, gold, emeralds, and other precious stones. Informed of Judith's presence, Holofernes emerged from behind the curtain, with silver lamps led before him. Judith stepped out before him and his attendants, and they were all stunned by her beauty. She fell down and kneeled before him, and his servants helped her to her feet.

(11) "Do not be afraid, woman," said Holofernes. "I have never harmed anyone who chose to serve Nebuchadnezzar, king of all the earth. But as for your people who reside in the hill country, if they had not slighted me, I would never have raised my spear against them. Now they have brought this upon themselves. But tell me, why have you fled from them and come to us? By doing so, you have saved yourself, so do not fear. No harm will come to you tonight or hereafter. You will be treated well, as are all those who serve my lord, King Nebuchadnezzar."

"Then hear the words of your slave," said Judith, "and allow your servant to address you. I will not speak falsely to my lord tonight. And if you follow the advice of your servant, God will accomplish a great deed through you; my lord will not fail in his plan. For as Nebuchadnezzar, king of the whole earth, lives, and as he rules who sent you to order all nations, not only do all people serve him on account of you, but even the beasts of the field and the cattle and the birds of the air live through your might for the greater glory of Nebuchadnezzar and all of his household. Indeed, we have heard of your wisdom and the clever strategies you have employed. Everywhere it is proclaimed that you alone in the whole kingdom are worthy and intelligent, and the most skilled military commander.

"But we have now also heard what Achior told you in council, since the men of Bethulia spared him, and he recounted to them the entire exchange. Do not disregard his advice, my lord and master, but take it to heart, for it is true. Our people can neither be avenged nor overpowered unless we sin against our God. But now, in order that my lord not be frustrated and fail to achieve his goal, death will descend upon them. They are in the grasp of a grave sin that will provoke their God to fury, as soon as they commit their sacrilege. When their food and water were depleted, they decided to turn to their cattle, consuming them entirely—even those portions that they had been commanded in God's laws not to eat; likewise the first fruits of wheat and the tithes of wine and oil, which are sanctified and reserved for the priests who serve in the presence of our God in Jerusalem. Even things that are not to be touched by anyone of the laity have also been consumed. They have even sent messengers to Jerusalem to ask permission from the Council, because they who dwell there have done the same things. And so when they return word to them and they act upon it, on that very day they will be given over to you for destruction. When I, your servant, found out that these things had occurred, I ran away from them, and God sent me to you to accomplish something so great that whoever hears about it the world over will be astounded, because your servant is indeed pious and serves the God of heaven night and day. For now, I shall remain with you, my lord, and go out by night to the valley to pray to God; he will tell me when they have committed this sin. I shall then return and report to you, and at that time you should march forth with your entire army. No one will stand in your way. Afterward, I shall lead you through the middle of Judea until you arrive at Jerusalem, where I shall set your seat in the midst of the town. You will lead them away like sheep without a shepherd, and no dog will so much as growl as you pass. All of this was proclaimed ahead of time and revealed to me, and I have been sent to announce these things to you."

Holofernes was very pleased to hear this, as were his attendants, and marveling at her wisdom, they said, "There is not another woman like her for beauty and intelligence in the entire world."

Holofernes turned to her: "God has done well in sending you from your people so that control may fall into our hands, for death will be the lot of those who ridicule my lord. You are both elegant in your appearance and refined in speech; if you do as you say, your god shall be my god, and you shall sit in the house of King Nebuchadnezzar and be famous throughout the world."

(12) Holofernes then commanded that she be brought into his tent, where his silver vessels were laid out, and ordered that she be served some of his delicacies and wine. Judith, however, declined. "I cannot eat from these," she said, "lest it be an offense to God, but I shall eat from the things that I brought with me."

"But if your provisions fail," Holofernes replied to her, "where shall we find food of a similar kind for you, as there is no one else here of your race."

"As you live, my lord," Judith assured him, "your servant will not use up what she has with her before the Lord accomplishes by my hand what he had planned."

Holofernes' servants then led her to her tent, where she slept until the middle of the night. Just before the morning watch she arose and sent word to Holofernes, "Command, I pray you, my lord, that your servant be allowed to go out for morning prayer." Holofernes therefore instructed the guards to give way to her and allow her to come and go. In this way she passed three days in the camp. Each night she made her way past the guard into the valley of Bethulia and bathed in the spring. When she came out of the water, she called upon the Lord God of Israel to direct her path for the victory of his people. Thus cleansed, she returned to camp and remained in her tent until she ate her evening meal.

On the fourth day, Holofernes made a feast for his servants alone and did not invite any of the soldiers on duty. He said to Bagoas, the eunuch who was in charge of all his affairs, "Go now and persuade the Hebrew woman in your charge to come join us for our feast. It would be a disgrace if we allow a woman such as this to pass through our fingers without enjoying the fruits of her company. If we cannot win her favors, she will surely ridicule us."

Taking leave of Holofernes, Bagoas proceeded to Judith's tent. "Such a fair young woman as you," he said to her, "should be only too glad to come to my lord to be honored in his presence and join us in wine and merriment. Today you can become like one of the Assyrian women who serve in Nebuchadnezzar's palace."

"Who am I to refuse my lord?" answered Judith. "I am anxious to do anything that pleases him; this will indeed bring me joy till my dying day."

She arose and arrayed herself in her garments, making herself up with every feminine charm. Her maid then went ahead of her and laid out lamb skins on the ground before Holofernes, which Bagoas had given her for her daily use when eating. Judith then entered and reclined upon them, and Holofernes, upon seeing her, was beside himself. He began to tremble with excitement, enflamed with the desire to lie with her. He had been waiting for just such an opportunity to seduce her from the first moment he saw her. "Drink up," he said, "and join us in revelry."

"Yes, I shall drink, my lord," replied Judith, "for this is indeed the greatest day of my life."

She then took what her maid had prepared for her, and ate and drank with him. Holofernes was gladdened by this and began downing his wine, consuming more than he had ever drunk before. (13) When evening came, his servants quickly retired; Bagoas closed the tent from the outside and dismissed Holofernes' servants, who, wearied from the long evening's festivities, went straight off to bed. Judith alone remained within, as Holofernes lay on his bed, his head now swimming in wine. Judith bade her maid stand outside the curtain and wait for her to emerge as she had done before. She had previously arranged for her to accompany her each morning to prayer, and Bagoas had also been informed of their intention to leave the tent during the night. Everyone, therefore, had now departed, and no one, whether master or slave, remained within the curtain. Standing beside the bed, Judith said in her heart, "O Lord, God of all power, look now upon the actions of my hands, which I perform for the exaltation of Jerusalem. Come now to the aid of your inheritance and accomplish my plan to destroy the enemies who have risen up against us." Stepping up to Holofernes' bedpost, she took down the sword hanging beside his head, and turning toward him, lifted his head by the hair. "Give me strength," she prayed, "O Lord God of Israel!" Then she struck him twice in the neck with all her might, severing his head from him. She then rolled his body off the bed and pulled down the curtain from its poles. Pausing but a moment, she stepped outside and handed the head of Holofernes to her maid, who placed it in her pouch.

The two of them then proceeded out as if to prayer, just as they had done in the past. They passed through the camp and traversed the edge of the valley, then climbed the mountain of Bethulia and came to its gates. From a distance Judith called out to the gatekeepers, "Open the gates, I beg you! Our God is with us, who brings forth his strength in Israel and his might against his enemies, as he has done today!"

When the men of the town heard her voice, they quickly gathered at the town gates and called together the elders. All came running, both great and small, astounded that she had indeed returned, and opened up the town gates to receive them. A fire was lit to see them, and everyone gathered round. "Praise God!" cried Judith. "Praise the God who has not withheld his mercy from the house of Israel but has destroyed our enemies tonight by my hand!" Drawing the head out of the pouch, she showed it to them and said, "This is the head of Holofernes, commander-in-chief of the Assyrian army! And here is also the curtain, behind which he lay in a drunken stupor! The Lord struck him down by the hand of a woman! As the Lord lives, who protected me as I went, it was my face that seduced him and led to his destruction, and yet, he never committed a sin with me to defile or shame me."

The people were all astounded and bowed down to God, crying out, "Blessed are you, O God, who on this day have humiliated our enemies!"

"My daughter," said Uzziah, "you are blessed by the Most High God above all women on earth, and blessed be the Lord God who created the heavens and the earth, who guided you to strike the head of the leader of our enemies! Those who abide in the strength of God will never lose sight of your hope. May God protect you and exalt you forever. You did not hesitate to risk your own life when you saw your people humiliated, but during our humiliation stepped forward and steadfastly performed God's will."

And all the people responded, "Amen, amen!"

(14) "Now listen to me, my brothers and sisters," said Judith, "Take this head and hang it on the parapet of your walls. When morning comes and the sun has risen over the earth, let every able-bodied man take up his weapons and assemble outside the town. Station a commander before you, as if you were going to charge down upon the plain into the camp of the Assyrian guards, but do not go down. They will then seize their weapons and go to their camp, where they will rouse the Assyrian generals. When they rush to Holofernes' tent, they will not find him there. They will fall into a panic and flee before us. All of you and all of those who live in every part of Israel will then cut them down in their flight. But before you go, bring to me Achior the Ammonite, so that he can identify the one who threatened the house of Israel and threatened him as well by sending him to us as though to his death."

Achior was then brought from the house of Uzziah, and when he came and saw the head of Holofernes, held aloft by one of the people gathered around, he fell faint before them. When they helped him to his feet, he threw himself down before Judith and did obeisance to her. "Blessed are you," he said, "in every tent of Judah, and among every people! When they hear your name, they will tremble! But tell me, what did you do during these past days?" And Judith recounted to him in the presence of all the people everything that she had done, from the time she had left until that very moment. When she stopped speaking, the people cried aloud, filling their town with sounds of joy. Seeing all that the God of Israel had accomplished, Achior also came to believe in God with all his heart. He was circumcised and has remained a member of the house of Israel until today.

So when morning came, they hung the head of Holofernes on the walls, and every man took up his weapons, and they all marched out in groups to the mountain passes. When the Assyrians saw them, they immediately sent word to their commanding officers; they, in turn, informed their superiors and generals and every other officer. When they came to Holofernes' tent, they said to his officer, "Rouse our lord quickly; these slaves have dared to take the field against us! Now they will be wiped out, once and for all!"

Bagoas then entered and tapped on the inner curtain of the tent, for he supposed that Holofernes was sleeping with Judith. When there was no response, he parted the curtain and went in, and there found Holofernes slumped over the stool, dead, with his head cut off. Screaming and wailing and tearing his garments, Bagoas ran to Judith's tent and went in, but did not find her there. He then rushed out of the tent and cried, "These slaves have deceived us! One Hebrew woman has shamed the house of King Nebuchadnezzar! Holofernes is lying on the ground, and his head is gone!" When the Assyrian generals heard this, they tore their garments and were seized with panic, as the camp filled with the sounds of wailing and crying. (15) Those who were in their tents were stunned when they heard what had happened. Struck with fear, to a man they lost their nerve and broke and ran, pouring out across the plain and over the hills. The Assyrian guards in their encampment on the mountainside were also set into flight, as the Israelite warriors descended upon them.

Uzziah sent messengers to Betomasthaim, Bebai, Choba, Kola, and throughout Israel to proclaim everything that had happened, so that everyone could overtake the enemy and destroy them. When the word came to all the Israelites, they attacked at once, cutting their ranks and pressing them as far as Choba. Those from Jerusalem and from the hill country also joined them, having heard what had happened in the Assyrian camp. Those in Gilead and Galilee, by outmaneuvering the enemy, were able to strike a decisive blow and drive them back beyond the borders of Damascus. The remainder of those who lived in Bethulia attacked the Assyrian camp and plundered it, taking away great riches. When the Israelites returned from their slaughter, they took away what was left of the plunder, as did those from the villages and towns in the hill country and the plain, who also took away a large share of booty.

Then Joakim the high priest and the Council of the Israelites who lived in Jerusalem came to commemorate what the Lord had done for Israel, and to laud Judith for her deeds. When they met her, they all blessed her and said, "Through you has come the exaltation of Jerusalem, through you Israel has been glorified! You are the pride of our people! What you have done is a mighty accomplishment by your own hand, a great deed for Israel that has pleased God greatly. May you be blessed by the Almighty Lord forever!"

And all the people said, "Amen."

For thirty days the people plundered the Assyrian camp. They handed over to Judith the tent of Holofernes, along with his silver vessels, his beds, his basins, and all his furnishings, which she loaded upon her mule and her wagons. All the Israelite women came running to see her; they blessed her, while some performed a dance in her honor. She took up garlanded wands and distributed them to the women, and they all crowned themselves with the olive branches, whereupon she led a procession of all the people, the women in front, the men behind fully armed, wearing garlands and singing songs of praise. Judith led the thanksgiving before all of Israel, as the people jubilantly sang with her this hymn:

(16) Raise up a song to my God with tambourines.
    Sing to the Lord with cymbals.
Raise for him a psalm of praise,
    Exalt and invoke his name.
For the Lord is a God who crushes war.
    Into his camps in the midst of the people
    He plucked me out of the hands of those who pursued me.

Assyria came out of the northern mountains with an army of thousands,
An army so great that they clogged the rivers,
Their horses covering the hills.
He gave command to burn all my land
And destroy my young men by the sword.
My nursing babes he commanded to cast to the ground,
To give over my infants for spoils,
And to defile my young women.
But the almighty Lord foiled them
By the hand of a woman.
Indeed, their leader was not undone by young men,
Nor did sons of the Titans strike him,
Nor mighty giants grab him;
But Judith, daughter of Merari,
Led him astray with the beauty of her face.
She took off her widow's garments.
For the lifting up of those struggling in Israel,
She made up her face with precious oils,
And fastened her hair with a tiara.
She chose out her linen garments to bring his downfall.
Her sandal bewitched his eye,
And her beauty captivated his heart,
While her sword sliced through his neck!
Persians quivered at her daring,
While Medes shuddered at her courage.
My oppressed people shouted in triumph,
And my weak people raised a cry as the enemy trembled,
They lifted up their voices and my enemies were turned to flight.
The sons of handmaids ran them through,
And beat them like runaway slaves.
They were broken by the battle line of my Lord.
I will now sing a new song to my God:
O Lord, you are great and glorious,
Marvelous in your strength, and invincible.
Let all creation serve you,
For you spoke, and it came to be.

You sent forth your spirit, and it built them up.
There is no one who can withstand your voice.
For the mountains shall be shaken by the roaring waters;
Before you rocks shall be melted like wax.
Yet for those who fear you,
You shall still show mercy.
For every sacrifice as a fragrant offering is a small thing,
And all fat for the burnt offering is a trifle to you.
But the one who fears the Lord is great forever.
Woe to the nations who oppose my people.
The Lord Almighty will take vengeance upon them on the day of judgment
He will place fire and worms in their flesh,
Causing them to scream in torment forever.

When they came to Jerusalem they bowed to God, and when the people were purified, they brought forth their whole burnt offerings and their free-will offerings and gifts. Judith offered to God all of the furnishings from Holofernes' tent which the people had given to her, and deposited the curtain she had taken from his bed as a votive offering. For three months, the people continued their celebration before the sanctuary in Jerusalem, and Judith remained there with them.

After this, the people returned to their own homes, and Judith went back to Bethulia to reside on her estate. In her day she remained famous throughout the world. While many men desired her, she gave herself to none for as long as she lived, from the time her husband Manasseh had died and was gathered to his ancestors. Her fame continued to grow, and she grew old in her husband's house, reaching the age of a hundred and five. She gave her maid her freedom, dividing her wealth among all the close relatives of Manasseh her husband and to all her relatives. She then died in Bethulia, and was buried in the tomb of her husband Manasseh. The house of Israel mourned her for seven days. And no one was able to strike terror among the Israelites while Judith was alive, nor for a long time afterwards.

## SUGGESTIONS FOR FURTHER READING

Alonso-Schökel, Luis. *Narrative Structures in the Book of Judith.* Berkeley, Calif.: Center for Hermeneutical Studies in Hellenistic and Modern Culture, 1974.

Craven, Toni. *Artistry and Faith in the Book of Judith.* Chico, Calif.: Scholars Press, 1983.

Garrard, Mary. "Judith." In *Artemisia Gentileschi: The Image of the Female Hero in Italian Baroque Art.* Princeton, N.J.: Princeton University Press, 1989.

Jacobus, Mary. "Judith, Holofernes, and the Phallic Woman." In *Reading Women: Essays in Feminist Criticism,* pp. 110–36. New York: Columbia University Press, 1986.

Moore, Carey A. *Judith.* Garden City, N.Y.: Doubleday, 1985.

Nickelsburg, George W. E. *Jewish Literature Between the Bible and the Mishnah,* pp. 105–9. Philadelphia: Fortress, 1981.

Stocker, Margarita. *Judith, Sexual Warrior: Women and Power in Western Culture.* New Haven, Conn.: Yale University Press, 1998.

VanderKam, James C., ed. *"No One Spoke Ill of Her": Essays on Judith.* Atlanta: Scholars Press, 1992.

Wills, Lawrence M. "The Book of Judith." In *The New Interpreter's Bible.* Ed. Leander E. Keck, pp. 3.1073–1183. 12 vols. Nashville: Abingdon, 1999.

———. *The Jewish Novel in the Ancient World,* pp. 132–57. Ithaca, N.Y.: Cornell University Press, 1995.

SIX

# THE MARRIAGE AND CONVERSION OF ASENETH

*The Marriage and Conversion of Aseneth* (also called *Joseph and Aseneth*) sweeps the reader up more effectively than do many of the other texts in this volume. There are two great movements in the plot, one contained inside the other. The story begins and ends as a romance of Joseph and Aseneth and includes the conflicts that arise between Joseph and his brothers and also within Pharaoh's royal house. Aseneth is a wealthy Egyptian woman of marriageable age, who rebuffs her parents' suggestion that she marry the Hebrew Joseph. Once she sees him, however, she is struck to the heart by his appearance and repents of ever having scorned him. This much is similar to the contemporary Greek novels, where "lovesickness" is often the motif that begins the narrative. In the middle section of this novel, however, the typical romance elements of wealth and class become fantastic and heavily laden with symbols. Aseneth lives in her tower and has never been seen by a man. Her tower consists of ten rooms, and she is waited on by seven virgins born on the same night as she. Her family's compound has four gates, beautiful fruit trees, and a spring that flows into a stream running through the courtyard. Such symbolic descriptions overwhelm the reader in this section, but there is no clear interpretive key to them, and none has yet been successfully put forward by scholars. Some of the symbols may reflect the appropriation of sun god symbols to a Jewish context, perhaps even to Jewish mysteries. Just as the Greek sun god Helios had been identified with Zeus, so also in many Jewish synagogues there was an identification of Helios with the Jewish God. At Heliopolis, or City of Helios, where this story takes place, Joseph is likened to the sun and the "man from heaven" is a messenger of the sun.

Whatever the connection with Helios, however, the symbols only become deeper and more mysterious in this middle section, as the narrative turns to Aseneth's prayer scene. It is typical of the Jewish novels to have a woman's prayer scene (see the introduction to the collection), but Aseneth's is the most rending of all of them, and also quite exaggerated; her praying and weeping last seven days and nights. At her lowest point, however, she is visited by a "man from heaven," who oversees a mystical conversion experience involving a ritual with a honeycomb and multicolored bees. (Aseneth in Egyptian means "consecrated to the goddess Neith," who was associated with the bee.) After that, however, we emerge from the conversion interlude and the story returns to the more typical romance narrative style. Aseneth's engagement to Joseph causes jealousy and treachery arising from Pharaoh's oldest son and from Joseph's own brothers as well. A battle ensues in which Aseneth is able to help Joseph's loyal brothers defeat them, Joseph and Aseneth are married, and he is made Pharaoh pro tem until Pharaoh's younger son comes of age.

This novel takes its point of departure from one clause in the Genesis story of Joseph in Egypt: "Pharaoh gave Joseph Aseneth, daughter of Potiphera, priest of On, as his wife" (41:45). There are several scholarly theories as to who wrote it. Certain motifs may arise from the interpretation of the text of Genesis, and until recently the consensus was that a Jewish narrative composed at about the turn of the era was afterward interlaced with other theological motifs, perhaps even from a Christian hand. Others have argued, however, either for an early Jewish composition that was set in the Jewish center of

Heliopolis in Egypt, or for a composition in the fourth century C.E. by a Christian. It is possible, and in my opinion likely, that the two plot lines—the adventure-romance narrative and the mystical interlude—represent two stages in the composition of this narrative. The older romance is Jewish and typical of the historical romances like those of Artapanus, *Tobiad Romance, Royal Family of Adiabene,* and the non-Jewish *Ninus and Semiramus.* It may date from the second century B.C.E. to the first century C.E. The intensely penitential conversion interlude was probably added to this romance (although some description of her conversion may have been present in the original); it dates from a later period and is probably Jewish but may perhaps reflect a Christian milieu.

There are several reasons for concluding that there is more than one layer in the text: the basic distinction between the tone of the romance adventure and that of the unreal, symbolic interlude; the contradiction between the statement at one point that every young man loved Aseneth because of her beauty (from the romance), and at another point that no man has ever seen her (from the interlude); corresponding to this, her statement at one point that she wants to marry the prince rather than Joseph (romance), and at another that she hates all men (interlude). Also, some passages would render a Christian authorship unlikely, such as the fact that the "firstborn son of the Great King"—the king being God—is Joseph and not Christ. Further, the theological tone of the last hymn argues against a Christian authorship.

Another interesting question is regarding the original text. As with most ancient novelistic literature, there are different ancient versions, and here they fall into two groups, a long version (b text) and a short version (d text). Scholars differ on which better represents the original narrative; here I have translated the long version but enclosed in brackets the significant sections that are lacking in the short version. The reader may note some trivial, but also some interesting differences between the two. For instance, Aseneth's prayers are almost three times as long in the longer version. They are also much more rending, with a focus on Aseneth's interior feelings. The longer version also at times appears to have a more male-oriented perspective.

## *The Marriage and Conversion of Aseneth*

(1) In the first year of the seven years of plenty, on the fifth day of the second month, Pharaoh sent Joseph out to tour the entire country of Egypt. In the fourth month of the first year, on the eighteenth day, Joseph arrived in the region of Heliopolis and began to gather the wheat found there, which was as plentiful as the sand of the sea. The governor of Pharaoh in that city was the most highly regarded of all his governors and noblemen, a very wealthy man, and both wise and kind. Having surpassed all of the other noblemen in wisdom, he had became the chief counselor to Pharaoh. His name was Pentephres, priest of Heliopolis.

Pentephres had a daughter, a virgin, who was eighteen years old, tall and comely, and more beautiful than any young woman on earth. Indeed, she bore little resemblance at all to Egyptian women but was in every way more like the women of the Hebrews: as tall as Sarah, as comely as Rebecca, as beautiful as Rachel. Her name was Aseneth, and reports of her beauty could be heard throughout Egypt and beyond, even to the ends of the civilized world. She was courted by the sons of all the noblemen, governors, and princes, all of them young and powerful, and this gave rise to much strife among them on her account; some were even prepared to go to war to win her hand.

When the eldest son of Pharaoh heard of her, he begged his father to give her to him as wife, saying, "Father, grant to me

Aseneth, the daughter of Pentephres, priest of Heliopolis, to be my wife."

"Why," asked Pharaoh, "do you wish to marry someone who is beneath you? You are crown prince of all Egypt. Is not the daughter of Joakim, king of Moab, betrothed to you? She is a princess and is also very beautiful; take her as wife instead."

(2) But Aseneth, for her part, despised and rejected all the men who courted her, and she was arrogant and superior to everyone. Indeed, no man had ever seen her, because she resided in a tower which adjoined Pentephres's house, tall and splendid, on top of which was a floor containing ten rooms. The first room was large and beautiful, paved with purple stones, with a many-colored mosaic of precious stones along the walls, and gold plate on the ceiling. Inside the room, mounted on the walls, were countless Egyptian gods made of gold and silver, which Aseneth worshipped and revered, placing before them many offerings each day. In the second room were Aseneth's chests and jewelry. There was much gold and silver, along with clothes interwoven with gold, rare stones, and exotic, beautiful threads, and all of the cosmetic accessories appropriate to a virgin. The third room served as Aseneth's storeroom, containing all the luxuries of the world. In the remaining seven rooms resided seven virgins, one in each room, who served Aseneth. They were all the same age, born on the same night as Aseneth, and she loved them dearly. They were as beautiful as the stars of heaven, and they had never been spoken to by boy or man.

Three windows opened off of the great room where Aseneth was being nurtured as a virgin. The first window, facing east, was very large and opened onto the courtyard. The second faced south, while the third faced north, overlooking a busy street. There was a golden bed standing in this room, facing the east window, covered in gold and purple material, interwoven with violet, purple, and white threads. This was the bed of Aseneth; other than she, no man or woman had ever sat upon it. A great courtyard surrounded the house, bounded on all sides by a high wall, constructed of huge stones. There were four gates to the courtyard, plated with iron, each guarded by eighteen stalwart, heavily armed guards. Along the wall of the courtyard were beautiful fruit trees of every kind bearing ripe fruit, for it was at this time the harvest season. On the south side of the court was a spring providing an abundance of flowing water, with a cistern below it to catch the overflow. A stream ran from it through the middle of the court, watering all the trees found there.

(3) And it happened during the first year of the seven years of plenty, in the fourth month, on the eighteenth day, that Joseph came into the region of Heliopolis to gather the abundant wheat of the region. As he approached the city, he sent twelve men ahead of him to Pentephres, the priest, saying, "I shall lodge with you, because it is now noon and time for my meal, and since the sun is hot, I would like to rest in the shade of your house."

Pentephres was overjoyed to hear this and said, "Blessed is the Lord God of Joseph, because my lord Joseph considered me worthy to lodge here." Summoning his chief servant, he said, "Hurry and prepare the house, and have a large banquet made up, because Joseph, the Mighty One of God, is coming here today."

When Aseneth heard that her father and mother, who had been away at the family estate for the harvest season, had returned, she was overjoyed and said, "I shall go to meet them, now that they are back." Aseneth hurried to her room, where her robes were kept, and dressed in a white linen robe with purple and gold threads. She also bound a golden sash around her, placed bracelets on her hands and feet, strapped on her golden sandals, and draped around her neck pendants of rare and precious stones which hung down on all sides. The names of the Egyptian gods were engraved on each of her bracelets and stones, and the faces of idols were also carved upon them. Next she placed a tiara upon her head and a diadem around her forehead, finally covering her entire head with a veil. (4) She then rushed down the stairs from her upper floor and met her father and mother, greeting them with a kiss. Pentephres and his wife rejoiced over their daughter Aseneth when they saw her adorned like a bride of God. They then brought out all of the good things that they had brought from their family estate and gave them to their daughter. She was delighted by all the good fruits—grapes, dates, peaches, pomegranates, and figs—all luscious and sweet.

"My child," said Pentephres to Aseneth.

"Yes, father?" she replied.

"Sit down here between your mother and me. I have something to say to you."

Aseneth sat down between them as her father, taking her right hand in his, kissed it and said, "Aseneth, my child."

"Yes, my lord and father," she replied. "Please tell me what it is."

"Joseph, the Mighty One of God, is coming here today. He is now prime minister of all Egypt. Pharaoh appointed him as ruler of the whole land to ration the grain for everyone and to save the land from the approaching famine. Joseph is a man who reveres God and is very prudent, and he is still a virgin, as you are. He is learned and most wise; the spirit of God is upon him and God's grace is with him. So, my child, I shall give him your hand in marriage; you will be his bride and he your groom, forever."

Upon hearing this, Aseneth's face grew red with anger. Glaring at her father in fury, she said, "How can my lord and father speak like this and say that he will take me like some captive and hand me over to a man who is a foreigner and a fugitive, and who was sold as a slave? Is he not a shepherd's son from the land of Canaan, and was he not caught in the act of sleeping with his master's wife? Was he not then also cast into a dungeon, until Pharaoh released him, simply because he could interpret dreams like the old Egyptian women? Would I not be better off marrying the king's eldest son? He is the crown prince of all Egypt!"

When he heard this, Pentephres was ashamed to speak any further with Aseneth about Joseph, for she had answered too boldly and in boastfulness and anger. (5) But at that point one of Pentephres's servants came running in and said, "Joseph is now standing outside the gates." As a result of her conversation about

Joseph, Aseneth fled from her father and mother and ascended to her upper floor. She entered her room and stood beside the large window facing east, hoping to catch a glimpse of Joseph as he entered the house.

Pentephres and his wife, with all his family, went out to meet Joseph. The gates of the courtyard facing east were opened and Joseph entered upon Pharaoh's second chariot, which was appointed with purest gold, and pulled by four horses white as snow, with golden bridles on their heads. Joseph was dressed in a splendid white tunic, with a purple robe wrapped around him, made of linen interwoven with gold. A gold crown was on his head, in which twelve precious stones were set, with twelve golden rays rising from them. He held a royal staff in his left hand, and in his right he extended an olive branch, heavily laden with fruit dripping with oil. Joseph entered the courtyard as the guards closed and secured the gates behind him, leaving every foreign man and woman outside the gates. Pentephres, his wife, and all his family, except for his daughter Aseneth, came forward and prostrated themselves on the ground before Joseph, and Joseph in response stepped down from the chariot and greeted them with his right hand.

(6) When Aseneth saw Joseph upon the chariot, she was cut to the heart. Her soul reeled, her knees grew weak beneath her, her entire body trembled. Frightened by her reaction, she gasped and said to herself:

What am I to do, oh wretch that I am!
Did I not just say that Joseph comes as the son of a shepherd from Canaan?
But now I see the sun come down to us from heaven, mounted on a chariot.
Today it has come into our home,
Illuminating it as the sun does the earth.
But I, foolish and much too bold, despised him
And said vicious things about him.

For I did not know that Joseph is the son of God.
Indeed, what mere mortal could beget such beauty?
Or what mother's womb give birth to such light?
But what a wretch and fool am I,
For I said vicious things about him to my father!
Where can I go now to hide from his presence,
So that Joseph, the son of God, would not see me
After I have said these vicious things about him?
Where can I hide, when he sees every hiding place
And nothing remains hidden from him, because of the great light within him?
Have mercy on me, Lord God of Joseph!
These vicious things that I said about him were spoken in ignorance.
Now, my father, give me to Joseph as a maidservant and slave,
And I will serve him forever!

(7) Joseph then entered the house of Pentephres and sat upon his chair. They washed his feet and set a table for his use alone, as he did not eat with the Egyptians, an act which would be an abomination to him. But when Joseph looked up, he saw Aseneth leaning down for a glimpse of him, and he said to Pentephres and his family, in a fearful voice, "Who is that woman standing upstairs beside the window? Get her out of this house, lest she try to harass me as well!" Indeed, all of the wives and daughters of the noblemen and governors of Egypt had pestered him to lie with them. All the wives and daughters of the Egyptians, whenever they laid eyes on him, suffered greatly over his beauty. Joseph, however, despised them, and the messengers the women sent bearing gold, silver, and precious gifts he rebuffed with threats of violent punishment. "I will never commit a sin against the Lord, God of my father Israel," Joseph had said to them, "nor against the vision of my father Jacob."

Joseph kept the face of Jacob his father continually before his eyes and remembered his commandments, for Jacob had said to his son Joseph and to all his sons, "Be on guard, my children, against associating with a foreign woman; relations with her will surely bring destruction and ruin." For all these reasons, then, Joseph had said, "Send this woman away from this house."

"But my lord," Pentephres responded, "the woman whom you saw standing at the top of the stairs is not a foreign woman, but our daughter, a virgin who hates every man. No man has ever seen her, except for you just now. If you wish, she will come down and greet you, for our daughter is like a sister to you."

Joseph was overjoyed to hear that she was a virgin who hated every man. He said to himself, "If she is a virgin who hates all men, she will never harass me." So Joseph said to Pentephres and all his family, "If she is your daughter and a virgin, let her come down, for she is my sister and from this day on I shall love her as my sister."

(8) Aseneth's mother went upstairs and came back with her daughter and stood her before Joseph, as Pentephres said to her, "Aseneth, greet your brother, for he is also a virgin, just as you are, and hates all foreign women, as you hate all foreign men."

"Greetings, my lord," said Aseneth, "You are blessed by the Most High God."

And Joseph responded, "The Lord God who gave life to all things will bless you."

"Now kiss your brother," said Pentephres to his daughter.

But as Aseneth tried to kiss him, Joseph held out his right hand and placed it upon her chest, [between her breasts, which were already standing up like ripe apples.] "It is not proper," he said, "for a man who worships God, and who blesses the living God with his lips, and eats the bread of life that has been blessed, and drinks from the cup of resurrection that has been blessed, and is anointed with the oil of incorruptibility that has been blessed, to then kiss a foreign woman who blesses dead, silent idols with her lips, eats bread of strangulation from their tables, drinks the cup of wickedness from their libation, and is anointed with the oil of destruction. No, a man who reveres God will kiss his mother, or sister, or a kinswoman from his family and clan, or his own wife, with whom he shares his bed, all of whom bless with their lips the living God. Just so for a woman who reveres God: it is not proper to kiss a foreign man, since that would be an abomination before the Lord God."

When Aseneth heard this, she was cut to the heart. She became quite distraught, and groaned loudly. She looked up reverently at Joseph, with her eyes fixed upon him, as they swelled up with tears. When Joseph saw this, he too was struck; he had mercy on her, because he was gentle and merciful, and revered God. Raising his right hand, he placed it upon her head, and said:

> O Lord, God of my father Israel,
> Most High, Mighty One of Jacob,
> Who gave life to all things,
> And summoned them out of the darkness into light
> And from error into truth,
> From death into life,
> O Lord, bless this virgin
> And renew her by your spirit.
> Form her anew by your hidden hand,
> Make her alive again by your life,
> Let her eat your bread of life,
> Let her drink from your cup of blessing.
> [Count her among your people,
> Whom you chose before creation.]
> Let her enter into your rest,
> Which you prepared for the elect.
> [Let her live in your eternal life forever.]

(9) Aseneth rejoiced exceedingly over Joseph's blessing. When she heard the words of this prayer, spoken in the name of the Most High God, she hurried to her upper floor alone and collapsed upon her bed, weak and covered with perspiration. She felt within her joy and grief, fear and trembling. Weeping loudly, she repented from the gods whom she had worshipped and spurned all her idols, and then waited for evening to come.

Joseph ate and drank, then said to his servants, "Harness the horses to the chariots; I am leaving to tour the entire land."

"But let my lord lodge here tonight," said Pentephres, "and then proceed along your way in the morning."

"I must go today," Joseph responded, "for this is the day on which God began to make all his creatures. On the eighth day, when this day comes around again, I shall return to you. Then I shall lodge here."

(10) So Joseph proceeded on his way, and Pentephres and all his family returned to their family estate. Aseneth alone remained, accompanied by her seven virgins, and was deep in gloom, weeping until dawn. She neither ate bread nor drank water, and when night came, and all those in the house with her fell asleep, she herself remained awake. Brooding and weeping, she struck her chest with her hand over and over again and trembled in fear. She arose from her bed and went quietly downstairs and out to the gate, where the woman gatekeeper was asleep with her children. Aseneth quickly took down from the window the skin which was used as a curtain, and filled it with ashes from the fireplace, and carried it back upstairs to the upper story, and set it on the floor. Closing the door firmly behind her and securing the iron bolt, she groaned and wept bitterly. Now one of the virgins, whom Aseneth loved more than all the virgins and had adopted as a sister, heard the groaning and immediately woke the others. They came to Aseneth's door but found it closed. Hearing her moaning and weeping, they called out, "What is wrong, mistress? Why do you sound so ill? Is something troubling you? Open the door so that we may see what is wrong!"

"My head is throbbing with pain," answered Aseneth through the closed door, "and I must lie quiet in my bed. I am not strong enough to rise and open the door, my body is so weak. But go, each of you, back to your rooms and rest, and allow me to lie quietly."

The virgins then returned to their own rooms. Aseneth arose and quietly opened the door and entered her second room, where the chests were that contained her beautiful garments. From one of her chests she took out a somber, black tunic of mourning, the same mourning tunic she had worn when her younger brother had died, [and carried it into her room, carefully closing the door behind her and bolting it.]

She then quickly took off her royal robe made of linen and gold thread and put on her black mourning tunic. She untied her golden sash and bound a rope around her waist in its place. She next removed the tiara from her head, along with her diadem, bracelets, and anklets, and placed everything on the floor. Then she took her beautiful robe, her gold sash, and the tiara and threw them all out the north window for the poor. The innumerable gods in the room, made of gold and silver, she also broke into pieces and threw through the north window for the poor and needy. Aseneth then took her royal dinner—choice beef, fish, and veal—and all the sacrifices of her gods and the vessels for the libations of wine, and threw them out of the window [facing north, to feed the foreign dogs, saying to herself, "My dogs shall never eat from my plate, nor from the sacrifices offered to idols. Let the foreign dogs have these."] Aseneth next took the skin filled with ashes and emptied it out upon the floor. After girding her waist with a piece of sackcloth, she loosened the clasp on her braid and let her hair down. She then sprinkled ashes over her head and spread them over the floor.[1] Over and over she struck her breast with both hands, weeping bitterly, and then fell upon the ashes. All night long she lamented loudly, moaning and weeping until dawn. At daybreak, when Aseneth got up, she saw that a great pool of mud had formed from her tears and the ashes. Falling on her face again in the ashes, she remained there until nightfall. In the same way she passed the next seven days; she did not eat bread or drink water in the seven days [of her humiliation].

(11) But when dawn came on the eighth day, the birds were

1. Ashes were strewn on the head during mourning, or in some cases a person might wallow in them (Jeremiah 6:26), and they become symbolic of penitence here and in the woman's prayer scene in *Greek Esther* and *Judith*.

singing and the dogs barking at passersby. Exhausted and spent from her fast of seven days, Aseneth was barely able to lift her head from where she was lying amid the ashes on the floor. [Placing her hand upon the floor for support, she managed to rise to her knees, but her head still hung down, and her hair was matted with ashes. She clasped her hands together and shook her head from side to side, then struck her chest with her hands, her head drooping down against her chest, and her face covered with tears. She groaned loudly and pulled at her hair, sprinkling ashes again over her head. Thoroughly spent, Aseneth had now become dispirited. She leaned against the wall beneath the east window, and dropped her head against her bosom. She clasped her fingers together over her right knee, and with her mouth closed, as she had for the seven days and nights of her humiliation, said to herself:

What shall I do, humbled as I am?
Where shall I go?
With whom shall I take refuge?
What shall I say?
I, a virgin and orphan, desolate, abandoned, and despised—
Now everyone hates me, even my father and mother!
I have come to hate their gods; I have destroyed them
And thrown them down to be trodden under foot.
Now my father and mother and all my family hate me
And have declared, "Aseneth is not our daughter, because she destroyed our gods."
Everyone hates me because I have loathed every man,
Especially those who have courted me.
Now in my humiliation everyone despises me
And gloats over my affliction.
But the Lord God Most High of the Mighty One, Joseph,
Hates all those who worship idols.
He is a jealous and terrible God towards all those who worship foreign gods.
Now he hates me too because I have worshipped dead and silent idols

And have blessed them.
I ate from their sacrifices.
My mouth is now defiled from their table,
And I do not dare to call upon the Lord God of Heaven,
The Most High, the Mighty One of the powerful Joseph,
Because my mouth has been defiled from the sacrifices of idols.
But indeed I have heard many people say that
The God of the Hebrews is a true and living God and a God of mercy:
Compassionate, patient, merciful, gentle,
Who does not reckon the sins of a humble person
And does not hold people accountable for their sins
When they have been greatly afflicted.
Therefore, I will pluck up courage and turn to him,
And take refuge with him,
Confessing to him all my sins
And pour out my prayer before him.
For who knows whether he will look upon my humiliation
And have mercy upon me?
Perhaps seeing my desolation, he will have compassion for me,
Or seeing that I am an orphan, will protect me.
Indeed, he is the father of orphans!
The protector of the persecuted!
A helper to the afflicted!
I will dare to call upon him.

Aseneth rose from beside the wall and turned and sat looking toward the east window. She sat straight up upon her knees and stretched her hands toward heaven but was still afraid to open her mouth and invoke the name of God. Leaning back against the wall, she sat there, striking her head and chest with her hand, and said to herself without opening her mouth:

A wretch am I, orphaned and desolate!
My mouth is defiled from the sacrifices of idols
And from the praises of the Egyptian gods.
Surrounded here by these ashes mixed with tears, and in the filth of my humiliation,

How could I open my mouth to the Most High?
How could I invoke his holy and terrible name?
Surely the Lord will be furious
If I call upon his holy name in my sins.
What then is such a wretch as I to do?
I will dare to open my mouth to him
And call upon his name!
And even if the Lord strikes me in his fury,
Surely he will heal me again,
And if he chastises me with his whips,
He will also turn his face to me in his mercy.
And if he is enraged over my sins,
He will be reconciled to me again and forgive each one.
Therefore I will dare to open my mouth to him.

Aseneth yet again arose from the wall where she was leaning and sat straight up on her knees. She extended her hands to the east and, looking toward heaven, opened her mouth and said,]

(12) Lord, God of the ages,
[Who created all things and gave them life,]
Who granted the breath of life [to your whole creation,]
And brought the unseen things to light,
Who made the things that exist and appear to us
From what is invisible and does not exist,
Who stretched out the heavens
[And secured them on a firmament upon the back of the winds,]
Who placed the earth upon the waters,
Who erected great rocks over the abyss of the water
So great they are still not covered,
[But jut out of the water like oak leaves.
They are living rocks
Who hear your voice, O Lord,
And keep the commandments which you have ordained for them.
Your laws they will never transgress,
But will obey your will forever.
You spoke, O Lord, and they were brought to life,
Because your word, Lord, is the word of life for all your creatures.

Therefore, I take refuge in you, O Lord.]
I will call out to you, [and pour out my prayer,]
Confessing my sins.
To you I shall render account for my trespasses.
[Spare me, O Lord, for I have committed many sins against you.]
I have sinned and been blasphemous, speaking many evil and unspeakable things in your presence.
My mouth is defiled from the idol sacrifices
And from the table of the Egyptian gods.
I have sinned against you in many ways, O Lord,
Committing many sins [in ignorance,]
Worshipping dead and silent idols.
Now I am not worthy to open my mouth before you, O Lord,
[And I, Aseneth, daughter of Pentephres the priest,
A virgin and of royal blood,
Once proud and arrogant,
And content in my riches beyond all people,
Have now become an orphan, forsaken and abandoned by all people.]
I take my refuge in you, O Lord,
And offer up my prayer and call out to you:
Save me before I am run down by those pursuing me!
For just as a little child who is afraid runs to her father,[2]
[And the father will reach down and snatch her up,
And hold her to his chest
While the child clasps her hands around her father's neck
To recover from her fear, resting at the bosom of her father
As the father smiles at her childish fear,]
So also you, O Lord, extend your hands to me as a benevolent father,
And snatch me up off the earth,
For now a savage old lion is after me—
The father of the Egyptian gods—
And his children [are those who are driven mad by idols.

2. Words for young children in Greek are neuter, as they are in many other languages that have a neuter gender. Choosing the feminine gender here in English emphasizes that it is Aseneth's experience, even though it is a metaphor for others' experiences as well.

I despise them because they are children of the lion,]
And I cast them away from me and destroyed them.
Their father, [the lion, is in a rage and pursuing me,]
But you, Lord, save me from his hands
And pluck me up from out of his mouth,
Lest he grasp me like a lion
And rip me to pieces,
And throw me into a roaring flame,
[And the fire throw me into the hurricane,
And the hurricane surround me with darkness,
And cast me out into the depths of the sea.
The eternal] sea monster will swallow me whole
[And I shall perish for all time.
Save me, Lord, before all these things overtake me.]
Save me, Lord, who am desolate and all alone,
For my father and mother have disowned me
[And said, "Aseneth is not our daughter,"]
Because I destroyed and broke their gods
[And despised them.]
I am now an orphan and desolate,
With no hope except in you, O Lord.
[I have no other refuge except in your mercy.]
You are the father of orphans,
A defender of the persecuted
And an aid to the afflicted.
[Have mercy on me, O Lord,
And protect me, a chaste virgin who is abandoned and an orphan,
Because you are the Lord, a good and sweet and gentle father.
What father is as sweet as you, Lord?
Or as quick to show mercy?
Or as slow to rise to anger for our sins?]
All of the gifts of my father, Pentephres,
[Which he gave to me as my estate,] are fleeting and transient,
But the gifts of your estate, O Lord, are imperishable and eternal.
(13) Consider my humiliation and have mercy on me.
I am but an orphan;
Show compassion on one so afflicted,

For I am fleeing everyone
And am taking my refuge in you, O Lord,
Who alone shows compassion.
Now I have forsaken all the good things of this earth,
And have come to you for refuge, O Lord,
Dressed in sackcloth and ashes,
Naked, an orphan, and forsaken.
I took off my royal robe of finest linen, interwoven with purple and gold,
And put on a black tunic of mourning.
I have also loosened my gold sash and cast it off from me
And girded myself with a rope and sackcloth.
My tiara and my diadem I flung from my head,
Sprinkling them with ashes.
The floor of my room, tiled with colored and purple stones,
Which was formerly sprinkled with perfumes
And wiped with bright linen cloths,
Is now sprinkled with my tears
And profaned, covered with ashes.
Now, Lord, from my tears and the ashes
A pool of mud has formed in my room,
As though it were the middle of the street.
I gave my royal banquet, Lord, [and my fine cereals] to the [foreign] dogs,
And for seven days and seven nights I fasted
And neither ate bread nor drank water.
My mouth became dry as a drum
And my tongue as dry as a horn.
My lips became parched like a potsherd.
My face is sunken
And my eyes are red with shame from the flow of tears.
[My strength has deserted me.
But all the gods which I once worshipped in ignorance
I now know to be dead and silent idols.
I have cast them out to be trampled underfoot,
For thieves to steal and melt down for the silver and gold.
And now I take refuge in you, O Lord my God.]

Please save me from all my sins of ignorance.
Pardon me, for I have sinned against you in ignorance,
While still only a virgin,
And have stumbled unwittingly
And spoken blasphemies against the Lord of Joseph,
Because I, a miserable wretch, did not know him.
I did not know that he was your son.
Everyone told me that Joseph was the son of a shepherd from Canaan,
And I, wretch that I am, believed them,
And erred as a result.
I hated him and said wicked things about him.
I did not know that he is your son,
But what human being is capable of giving birth to one of such beauty,
Or of such wisdom, virtue, or power as the most excellent Joseph possesses?
Lord, I commit him to your keeping,
Because I love him more than my own life.
Protect him, therefore, in the wisdom of your grace,
And commit me to his keeping, O Lord, as a maidservant and slave.
I shall make his bed and wash his feet and wait on him
And will be his slave and serve him forever.

(14) As Aseneth finished her confession to the Lord, the morning star rose in the east, and she was overjoyed at its sight. "The Lord God has now heard my prayer," said Aseneth, "because this star has risen as a messenger and herald of the light of the great day."

And as Aseneth was watching, near the star the heavens split, and there appeared a great and indescribable light. Aseneth fell down upon her face in the ashes, and a man came to her from heaven and stood beside her head, calling "Aseneth, Aseneth."

"Who is calling me?" she asked, "The door of my room is locked, and this room is high above the ground. How did he enter my room?"

But the man called to her a second time, "Aseneth, Aseneth."

"Here am I, Sir," she answered. "Please tell me who you are."

"I am the one who rules over the Lord's house, the one who leads the army of the Most High. Rise up on your feet and I shall speak to you."

Raising her head, Aseneth beheld a man like Joseph in every respect—his robe, his crown, his royal staff were the same. His face, however, was like lightning, his eyes like the rays of the sun; [his hair was like the flame of a burning torch,] and his hands and feet like glowing hot iron, with sparks flying from them. When Aseneth saw him, she fell on her face at his feet, frightened, her whole body trembling.

"Have courage and do not fear," the man said to her. "Stand up on your feet and I shall speak to you." Aseneth rose to her feet and the man continued. "Go now into your second room and take off your black tunic of mourning and take the sackcloth from your waist. Shake the ashes from your hair and wash your face and hands with living water.[3] Then put on a special new linen robe which has never been worn, and tie a new sash around your waist, a double sash which shows your virginity. When that is done, return to me and I shall tell you more."

Aseneth hurried into the second room where she kept her chests of beautiful garments, and opened one of the chests and took out a new linen robe which had not been worn. Taking off her black tunic of mourning and removing her sackcloth sash, she put on her new linen robe and placed around her the double sash of virginity, one sash around her waist and the other around her breasts. She shook out the ashes from her hair and washed her hands and face with living water, then covered her head with a beautiful linen veil that had never been worn.

(15) Returning to the man in the first room, she stood before

3. Living water is an evocative symbol (cf. John 4:10), but it is also a standard term in Greek for flowing water or spring water, as opposed to stagnant or salt water, and therefore safe to drink.

him. He said to her, "Take the veil off of your head. Why did you put this on? Today you are a chaste virgin, and your head is like a young man's."[4] So Aseneth took off the veil from her head, and the man continued, "Have courage, Aseneth, chaste virgin. I have heard all the words of your confession [and prayer. I have also seen the humiliation and affliction of your seven days of fasting. From your tears and these ashes, a pool of mud has now formed before you.] Have courage, Aseneth, [chaste virgin.] Your name has been inscribed in the Book of Life [in heaven; at the very beginning of the book your name has been inscribed by my hand,] never to be erased. From this day forth you shall be made new, reformed, given a new life, eating [blessed] bread of life, drinking from the [blessed] cup of immortality, and anointed with the [blessed] ointment of incorruptibility. Have courage, Aseneth, [chaste virgin.] I have given you today as a bride to Joseph, and he shall be your groom forever. Your name shall no longer be Aseneth, but City of Refuge, because in you many nations will seek refuge in the Lord God Most High. Under your wings many peoples who believe in the Lord God will be sheltered. Within your walls will be guarded those who devote themselves to the Most High God through repentance, for Repentance is a [fair and beautiful] daughter of the Most High, [and resides in heaven.] She herself entreats the Most High God every hour on your behalf, and for all those who have repented [in the name of the Most High God,] since he is the father of Repentance. She is the guardian of all virgins, [and loves you very much;] every hour she intercedes for all of you with the Most High, [and has prepared a place of rest in the heavens for all of those who repent. She will renew them] and serve them forever.

4. In the religious texts of this period, virginity was often a metaphor for a special, ascetic spiritual state, and it was sometimes described as "becoming male." As a male, she would not have to wear a veil.

Repentance is a beautiful and chaste virgin, [always laughing,] gentle and meek. For this reason, the Most High Father loves her, and all the angels show her respect. [I also love her very much, because she is my sister. And because she loves you virgins, I love you too.]

"Now I am going away to Joseph to tell him everything that has happened to you, and Joseph will come to you today, and when he sees you, he will rejoice over you and love you and be your groom, and you will be his bride forever. Listen to me now, Aseneth, chaste virgin, and put on your marriage robe, the ancient robe, which was the first robe placed in your room from the very beginning. Put on as well all of your beautiful jewels and cosmetics. Beautify yourself as a beautiful bride, and go to meet Joseph. He will be here today and will rejoice when he sees you."

When the man finished speaking, Aseneth was overjoyed at what he had said, and she fell upon his feet, [prostrating herself before him] and said, "Blessed is the Lord your God, [the Most High,] who sent you to save me from darkness, leading me [out of the depths of the abyss.] Blessed be your name forever. [What is your name, O Lord? Tell me so that I may sing praises and glorify you forever."

"Why do you want to know my name?" he said. "My name is in heaven in the book of the Most High, inscribed by the hand of God at the beginning of the book before all the others, because I rule over the house of the Most High. All names inscribed there are unspeakable, and it is not permitted for anyone in this world to say or to hear them, because these names are great and marvelous and highly praised."

"Lord," said Aseneth, "if I have found favor in your eyes and believe that you will do everything you say, pray let your maidservant speak to you."

"Speak," said the man.

And Aseneth extended her right hand and placed it upon his knees and said to him, "This bed is pure and undefiled, and no man or woman has ever sat upon it.] I beg you, Lord, sit a while on this bed. I shall set a table for you and bring to you bread to eat, and bring the best aged wine from my storeroom for you to drink, with an aroma so beautiful it will reach up to heaven. After this, you can go on your way."

"Go at once and bring them here," he replied.

(16) Aseneth hurried and prepared a new table for him, and went to fetch the bread. The man said to her, "Bring me also a honeycomb." Aseneth stopped and became troubled, for she had no honeycomb in the storeroom. The man said to her, "Why have you stopped?"

She replied, "I shall send a slave out to the village, because our family estate is near, and he can quickly return with a honeycomb for me to serve you."

"Go now to your storeroom," he said, "and you will find a honeycomb sitting on the table. Bring it back here to me."

"But Lord," said Aseneth, "there is no honeycomb in the storeroom."

"Go there and you will find it," he said.

So Aseneth entered the storeroom and found a honeycomb lying upon the table. It was [large and] white as snow, and full of honey. [The honey was like the dew of heaven,] and the aroma was like the breath of life. [Aseneth was amazed, and said to herself, "Why, this honeycomb must have come out of this man's mouth, because its aroma is just like his breath."] Then Aseneth took the honeycomb and brought it to the man [and placed it on the table that she had set before him.]

The man said to her, "Why did you tell me there was no honeycomb in your storeroom, when you have brought me a marvelous comb?"

"Lord," said Aseneth, [now frightened,] "I had no honeycomb in my storeroom, but you spoke and it appeared! Could this have come forth from your mouth? Its aroma is just like your breath."

The man [smiled at Aseneth's understanding. He called her over to him,] and extending his [right] hand, held her head [and shook it. Aseneth, however, was frightened of his hand, because sparks were shooting forth from it, as though from glowing iron. She continued watching intently, however, keeping her eyes fixed on the man's hand. The man saw this and smiled,] saying, "Blessed are you, Aseneth, because the secret mysteries of the Most High have been revealed to you, and blessed are all those who attach themselves to the Lord God in repentance, because they eat from this honeycomb. This honeycomb is [the spirit of life,] made by the bees in the Garden of Eden [from the dew of the roses of life which are there.] All the angels of God eat of it, [as do all the elect of God and all the children of the Most High, because it is the honeycomb of life,] and anyone who eats from it will never die."

With his right hand the man broke a piece off of the comb and took a bite from it, then placed the rest in Aseneth's mouth [and said, "Eat," and she ate. "Now," he said, "you have eaten the bread of life and drunk from the cup of immortality and have been anointed with the ointment of incorruptibility. From this day forth, your flesh will flourish like the flowers of life sprouting up from the ground of the Most High, your bones will grow strong like the cedars of the Garden of Eden of God, and unceasing powers will course through you. You will never see old age, and your beauty will never fade. You will be like a walled city for all those who take refuge in the name of the Lord God, Eternal King." With his right hand the man touched the comb where he had broken it, and it was immediately restored and filled out as it had been.]

The man then extended his right hand again and placed his finger on the corner of the comb which faced eastward, [and drew his finger across the comb to the corner facing west,] and it left a mark which was like blood. Then he extended his hand a second time and placed his finger on the corner of the comb facing north [and drew his finger across the comb to the corner facing south,] leaving another mark like blood.[5] Aseneth stood by his left side and watched everything that he was doing. [The man then said to the comb, "Come,"] and bees rose up out of the cells of the comb, [cells which were so numerous that they could not be counted, thousands upon thousands upon thousands.] The bees were white as snow, with wings shimmering of purple, hyacinth, [scarlet,] and linen interwoven with gold threads, while golden diadems were on their heads. Although they did not attempt to injure anyone, their stings were sharp, and they swarmed around Aseneth from head to toe. Other bees, as large and beautiful as queen bees, [emerged from the broken part of the comb] and swarmed around Aseneth's face, [and upon her mouth] and lips [they made a comb similar to the comb which lay before the man. All those bees ate from the comb which was on Aseneth's mouth,] and then the man said, "Go now to your place." [The bees then rose up and flew into heaven, but any of them that tried to sting Aseneth] fell to the floor and died. The man [extended his staff over the dead bees] and said, "Arise, now, and go to your place as well." The [dead] bees arose and flew out to the court [beside the house and collected in the fruit trees.]

(17) "Have you seen what I have done?" the man asked Aseneth.

"Yes, Lord, I have seen everything."

"Thus shall it be with everything which I have said to you today." The man extended his right hand for the third time and touched the comb where it had been broken, and fire immediately flew out of the table and consumed the comb, but the table was not burned. The aroma from the burning comb filled the room.

5. Although the cross thus created might be taken to be a Christian symbol, that is not likely the case. A cross such as this has been found in ancient Jewish representations of the sun god Helios, and that is more likely its association here. See Kraemer, *When Aseneth Met Joseph,* 166–67, in the Suggested Reading.

Aseneth said to the man, "Lord, seven virgins, born on the same night as I, and raised with me from my youth, are here. They serve me, and I love them [as my sisters.] Allow me to call them so that you may bless them as you have me."

"Call them," he said.

So Aseneth called [the seven virgins and presented them to the man,] who blessed them and said, "May the Lord God Most High bless you, [and may you become the seven pillars of the City of Refuge, and all the fellow citizens of the elect in that city will take their rest in you] forever and ever." Then the man said to Aseneth, "Now remove this table." Aseneth turned to put the table away, and the man disappeared from before her eyes. She saw, however, something like a chariot, [pulled by four horses,] proceeding into heaven toward the east. [It was like fire, and the horses were like lightning, with the man at the reins.

"How foolish and bold I have been!" said Aseneth. "I have spoken too boldly and said that it was a man who came into my room from heaven, but little did I realize, it was a god who came to me, and now he is returning to his abode in heaven!"] She said to herself, "Lord, I pray, be merciful to your slave, and spare your maidservant. I have spoken too boldly in your presence, but all my words were uttered in ignorance."

(18) As Aseneth was speaking these words, a servant of her father's arrived and said, "Joseph, the Mighty One of God, is coming today, and his messenger is now standing outside the gates of the court."

Aseneth then summoned her guardian, who managed all the household affairs, and said, "Hurry and prepare the house and arrange a banquet, for Joseph the Mighty One of God is arriving here today."

[Her guardian then noticed her face, which was sunken from the trials, the weeping, and the fasting of the previous seven days. Greatly disturbed, he cried and took her right hand and kissed it and said, "What has happened to you, my child, to give you such a sunken face?"

"My head has reeled with turmoil," she replied, "and my eyes have not slept; thus my face is sunken."

So her guardian left to prepare the house and dinner. Aseneth recalled the man who had visited her and his commandments,] and hurried off to her [second] room, [where her chests of beautiful garments were kept.] There she opened her large chest and took out her best [wedding] robe, which was like lightning in appearance, and put it on. She also put on her royal golden sash, made with precious stones, and placed golden bracelets on her hands and golden sandals on her feet, and around her neck she placed a necklace, [from which hung innumerable priceless jewels.] On her head she placed a golden crown, [on the front of which was a great sapphire,] surrounded by [six] valuable stones. She covered her head with a veil [like a bride, and held a sceptre in her hand. But when Aseneth recalled that her guardian had told her that her face was sunken, she became upset. "Oh, that this should happen to such a humbled woman as I! Now Joseph will see me and despise me!"] She turned to one of her [adopted sisters,] "Bring me some clean water from the spring [to wash my face."

The maid brought the clean water from the well and poured it into a basin.] When Aseneth leaned over to wash her face, she saw her face in the water. It was like the sun, and her eyes like the rising morning star, [her cheeks like fields of the Most High, with a blush as red as blood, her lips were like a rose of life, rising out of its greenery, and her teeth like soldiers standing in battle array. The hair of her head was like a vine in the Garden of Eden, bearing abundant fruit, her neck like a towering cypress, her breasts like the mountains of the Most High God. When Aseneth saw herself in the water, she was amazed and rejoiced and did not wash her face, "lest," she said, "I wash away this great beauty."

When her guardian returned to tell her that everything had been prepared as she had ordered, he saw her and was startled. Speechless and frightened, he fell at her feet and said, "What has happened, my lady? Where did this great and marvelous beauty come from? Can it be that the Lord God of Heaven has chosen you to be the bride of his firtborn son Joseph?"]

(19) While they were speaking, a servant entered and said, "Joseph is now standing at the gates of the court." Aseneth immediately descended the stairs with her seven virgins to meet Joseph, [and stood in the entryway of the house. Joseph entered the court, and the gates were closed, with all the foreigners remaining outside the gates. Aseneth went out of the entryway to meet Joseph, and when he saw her, he was amazed at her beauty and said, "Please tell me, who are you?"

"I am your servant, Aseneth," she replied, "I have cast out all my idols and destroyed them. Today a man came to me from heaven and gave me bread of life which I ate, a cup of blessing which I drank, and he said to me, 'Today I have given you to Joseph to be his bride, and he will be your groom forever. You shall no longer be called Aseneth, but City of Refuge, and the Lord God will rule over many nations forever, because in you many nations will take refuge with the Lord God Most High.' The man also said, 'I shall go now to Joseph and tell him about you.' So now you know, my lord, if the man came to you and told you about me."

"Blessed are you by the God Most High," said Joseph, "and blessed is your name forever, because the Lord God has set the foundations of your walls in the heights. Your walls are adamantine walls of life, because the children of the living God will dwell in your City of Refuge, and the Lord God will rule over them forever. That man came to me today and told me these things about you.] Come to me, chaste virgin. [Why do you stand so far off?"]

He extended his hands [and called Aseneth with his eyes, and Aseneth extended her hands and ran to Joseph and fell upon his chest.] Joseph held her in his arms, as they clung to each other for a long time, and their spirits came to life. [Joseph kissed Aseneth and gave her the spirit of life, then kissed her again and gave her the spirit of wisdom, and kissed her a third time and gave her the spirit of truth. (20) They sat entwined in each other's arms for a long time, and locked their hands together as if in bonds.] Aseneth then said to Joseph, "Come, my lord, and let us go into the house, [for I have prepared the house and have set out a great feast.]"

She took his right hand and led him into the house, setting him upon the chair of Pentephres. She then brought water to wash his feet, but Joseph said, "Have one of the virgins come and wash my feet."

["You are my lord from now on," Aseneth replied, "and I your servant. Why do you say that another virgin should wash your feet?] Your feet are my feet, your hands are my hands, [your soul is my soul.] No other woman will ever wash your feet." Thus she insisted, and proceeded to wash his feet. [When Joseph saw her hands, they were like hands of life, and her fingers delicate like those of a skilled scribe.] When she had finished, Joseph took her [right] hand and kissed it, and she kissed his head [and sat at his right.]

Aseneth's father, mother, [and family] meanwhile returned from their family estate and saw Aseneth sitting with Joseph dressed in her wedding garment. She was [a vision of light, and her beauty was like a heavenly beauty. Awed by her appearance,] they rejoiced and praised the God [who brings life back to the dead.] Then they all ate and drank together in celebration. Pentephres said to Joseph, "Tomorrow I shall invite all the nobles and governors of Egypt to the wedding which I shall provide for you, and you will take my daughter Aseneth as wife."

But Joseph responded, "I must go tomorrow to Pharaoh, the king, because he is like a father to me, [and appointed me prime minister of all Egypt. I shall speak to him directly about Aseneth,] and he will grant her to me as wife."

["Go in peace," said Pentephres.]

(21) Joseph remained that day at the house of Pentephres but did not sleep with Aseneth, for to Joseph it was not fitting for a man who reveres God to sleep with a woman before they were married. Joseph arose early and proceeded to Pharaoh, to whom he said, "Grant to me Aseneth, daughter of Pentephres, priest of Heliopolis, as wife."

[Pharaoh was overjoyed at this and said to Joseph, "But was she not already betrothed to you from eternity? She shall be your wife from now on, forever."] So Pharaoh sent and summoned Pentephres, who came with Aseneth and presented her to Pharaoh. When he saw her, he was also awed by her beauty, saying, "May the Lord God of Joseph bless you, child, and your beauty remain forever, for the Lord God of Joseph has justly chosen you as a bride for him; he is the firtborn son of God. You shall be called daughter of the Most High, and bride of Joseph from now on forever." Pharaoh then placed golden crowns upon Joseph and Aseneth, [which had been in his household from the very beginning, and stood Aseneth to Joseph's right.] He then placed his hands on their heads, [his right hand on Aseneth's,] and said, "May the Lord God Most High bless both of you, bring you happiness and prosperity, and glorify you forever." He then turned them toward each other and brought their mouths together, lips to lips, and they kissed. After this, Pharaoh made a wedding feast and banquet, with much eating and drinking for seven days. All the governors of Egypt and the kings of all the nations were invited, and Pharaoh issued a proclamation to all Egypt, which said: "Any person who performs any labor during the wedding celebration of Joseph and Aseneth shall be put to death."

Joseph and Aseneth then came together to consummate their marriage, and she became pregnant by Joseph and bore in the household of Joseph Manasseh and Ephraim, his brother. [She then began her confession to the Lord God and gave thanks, praying for all those who were deemed acceptable by the Lord:

I have sinned, O Lord, I have sinned!
I have committed many sins in your sight.
I, Aseneth, daughter of Pentephres, priest of Heliopolis, who oversees all things.

I have sinned, O Lord, I have sinned!
I have committed many sins in your sight.
I rested contentedly in the house of my father
And was a proud and arrogant virgin.

I have sinned, O Lord, I have sinned!
I have committed many sins in your sight.
I worshipped foreign gods without number,
And ate the bread of their sacrifices.

I have sinned, O Lord, I have sinned!
I have committed many sins in your sight.
I ate the bread of strangulation,
And the cup of treachery I drank from the table of death.

I have sinned, O Lord, I have sinned!
I have committed many sins in your sight.
I did not know the Lord God of Heaven
Nor place my trust in the Most High God of life.

I have sinned, O Lord, I have sinned!
I have committed many sins in your sight.
I placed my trust in the wealth of my glory and my beauty,
But was proud and arrogant.

I have sinned, O Lord, I have sinned!
I have committed many sins in your sight.
I despised every man in the world;
No one could do anything for me.

I have sinned, O Lord, I have sinned!
I have committed many sins in your sight.
I hated all those who came courting me;
I despised them and spat upon them.

I have sinned, O Lord, I have sinned!
I have committed many sins in your sight.
I spoke bold words in vain
And said that no prince on earth could loosen the sash of my virginity.

I have sinned, O Lord, I have sinned!
I have committed many sins in your sight.
But now I shall be the bride of the firstborn son of the Great King.

I have sinned, O Lord, I have sinned!
I have committed many sins in your sight.
Until Joseph came, the Mighty One of God.

He pulled me down from my noble perch
And humbled me from my haughtiness.

With his beauty he snared me,
With his wisdom he caught me like a fish on a hook,
With his spirit he lured me into his trap as though with the bait of life.

By his power he strengthened me
And led me to the eternal God,
To the one who rules over the house of the Most High.

He granted to me to eat the bread of life
And to drink the cup of wisdom.
I became his bride for all time.]

(22) Later, when the seven years of plenty had ended, the seven years of famine began. Jacob heard about Joseph his son, and Israel came to Egypt with all his family in the second year of the famine, during the second month, on the twenty-first day, and sojourned in Goshen. Aseneth said to Joseph, "I shall go and see your father because your father Israel is like a god and father to me."

"Come with me," said Joseph, "and you will meet my father."

As Joseph and Aseneth arrived in the land of Goshen to see Jacob, Joseph's brothers met them there and prostrated themselves before them. When they entered to meet Jacob, [he was sitting on his bed, an elderly man in his golden years. When she saw Jacob, Aseneth was struck by his beauty, for Jacob was very handsome, and indeed still looked like a handsome young man. His hair was white as snow, yet still thick and full, like an Ethiopian's, and his beard was also white, reaching to his chest. His eyes were bright and cheerful, darting back and forth like lightning, and the sinews in his shoulders and arms were like an angel's, his thighs, calves, and feet like those of a giant. Jacob was truly like a man who had wrestled with God. Aseneth, amazed, prostrated herself before him. "Is this my daughter-in-law, your wife?" Jacob asked Joseph. "May she be blessed by the Most High God." Jacob called her over to himself] and blessed her and kissed her. Aseneth then [extended her hands and embraced

Jacob around the neck, hanging onto him just as a son would embrace his father when he returns from war and first enters the house.] Then she kissed him. Afterward, they ate and drank, and Joseph and Aseneth proceeded to their own home.

Simeon and Levi, Joseph's brothers and the sons of Leah, escorted them, while the sons of Zilpah and Bilhah, the maids of Leah and Rachel, had become envious and bitter and did not accompany them. Levi rode on Aseneth's right side, and Joseph on her left. Aseneth took Levi's hand; [she loved him more than all of Joseph's brothers because he was a prudent man,] devoted to the Lord and a prophet [of the Most High, possessed of eyesight so sharp that he even saw letters written in the heavens by the finger of God, and knew the unspoken mysteries of the Most High God,] which he revealed to Aseneth in secret. [Levi also loved Aseneth very much] and saw her place of rest in the highest heavens, [her walls like eternal stone, and her foundations set upon rock in the seventh heaven.]

(23) And it happened as Joseph and Aseneth were returning that Pharaoh's firstborn son saw them from the city wall. Struck to the quick at the sight of Aseneth's beauty, he became heartsick and despondent over her. "May this not happen!" he said to himself, and decided to send mesengers to summon Simeon and Levi. When they arrived and stood before him, he said, "I am well aware that you are stronger than any men on earth, and that with your right hands you destroyed the city of the Shechemites, and with these two swords you cut down thirty thousand men.[6] I invite you, therefore, to ally yourselves with me, and I shall give you much gold and silver, male and female servants, houses and great estates, provided you have mercy on me and agree to do one thing: I have been greatly wronged by your brother Joseph,

6. See Genesis 34. Although there and in Genesis 49:5–7 the violence of Simeon and Levi is condemned by Jacob, at *Judith* 9:2–4 Simeon's revenge is also viewed positively.

for he took Aseneth as wife, who was betrothed to me from the very beginning. Throw in with me then, and we shall make war against him. I shall slay him with my sword and take Aseneth as my wife. If you will do this one thing, you will become my trusted friends, like brothers to me, but if you shrink from it and oppose my plan,"—he bared his sword to them as he spoke—"I assure you, my sword lies ready to slay you."

Simeon and Levi were dumbfounded that the Pharaoh's son had assumed such a tyrannical air, but Simeon, a bold and daring man, was already resolved to lay his hand upon his sword, draw it from its sheath, and strike Pharaoh's son in response to his menacing tone. Levi, however, a prophet who could see clearly, both with his mind and with his eyes, what was written in a person's heart, had already perceived Simeon's intention. He placed his foot on Simeon's, pressing it to signal that he should contain his wrath. Then quietly Levi said to him, "Why are you so furious with this man? Are we not men who revere God? It is not fitting for us to repay anger with anger."

Levi turned to Pharaoh's son and spoke fearlessly, yet with gentleness and warmth and no hint of anger: "Why does our lord speak like this? We are men who revere God; our father is a friend of the Most High God, and our brother Joseph is like the firstborn son of God. How could we do such an evil thing, sinning before our God, our father Israel, and our brother Joseph? [This is our reply: it is not fitting for a man who reveres God to attack anyone. And if anyone chooses to attack a man who reveres God, he does not avenge himself, but refuses to take up the sword.] Now make sure that you say nothing more against our brother, for if you persist in your wicked plan, be assured of this: our swords stand ready." Simeon and Levi then drew their swords from their sheaths. "Do you see our swords? With these the Lord God punished the arrogance of the Shechemites, when Shechem, son of Hamor, shamefully abused the Israelites by defiling our sister Dinah."

When the Pharaoh's son saw their drawn swords, [flashing like flames of fire,] he became very frightened. His entire body trembled and his eyes grew dim. He fell down upon his face at their feet, whereupon Levi extended his [right] hand and helped him to his feet, saying, "Rise up now, and do not be afraid. But remember this: make no more wicked suggestions concerning our brother Joseph." Then they took their leave of the son of Pharaoh.

(24) Pharaoh's son was overcome with fear and grief; he feared Joseph's brothers Simeon and Levi, and yet he still grieved over the beauty of Aseneth. How he grieved for her! His servants then said to him, "The sons of Bilhah and Zilpah, the maids of Jacob's wives, Leah and Rachel, are hostile to Joseph and Aseneth and are envious of them. They can easily be manipulated to your will."

So the son of Pharaoh sent messengers to summon them to come before him, and in the first hour of the night they arrived and presented themselves. He said to them, "I have called you here because you are very powerful men."

Dan and Gad, the two eldest brothers, replied, "Let our lord say to us, his servants, whatever he wishes; we shall hear and obey."

Pleased at their response, the son of Pharaoh turned to his own servants and said, "Withdraw from us for now, for I have private matters to discuss with these men." When the servants had all departed from him, he lied to Joseph's brothers and said, "I now place a blessing and death before you; therefore, choose the blessing and not death, because you are powerful men and you will not die like women, but will play the man and avenge your enemies. I have heard Joseph, your brother, say to my father, Pharaoh, 'Dan, Gad, Naphtali, and Asher are children of my father's maidservants and are not my true brothers. I shall only await the death of my father and then wipe them and all their offspring off the face of the earth, lest they also receive a share of our inheritance. They are only children of slaves and are the same ones who sold me to the Ishmaelites. Now, waiting only until my father dies, I shall repay them for the evil which they did to me.' My father, Pharaoh, praised him and said, 'You have spoken truly, my son. Now take some of my valiant men and attack them in the same way that they did to you. I shall help you.'"

When the brothers of Joseph heard this, they were greatly troubled. "We beg you, lord, help us!" they said to him.

"I shall come to your aid," he said, "if you heed my request."

"We are your servants, at your disposal. Merely say the word, and we shall do whatever you wish."

"I intend to kill Pharaoh this very night, because although he is my father, he acts more the father to Joseph, saying that he would help him against you. Therefore, kill Joseph, and I shall take Aseneth as my wife. If you help me in this one task, you will also become my brothers and fellow-heirs in all that I possess."

"Today we have become your servants," Dan and Gad responded, "and will do all that you have commanded. Indeed, we have just heard Joseph say to Aseneth, 'Tomorrow go to your family estate, for it is now time for the grape harvest.' He provided for her six hundred valiant armed warriors and fifty messengers as escort. Listen to us now and we shall propose a plan to you, our lord." They then stepped closer and said to him in secret, "Give us also valiant warriors, ready and able to fight." The son of Pharaoh then gave to the four brothers five hundred men each, and appointed commanders and leaders for them, and Dan and Gad said, "Today we are your servants and shall do all that you have commanded. We shall leave tonight and, hiding among the reeds, set up an ambush. Take also fifty mounted archers and ride before us, staying at a distance. Aseneth will come and fall into our trap; we shall cut down the men with her, but she will flee on her chariot to where you are waiting. Do with her according to your desire. After that, we shall kill Joseph, who by then will be grieving over Aseneth, and also kill his children before his very eyes."

Pharaoh's son was very pleased with this plan, and sent them off with two thousand soldiers under their command. They came to a riverbed and hid in the reeds, dividing their troops into four groups: some were stationed on one side of the riverbed where it met the road, five hundred men on either side of the road, while the rest hid among the reeds on the far side of the river, with five hundred men on each side of the road there as well. The road between them was broad and open.

(25) In the middle of the night, the son of Pharaoh arose and went to his father's room with sword in hand to kill him, but the Pharaoh's guards did not allow him to enter the room. "What is your business, lord?" they asked.

"I am leaving to harvest my new vineyard," the son of Pharaoh replied, "and I wish to see my father."

"Your father is suffering from a headache," said the guards, "and has been awake all night. Now he is resting a bit and has instructed us not to admit anyone, not even his firstborn son."

When he heard this, the Pharaoh's son immediately left, taking fifty mounted archers with him, and led them to the place Dan and Gad had named.

The younger brothers, however, Naphtali and Asher, said to Dan and Gad, "Why are you once again acting wickedly against your father Israel and your brother Joseph? The Lord is protecting him like the apple of his eye. Did you not once sell him, and now he is prime minister of all Egypt, the benefactor and provider of wheat? But if you are tempted once again to act wickedly against him, he will call out to the Most High, who will send fire down from heaven to consume you, and the angels of God will wage war against you for his sake."

"Then shall we die like women?" said the older brothers Dan and Gad, enraged. "Surely not!" They then proceeded out to intercept Joseph and Aseneth.

(26) Aseneth arose early and said to Joseph, "I shall go as you said to our family estate, but my soul is very anxious because we shall be apart."

"Have courage," said Joseph, "and do not be afraid, but proceed as we planned. The Lord is with you, and no matter what evil may befall you, he will protect you, like the apple of his eye. I myself shall continue distributing wheat, giving bread to all the people, so that the earth not vanish from the sight of the Lord."

So Aseneth set out on her way, and Joseph left to dispense wheat. As Aseneth with her escort of six hundred men approached the riverbed, suddenly the waiting soldiers sprang up from their hiding places and attacked Aseneth's men, cutting them down with their swords, and killed her messengers as well. Aseneth, however, escaped on her chariot.

Meanwhile, Levi son of Leah, being a prophet, knew through the spirit everything that was happening, and he sent to his brothers, the sons of Leah, and informed them of the danger to Aseneth. Strapping their swords to their thighs, and taking up their shields on their arms, they grasped their spears in their right hands and set out at a run to intercept Aseneth. She, however, in her flight was met by Pharaoh's son with his fifty horsemen. Frightened and trembling over her entire body, she called upon the name of the Lord her God. (27) Benjamin was seated to her left in the chariot. Now Benjamin was eighteen years old, still a lad, but large and powerful, handsome beyond description, strong as a lion cub, and very devoted to the Lord. Jumping down from the chariot, he picked up a smooth stone from the riverbed, gripped it firmly, and hurled it at the Pharaoh's son. It struck him on the left temple, inflicting a heavy wound. Pharaoh's son fell from his horse onto the ground, half dead. Benjamin then leapt up onto a rock and called to Aseneth's charioteer, "Give me stones from the riverbed!" and he brought him fifty stones. Hurling the stones, he killed the fifty men who had accompanied Pharaoh's son, striking each in the temple. Then the sons of Leah—Reuben, Simeon, Levi, Judah, Issachar, and Zebulun—pursued the men who had attacked Aseneth, took them by surprise, and cut them all down, the six of them slaying two thousand.

Their brothers, however, the sons of Bilhah and Zilpah, fled from them saying, "We have been destroyed by our brothers! Pharaoh's son has been killed by the lad Benjamin, who has also killed his soldiers. Let us then kill Aseneth and Benjamin and flee into the thicket of reeds."

They came upon Aseneth, their drawn swords covered with blood, and when Aseneth saw them, she said in her fright, "O Lord, my God, who gave me new life, saving me from my idols and the corruptibility of death, and who said 'Your soul will live forever,' save me from the clutches of these evil men!" The Lord God heard the voice of Aseneth, and their swords fell from their hands upon the ground and were immediately turned to ashes.

(28) When the sons of Bilhah and Zilpah saw this, they were filled with deathly fear and said, "The Lord is taking Aseneth's side against us!" They fell upon their faces, prostrating themselves before Aseneth. "Have mercy upon your slaves! You are our lady and mistress! We acted wickedly against you, and against our brother Joseph, and now the Lord has repaid us according to our deeds. We beg of you, have mercy upon your slaves and save us from the hands of our brothers, who are avenging the insult done to you. Here they come now, with swords drawn! [We know that our brothers revere God and do not repay anyone evil for evil. We beg you, lady, show mercy to your slaves in their presence."]

"Have courage," replied Aseneth, "and do not be afraid of your brothers. They are men who revere and fear God and show due respect for everyone. Go and hide among the reeds until I can still their wrath and appease them on your behalf, for you have greatly offended them. But have courage, and do not fear; it is the Lord who will judge between you and me." Dan, Gad, and all their brothers then fled into the reeds, as the sons of Leah came running, swift as deer, in pursuit. Aseneth descended from the chariot which had been her protection and greeted them with tears, while they prostrated themselves upon the ground. They cried out loudly, seeking their brothers, the sons of their father's maids, in order to kill them. But Aseneth said to them, "I beg of you, spare your brothers and do not repay them evil for evil, for the Lord protected me from them, knocking their swords from their hands and melting them upon the ground like wax in a fire. The Lord opposed them for my sake—let this be enough! Spare them because they are your brothers, and the flesh and blood of your father Israel."

But Simeon said to her, "Why would our mistress speak on behalf of our enemies? Should we not rather cut them down with our swords, because they first hatched this evil plan against us, against our father Israel, against our brother Joseph—now for the second time!—and also against you today, our lady and mistress?"

Aseneth, however, [extended her right hand and touched Simeon's beard and kissed him,] saying, "Brother, you should not repay your neighbor evil for evil. Surely you will say that it is for the Lord to punish their crime, and these men are your brothers, part of the family of Israel. Now, however, they have fled far away from you, so grant them pardon." Levi came to her and kissed her right hand, [realizing that she had said this to save these men from their brothers' wrath and thus preserve them, and that they were at that time nearby in the stand of reeds. Levi knew this but did not tell his brothers, because he was afraid that in their anger they would cut them down.]

(29) Meanwhile, the son of Pharaoh stirred and sat up, spitting the blood from his mouth that had flowed down from his temple. Benjamin ran over to him and drew his sword from its sheath, since he carried none of his own, and was about to strike him in the chest when Levi ran up and stayed his hand. "Do not do it, brother," he said, "We are men who revere God, and it is not fitting for such a man to repay evil for evil, nor to trample one who is fallen, nor to afflict an enemy to the point of death. Put your sword back in its sheath, and help me soothe his wound. If he lives, he will become our friend, and his father will be as our own father." Raising the son of Pharaoh to a sitting position, Levi washed the blood from his face and tied a bandage around his wound. Mounting him on his horse, he took him to Pharaoh, and when he had told Pharaoh all that had happened, Pharaoh rose from his throne, prostrated himself before Levi, and blessed him.

On the third day following, the son of Pharaoh died from the wound inflicted by the lad Benjamin. Pharaoh mourned his firstborn son greatly, so greatly that he became ill and died. He was a hundred and nine years old. He passed his diadem to Joseph, who ruled over Egypt for forty-eight years, after which he passed the diadem on to Pharaoh's younger son, who was but a nursling when Pharaoh died. Joseph was like a father to the younger son of the Egyptian Pharaoh all the days of his life.

## SUGGESTIONS FOR FURTHER READING


Barclay, John M. G. *Jews in the Mediterranean Diaspora: From Alexander to Trajan (323 BCE–117 CE),* pp. 204–16. Berkeley: University of California Press, 1996.

Bohak, Gideon. *Joseph and Aseneth and the Jewish Temple at Heliopolis.* Atlanta: Scholars Press, 1996.

Burchard, Christoph. "The Present State of Research on Joseph and Aseneth." In *Religion, Literature, and Society in Ancient Israel, Formative Christianity, and Judaism,* pp. 31–52. Ed. Jacob Neusner et al. Lanham, Md.: University Press of America, 1987.

Chesnutt, Randall D. *From Death to Life: Conversion in Joseph and Aseneth.* Sheffield: Sheffield Academic Press, 1995.

Collins, John J. *Between Athens and Jerusalem: Jewish Identity in the Hellenistic Diaspora,* pp. 89–91, 211–18. New York: Crossroad, 1983.

Gruen, Erich. *Heritage and Hellenism: The Reinvention of Jewish Tradition,* pp. 89–99. Berkeley: University of California Press, 1998.

Kee, Howard Clark. "The Socio-Cultural Setting of Joseph and Asenath." *New Testament Studies* 29 (1983) 394–413.

Kraemer, Ross S. *When Aseneth Met Joseph: A Late Antique Tale of the Biblical Patriarch and His Egyptian Wife, Reconsidered.* New York: Oxford University Press, 1998.

Nickelsburg, George W. E. *Jewish Literature Between the Bible and the Mishnah,* pp. 258–63. Philadelphia: Fortress, 1981.

Philonenko, Marc. "Joseph and Aseneth." In *Encyclopedia Judaica,* p. 10: 223. 16 vols. New York: Macmillan, 1971–72.

Standhartinger, Angela. *Das Frauenbild im Judentum der hellenistischen Zeit: Ein Beitrag anhand von "Joseph und Aseneth."* Leiden: Brill, 1995.

Wills, Lawrence M. *The Jewish Novel in the Ancient World,* pp. 170–84. Ithaca, N.Y.: Cornell University Press, 1995.

# PART II

## *Jewish Historical Novels*

SEVEN

# ARTAPANUS, ON MOSES

Artapanus was a Jewish historian living in Egypt who wrote in the third to second century B.C.E. Artapanus's writings and *The Marriage and Conversion of Aseneth* are unlike the other novels and historical novels in that they treat important figures from the period of the patriarchs—albeit in a free-spirited way—instead of fictional characters or characters from the recent past. Unfortunately, the fragments of Artapanus's history that we possess are known only from excerpts by other authors. These excerpts include Artapanus's accounts on Abraham, Joseph, and Moses, but only the section on Moses survives in a form long enough to contain a significant amount of narrative.

Moses has a larger role as public benefactor here than in the Hebrew Bible, and the work begins with a surprisingly ecumenical spirit. He is identified with the Greek Musaeus, teacher of Orpheus, makes many important inventions for the Egyptians, but even more surprisingly, is credited with establishing the provinces of Egypt and the animal worship practiced in each. Moses is later even identified with Hermes and is given divine honors by the Egyptian priests, and his rod is adopted as a symbol in the temples of the goddess Isis. The import is clear: Moses is a benefactor of the people, even in their religious observances, and the Pharaoh could not govern such a flourishing empire without him. A series of intrigues occurs, the result of the Pharaoh's insecurity and petty jealousy, but

Moses rises above them all. The successes of the protagonist here are guided by a providential hand, a theme we have seen in most of the other texts collected here.

This narrative comprises an interesting combination of plot elements from the Exodus story of Moses and otherwise unknown embellishments. In the middle of invented events concerning Moses' exploits in Egypt, for example, Moses suddenly finds himself before the burning bush and is commanded to return to Egypt to lead the Jews out. The story of Exodus is thus taken up, but in Moses' interactions with the Pharaoh we also find new elements. Moses at one point whispers the name of God into Pharaoh's ear, causing him to collapse until Moses revives him. It is this spirit of history combined with magic and adventure that propels this story.

If *The Marriage and Conversion of Aseneth* focuses on the domestic drama and inner-family conflict of Joseph's household, Artapanus is more like some of the non-Jewish "national hero romances" that have survived from antiquity, such as the *Alexander Romance,* the *Story of Ahikar,* or *Ninus and Semiramus.* More specifically, it fits into a period in which many indigenous ethnic groups were writing competitive histories that glorified the past heroes of their own people and credited them with important contributions to civilization. Some of Artapanus's more unexpected attributions to Moses respond directly to calumnies against Moses found in these other competitive ethnic histories. For example, one history asserts that Moses forbade the Jews to worship the Egyptian gods, but Artapanus shows that it was in fact Moses who established these cults. In a similar vein, whereas in Greek tradition Orpheus taught Musaeus, here Musaeus—or Moses—taught Orpheus.

Artapanus moves far beyond the usual limits of fanciful Jewish literature in associating Moses with pagan cults, but throughout this narrative the emphasis is on the explanation of all Egyptian practices as the gift of Moses, and after Pharaoh turns on him, Moses' successes also include the destruction of the cults he established. There is a sense that Moses' benevolence was spurned by the Pharaoh and that the latter's ill will turned his people against him, with some destruction of the very cults he should support. Ultimately, however, this text argues that Moses began as a benefactor and that this is the role which, left to his own devices, he would have maintained.

## Artapanus, *On Moses*

After Joseph and his son Mempsasthenoth died, the king of Egypt also died, and he was succeeded on the throne by his son Palmonothes, who constantly mistreated the Jews.[1] It was he who constructed the temple at Sais and also the temple at Heliopolis. He fathered a daughter, Merris, and betrothed her to a certain Chenephres, who ruled over the regions above Memphis. (In those days there were many such rulers in the land.) Since she was unable to conceive, she adopted a child of one of the Jews, whom she named Moses. Upon reaching the age of maturity, however, he was named by the Greeks Musaeus, and he became the teacher of Orpheus. As a grown man he was the source of many great inventions for humankind: ships, cranes for lifting large stones, Egyptian weaponry, devices for lifting water and for war, and philosophy. He was also responsible for dividing the country into thirty-six nomes, appointing to each the appropriate god to be worshipped, whether cats, dogs, or ibises, and appointing sacred scriptures for the priests as well. In addition, he set aside certain tracts of land specifically for the priests. All of

1. The beginning of the text as quoted by Eusebius (*Preparation for the Gospel* 9.27) is unclear, and the present translation reflects an attempt at a plausible introduction to the story.

these changes he instituted to solidify Chanephres's rule and make it more secure, for prior to this the people had been quite disorganized and would depose or establish rulers at will, at times reinstalling former rulers, at other times elevating new ones. Moses was for this reason well loved by the people, and so highly esteemed by the priests that they considered him divine, calling him Hermes on account of his ability in the interpretation of holy scripture.

When Chenephres, however, saw what virtues Moses possessed, he became jealous and sought some pretext on which to kill him. And so it happened that when the Ethiopians invaded Egypt, Chenephres supposed that he had found his opportunity and sent Moses against them as a general of one of his armies. The army that he had mustered consisted mainly of farmers, and Chenephres rashly assumed that Moses would be destroyed as a result of his soldiers' inability. Moses advanced to the nome called Hermopolis with about 100,000 farmers, and encamped there. He sent out as generals those who would later rule over this region, and they prevailed in every battle with distinction. The war, according to those in Heliopolis, lasted ten years. Because of the size of their army, those who fought with Moses founded a city there called Hermopolis, with the ibis as its sacred symbol because it kills animals that are harmful to humans. Thus although the Ethiopians had formerly been enemies, they came to love Moses, and even learned from him the practice of circumcision—and not only the Ethiopians, but all of the priests as well.

When the war was over, Chenephres pretended to receive Moses back but in reality continued to plot against him. First Chenephres took command of Moses' army and divided it in half, sending one detachment to the border with Ethiopia to establish a defense garrison. The rest he commanded to destroy the temple in Diospolis, built with baked bricks, so that by quarrying a nearby mountain, he could construct another made of stone in its place. Nacheros was placed in charge of the construction, and when he and Moses reported to Chenephres at Memphis, the king asked Moses whether there might be anything else useful for humankind. He replied that a new breed of cattle would be useful for tilling the ground. Chenephres therefore named a bull "Apis" and commanded that the people consecrate a temple to it, while at the same time ordering that all of the animals consecrated by Moses be brought there to be buried, trying to conceal all of his marvelous inventions. Soon, however, Chenephres began to fall out of favor with the Egyptian populace, and he exacted an oath from his friends not to allow Moses to find out about the conspiracy that was brewing against him. Chenephres had commanded a number of men to kill Moses, but when none of them followed through, he reprimanded Chanethothes as the one specially assigned by him for the task. Smarting from the censure, Chanethothes vowed to carry out the assassination, once he found an opportune moment.

In the meantime, however, Queen Merris died, and Chenephres ordered both Moses and Chanethothes to transport her body to Upper Egypt for burial, supposing that Moses would be killed by Chanethothes along the way. But as they were proceeding, one of the men who were part of the conspiracy informed Moses about it. Moses, exercising great caution, first buried the body of Merris and named both the river and the city there Meroë. People in that region came to honor Merris no less than Isis. When Aaron, the brother of Moses, learned of the plot against him, he counseled him to flee into Arabia, and Moses, finally persuaded, sailed from Memphis across the Nile and took refuge in Arabia. But when Chanethothes found out that Moses had fled, he lay in wait for him in order to kill him there. When he saw Moses approaching, Chanethothes drew his dagger, but Moses responded quickly; he seized Chanethothes's arm, drew his own sword, and slew him. Moses then continued his flight into Arabia, where he took up with Raguel, the leader of that region, and married his daughter. Raguel was prepared to declare war against the Egyptians, returning Moses from exile to establish a dynasty there for his daughter and son-in-law. Moses, however, would not allow such talk, out of concern for his own people. Accordingly, Raguel forbade a full-scale military expedition against Egypt but ordered the Arabs to plunder them instead.

At about this time Chenephres became the first man ever to contract elephantiasis, and he died soon after. He was afflicted with this disease for commanding the Jews to wear linen and not woolen garments, so that they would be easily marked for persecution by him. Moses prayed to God that the people might have relief from their sufferings, and as he was still praying, fire sprang up suddenly from the earth, burning brightly even though there was no wood or other flammable substance nearby. Frightened at this sight, Moses began to flee, but a divine voice spoke to him, commanding him to wage war against Egypt and to save the Jews and lead them into their ancient homeland. So Moses, emboldened by this, resolved to lead an army against the Egyptians, but went first to his brother Aaron. When the new king of the Egyptians heard that Moses had returned, he summoned him and asked him why he had come. Moses answered that the master of the world had commanded him to return in order to release the Jews from captivity. When he heard this, Pharaoh threw him into prison. But when night came, all of the doors of the prison opened by themselves. Some of the guards died, while others were overcome with sleep, their weapons shattered into pieces. Moses walked out of the prison and went to the palace. Finding all of the doors open, he entered the palace, walking past the guards who lay asleep all around him, and woke up the king. Startled at this, the king commanded that Moses tell him the name of the god who had sent him, mocking him all the while. Moses bent over and whispered the name into the king's ear, and the king, upon hearing it, fell over without uttering a sound. Moses, however, lifted him up again, and he came back to life. After this, the king wrote the name that Moses had told him on a tablet and sealed it securely, but one of the priests, who treated the letters written on the tablet with contempt, was seized by convulsions and died.

The king then asked Moses to perform some sign for him, and Moses in response threw down the rod in his hand, and it turned into a snake. Everyone was terrified at this sight, so Moses picked up the snake by the tail, and it became a rod again. Moses then walked over to the Nile, touched it with his rod, and caused the river to flood, inundating all of Egypt. (This was the beginning of the flooding of the Nile.) Once it collected into pools, it began to reek; the animals in the water soon perished, and the people as well as thirst overtook them. When the king saw all of these wonders, he agreed that if Moses would restore the river to its banks, he would release the people after one month. Moses once again struck the water with his rod and the water returned to its proper level. The king then summoned the priests from above Memphis and threatened to execute them and destroy their temples unless they could perform some sign as well. So using magical charms and incantations, they created a great serpent and changed the color of the Nile. This bolstered the king's pride, causing him to become arrogant, and he mistreated the Jews with every conceivable harsh punishment. Moses in response performed more signs, by striking the ground with his rod and raising winged animals to scourge the Egyptians. Their bodies all broke out in sores, and while the Egyptian doctors were unable to cure those who were afflicted, the Jews once more found relief from their sufferings. Moses again proceeded to use his rod, and raised up frogs, as well as locusts and lice. Because of this, Egyptians set up a rod in every temple, especially in the temple of Isis, since the earth is Isis and it brought forth these wonders when it was struck with the rod.

The king, meanwhile, persisted in his foolish course, and so Moses caused hail and earthquakes throughout the night; those who tried to flee the earthquakes were killed by the hail, and those who took refuge from the hail were killed by the earthquakes. As a result, all of the houses and a great many of the temples collapsed, and the king, after witnessing such unrelenting disasters, finally released the Jews. Procuring from the Egyptians many drinking vessels, a plentiful supply of clothing, and all sorts of treasures, they departed, crossing the rivers toward Arabia, and made good time, arriving at the Red Sea in three days. The people of Memphis say that since Moses was familiar with the region, he waited for the low tide and then led the people through the dry part of the sea. The people of Heliopolis, however, say that Pharaoh swooped down upon them suddenly with his entire army, even bringing their sacred animals with them because the Jews had taken with them the property that they had obtained from the Egyptians. Moses, however, heard a divine voice, instructing him to strike the Red Sea with his rod and divide it. He heeded the voice and touched the water with his rod. The water then divided, while his force passed over on dry land. But when the Egyptians followed close behind, a fire blazed up ahead of them, while the sea flooded in again over their path. By fire and the flood, therefore, the Egyptians were all destroyed.

After the Jews had escaped this danger, they passed forty years in the desert, eating the food that God rained down upon them, similar to millet, and in color like snow. Moses, who performed all these great things when he was eighty-nine years old, was tall, ruddy, and dignified, with long, flowing white hair.

## SUGGESTIONS FOR FURTHER READING

Barclay, John M. G. *Jews in the Mediterranean Diaspora: From Alexander to Trajan (323 BCE–117 CE)*, pp. 127–32. Berkeley/Los Angeles/London: University of California Press, 1996.

Braun, Martin. *History and Romance in Graeco-Oriental Literature*, pp. 26–31, 99–102. New York: Garland, 1987.

Collins, John J. *Between Athens and Jerusalem: Jewish Identity in the Hellenistic Diaspora*, pp. 32–38. New York: Crossroad, 1983.

Fraser, P. M. *Ptolemaic Alexandria*, pp. 1.52–87, 280–301, 674–716. 3 vols. Oxford: Oxford University Press, 1972.

Gruen, Erich. *Heritage and Hellenism: The Reinvention of Jewish Tradition,* pp. 155–60. Berkeley: University of California Press, 1998.

Holladay, Carl R. *Theios Aner in Hellenistic Judaism: A Critique of the Use of This Category in New Testament Christology,* pp. 199–232. Missoula, Mont.: Scholars Press, 1977.

Tiede, David L. *The Charismatic Figure as Miracle Worker,* pp. 317-24. Missoula, Mont.: Scholars Press, 1972.

EIGHT

# THIRD MACCABEES

This historical novel early on acquired the title *Third Maccabees,* even though it does not mention the Maccabees or the Maccabean Revolt. The common theme of persecution and vindication evidently brought this text into the same orbit as the other Maccabee literature found in the Apocrypha, and it was canonized as part of the Eastern Orthodox Bible. It was likely written in Alexandria, Egypt, in the first century B.C.E. or first century C.E. This narrative recounts the persecution of the Jews in Egypt by the Hellenistic king Ptolemy IV Philopator (222–203 B.C.E.). However, the Jewish historian Josephus (*Against Apion* 2.53–56) describes a similar event during the reign of Ptolemy VIII Physcon (Euergetes II, 145–117 B.C.E.). It is possible that an incident in the reign of the latter Ptolemy was retrojected back to the time of the former, although it is not clear that either *Third Maccabees* or Josephus are treating anything more than legend. Most scholars also agree that the beginning of the narrative must be missing. The text begins abruptly, almost mid-sentence, and characters described later in the story as "mentioned above" are in fact being introduced for the first time. The narrative is divided into three movements: military campaigns of Ptolemy in which the king perceives the Jews positively, the attempt of Ptolemy to worship at Jerusalem and enter the forbidden Holy of Holies and his subsequent punishment by God, and the persecution of the Jews that followed, which ends in a miraculous deliverance and the king's recognition of the Jews' rights.

Though similar in some ways to the other Maccabee literature, *Third Maccabees* differs in two respects: the miracles are more outrageous, even laughable by our standards, and the writing style is overly florid. Like other novels in this collection, this one requires the reader to enter into the high spirits of the narrative. In addition to the comical depiction of the king (he mysteriously oversleeps at one point, causing the postponement of the execution of Jews), the most important plot reversal—the king's change of heart toward the Jews—remains completely unmotivated, except by implication as part of the providential operation of God. Contained within the whimsical plot is a satire not just of the Hellenistic king, but of the Dionysos cult in particular. This cult, a favorite of Ptolemy IV, included wine drinking, the ivy leaf design, and especially the motif of "divine madness." All of these elements are explicitly present in the narrative, and we see that in God's providential plan the Dionysiac elements backfire on the Ptolemaic king: the elephants become inebriated and trample their Egyptian handlers.

Though somewhat more extreme than the other Jewish novels, *Third Maccabees* does not differ from them in terms of the typical themes. The persecution of Jews is initiated by a short-sighted monarch, it is encouraged by some part of the surrounding peoples who have been looking for such an opportunity, it is reversed by the implicit or explicit providence of God, the monarch realizes the value of the Jews within his kingdom, and the villainous elements are punished. There is a conflict of loyalties for the Jews, as they must decide between loyalty to their God or obedience to the king, but it is not a continuing tension or a tragic conflict; it is resolved through the actions of God into a harmonious relationship.

The herding of Jews together, however, along with the registration of them in official documents and the dust clouds that rise over the huddled detainees, conjure eerie images of the Holocaust, despite the overall humorous tone. The position of Jews in the Greco-Roman world was in some ways similar to that in early twentieth-century Europe. They were a sizable minority that had not assimilated into a more "universalistic" culture. *Third Maccabees,* like *Greek Esther,* senses anti-Judaism and dramatizes it in a pseudo-historical scenario. As in the decree of Haman in *Greek Esther,* there is reflected here an acute awareness of the inner ethos of anti-Judaism, projected onto the pagan people and rulers: gentiles see Jews as odious and set apart in regard to their food laws, and rumors are spread that Jews are not allowing others to practice their religion. Yet the Greco-Egyptian people are forgiven magnanimously by the Jews, while Jews who renounced their religion and joined in the pagan sacrifices are in the end executed by the pious Jews who did not waver.

And yet it is ironic that the negative attitude toward assimilation is expressed in such pretentious Greek. There is a simple sentence structure, but a preponderance of double adjectives and many rare and otherwise unknown Greek words. The goal of the text is to entertain at the same time that a staunch Jewish piety is affirmed in the face of opposition by the surrounding peoples. Still, this aspect makes the text difficult to translate. How does one try to duplicate this in English? Here I have attempted merely to communicate a style bent on entertainment and wonder, and have not sought out unusual or bombastic English equivalents.

One question remains. Although the narrative is unbelievable to us, and we can detect no solid connection to the historical events in the Ptolemaic kingdom, was it composed as a historical account or read as history by its early audiences? Contrary to what we might assume, the presence of the miraculous does not necessarily imply that we have left the genre of history behind. Many of the Greek, Roman, and Jewish histories included miraculous interventions of the gods. If the text was canonized as sacred scripture by the Eastern Orthodox Church, it was likely read by some as a true account of perseverance and miraculous deliverance. (Compare also Josephus's incorporation of Esther and Daniel into his history). However, that does not prove that it was *originally* received as historical. When we look to the ending of *Third Maccabees,* we detect a happily-ever-after tone that perhaps indicates a fictitious mode; there is no interweaving of the events of this narrative into the larger flow of history, as generally occurs at the end of ancient histories. It was thus likely first read as fictitious, even if similar texts such as *Second Maccabees* were read as historical.

## *Third Maccabees*

(1) When Philopator learned from those who had just returned that Antiochus had seized the regions formerly under his control, he marshalled all his forces, both infantry and cavalry, took with him his sister Arsinoë, and marched out to the area of Raphia, where Antiochus's army was camped. Now a certain Theodotus, determined to carry out a scheme he had concocted, took with him the best soldiers that Philopator had placed under his command and came by night to the tent of Philopator to kill him single-handedly and thus bring the war to an end. But Dositheus, known as the son of Drimulus, a Jew by birth but who had later converted from this religion and abandoned his ancestral beliefs, led Philopator away and in his stead had some insignificant man lie in his bed in the tent. Thus this man received the punishment intended for Philopator.

When the bitter battle was engaged, the tide appeared to be moving in Antiochus's favor, but Arsinoë went out before the troops, and with her hair loose and disheveled, exhorted them with tears to defend bravely both themselves and their wives and children, and promised to give each of them two minas of gold if they should prevail. And so it happened that the opposing forces were wiped out in the ensuing battle, and many prisoners were taken. Having now foiled the plot against him, Philopator decided that he should go through the neighboring cities and give them encouragement. By doing this, and by distributing gifts to their sacred precincts, he bolstered their spirits.

The Jews sent to him representatives to bring greetings on behalf of the council and elders and congratulations for his recent victories, and they also bore gifts of welcome. As a result, Philopator wanted all the more to come to them as soon as possible. Arriving in Jerusalem, he offered a sacrifice to the highest God, presented thank offerings, and performed other acts appropriate for the sacred precincts. No sooner had he entered the Temple than he was struck by its solemnity and dignity. He also marveled at the good order of the Temple and decided that he would like to enter the inner sanctuary, but they told him that this was not permitted. No one from their own people could enter, not even the priests—except for the high priest alone, who took precedence over all, and even he only once a year—and yet Philopator was still not persuaded. Even after the law concerning it had been read to him, he continued to maintain that he should enter, saying, "Even if others are denied this honor, this should not apply to me." Why was it, he inquired, that when he entered any other temple, none of those attending prevented him. One of the men present imprudently answered that this was hardly to be interpreted as a portent that he should enter. "But since for some reason it has in fact come about in just this way," he said, "should I not enter the Temple whether the people here wish it or not?"

Then the priests, dressed in their sacred robes, fell on the ground and filled the Temple with their wailing and tears. They begged the greatest God to come to their aid in this matter and to stop the progress of this ill-conceived plot. The residents of the city outside the Temple walls fell into a panic and ran out into the streets, thinking that something mysterious was occurring. Young girls who had been secluded within their own chambers rushed out with their mothers, sprinkled their hair with dust, and filled the streets with wailing and lamentations. The young women who had recently been prepared for marriage abandoned the bridal chambers set aside for their wedded union and, forsaking all sense of modesty, thronged together in a mad rush throughout the city. Newborn babies could even be found abandoned along the way by their mothers and nurses, some here, some there, some in the houses and some in the city streets, as the women crowded heedlessly around the Temple that towers over all.

All manner of prayers were sent aloft by those who had come together on account of the profane designs of the king. Among those gathered were also the more courageous citizens who would not allow him to carry out his plan and fulfill his desired goal. Calling out for those present to take up arms and valiantly die for their ancestral law, they created a great uproar in the Temple area. Scarcely restrained by the old men and elders, they joined in the same posture of supplication as the others. The crowd as a whole continued praying as before. The elders who were with the king tried in many ways to convince him to abandon the arrogant scheme that he had concocted. But he, now even more emboldened, only dismissed all attempts at restraint and began to make his approach, believing that he would attain his aforementioned goal. When those around him saw this, they, together with our people, turned to call upon the one who had the power to come to their aid in the present straits and not overlook this arrogant and wanton act. From the incessant and woeful cry of the crowd there arose, now resounding as one, an indescribable shout, for now it seemed that not only the people, but also the very walls and foundation of the Temple began to resound in unison, since indeed all would at that time accept death over the defilement of the Temple.

(2) Then the high priest Simon, facing the Temple in solemn dignity, bent his knees and extended his hands. He uttered the

following prayer: "Lord, Lord, king of the heavens and ruler of all creation, holiest of all, sole ruler, almighty, give heed to us who are weighed down with suffering at the hands of a profane and impious man, bloated with his own pride and power. For you, the creator of all things and master of all, are a just ruler, and you judge those who act in arrogance and insolence. You destroyed those who in past times committed acts of injustice, even those who were giants and trusted in their own strength and courage, by bringing upon them a flood of immeasurable proportions. The people of Sodom, who acted arrogantly and became famous for their wickedness, you burned up with fire and brimstone, making them an example for those who would follow. You demonstrated the extent of your power to all by inflicting many and varied punishments upon the haughty Pharaoh, who had enslaved your holy people Israel. And when he pursued them with chariots and hosts of armies, you washed him into the depths of the sea, while at the same time delivering to safety those who trusted in the one who rules all of creation. Upon seeing the works of your hands, they praised you as the almighty God.

"You, O king, when you created the boundless, immeasurable world, chose this city and sanctified this place for your name, even though you have no need of anything, and by glorifying it by your magnificent presence, you laid a firm foundation there for the glory of your great and much-honored name. Because you love the house of Israel, you promised that if we should turn away and tribulations should overtake us, we could come to this place and pray, and you would hear our petition. And indeed you are faithful and true. And since you have in the past often come to the aid of our forebears in their hour of tribulation and humiliation, and delivered them from great evils, behold now, O holy king, how because of our many great sins we are weighed down with suffering and oppressed by our enemies and have succumbed to our own helplessness. This arrogant and profane man, with the reversal of our fortunes, would violate the holy place on earth dedicated to the glory of your name. Indeed, your real home is in the highest heavens, unapproachable by mere humans, but since you have thought it good to allow your glory to reside among your people Israel, you have sanctified this place. Do not punish us, therefore, by means of the defilement of others, nor chastise us with their uncleanness, lest these lawless men should boast in their anger and exult in the arrogance of their tongues, saying, 'We have trampled upon the house of the sanctuary as the houses of abominations are trampled down.' Rather, wipe away our sins, scatter our iniquities; reveal now your mercy. Let your compassion rest upon us and put praise in the mouths of those who have fallen and are broken in spirit. Grant us peace."

At this, the all-seeing God, forefather of all, holiest of the holy, heeded the reverent prayer and scourged the man who had so exalted himself in arrogance and audacity. First on one side and then the other, he shook him as a reed is shaken by the wind, so that he lay helpless on the ground, all his limbs paralyzed, unable to speak because he was afflicted by a righteous judgment. As a result, his friends and bodyguards, when they beheld the sudden punishment that he had received and fearing that he would soon perish, quickly dragged him away, while still themselves in the grip of an overwhelming dread. Not long afterward he recovered, and although he had received such a punishment, still he did not repent but departed with bitter threats on his lips.

When he came to Egypt, he only increased the number of his evil deeds, joined now by his previously mentioned drinking companions and friends,[1] who were themselves alien to everything just. He was not satisfied with the countless wanton acts but proceeded to such arrogance that he initiated rumors in various places, and many of his friends, observing carefully the king's purpose, followed his example. He took it into his mind

1. Contrary to the text, these friends have not been mentioned before. This is one piece of evidence that the beginning of the story may be missing. See the introduction.

to inflict a public disgrace upon the Jewish people by erecting on the tower in the courtyard the following inscription: "All those who refuse to offer sacrifice shall not be allowed to enter their Temple, and all Jews shall be reduced to slavery and are now subject to the poll tax. Those who speak against this edict shall be forcibly taken into custody and executed. Those who have sacrificed and have been properly registered will be branded by fire on their bodies with an ivy leaf, the symbol of Dionysus, and listed in the records as retaining their former status." So that he would not appear prejudicial toward all Jews, he also had inscribed: "If any of the Jews choose to participate in the mysteries and join the initiated, they will receive equal rights with the citizens of Alexandria."

Some Jews, who were loath to pay the high price exacted by their reverence of Jerusalem, easily gave themselves over, hoping to gain prestige from the association they would enjoy with the king. Most, however, persevered with a noble spirit and did not forsake their religion. By offering money in exchange for their lives, they valiantly attempted to save themselves from the registration, remaining ever hopeful that they would find relief. They despised those who had separated themselves from them, considering them enemies of their people, and excluded them from any companionship or mutual assistance.

(3) When that impious man became aware of this, he became so angry that he not only fumed at those in Alexandria, but was also even more enraged at those in the countryside as well. He decreed that they should all immediately be gathered together at the same site and be put to death by the worst means possible. While these things were being arranged, a malicious rumor began to be circulated against the Jews by people who had conspired to do them harm, giving as a pretext that the Jews had hindered them from observing their laws. And while the Jews resolutely maintained their goodwill and unswerving fidelity toward the Ptolemaic house, they nevertheless feared God and lived their lives according to his law; they held themselves apart in the matter

of food, and for this reason appeared odious to some. By ordering their lives by the faithful practice of righteous deeds, they established a good reputation among all the people. Those of other races,[2] however, showed no respect for the general good practices of this people recognized by all, but took more account instead of the differences in regard to worship and dietary practices, saying that they were bound neither to the king nor to the governing authorities but were hostile and in every way opposed to his interests. Thus it was no small charge that they were laying at their feet. When the Greeks of the city, in no way themselves injured, beheld the unexpected tumult taking place and the people being herded together for no apparent reason, they were not strong enough to offer help, for they lived under a tyranny. However, they tried to comfort them and were very distressed at their plight, and they supposed that these things would pass, for it seemed that so great a nation would not be abandoned when it had done nothing wrong. Already some of their neighbors and friends and business associates had taken some aside secretly, offering pledges to protect them and to give their all on their behalf.

Meanwhile, the king, exulting in his present success and oblivious to the power of the greatest God, supposed that he could continue in his present designs, and he wrote the following letter against the Jews:

> King Ptolemy Philopator to his generals and soldiers in Egypt, greetings and good health:
>
> I myself am in good health and our rule is prospering. Now that our expedition to Asia, of which you are aware, has been

2. Just who is meant is unclear, and this sentence seems to contradict the previous one. It is possible that a distinction is being drawn between Greeks and native Egyptians, the latter being perhaps more directly in competition with Jews in the Greek-controlled city of Alexandria. In any case, the author is probably not overly concerned with consistency.

brought to a conclusion, according to plan and by the deliberate alliance of the gods, we supposed that we should nurture the care of the peoples of Coelesyria and Phoenicia, not at the point of the spear, but through gentleness and benevolence, graciously granting them benefits. After we had granted large revenues to the temples in each city, we came also to Jerusalem, and went up to do honor to the temple of this abominable people who never cease from their folly. Although they pretended to welcome our presence with their mouths, in fact they were being deceitful, for when we were eager to enter into their sanctuary and honor it with the most beautiful and splendid offerings, they shut us out, carried away by their ancient delusions. Nevertheless, on account of the benevolence that we have for all people, they were spared the full force of our arms. By the ill will that they show toward us they demonstrate that they are the only nation to resist their kings and benefactors, and accept no overtures as sincere.

We accommodated ourselves to this folly and, returning to Egypt with victory in hand, met all nations with benevolence, as was proper for us to do. Among our actions, we made known to all our amnesty for the Jews' fellow countrymen in Egypt on account of our alliance with them and the many matters generously entrusted to them from of old, and we decided to institute a change whereby we would deem them worthy of Alexandrian citizenship and full participation in our religious rites. They, however, received this in a way opposite to that intended, and in their inborn maliciousness rejected what was good, and chose, as ever, what was bad. Not only did they reject the invaluable citizenship, but both by their words and by their silence they show their contempt for the few among them who are genuinely disposed to us. In each case they nurture the secret hope that because of their infamous manner of life we shall soon reverse our actions.

Therefore, since we are firmly convinced by all the evidence that these people are opposed to us in every way, and we are apprehensive that, if some sudden disturbance should hereafter arise against us, we would find these impious people at our rear as traitorous and barbarous enemies, we have therefore ordered that as soon as this letter reaches you, you should send to us those who live among you, together with their wives and children, chained and shackled in irons, with every sort of punishment and harsh treatment, to receive the inexorable, shameful death that befits those hostile to us. When they are all thus punished, we believe that our government will be perfectly established in stability and harmony for all time. If anyone should shelter any Jew, from old to young—even an infant—that person and the entire family will be tortured to death with the most horrible punishments. Anyone who so desires may inform against transgressors and, as a result, receive the property of the one who incurs punishment and two thousand drachmas from the royal treasury, and in addition be crowned at the festival of Dionysus.[3] Any place whatsoever in which it is ascertained that a Jew has received shelter will be declared impassable and burned with fire; it will be rendered uninhabitable for all time for every living creature.

Thus Philopator wrote concerning the Jews, (4) and in every place where the decree arrived, a feast was instituted at public expense for the various peoples, celebrated with joy and gladness. The hatred that had long since hardened within their hearts had now found open expression. For the Jews there was now incessant grief and mournful cries, filled with tears. Their hearts burned with the groans and lamentation, as they bewailed the unexpected destruction that was now suddenly decreed for them. What region or city, what streets—or indeed what inhabited place whatsoever—was not filled with wailing and groans for them?

With a bitter and merciless spirit they were sent away all at the same time by the generals in each city, with the result that their extraordinary punishments made even some of their enemies, when they beheld such a pitiful display before their eyes, reflect on the uncertain reversals of life and weep at the miserable expulsion of this people. A host of old people, covered with gray

3. The text says "crowned at (or with) freedom," but the latter is also a name for a festival of Dionysus. In view of the evident satire of all things Dionysian in Third Maccabees, the text as read here seems more likely.

hair, were led away; their feet, though slowed by age, were violently and shamelessly whipped into a swifter pace. Young women who had only recently entered the bridal chamber to begin wedded life exchanged their joy for wailing, and the myrrh that perfumed their hair for ashes, and were now being driven, exposed without their veils. In place of the wedding songs, with one voice they chanted a dirge, as though they were being rent by the pagan strokes. In bonds they were publicly and forcibly dragged to the docks where they would be boarded on boats. Their husbands as well, still in the very bloom of youth, in place of garlands wore ropes around their necks, and in place of their celebrations and revelry passed the final days of their wedding feasts in mourning, gazing at Hades opening up in front of them. They were driven on board like animals, confined with iron fetters, some fastened to the rowers' benches by their necks, others secured by their feet with unbreakable shackles. Enclosed below under a solid deck, they proceeded in total darkness, receiving the treatment throughout the entire trip that would normally be accorded to traitors.

When they reached a place called Schedia, the voyage was brought to an end just as the king had decreed, and he ordered that they should be confined in the hippodrome just outside the city. It had been constructed with an immense and imposing wall around it and was as a result well suited to make a public spectacle of the Jews for all those who happened to be traveling on a journey to or from the city. The Jews within were thus unable to communicate with the king's armies and could not claim the same rights as those Jews who were in the city. But no sooner were these arrangements completed than the king heard that the Jews from within the city were coming out secretly to mourn bitterly the shameful state of their brothers and sisters. He became enraged and ordered that they should without exception receive precisely the same punishment as the others. The whole people was to be registered by name, not only for the hard labor that was described above, but also to be tortured by the punishments he had ordained, and finally to be killed in the space of one day. The registration of these people was therefore carried out with hateful zeal and methodical diligence, from the rising of the sun till its setting, for a period of forty days, and even then remained unfinished.

The king was now filled with a great and continuous joy, instituting revels before all of his idols, polluting his lips and allowing his mind to stray even further from the truth, praising things that were mute and unable to speak or offer assistance, and uttering things inappropriate before the greatest God. But after the aforementioned period of time the scribes reported to the king that, because there were so many Jews, they were not yet able to complete the registration, and there were yet many more residing in the countryside, some in their homes and some still on the journey. It would be an impossible task even for all the generals in Egypt. The king reproached them with harsh threats, assuming that they had been bribed to allow some a means of escape, but he was given a sure proof on this point when they showed him that the paper and writing utensils which they had been using had already run out—this, of course, being in fact the result of the workings of that invincible providence that comes from the one who helps the Jews from heaven.

(5) The king then summoned Hermon, the keeper of the elephants, and consumed now by an overwhelming rage and incapable of exhibiting any hint of compromise, commanded that on the next day he ply the elephants—five hundred in all—with large handfuls of frankincense and copious amounts of strong wine, and after they had been driven mad by the abundance of drink, lead them in to seal the fate of the Jews. Once these orders had been given, he turned to his feasting, gathering around him those of his friends and generals who were especially hostile to the Jews. Meanwhile, Hermon, the keeper of the elephants, followed his instructions to the letter. Those in charge of the Jews went out in the evening and bound the hands of their wretched prisoners, keeping them securely through the night,

supposing that their race would all meet their end at one time Since they were confined on every side and bound in shackles, the Jews seemed to the gentiles to be bereft of any hope of aid. But with tears and in a voice that could not be silenced, they all cried out to the almighty Lord, the one who rules over every power, their merciful God and Father, praying to him to divert the unholy plan hatched against them and with a magnificent manifestation of his presence save them from the fate that lay before them. Thus their fervent prayer ascended to heaven.

When Hermon had drugged the pitiless elephants, filling them with huge drafts of wine and large quantities of frankincense, he appeared at the court early in the morning to report to the king concerning these things. But the Lord had also apportioned upon the king a measure of sleep, that fair creation of old, which night and day is graciously bestowed by its author on whomsoever he wishes. The king was thus overcome by a deep, sweet sleep through the workings of the Lord, and as a result he was frustrated in his lawless plan, thwarted in the dogged pursuit of his goal.

And the Jews, when they survived the appointed hour, gave praise to their holy God and again besought the one who is quick to be reconciled to show the arrogant gentiles the might of his all-powerful hand. But now, since it was nearly the middle of the afternoon, the official in charge of the invitations, seeing that the guests had arrived, went in and shook the king. Only with great difficulty could he rouse him; he explained what was happening and that the hour of the festivities was already slipping by. The king considered this and then, returning to his drinking, commanded that those present take their seats opposite him. Once they were seated, he encouraged them to give themselves over to revelry and to enjoy the present portion of the festivities by celebrating all the more. When the party had gone on for some time, the king summoned Hermon and, interspersing many threats, asked why the Jews had been allowed to survive that day. But when he pointed out that he had carried out the king's instructions to the letter on the previous night, and his account was supported by the king's friends, the king fell into the grip of a savagery worse than that of Phalaris.[4] He declared that the Jews owed their thanks for escape that day to sleep, "but as for tomorrow," he added, "go without delay and prepare the elephants in the same way for the destruction of the lawless Jews." When the king said this, all those present with one voice applauded joyously, and all returned to their own homes. They did not, however, devote the night hours to sleep as much as to devising every insult imaginable for those they deemed wretched.

When the cock crowed, announcing the dawn, Hermon dressed out the elephants in their finery and began to drive them through the great colonnade. Large crowds, eagerly awaiting the morning light, had gathered around the city to see the pitiful spectacle. But the Jews, breathing their last gasp—for their time had run out—made a tearful supplication amid mournful cries, extended their hands to heaven, and prayed again to the Greatest God and begged for immediate deliverance. The rays of the sun had not yet spread over the earth when the king began welcoming his friends. Hermon presented himself to the king and reported that it was time to go forth to the festivities; everything that the king desired lay ready to be carried out. But when the king heard these words he was very perplexed at the unusual invitation to go forth—he was, in fact, completely oblivious to everything that was happening. He asked Hermon what it was that was being prepared so zealously for him—this was also the working of the God who rules over all things, to place in the king's mind a forgetfulness of all the things he had devised. Hermon and all the king's friends explained to the king, "Sire, the beasts and the soldiers have been marshalled in response to your urgent plan." But the king began to seethe with a deep anger at

4. Phalaris was a king of Agrigentum in the sixth century B.C.E. who was famous for his cruelty and tortures.

these words; by the providence of God all his power of reason had deserted him.

The king looked at him intently and with a threatening tone said, "Had your parents or children been present here, I would have served them up as a rich feast for the wild beasts in place of the Jews, who are blameless before me and at every turn have shown me and my ancestors a complete and abiding loyalty. And indeed if it had not been for your service and the affection that derives from our common origins, you would have forfeited your life for theirs." Thus Hermon encountered a dangerous and unexpected threat, and his countenance fell in shame. Each of the king's friends slunk away sullenly and dispersed the assembled audience to return to their business. But when the Jews heard what had happened to the king, they praised the Lord, the manifest God and King of kings, because they had received this help as well.

Yet once again the king laid plans for a banquet according to the same arrangements, and he invited everyone to enjoy the festivities. To Hermon he said in a menacing tone, "How many times, you pitiful wretch, must I give you these same orders? Now dress out the elephants so that tomorrow they may destroy the Jews."

But the king's officials who reclined at dinner with him were shocked by his erratic mental state and said, "O king, how long are you going to test us as though we were fools? This is now the third time that you have given orders to destroy this people, yet when the matter is about to be concluded you change your mind and cancel what you have decreed. The city is now in turmoil as a result. Everywhere there are people assembled and there is a constant danger of looting."

Then the king, who was in every way like Phalaris, took total leave of his senses; the vacillations concerning his treatment of the Jews he completely disregarded, but instead swore an oath—solemn, yet impossible to fulfill—that he would inexorably consign the Jews to Hades, crushed under the legs and feet of the beasts, and after that direct a campaign against Judea and raze it to the ground forthwith by fire and sword, burning down the Temple that had formerly been inaccessible to him, rendering it forever deserted of any who would offer sacrifices there. His friends and officials, confident and in high spirits, took their leave and proceeded out, commanding their soldiers to take up the most strategic posts around the city to keep order.

The beasts had now been accoutered fearfully in military fashion, and the keeper of the elephants began driving them, one might say, nearly to the point of madness, with pungent drafts of wine mixed with frankincense. By dawn, when the city was already crowded with innumerable throngs of people streaming into the hippodrome, the keeper of the elephants entered the court and aroused the king for the task at hand. His impious mind now filled with an intense fury, he set off marching stridently at the side of the beasts and wanted now to gaze pitilessly with his own eyes on the wretched, forlorn end of those people described above. When the Jews saw the cloud of dust raised up by the elephants coming through the gate of the hippodrome, the armed soldiers following behind and the tramping of all the crowds, and when they heard the thundering noise, they supposed that this was the final moment of their lives, the resolution of all their worst fears. They then turned to wailing and lamentations, kissed each other and embraced their relatives, holding them tightly, parents hugging their children and mothers their daughters, others suckling at their breasts their newborn babes, who drew milk for the last time. Nevertheless, they considered also all the times in the past when they received assistance from heaven, and with one accord threw themselves upon the ground. Pulling the newborns from their breasts they cried out loudly to the one who rules over every power, begging him, by a manifestation of his presence, to take pity on them, who were already standing at the very gates of Hades.

(6) At this time a certain Eleazar, a known and respected priest from the countryside, who had now reached old age and

comported himself throughout his life with every virtue, instructed the elders around him to cease calling upon the holy God and began himself to pray as follows: "O most powerful King, Most High, Almighty God, who governs the whole creation with mercy, look now upon the seed of Abraham, the children of Jacob—the one you have sanctified—the people who constitute your holy portion, strangers in a strange land, who are perishing unjustly, O Father. Pharaoh, the former ruler of this land Egypt, who had an abundance of chariots and was exalted by his lawless outrage and boasting tongue, you destroyed, together with his arrogant army, by drowning them in the sea, and shined the light of your mercy on the people Israel. And you, when Sennacherib, the oppressive king of the Assyrians, had vaunted himself arrogantly with his innumerable armies, had put the entire world under the control of his spear, and rose up against your holy city, muttering threatening words in boasting and arrogance—you, O Lord, shattered him into pieces, demonstrating your power to many nations. And when Daniel's three companions in Babylon freely chose to surrender their lives to the flames rather than worship empty idols, you changed the fiery blast into dew and thus saved them. Not even a hair on their head was singed in the furnace, which you then turned upon their adversaries. And you, when Daniel, because of envious accusations, was cast to the lions underground to become meat for wild beasts, brought him up again into the light unharmed. When Jonah was languishing in the belly of the monster of the deep, you looked down on him, O father, and restored him to his family unharmed.

"And now, O enemy of every outrage, merciful guardian of the entire world, quickly reveal yourself to those of the people Israel who are being abused by the abominable and lawless gentiles. If our lives have been taken up in impious deeds while we have been in our foreign exile, deliver us from the hand of our enemies, O Lord, and only then destroy us by whatever fate you choose, but do not let those with vain minds give blessings to their vain gods by destroying those who love you, saying, 'Their God did not save them.' No, you, Eternal One, who possess all might and all power, look upon us. Have mercy upon us who are being forced to leave this life like traitors, executed by the mad insolence of lawless men. Let the gentiles cringe today in fear before your invincible might, O most honored one, who have the power to bring salvation to your people Jacob. This great throng of babes, together with their parents, are begging you with their tears. Let it be shown to all the gentiles that you are with us, O Lord, and you have not turned your face from us, but as you have said, 'Not even when they were in the land of their enemies did I forget them.' Thus make it so, O Lord."

Just as Eleazar was concluding his prayer, the king, with the wild beasts and arrogant armies, made his way into the hippodrome. When the Jews saw them, they cried out so loudly unto heaven that the valleys round about echoed it back and caused an uncontrollable shudder among the troops. Then the true, almighty, and glorious God, revealing his holy face, opened the gates of heaven and out came two mighty angels of horrifying aspect, visible to all except the Jews. They faced the army of their adversaries and filled them with tribulation and terror, binding them with immovable shackles. A great fright seized the body of the king as well, as he forgot everything of his former insolence. The elephants also turned back upon the armed soldiers who followed them and began to trample and destroy them.

The wrath of the king then turned to compassion and tears for all the things he had devised. When he heard them crying and beheld them all prostrate awaiting their destruction, he wept, and in a fury threatened his friends: "You are committing treason, surpassing even the tyrants in your cruelty. By secretly plotting things that are destructive of my administration you are even attempting to deprive me, your benefactor, of my kingship and my very life. Who has driven from their homes those who have so faithfully guarded the fortresses of the country, and foolishly gathered them all here? Who has so lawlessly heaped indignities on those who from the beginning surpassed all the other nations in goodwill toward us, and who were often subject to the worst dangers that human beings are exposed to? Release them from their undeserved chains! Send them home in peace, begging their forgiveness for all that you have done to them. Set free these children of the all-powerful, living God of heaven, who from the time of our ancestors until now has bestowed upon our administration an unimpeded glory and stability."

Thus the king spoke, and the Jews were instantly released. Having just escaped death, they praised the holy God who delivered them.

Upon returning to the city, the king then summoned the official in charge of revenues and commanded him to provide wine and all other things necessary for a feast of seven days, and declared that it was appropriate that in the very place where they expected to meet their destruction, there they should celebrate their deliverance with much joy and happiness. And so they, who had just been treated so shamefully and brought down to the very edge of Hades, were now, instead of meeting a bitter and mournful fate, arranging a festival of deliverance; in the very place that had been prepared for their fall and interment they hallowed spaces for festive celebration. They put an end to the pitiable sounds of dirges and took up instead their ancestral song praising their God and savior who worked wonders. Rejecting all wailing and lamentation, they joined in dancing as a sign of their newfound peace and joy. The king also arranged a great banquet to celebrate these events, unceasingly giving his heartfelt thanks to heaven for his unexpected deliverance. But those who had before assumed that the Jews were destined for death and to be picked over by birds and had registered their names with such glee now shuddered, overwhelmed with shame, and the fires of their temerity had been ingloriously doused. But the Jews, as we have said, instituted the aforementioned dance and spent their time in celebration with joyful hymns of praise, establishing a common rite for their whole community throughout the generations. They constituted the aforementioned days as a festival of celebration, not for drinking and gluttony, but to mark the deliverance that God had granted them. Then they prevailed upon the king to allow them to be dismissed to their homes.

The registration of the Jews had taken place from the twenty-fifth of Pachon until the fourth of Epeiph, forty days, and their destruction had been decreed from the fifth day of Epeiph to the seventh, three days. It was on these days that the glorious ruler of all manifested his mercy and delivered each and every one of them unharmed. They joined in feasting, with all the things necessary supplied by the king, until the fourteenth, when they petitioned the king to be allowed to go home. The king consented to their petition and wrote the following letter on their behalf to the generals in each of the cities, magnanimously expressing his position:

> (7) King Ptolemy Philopator to the generals in Egypt and to all government officials, greetings and good health:
>
> We are well, as are our children, the great God directing our affairs, as is our desire. Some of our friends, because of the thoroughgoing malignity of their disposition, persuaded us to gather together the Jews in the kingdom into one body to punish them by the extraordinary measures normally applied to traitors, arguing that our government would never be stable because of the hostility they bear for all nations, until this situation is resolved. As a result, they brought them together in shackles, with harsh punishments, like slaves, or rather, like conspirators, and sought to execute them without any legal procedure or examination, exhibiting a cruelty more savage than the custom of the Scythians. We reprimanded them severely for this and only allowed them to escape with their lives, on account of the kindness that we show toward all people. And because we are now firmly convinced that the God of heaven will shield the Jews from all harm, being their ally always as a father protects his children, and on account of the strong affection and friendship that they have shown for us and our ancestors, we have examined the case and justly absolved them of all blame whatsoever. We have therefore decreed that they all

> return to their own homes, and that no one should harm them in any way nor reproach them for things they suffered without just cause. Know, therefore, that if we devise any evil against them or bring them into any harm whatsoever, we shall be opposed not by a human adversary but by the master of all power, the most high God, who will most assuredly exact a just punishment for all our deeds. Farewell.

When the Jews received this letter, they did not proceed immediately back to their homes, but laid a further request before the king, namely, that those Jews who had willingly transgressed against the holy God and his law should receive from them the punishment they deserved. They argued that those who had transgressed the divine ordinances for the sake of their stomachs would at any rate never be supportive of the king's affairs. The king voiced his agreement with their suggestion and praised them for it, granting them full immunity so that they might wipe out those throughout his kingdom who had transgressed the law of God, openly and with no danger of an inquiry or interference from the royal authority. Then they, for their part, both the priests and the whole people, as was proper, applauded what he said, and as they departed shouted with joy "Hallelujah!" Any of their own people whom they met who had allowed themselves to be defiled they punished with an ignominious death. On that day they killed more than three hundred men, and kept it as a day of celebration, having destroyed those who were polluted. Those, however, who held fast to God even to the point of death took the full enjoyment afforded by their deliverance; they departed the city crowned with all sorts of fragrant blossoms, shouting out in celebration, and gave thanks to the eternal God of their fathers, savior of Israel, with songs and hymns of praise.

When they reached Ptolemais, which is called "rose-bearing" after the nature of the place, the fleet waited for them there for seven days, as was their common wish, and there they held a banquet to celebrate their deliverance, for the king had magnanimously provided all the things for the journey until they had all arrived at their own homes. Having arrived in peace with all the appropriate confessions of praise, there too in similar fashion they decided to celebrate those days as a joyous festival during the time of their stay. They inscribed them as holy days on a pillar and established a house of prayer at the site of the banquet, and then by the decree of the king they departed, unharmed, free, jubilant, having been brought safely by land, sea, and river to their own homes. They acquired even greater standing than before among their enemies, instilling awe and fear, and were never threatened again with being dispossessed. They received back all of their possessions in accordance with the registration; those who had taken it returned it with great tribulation. Thus the supreme God perfectly accomplished great things for their deliverance. Blessed be the one who delivers Israel forever and ever! Amen.

## SUGGESTIONS FOR FURTHER READING

Barclay, John M. G. *Jews in the Mediterranean Diaspora: From Alexander to Trajan (323 BCE–117 CE),* pp. 192–203. Berkeley: University of California Press, 1996.

Collins, John J. *Between Athens and Jerusalem: Jewish Identity in the Hellenistic Diaspora,* pp. 104–11. New York: Crossroad, 1983.

Gruen, Erich. *Heritage and Hellenism: The Reinvention of Jewish Tradition,* pp. 222–36. Berkeley: University of California Press, 1998.

Hadas, Moses. *The Third and Fourth Book of Maccabees.* New York: Ktav, 1953.

Nickelsburg, George W. E. *Jewish Literature Between the Bible and the Mishnah,* pp. 169–72. Philadelphia: Fortress, 1981.

Wills, Lawrence M. *The Jewish Novel in the Ancient World,* pp. 201–6. Ithaca, N.Y.: Cornell University Press, 1995.

NINE

# THE TOBIAD ROMANCE

*The Tobiad Romance* is a name that scholars have applied to a section of Josephus's Antiquities (12.4.1–11 §154–236) that appears to be derived from an older historical novel (see also *The Royal Family of Adiabene*). Josephus wrote at the end of the first century C.E., but the older account was likely written during the early second century B.C.E. concerning events at the end of the third century B.C.E. (although Josephus incorrectly places the events somewhat later).

The *Tobiad Romance* concerns the wealthy and powerful Tobiad family of Jews, who were probably descended from Tobiah the Ammonite (Neh 2:10, 19). This family traded for at least three hundred years between Judah and Samaria and the lands to the east, including Ammon (thus "the Ammonite," even though Tobiah was Jewish). Archaeological remains have been discovered of this family's eastern estate, and so we are fortunate to have a number of different sources to catalog this ancient Jewish dynasty. This is the same family that may have produced *Tobit,* but if the *Tobiad Romance* and *Tobit* were produced by the same family, it is remarkable how different the intentions of the authors are. In the *Tobiad Romance* we find a focus on one wing of the family, Joseph and his son Hyrcanus. They are rendered in a thoroughly positive way, while others from the Tobiad family, including Joseph's other sons (Hyrcanus's half-brothers), are described quite negatively, as unworthy of warmth and respect. They are even involved in plots against Joseph and Hyrcanus. Thus while *Tobit* greatly magnifies and romanticizes family relations, the *Tobiad Romance* presents the inner-family relations as internecine warfare. This should perhaps not be so surprising as a narrative theme, however, when one considers the struggle between brothers in the Hebrew Bible, especially Joseph and his brothers in Genesis 37–50 and its even more conflictual retelling in *The Marriage and Conversion of Aseneth.*

There is likely a historical explanation for the clear lines of division within the Tobiad family. The Greek rulers of Egypt, the Ptolemies, and the Greek rulers in Syria, the Seleucids, both successor-dynasties of Alexander the Great, were vying at this point in history for control of the Judean buffer zone. It appears that some members of the Tobiad clan—doubtless because of trade relations—favored Ptolemaic control, while others for the same reason favored Seleucid control. This drama is also played out in *Second Maccabees* 3–4. It is the rhetorical design of the storyteller that colors each wing of the family in such strongly moral terms. The positive depiction of Joseph and Hyrcanus in *Tobiad Romance* is at times offensive to modern sensibilities, since the pair rise to prominence by tax-farming; that is, they purchase the rights to collect taxes forcibly from the populace and give a required portion of it to the Ptolemaic kings. This is a far cry from the litany on alms-giving found in *Tobit,* but the reader must take the author's perspective into account. In the moral world of this text, Joseph and Hyrcanus are the "protectors" of the people. The prevailing ethos of the book is the ancient patronage system, in which every person seeks to become a patron to as many clients as possible, and a client to some more powerful patron. Joseph and his son Hyrcanus manage to become patrons of the Jewish people in several important areas, partly by successfully insinuating themselves as clients to the Ptolemaic king and queen in Egypt. The ethos of patronage may explain the strange and abrupt ending of the text as well. Although we cannot know for certain how the original book ended before Josephus excerpted it, the present text ends with the suicide of Hyrcanus, who had formerly been depicted as so brash. When the control of the Egyptian kings receded at the end of the third century, and influence swung in the direction of the Seleucids, Hyrcanus found himself without a powerful patron and his economic empire collapsed. With that he took his life.

The building blocks of the narrative consist of stories that glorify the wit, pluck, determination, and resourcefulness of Joseph and Hyrcanus. It is a series of major and minor triumphs in repartee and cunning, told with obvious satisfaction but without satire or cynicism—these Tobiads supposedly have the best interests of their clients at heart. The use of shorter anecdotes as building blocks is a common technique in popular literature contemporary to *Tobiad Romance;* one may compare *Susanna* and *Bel and the Serpent* in the growing Daniel tradition (see the introduction to those texts), the formation of each of the gospels and Acts in the Christian tradition, and *Life of Aesop* and the *Alexander Romance* in the tradition of the Greco-Roman novel. The similarity of technique across cultural borders can be seen by comparing the dinner scene near the beginning of *Tobiad Romance* with *Alexander Romance* 2.15.

Some of the episodes are also clearly modeled on biblical narratives, however, presumably to invest the characters with some of the authority of their biblical counterparts. For instance, when Joseph becomes infatuated with a non-Jewish dancing girl, his brother tricks him while drunk into sleeping with his own daughter. This calls to mind the biblical story of Jacob and Laban (Genesis 29). Further, as was noted earlier, the jealousy of Hyrcanus's brothers is reminiscent of the Joseph story of Genesis 37–50. Yet it is perhaps the sheer bravado of an author who could celebrate such characters as the Tobiad offspring that renders the work entertaining even today.

## *The Tobiad Romance*
## (From Josephus, *Antiquities* 12.4.1–11)

(1) Antiochus the Great of Syria, upon signing a treaty with King Ptolemy of Egypt, gave his daughter Cleopatra to him in marriage, providing as dowry the regions of Coele-Syria, Samaria, Judea, and Phoenicia. The tribute from these regions, however, was to be divided between Ptolemy and his new queen Cleopatra. The leading citizens of each province purchased the rights to collect taxes, and once they had gathered the revenues, paid what was due into the treasuries of the royal pair. It was during this period that the Samarians, who were flourishing, inflicted many setbacks on the Jews by raiding the countryside and seizing slaves. All this occurred during the high-priesthood of Onias. (When Eleazar had died, his uncle Manasses had acceded to the position of high priest, and when he died, the office fell to Onias, son of Simon, called "the Just.") This Onias, however, was petty and a slave to his own greed, and as a result he failed to pay on the people's behalf the required tribute of twenty talents of silver; his predecessors, in fact, had always rendered this money from their own funds. As a result, King Ptolemy became furious and dispatched an envoy to Jerusalem to call Onias to account for withholding the tribute, threatening at the same time to divide up the land and parcel it out to his soldiers if he did not receive it. When the Jews heard of this threat, there was great consternation among them, but Onias, for his part, was so consumed by avarice that he was unconcerned.

(2) There was also at this time a certain young man named Joseph, son of Tobias, whose mother was a sister of Onias. Though still young, he enjoyed a reputation for uprightness among the citizens of Jerusalem as a result of his reverence and foresight. Although away in the village of Phicola at the time of this incident and far removed from Jerusalem, Joseph was nevertheless informed by his mother of all that had happened. He returned to the city and severely rebuked Onias for his obliviousness to the welfare of the people and for willingly placing the nation in dan-

ger by refusing to pay the tribute. Indeed, it was for this very purpose that Onias had become the patron of the people and risen to the office of high priest. Joseph advised him that if his passion for money was so great that for the sake of it he could stand by and watch his fellow citizens suffer any injury whatsoever, he should go to the king and ask him to forego all, or at least a portion, of the payment due to him. Onias, however, answered that he was not interested in retaining his patronage and that if he could, he would gladly give up the high priesthood. He still, however, did not intend to approach the king, since he was not genuinely concerned about the consequences. Joseph thereupon asked Onias whether he himself could act as envoy to Ptolemy on behalf of the people. Onias replied that he would allow it, and Joseph went up to the Temple and called the people together into an assembly, assuring them that they should not be troubled or frightened because of his uncle Onias's lack of concern for their well-being. He further exhorted them to remain hopeful and not to allow their minds to be clouded by fears of a catastrophe. He promised them that he would go before the king to persuade him that they were not themselves at fault. When the gathered people heard this, they gave Joseph their heartfelt thanks. He then came down from the Temple and received the envoy sent by Ptolemy most warmly, laying opulent feasts before him each day, while also bestowing upon him the most lavish gifts. He then sent him back to the king, saying that he himself would follow. Joseph was now even more anxious to proceed to Alexandria to meet the king; the envoy had indeed urged him strongly to proceed to Egypt and had assured him that whatever he asked of Ptolemy he would receive. The envoy had, in fact, come to admire Joseph greatly for the dignity of his bearing and his high-minded liberality.

(3) When the emissary returned to Egypt, he laid before the king an account of Onias's boorishness but at the same time informed him how gracious Joseph had been. He further explained that Joseph was on his way to see him in order to seek

royal forbearance for the misdeeds of the people; Joseph had indeed now become their patron. Setting aside his normal restraint, the emissary began to employ such an abundance of praises in describing the young man that both the king and his wife Cleopatra felt as if they knew him well, even before he arrived.

Meanwhile, Joseph sent word to friends in Samaria, and from them obtained money on loan to procure the necessities for the journey: clothes, drinking vessels, draft animals—the whole amounting to about twenty thousand drachmas—and thus came to Alexandria. All the leading citizens of the cities of Syria and Phoenicia were at this time making their way there as well for the auctioning of the rights to collect taxes, for these were sold annually by the king to the wealthiest citizens of each city. When they saw Joseph on his way to Alexandria, they mocked at his poverty, deriding him as a country bumpkin. When he arrived in Alexandria, however, he heard that Ptolemy was in Memphis, and he proceeded there to meet him and introduce himself. The king was seated on his chariot with his wife and Athenion, his friend—this was the man who had served as envoy to Jerusalem and was received so well by Joseph. Upon seeing Joseph, Athenion immediately introduced him to the king and noted that this was the same young man whom he had described to the king upon his return from Jerusalem as being dependable and showing such promise. Ptolemy first greeted him, then invited him to join him on the chariot. No sooner was Joseph seated, however, than Ptolemy began to rail against the actions of Onias. "Please excuse him on account of his age," said Joseph, "for surely the king has noticed that old people and infants have much in common with respect to their mental capacities, but with those who are in the prime of their lives you will be well pleased and find no fault whatsoever." Quite taken with his charm and urbane wit, Ptolemy grew even fonder of the young man, as if in fact he were already a trusted friend, and as a result commanded that he be a guest in the palace and share the king's table every day. When the king returned to Alexandria, however, and the leading men of Syria saw Joseph dining regularly with the king, they were very upset.

(4) Soon the day arrived on which the tax rights were to be sold, and all the wealthy citizens in the provinces came to place their bids. When the sum of the bids for Coele-Syria, Phoenicia, and Judea with Samaria was tallied at eight thousand talents, Joseph came forward and accused those bidding of having conspired ahead of time to keep the bidding low; he himself would pay twice that figure, and in addition hand over to the king the property of those who were in arrears to his house—for this right of seizure was sold along with the rights to collect taxes. The king was, of course, pleased to hear this, and in the hopes of thus increasing his income, granted Joseph the tax-farming rights. When he asked, however, whether Joseph could also provide guarantors for his bid, the young man cleverly responded, "I shall provide for you guarantors of sterling character, in whom you will have complete faith." And when the king asked who they might be, he answered, "Why, you yourself, O king, and your wife. Each of you shall stand as guarantor for the other's portion." At this Ptolemy began to laugh, and he granted Joseph the tax rights without requiring guarantors. Those who had come to Egypt from the various cities were now quite vexed, however, feeling humiliated by Joseph, and returned shamefaced to their own provinces.

(5) Joseph next procured two thousand soldiers from the king—he had asked for assistance in order to deal with those in the cities who might treat him with contempt—and borrowed five hundred talents from the friends of the king; with these he set out for Syria. Arriving in Ashcalon, he demanded the tribute from the people of the city. They, however, not only refused to pay him the money, but also proceeded to treat him insolently. He therefore arrested about twenty of the leading citizens and executed them, then confiscated their property, worth about one thousand talents, and sent it to the king, along with an explanation of his actions. Ptolemy, impressed by his cleverness, praised

his handling of affairs and granted him permission to do whatever he wished.

When the Syrians heard of these things, however, they were in a state of shock. With the execution of the men of Ashcalon as an example before their eyes, they gladly opened their gates to Joseph and paid him the required tribute. But when the citizens of Scythopolis also tried to insult him and refused to pay him the tribute which had always been rendered willingly in the past, he executed the leaders there as well, and sent their property on to the king. Having thus raised great sums of money and amassed wealth from the collection of taxes, he used it to secure his new-found power. It would be wise at this juncture, he thought, to protect the source of his good fortune, and so he used the vast means which he himself had acquired to send many secret gifts to the king, to Cleopatra, and to their friends and to all the leading figures at court; by this he hoped to obtain their goodwill.

(6) For twenty-two years Joseph enjoyed this good fortune, becoming the father of seven children by one wife, and the father of another son by the daughter of his brother Solymius, whom he named Hyrcanus. This marriage came about in the following way. On one occasion when Joseph made the journey to Alexandria, he was accompanied by his brother Solymius, who had brought his daughter along with him. She had come of age, and he hoped to arrange a marriage for her to one of the leading Jews of the city. While Joseph was dining with the king, a beautiful dancing girl entered into the banquet hall, and Joseph was immediately smitten. Since Jews are forbidden by law to have relations with foreign women, Joseph told his brother of his predicament and entreated him to help him, not only by concealing his sin but also by arranging an opportunity for him to satisfy his desire. His brother readily agreed to help him, but he dressed his own daughter in beautiful clothes and brought her by night to sleep with him. Joseph, for his part, was too drunk to recognize her and slept with his brother's daughter. After this had happened a number of times, he fell even more madly in

love with her. He told his brother that he was endangering his life by falling in love with a dancing girl, whom the king might not be willing to give up to him. His brother then urged him to be anxious no longer, but rather to take joy in this woman whom he loved without fear and to take her as his wife. He told Joseph the truth: he had chosen to bring his own daughter into disgrace rather than allow him to come to shame. Joseph then praised him for his devotion and agreed to marry his daughter, by whom he fathered Hyrcanus.

Hyrcanus, while still only thirteen years of age, already showed such natural courage and intelligence that his brothers became jealous of his superior qualities. Once, when Joseph wanted to learn which of his sons exhibited an excellence of character, he sent them in turn to the most famous teachers of the day. The older brothers, because of their laziness and aversion to work, returned as foolish and unlearned as when they had left. Afterward, however, he sent his youngest son, Hyrcanus, a two days' journey into the wilderness to till the ground; he gave him three hundred yoke of oxen for the task but hid the yokestraps. When Hyrcanus realized that the yokestraps were missing, he ignored the advice of the oxdrivers to send someone to fetch them; this would only waste time as they awaited the return of the messengers. Rather, he conceived a plan that proved him wise beyond his years: he slaughtered ten yoke of oxen and, after distributing the meat among his hired workmen, cut the hides into straps, and with these he fastened the yokes. After he had thus tilled the ground which his father had assigned him, he returned. Joseph was well pleased with his cleverness; he praised his sharpness of mind and bold spirit and loved him even more, as if he were his only true son. As a result, Hyrcanus's brothers grew to despise him.

(7) It was at about this time that Joseph heard the news that a son had been born to King Ptolemy. All of the leading citizens of Syria and of Ptolemy's subject lands were setting out with great fanfare for Alexandria to celebrate the birth of the child.

Although Joseph himself was prevented on account of his age, he inquired of his sons whether one of them would go to the king's festivities. The older brothers all declined, saying their manners were too rustic for such society, but they suggested that he send Hyrcanus. Joseph heartily agreed and, calling Hyrcanus, asked him whether he was ready and willing to make the journey to the king. Hyrcanus replied that he was and added further that he would live well within his means and only require ten thousand drachmas for the trip. Such moderation pleased Joseph very much.

Soon afterward Hyrcanus suggested to his father that rather than send gifts from their residence in Jerusalem, he should instead send a letter to the slave in charge of his affairs in Alexandria,[1] so that he might provide Hyrcanus upon arrival with money to buy the most beautiful and lavish gifts he could find. Joseph, supposing that the cost of the gifts for the king would be ten talents, praised his son for his wise advice. He then proceeded to write a letter to Arion, the slave who managed all of the wealth that he had in Alexandria, the value of which was not less than three thousand talents. (Joseph's practice had been to send the money he had collected from Syria to Alexandria, and when the day approached on which his tribute was due to the king, to write to Arion to render payment.) With letter in hand, Hyrcanus set out for Alexandria. While he was on his way, however, his brothers wrote to all the friends of the king to kill him.

(8) Arriving in Alexandria, Hyrcanus delivered the letter to Arion. Arion asked him how many talents he would require—he expected that he would request ten talents or perhaps a bit more—but Hyrcanus replied that he would need a thousand. At this Arion became indignant, castigating him for choosing to live

1. Although Arion is a slave, like many stewards who managed the affairs of their masters in other cities, he could possess a great deal of authority on behalf of his master. It is one of the points of this episode, however, that Hyrcanus returns Arion to his rightful place.

so irresponsibly and reminding him how his father had amassed his fortune through hard work and the control of his desires; he should, in fact, follow the example of the very one who had given him life. No more than ten talents would he give him, and that for the sole purpose of purchasing gifts for the king. Hyrcanus, in response, became furious and had Arion thrown into chains. Queen Cleopatra, however, held Arion in the highest esteem, and so Arion's wife informed her of his imprisonment and begged her to rebuke the young Hyrcanus. Cleopatra accordingly made the entire matter known to the king. He sent a message to Hyrcanus and told him that he was amazed that, first of all, although he had been commissioned to come by his father, he had not yet appeared before him, and beyond that, he had imprisoned his father's manager of affairs. He commanded him to come and explain his conduct. But Hyrcanus—so it is reported—instructed the king's messenger to inform him that there was a law among his own people that prevented a person from partaking of a birthday sacrifice until he had entered the temple and made an offering to God.[2] It was for this reason that he himself had not at first come to him but had waited before he brought the gifts to the man who was his father's own benefactor. As for the slave Arion, he had punished him for disobeying the orders which he had been given. "It makes no difference," he added, "whether one is master over a few or master over many; if we do not punish such kind as this, you can be sure that even you will come to be treated shamefully by your subjects." When Ptolemy heard this, he erupted with laughter and greatly admired the high spirit of the lad. (9) When Arion learned that the king was so disposed, and that no help was likely to be forthcoming, he

2. How a Jew whose temple is in Jerusalem is supposed to make an offering to God is not clear. There were Jewish temples established in Egypt, but in this text his explanation is perhaps better understood as another ruse on the part of Hyrcanus.

paid over to Hyrcanus the thousand talents he had requested and was released from his chains.

Allowing three days to pass, Hyrcanus came by to greet the king and queen. They received him most graciously and entertained him generously on account of their regard for his father. But afterward, Hyrcanus went secretly to the slavedealers and purchased from them one hundred males for a talent each, well educated and in the prime of their youth, as well as one hundred females at the same price. When he was next invited with the leading citizens of the country to feast with the king, he found himself placed at the foot of the table, slighted on account of his youth by those who assigned places according to social rank. Further, all of those who reclined at table with him, after consuming the meat from their portions, heaped up the bones before him with the result that they covered his place at the table. Tryphon, the king's jester who was appointed to regale the guests with jokes during the drinking, saw this and, egged on by those reclining, stood up before the king and said, "My Lord, do you see the bones lying here before Hyrcanus? From this you might surmise that his father has stripped all of Syria, as his son has stripped these bones of their meat." The king laughed at Tryphon's words and asked Hyrcanus why so many bones were lying on the table before him. "It is quite understandable, my lord," responded Hyrcanus. "These men here are like dogs and eat the bones together with the meat." With this he pointed to the clean table on every side of him. "Human beings, on the other hand, consume the meat and throw the bones away, just as I, being a man, have done." The king was very impressed by his clever response, and to demonstrate approval of his urbane wit, he ordered everyone present to applaud.

On the next day, Hyrcanus paid a call to each of the king's friends and to everyone who held influence in the court and greeted each one. Of the servants at each household, however, he inquired what gift each of their masters was planning to bestow upon the king for his son's birthday. Some said their masters were planning to offer gifts worth ten talents, while others, whose masters were of especially high rank, said the gifts would be in proportion to their wealth. Hyrcanus, however, pretending to be upset at this, said that he could not match such splendid gifts; he had no more than five talents.

The servants, upon hearing this, reported it to their masters, who were only too pleased to hear that Joseph would fall from grace and offend the king with such a paltry gift. So when the day arrived and all the other leading citizens brought their gifts to the king—some believing they were quite magnanimous even though their gifts amounted to no more than twenty talents—Hyrcanus led out before them the male and female slaves he had purchased and gave to each of them a talent to carry; the boys he presented to the king, the girls to Cleopatra. While everyone, even the king and queen themselves, marveled at the unexpected lavishness of the gifts, Hyrcanus bestowed upon the friends of the king and those who waited upon him gifts worth many talents, so as to avoid any reprisal on their part. (It was, in fact, to these people whom Hyrcanus's brothers had written to destroy him.) Then Ptolemy, in admiration of the young man's generosity, commanded him to take whatever gift he wished. He asked for nothing more for himself than that the king write to his father and brothers concerning him. The king, in response, bestowed upon him both high honors and magnificent gifts, and wrote to his father and brothers and to all the administrators and government officials. Then he sent him away.

But when his brothers heard that Hyrcanus had been exalted so highly by the king and was returning home with such honors, they went out to intercept him and do away with him, even though their father knew of their plan. For although Joseph had hidden his displeasure for fear of the king, he was also exceedingly angry at Hyrcanus for spending such vast sums of money on the gifts, and he made no attempt to protect him. But when the brothers met up with him to do battle, he killed two of the brothers, along with many of the men with them, while the others escaped and took refuge in Jerusalem with Joseph. Hyrcanus also entered Jerusalem, but since no one would receive him and he feared for his life, he departed for the country beyond the Jordan River, and there remained, collecting tribute among the barbarians.

(10) It was at this time that Seleucus, surnamed Soter, began to rule over Asia; he was the son of Antiochus the Great. Hyrcanus's father, Joseph, also passed away, a truly worthy and high-minded man who, in his twenty-two years in the post of collecting the taxes of Syria, Phoenicia, and Samaria, raised the Jewish people from a level of poverty and weakness to a new period of opportunity and a more splendid way of life.[3]

(11) When Joseph died, however, strife arose among the people on account of his sons, for the elder brothers made war on Hyrcanus, the youngest of Joseph's children, thus dividing the people into two camps. The majority of the people joined forces with the elder brothers, as did Simon the high priest, since he had closer relations with them. Hyrcanus, on the other hand, could no longer entertain the hope of returning to Jerusalem and settled instead in the country across the Jordan River. There he fought continuously with the Arabs, killing many of them and taking others prisoner. He had a strong fortress built, constructed entirely of white marble up to the roof, with gigantic animals carved in it, and he enclosed the whole with a broad, deep moat. Cutting through the rockface of the mountain opposite his fortress, he hollowed out caves many stades in length. In these he made a number of rooms, some used for banqueting and others for sleeping and living quarters, and he made water abundantly available in them, both for enjoyment and for the decoration of the open spaces. But the entrance of the caves was made narrower, so that no more than one person could pass at a

3. Omitted in this translation is a short digression in which Josephus included a letter from Onias III to the Spartans, taken from *First Maccabees* 12:20.

time. This he had introduced as a precaution against the possibility of being besieged and taken by his brothers. He also created huge courts, in which he cultivated large, beautiful gardens, and the whole, when finished, he named Tyre. It is located between Arabia and Judea, beyond the Jordan River, not far from Heshbon.

Hyrcanus ruled this region for seven years, while Seleucus reigned over Syria, but when Seleucus died, his brother Antiochus, surnamed Epiphanes, came to power. Meanwhile Ptolemy, king of Egypt—also surnamed Epiphanes—died as well, leaving two sons who were still quite young. The elder was called Philometer and the younger Physcon. Hyrcanus, aware of Antiochus's tremendous power, and afraid that he would be captured and punished for what he had inflicted upon the Arabs, ended his life by his own hand. Antiochus then took possession of all his property.

## SUGGESTIONS FOR FURTHER READING

Collins, John J. *Between Athens and Jerusalem: Jewish Identity in the Hellenistic Diaspora,* pp. 73–75. New York: Crossroad, 1983.

Goldstein, Jonathan A. "Tales of the Tobaids." In *Christianity, Judaism, and Other Greco-Roman Cults,* pp. 85–123. Ed. Jacob Neusner. 3 vols. Leiden: Brill, 1975.

Gruen, Erich. *Heritage and Hellenism: The Reinvention of Jewish Tradition,* pp. 99–106. Berkeley: University of California Press, 1998.

Niditch, Susan. "Father–Son Folktale Patterns and Tyrant Typologies in Josephus' *Ant* 12:160–222." *Journal of Jewish Studies* 32 (1981): 47–55.

Wills, Lawrence M.. *The Jewish Novel in the Ancient World,* pp. 187–93. Ithaca, N.Y.: Cornell University Press, 1995.

TEN

# THE ROYAL FAMILY OF ADIABENE

When Rome could no longer control the Hellenistic kingdoms to the east, they became independent, at times allying with, at times fighting against Rome. Adiabene was one such kingdom. In his Jewish history *Antiquities* (20.2.1–4.3 §17–96), Josephus recounts the dramatic story of the royal family of Adiabene, who converted to Judaism, sided with Rome, and became patrons of public works in Jerusalem during the first century C.E. It is generally agreed by scholars that the narrative is based on a family chronicle much like *The Tobiad Romance,* and the present title has been applied to it for convenience.

The major characters are Queen Helena and her son Izates, who rises to become king. It is actually the conversions, first of Helena and then of Izates and his family, that precipitate a crisis. The conversion of the royal family sets off prejudices, petty jealousies, and opportunism that result in full-scale military campaigns. There is a pattern in how these conversions occur that is common in ancient literature. The aristocratic women become enamored of the new religion first. This is a common motif in the literature of this period: it is often stated, whether positively or negatively, that it is the wealthy women who welcome new religious practices. Scholars are not certain whether this motif reflects the historical pattern of the movement of some religions or is a literary topos based on a stereotype. Still, there may well be some historical kernel to this text; we do hear elsewhere of Queen Helena's conversion and benefactions to Jerusalem (Mishnah *Nazir* 3:6, *Yoma* 3:10; compare Pausanias 8.16.5). It would also be difficult for Josephus to falsify circumstances concerning an eastern monarch from the recent past.

The question of realism arises about another aspect of the conversions as well. A fascinating element of this narrative is the drama of the two Jewish travelers who come in succession to Adiabene and ultimately convert the royal family. The first traveler takes a more lenient view of the degree of observance required for a proselyte; the second is stricter in his interpretation and insists that Izates must be circumcised to be fully Jewish. These two have been likened to Paul and Peter in early Christianity, and the story is often used as evidence of two views of Jewish observance that were prevalent in this period. However, the correspondence to historical conditions of Jewish observance and types of missionary activity should not be pressed too far. There is a morality play at work here, and the first, more lenient spokesperson for Judaism may be a mere foil for the second. Izates' own courageous stand is based on a full commitment to the signs of Jewish identity. There is a certain similarity here to the view expressed in *Third Maccabees:* a fearless public commitment is necessary for Jewish identity in the Greco-Roman world. There should be no closet Jews. Further, God's providential eye will safeguard those Jews who faithfully exhibit their religious identity.

As with most of the narratives here, the characters' motives are always clear: the protagonists have pure motives and act from a devotion to God, the antagonists have base motives arising from their selfish desires. Izates' interactions with some of the eastern monarchs serve to reveal his generosity of spirit, pure motives, and above all, his wisdom. His recognition of the vicissitudes of life, even for those who are kings, sets him above the common ancient stereotype of the eastern monarch and closer to that of philosopher. (Compare, for instance, Solon before King Croesus of Lydia in Herodotus 1.29–33.)

Though the king had an older son by Helena, also named Monobazus, and indeed other children by his other wives, Izates was clearly his father's favorite, as though he were an only child. As a result, all of his half-brothers soon became envious; their resentment of their brother ran so deep that before long, it had turned to loathing. Although Monobazus perceived this, he excused their behavior, preferring to attribute their ill will not to any base motive on their part, but to their natural desire to win their father's affections. Fearing that Izates might nevertheless fall victim to his brothers' hatred, Monobazus decided, after bestowing a number of generous gifts upon him, to send him off to the king of Charax Spasini, Abennerigus, to whom he entrusted the boy's safety. King Abennerigus not only received the boy enthusiastically but offered him the hand of his daughter, Symmacho, in marriage, and he included in the dowry the control of a region which would provide Izates a substantial income.

(2.2) When Monobazus was old and saw that he had little time to live, he decided that it was time to see his son again before he died. He sent for him, and when he arrived, greeted him most warmly, granting to him a district called Carron, where Izates resided until his father's death. When that day came, Queen Helena summoned the nobles and satraps of the kingdom, along with the generals who had been set over the armies, and when they arrived, sounded them out on the issue of Izates' return: "You are well aware," she said, "that it was my husband's wish that Izates succeed him on the throne and that he considered Izates worthy of this honor. I, however, await your decision in this matter. For blessed indeed is he who receives rulership, not by the will of one, but when the majority wish him to have it." When she had spoken, they prostrated themselves before her as was their custom and replied that they would affirm the king's decision and gladly obey the young man, who had after all been rightly named as successor ahead of all the other brothers, just as all those present had in fact prayed he would. They further said that it was their wish that all of his brothers and relatives be executed before Izates was crowned, so that he might occupy the throne more securely. Putting all the relations to death would remove any anxiety Izates might suffer from the hatred and envy which they bore him. Helena thanked them on her own and Izates' behalf, but at the same time urged them to postpone any decision concerning the execution of the brothers until Izates might arrive to confirm it. Since, however, they could not convince her to carry through the execution, they entreated her instead for their own safety to keep the brothers under guard until his arrival. They also counseled her in the meantime to appoint some individual in whom she had the greatest trust to rule in his place. This seemed good advice to Helena; she placed her oldest son Monobazus on the throne, setting the diadem upon his head, giving him his father's signet ring and what they refer to as the *sampsera,* and urged him to take the reins of government until his brother arrived. When Izates heard that his father had died, he quickly returned and succeeded his brother Monobazus, who readily stepped aside for him.

(2.3) Before Izates returned, however, while he was still in Charax Spasini, a Jewish merchant named Ananias passed through and, after meeting on several occasions with the king's wives, taught them to worship God according to Jewish tradition. They in turn introduced him to Izates, whom he also won over with their assistance. Thus when Izates was summoned back to Adiabene to assume the throne, he urgently entreated Ananias to accompany him, which he did. As it also happened, Helena, Izates' mother, had been similarly instructed by another Jew, and she converted to the observance of their laws. When Izates arrived and acceded to the throne of Adiabene, and found his brothers and other kinsmen imprisoned, he became very upset over this state of affairs. Considering it on the one hand impious to kill them or to leave them bound in prison, and yet too risky to release them—for they surely harbored much resentment—he sent some of them along with their children to Claudius Caesar in Rome as hostages, and the rest to Artabanus, king of Parthia, under the same agreement.

(2.4) When he learned that his mother was very happy with

her observance of Jewish practices, Izates resolved to convert himself, though he assumed that he would not truly be a Jew unless he was circumcised, and he was prepared to follow through with that as well. When his mother learned of this, however, she tried to prevent him, saying that it would place him in a dangerous situation, for since he was a king, his subjects would surely rise in protest when they found that he was now devoting himself to strange and foreign observances, and they would never acquiesce to being ruled over by a Jew. She presented such arguments to him, and by every other means tried to prevent him from being circumcised, but Izates decided to place the whole question before Ananias for resolution. Ananias, it seems, not only agreed with the Queen-mother but went so far as to threaten to leave the country if he could not persuade Izates. He was afraid, he said, that if the conversion became generally known, he himself would likely be punished as the one guilty of teaching the king disreputable practices. He further pointed out that the king could worship the Divine without undergoing circumcision if he had sincerely decided to devote himself to the ancestral traditions of the Jews, for indeed they were more important than circumcision. Would not God pardon him if he acted thus out of compulsion and fear of his subjects? King Izates was for the time being persuaded by his arguments.

Nevertheless, he had not wholly given up his desire to be circumcised, and soon another Jew, named Eleazar, passed through from Galilee; he was considered much stricter in the observance of Jewish ancestral laws than was Ananias. When he arrived at court to offer greetings to the king, he came upon him reading the law of Moses and said, "Unknowingly, O king, you have violated the greatest precepts of the law, and as a result are guilty before God, for it is necessary not only to read the law, but to observe what is commanded in it. For how long will you remain uncircumcised? If, indeed, you have not yet read the law concerning circumcision, read it now, so that you may know how impious you have been." When the king heard this, he delayed no longer, but retired to another room, summoned his physician, and there had the rite performed.[1] Sending for his mother and his teacher Ananias, he confided to them that he had been circumcised. They were both immediately gripped with fear. If it became known that he had been circumcised, Izates would run the danger of losing his throne, since his subjects would not endure having a man as king who was so enamored of foreign practices, while Helena and Ananias would also be in danger; the blame for his conversion would surely fall upon them. God, however, saw to it that their worst fears were not realized, for although both Izates himself and his children were threatened with many dangers, God delivered them from their desperate plight by providing a means of deliverance. In this way, God proves that for those who abide in him, trusting in him alone, there will always be a reward for their piety.

(2.5) When Helena, Izates' mother, saw that the kingdom was enjoying a period of great peace and that her son was blessed and admired by all, even foreigners, on account of the foresight that God had bestowed upon him, she decided that she wanted to journey to Jerusalem to worship at the Temple of God, well-known to people everywhere, and to present thank-offerings there. She asked her son for permission, which he offered enthusiastically. He made the preparations for her journey and bestowed on her a large sum of money, escorting her much of the way. Her arrival in Jerusalem was advantageous for the citizens of that city, for at that time there was a severe famine, and many were perishing from lack of funds to purchase food. Queen Helena sent her servants, some to Alexandria to purchase grain at great expense, and others to Cyprus to bring back a cargo of dried figs. They quickly returned, loaded with provisions, which she proceeded to distribute to those who were hungry. For this

1. A slightly different account of the conversion of the royal family is found in *Midrash Rabbah* 46:10 on Genesis 17:11.

act of generosity she has left a very great name among our whole people. Her son Izates, upon hearing of the famine, also sent large sums of money to the Jerusalem leaders to distribute among the poor for relief from the severe conditions of the famine.

(3.1) It also happened that Artabanus, king of Parthia, discovered that his governors had entered into a conspiracy against him. Realizing that it was no longer safe for him to remain there, he repaired to the court of Izates, hoping thereby to secure his protection, and if possible a base from which he could regain his throne. He arrived there with about a thousand of his family and attendants, meeting Izates by chance along the way. Although he easily recognized Izates, the latter did not recognize him, and so after Artabanus halted close by him, he prostrated himself according to his native custom and said, weeping, "O king, do not ignore my plea, nor scorn your servant. Humbled by circumstances, I find that I, though recently a king, am now but a private citizen and very much in need of your help. If you also consider how unpredictable is one's good fortune, you may find that a little foresight would help us both, for if you do not offer me protection and help me to avenge myself, many other citizens will be emboldened to rise up and strike at their kings as well."

Though his head was bowed low, when Izates heard his name and saw him standing before him as a suppliant, wailing indignantly, he quickly dismounted from his horse and said, "Have courage, O king, and do not consider this reversal to be final; you will soon experience another. I shall be a better comrade-in-arms than you might have hoped for; I shall either reestablish you over the throne of Parthia, or lose my own."

(3.2) When Izates had said this, he helped Artabanus back upon his horse and proceeded along beside him on foot, honoring him in this way as the greater king. Artabanus, however, even more distressed to see this, swore both by his recent misfortunes and by the honor now shown him that he would dismount also unless Izates remounted his horse and rode before him. Acceding to his request, Izates jumped back on his horse, and led him to his kingdom. There he assigned him positions of honor in his councils and banquets. He did not judge him by his present circumstances, but by his former glory, considering reversals of fortune to be the common lot of humanity.

Izates next wrote to the Parthians and urged them to receive Artabanus back, swearing solemnly that he would guarantee a general amnesty from Artabanus for what they had done. The Parthians, although themselves willing to reinstate Artabanus, declared that they were unable to do so, since they had already entrusted the rule to another by the name of Cinnamus; they feared that to support Artabanus now would only embroil the country in civil war. When Cinnamus learned of their decision, however, he wrote to Artabanus himself. He had, so it happened, been raised by Artabanus and was marked by a kind and noble character. He therefore urged Artabanus to place his trust in him and return to reclaim his throne, which he did. Upon his return, Cinnamus met him and prostrated himself. He then addressed him as king, taking the royal diadem off of his own head and placing it on that of Artabanus.

(3.3) Thus it was through the intervention of Izates that Artabanus was again placed upon the throne, after having been previously removed by the leading citizens. Artabanus always remembered the benevolent actions of Izates and had opportunity to bestow upon him the highest honor he could offer: Izates was permitted by him to wear the tiara upright and to sleep on a bed of gold, distinctions that are normally reserved for the kings of Parthia. He also handed over to him control of a large and fruitful region called Nisibis, which was formerly part of Armenia, where the Macedonians had established Mygdonian Antioch. In this way Izates received many great honors from the Parthian king.

(3.4) Not long afterwards, Artabanus died, and his kingdom passed to his son Vardanes, who approached Izates and proposed that he join him in a campaign against the Romans. Izates however, would have nothing of it, since he knew well the might and successes of the Romans, and he thought Vardanes was attempting the impossible. What is more, he had already sent five sons, still quite young, to Jerusalem to be thoroughly trained in Jewish language and learning, as well as his mother, who had gone to worship at the Temple; he was thus reluctant to antagonize the Romans. He further attempted to discourage Vardanes from his plan by continually describing the strength and remarkable achievements of the Romans. This, he thought, would be sufficient to frighten him and cool his desire to make war upon them, but Vardanes reacted instead with outrage and immediately declared war on Izates. Nevertheless, what he hoped to gain from such a venture eluded him, as God dashed all of his hopes of glory. For when the Parthians heard of Vardanes' plans to attack Rome, they assassinated him and turned control of the government over to his brother, Gotarzes. Not much later, a court conspiracy claimed his life as well, and another brother, Vologeses, succeeded to the throne. He entrusted positions of power to his two brothers by the same father; to the elder, Pacorus, he gave Media, and to the younger, Tiridates, he gave Armenia.

(4.1) When Izates' brother Monobazus and his relatives saw that Izates had won the admiration of people everywhere on account of his reverence of God, they were also eager to forsake their own ancestral customs and take up those of the Jews. When this became generally known, however, the leading citizens became furious. Nevertheless, they concealed their ill will for the moment until they could find an opportunity to exact punishment on them. They soon wrote to Abias, king of the Arabs, promising large sums of money to him if he would agree to send an expeditionary force against their king. For their part they assured Abias that they would withdraw from Izates at the first sign of battle and in this way punish him for despising their ancestral customs. Swearing oaths of loyalty to each other, they urged Abias to move as quickly as possible. The Arabian king agreed to their plan and, setting out with a large army, arrayed his men against the army of Izates. As they were about to engage each other, the Adiabenian nobles, as they had agreed, withdrew from

Izates and turned tail and ran, pretending to be caught up in some dreadful panic. Izates, though now realizing that the nobles were involved in some treachery, did not succumb to fear. When he returned to camp, he discovered by inquiries that the nobles were in league with the Arab king, and he executed those implicated. On the next day he took the field and killed a great number of the enemy, putting the rest to flight. Pursuing the king himself, he drove him into a fortress called Arsamus and, after laying an unrelenting siege, finally took it. He plundered it of its great wealth and returned to Adiabene. Abias, however, was not taken alive, for when he found himself totally surrounded, he chose to kill himself rather than fall into the hands of Izates.

(4.2) Although the nobles of Adiabene had failed in their first attempt—God having delivered them over to the king—others lost little time in writing again, this time to Vologeses, king of the Parthians, urging him to kill Izates and establish someone of Parthian descent on the throne. They despised their own king, so they said, for abrogating their ancestral religion and becoming a devotee of foreign practices. When the Parthian king heard their offer, though ready himself to act, he still lacked any plausible pretext for initiating hostilities. He therefore sent to Izates and demanded back the honors which his father had heaped upon him, and threatened war if he did not comply. Although greatly disturbed to hear this, Izates was convinced that returning the gifts would bring general disapproval, since it would appear that he had done so out of fear. He also knew that even if the Parthian king got his demands, he would still take action, and so in this hour of danger he decided to commit his life into the hands of God the protector. He was convinced that God had been his greatest ally, and he placed his wives and children in his strongest fortress, put all his grain in storehouses, burned the grass that stood in the fields and the pastures, and awaited the enemy's arrival.

The Parthian king, by forced march, arrived sooner than expected with a large army of infantry and cavalry. At the river bounding Adiabene and Media, he erected makeshift fortifications, while Izates took the field with six thousand cavalry and set up his own encampment not far off. A messenger, dispatched by Vologeses, arrived at Izates' camp and proceeded to recount to him the immense power of the Parthian Empire, how it stretched from the Euphrates to Bactria, and how many client-kings were subject to it. Izates, he threatened, would pay the just penalty if he were found to be ungrateful to his masters, and not even the God whom he worshipped would be able to rescue him from the king's hands. When the messenger had finished, Izates replied that, although he was aware that the power of the Parthian army was greater than his own, he knew that God was greater still than all human might. With such a reply, he turned to the supplication of God. He threw himself upon the ground and befouled his head with ashes, and then fasted, together with his wife and children, calling upon God all the while: "Surely it is not for nothing, O Lord and master, that I have been allowed to taste of your bounty, and came to consider you truly as the first and only Lord of all things. Come, be my defender and ally, protecting me from my enemies, not only for my sake, but because they have dared now to challenge your power." Izates thus lamented loudly, through tears and moans, as God heard his cry.[2] On that very night, Vologeses received letters bearing the news that a large army of Dahae and Sakae, taking advantage of his absence, had invaded and begun to lay waste to Parthia, leaving Vologeses to break camp and retreat without attaining his goal. Thus protected by the providence of God, Izates escaped the threat of the Parthian army.

(4.3) It was not long after this that Izates passed away. He had been king for twenty-four of his fifty-five years, leaving twenty-four sons and twenty-four daughters at his passing. He com-

2. Although there are similarities between Izates' prayer and that of Hezekiah in 2 Kings 19:15–19, the former is clearly more personal and rendered along the lines of the women's prayers in the novels in the present collection.

manded that his brother Monobazus succeed to his throne, since he should be rewarded for faithfully safeguarding the throne for him after his father's death while he was still away. His mother, Helena, very grieved when she heard of the death of her son—as one would expect when a mother is deprived of a son so pious—nevertheless received some consolation when she heard that the succession would pass to her older son, and she hastened to his side. Soon after arriving in Adiabene, however, weighed down by her age and the pain of her grief, she breathed her last and also passed away. Taking the bones of his mother and brother, Monobazus sent them to Jerusalem with instruction to bury them in the three pyramids that Helena had constructed a half-mile from the city.

## SUGGESTIONS FOR FURTHER READING

Collins, John J. *Between Athens and Jerusalem: Jewish Identity in the Hellenistic Diaspora,* pp. 163–67. New York: Crossroad, 1983.

Neusner, Jacob. "The Conversion of Adiabene to Judaism." *Journal of Biblical Literature* 83 (1964): 60–66.

Schiffman, Lawrence H. "The Conversion of the Royal House of Adiabene in Josephus and Rabbinic Sources." In *Josephus, Judaism, and Christianity,* pp. 293–312. Ed. Louis H. Feldman and Gohei Hata. Detroit: Wayne State University Press, 1987.

Wills, Lawrence M. *The Jewish Novel in the Ancient World,* pp. 206–11. Ithaca, N.Y.: Cornell University Press, 1995.

# PART III

## *Jewish Novelistic Testaments*

ELEVEN

# TESTAMENT OF JOSEPH

The *Testament of Joseph* is one of the *Testaments of the Twelve Patriarchs,* a collection of what purport to be the last will and testament of each of the twelve sons of Jacob. The testament motif is found in the Hebrew Bible (for example, Genesis 49–50, Deuteronomy 31–34) but became very popular as an independent genre among Jews. There is evidence of increased use of wills at this time in Hellenistic culture, and testaments of famous Greek philosophers were being composed as well. Just as in Greek culture a testament of a revered figure from the ancient past was the perfect vehicle to exhort the audience to certain virtues, so also in Jewish culture. Jewish literature from the Greco-Roman period includes more testaments than any other genre except apocalypses.

Although testaments vary considerably in their execution (a comparison of the three testaments in this collection demonstrates that), there is generally a common outline to them. As a patriarch's death approaches, he calls together his children and makes his testament. He recounts aspects of his life story, emphasizes certain virtues, predicts future events, and then the text concludes with an account of his death and burial. This outline of the typical testament would not immediately remind one of the novel, but the combination of virtue, psychology, and the events of a person's life naturally gave rise to an exploration of some of the same issues the novels of the period dealt with. *Testament of Joseph* demonstrates how this process occurs: the testament outline is simply opened up to include more and more narrative detail. It is thus clearly transitional to the novel, and it is not a large step to the much more thoroughly novelistic *Testament of Job* and *Testament of Abraham* that follow.

The *Testament of Joseph* recounts part of the story of Joseph as known from Genesis 37–50. It falls into separate parts illustrating two different virtues: self-control (*sophrosune*) in the first half and patient endurance (*hypomone*) in the second. It has also been argued that these two parts derive from different hands, and there is certainly much to be said for this multiple authorship. In the first, Joseph is a stalwart hero of resistance to the temptations of Potiphar's wife, which are enumerated and described beyond what was present in Genesis. In the second, which actually comes from an earlier point in the biblical Joseph story, he is a much more passive and introspective victim, mysteriously refusing to tell anyone that he is not a slave but a free man, even when he clearly could. There is a sort of ascetic ideal being presented in this second half, in which Joseph chooses to sacrifice his own self-interest to that of others, even if they do not deserve it. Joseph reflects directly on his self-sacrifice, which is above and beyond the call of family duty: "I wanted to weep, but held back my tears, because I did not want to bring shame upon my brothers. 'I know nothing about this,' I told them. 'I am a slave.'"

The irregularities in the narrative order of events in *Testament of Joseph* indicate that the novel form was not full-blown here but only present in a larval stage. Note, for example, that not only are the two halves reversed relative to the Genesis account, but even in the details there is an illogical order: Potiphar's wife, in order to trick Joseph into lying with her, pretends to love him as a mother at one point, even though in the previous scene she has openly propositioned him. All of the actions in this text are meant to be typical and not linear. The logic of this testament is based on the demonstration of virtues, not the chronological order of events.

Still, though the driving logic is not yet that of a novel, there are already clear parallels to the later Greek novels. Joseph's resistance to Potiphar's wife is similar to the many scenes in Greek novels that were influenced by the Phaedra legend in Euripides' *Hippolytus.* Joseph's encounters with Potiphar's wife reflect eroticism, but also the psychological exploration of the driven woman. As in the Greek novels she is the victim of "lovesickness" as she threatens the morally upright protagonist. The second half has fewer direct parallels to Greek novels but nevertheless manages to create an almost claustrophobic sense of the passive hero as an insect caught in a web. It may relate to the ascetic ideal of *Testament of Job* and later Christian asceticism and is evidently satirized in the passive hero of *Testament of Abraham.*

Scholars have debated the original language of the *Testaments of the Twelve Patriarchs,* their date, and whether they were originally Jewish or Christian. Jewish testaments are known in Hebrew and Aramaic, but *Testaments of the Twelve Patriarchs* was probably composed in Greek. The date, however, is uncertain; they could have been written anytime between the second century B.C.E. and the second century C.E. These Jewish texts were also preserved and transmitted by Christians, who added occasional theological embellishments. The *Testament of Joseph,* however, is evidently wholly Jewish, except for one dream vision near the end (not included here).

## *Testament of Joseph*

(1) A copy of the testament of Joseph.

When he was about to die, he called his sons and his brothers together and said to them:

My brothers and my children,
Listen to Joseph, the one who is loved by Israel.
Pay close attention to what I have to say to you.
I have seen, in the course of my life, both envy and death,
But I did not stray; I persevered in the truth of the Lord.
My brothers here despised me, but I was beloved by the Lord.
They tried to kill me, but the God of my fathers protected me.
They lowered me into a pit, but the Most High raised me up.
They sold me into slavery, but the Master of all set me free.
I was taken captive, but his strong hand came to my aid.
I was overcome with hunger, but the Lord himself nourished me.
I was alone, but God comforted me.
I was weak, but the Lord watched over me.
I was in prison, and the Savior acted graciously toward me.
I was in bonds, and he released me.
I stood accused, and he testified on my behalf,
I was accosted by the bitter words of the Egyptians, and he rescued me.
I was a slave, and he exalted me.

(2) A chief officer of Pharaoh entrusted his household to me. I was engaged in a struggle with a shameless woman, who pressed me hard to transgress with her, but the God of my father rescued me from a scorching flame. I was imprisoned, beaten, mocked, but the Lord showed me mercy in the eyes of the prison-keeper.

For the Lord will not abandon those who fear him,
Neither to darkness, nor chains, nor sufferings, nor difficult circumstances.
For God does not act shamefully, as does a man,
Nor shrink in fear, like a son of man,
Nor like one born of earth is he weak or frightened,
But in all these things he stands firm
And offers comfort in many ways,
Even though he may withdraw for a time in order to test the disposition of the soul.
With ten temptations he proved me worthy.

In all of these I persevered,
For perseverance is a powerful medicine,
And endurance offers many blessings.

(3) How often the Egyptian woman threatened me with death! How often did she hand me over to her punishments, only to call me back and threaten me! I never agreed to lie with her, but all the while, she would say to me, "You can become the master of my entire household and rule over all of us, if you will only give yourself up to me." But I recalled the words of my father and, returning to my chamber, wept and prayed to the Lord. During those seven years I fasted, and yet I appeared to the Egyptians as one who lived in luxury—for those who fast out of reverence for God take on a radiant glow. While my master was away, I drank no wine. For three days at a time I took my food and gave it to the poor and ill. Each morning I awoke early and prayed to the Lord, weeping over the Egyptian woman from Memphis, for she never gave me a moment's rest, even entering my chambers at night on the pretext of visiting with me. Because she herself had no male offspring, she pretended to consider me as her son. For a time she would embrace me as a son, but I became aware that she was trying to lure me into her bed. When I realized this, I was tormented to the point of death. When she departed, I regained my senses, and realizing then the depths of her conceits, I grieved for her for many days. I spoke to her words of the Most High, hoping that he might turn her away from her evil desire.

(4) How often, indeed, did she flatter me by addressing me as a holy man, deceitfully praising my self-control in the presence of her husband, only to try to seduce me when we were alone. She would honor me publicly, as a man of true continence, but when we were alone would say to me, "Do not worry about my husband! He is now so totally convinced of your restraint that even if someone were to tell him about us, he would never believe it." During all these trials I prostrated myself, begging God to rescue me from her treachery. But when she could not prevail

in these matters, again she came to me, this time for instruction in the word of God, saying to me, "If you want me to forsake all my idols, lie with me; I shall persuade my husband to abstain from idols, and we shall live in accordance with the law of your Lord."

But I said to her, "The Lord has no desire for people to worship him in uncleanness, nor does he accept adulterers, but rather those who approach him with a pure heart and undefiled mouth." But she was consumed with jealousy, still wanting to fulfill her desire. I, however, continued all the more to fast and pray that the Lord would rescue me from her.

(5) On another occasion she said to me, "If it is adultery you are opposed to, I shall kill my husband with poison, and then take you as my husband."

"Madam, show due reverence for the Lord!" I said, tearing my robe. "Do not do this wicked thing, lest you be utterly destroyed! Rest assured that I shall tell everyone of the evil you have planned!" She then became afraid and, begging me to tell no one of her wicked scheme, departed from my room. She continued, however, to ply me with gifts and all sorts of pleasantries.

(6) Afterward, she sent me food mixed with magical enchantments, but when the eunuch entered carrying the bowl, I looked up and perceived instead a horrific man, holding out to me a sword with the bowl, and I realized that it was a trick to lead me astray. After he left I wept, having tasted none of the food that he brought. A day later she came to me, and when she saw the food said to me, "Why have you not eaten any of this food?"

"Because," I said to her, "you have filled it with deadly enchantments. How could you say, 'I will never approach idols but only the Lord'? Now then know that the God of my father revealed your evil to me through an angel, but I have kept the food for this reason: it is a testimony against you, so that if you see it you might repent. But so that you may learn that the evil of the irreligious cannot overcome the self-control of those who revere God, now I shall take some of this and eat it in your presence." And when I had said this I prayed, "May the God of my fathers and the angel of Abraham be with me." And then I ate. When she saw this, she fell down upon her face at my feet and began to weep. I helped her to her feet and admonished her, and she agreed that she should no longer commit this impiety.

(7) But her heart was still inclined toward evil, and she continued devising ways to ensnare me. At one point she collapsed, groaning, even though she was not ill. When her husband saw her thus, he said to her, "Why are you so grieved?"

"I am heartsick," she replied, "and I am suffering deep within my soul." He tried to cure her by reasoning with her, but she found an opportunity while her husband was outside to run in to my chambers and she said, "If you will not lie with me, I shall hang myself, or else throw myself off a cliff!"

I realized that the spirit of Beliar had possessed her, and so I prayed to the Lord and said to her, "You wretched woman, why are you so addled and confused, and blinded by sin? You know very well that if you kill yourself, then Astetho, your husband's concubine who is so envious of you, will beat your children, and you will wipe all memory of yourself off the face of the earth."

"See then," she cried out, "you do love me! It is enough for now that you are concerned for my welfare and that of my children, and I shall keep alive some hope of satisfying my desire." She did not realize, however, that it was on account of my God that I said this, rather than her, for when people fall under the spell of lustful desires and are enslaved by them, as she indeed was, even if they were to hear some good word spoken, they perceive it as supporting their own twisted obsession. (8) So I tell you, my children, it was about the sixth hour when she left my room. I knelt and prayed to the Lord the whole day and night, crying and entreating the Lord to release me from her. Then at dawn I arose.

Finally, it happened that she grabbed hold of my garments and tried to force me to lie with her. I could tell that she was mad when she grabbed my tunic, so I shook loose, left it behind and ran away naked. She, however, kept it and brought false accusations against me, and her husband came and threw me into prison in his house. On the next day he had me whipped and sent me to the Pharaoh's prison. While I was in bonds, the Egyptian woman was overcome with grief. She came and heard about me, that though I was kept in the house of darkness, I gave thanks to the Lord, sang songs of praise, and rejoiced with a glad heart, glorifying my God because through her false accusation I was set free from this Egyptian woman.

(9) She often continued, however, to send word to me, saying, "Please fulfill my desire. I shall release you from prison and bring you up out of your darkness." But I did not even consider yielding to her, for God loves the person more who is faithful in his self-control while in the pit of darkness than him who feasts luxuriantly in royal chambers. And if one lives with self-restraint, and at the same time longs for glory—and if the Most High considers that it is an appropriate reward—then God bestows this as well, as he did for me.

And often, in the dead of the night, although she was ill, she would come down to my prison cell and listen to me as I prayed, and whenever I became aware of her sighs and groans, I ceased praying. For when I was in her house, she used to come to me, uncovering her arms and legs so that I might lie with her. And she was indeed very beautiful—especially when she had made herself up to lead me astray! But the Lord protected me from all her designs.

(10) See, then, my children, how many things patient endurance, prayer, and fasting can accomplish. Thus you also, if you pursue self-control and purity, patience and prayer and fasting with a humble heart, the Lord will dwell among you, because he loves self-control. Wherever the Most High dwells, even if you should encounter envy, or slavery, or false accusation, the Lord who abides with the one who practices self-control will not only save him from these ills, but will also exalt and glorify him as he did me. For these problems arise for all people, whether in deed or word or thought.

Although my brothers knew well how my father loved me, I was never conceited. Even for one so young I revered God in my thoughts, understanding as I did that all things must eventually pass away. I was not aroused by evil notions, but I honored my brothers, even remaining silent for their sake when they sold me to the Ishmaelites, did not let on that I was a son of Jacob, a very important and righteous man. (11) And you, then, my children, in every act keep the reverence of God before your eyes and honor your brothers, for everyone who does the law of the Lord will be loved by him.

When I was taken away by the Ishmaelites, they asked me, "Are you a slave?"

"I am a slave of their household," I replied, so as not to bring shame upon my brothers.

But their leader said, "You are no slave, for I can tell that from your appearance." I told them, however, that I was their slave, and so when we arrived in Egypt, they began to fight among themselves to see who would put up his money and lay claim to me. They all agreed, however, to deposit me in Egypt with the merchant in charge of their trading post until they returned again with their goods. The Lord disposed the merchant very favorably toward me, and he entrusted to me the running of his household. God blessed him through all my efforts and greatly increased his profits in gold, silver, and trade. There I remained for three months.

(12) At that time, however, the woman from Memphis, Potiphar's wife, arrived in a covered chariot with great splendor, because she had heard about me from her eunuchs. She said to her husband, "It is through the services of a certain young Hebrew man that this merchant has become so rich. They say that, in fact, he was stolen out of the land of Canaan. Now you can take this opportunity to render justice by confiscating him and taking him into our household. The God of the Hebrews will bless you, because it is heaven itself which is smiling upon him."

(13) Believing her words, Potiphar ordered the merchant to be brought forward and then said to him, "What is this I hear, that you steal persons from the land of Canaan and sell them as slaves?"

The merchant immediately fell upon his face and said, "I beg of you, Lord, I have no idea what you are talking about!"

"Where then did you get this Hebrew slave?" demanded Potiphar.

"The Ishmaelites deposited him with me until they returned," replied the other, but Potiphar was not convinced, and commanded that he be stripped and beaten.

When, however, the man persisted in his account, Potiphar said, "Bring the slave here."

When I was brought to Potiphar, I prostrated myself before him, for he was third in rank of all Pharaoh's officers. Then taking me aside from the trader, he asked, "Are you a slave or a free man?"

"A slave," I answered.

"Whose slave are you?" he asked.

"The Ishmaelites'."

"How did you become their slave?" he inquired further.

"They bought me in the land of Canaan."

"It is clear you are lying!" he said, and immediately commanded that I also be stripped and beaten.

(14) But when the Egyptian woman through her door saw me being whipped—for her residence was nearby—she sent to her husband and said, "You are committing a grave injustice! It is a free man who was kidnapped that you are punishing, as though he were guilty of some crime!"

Since I did not alter my account even though I was being beaten, he commanded instead that I be confined in prison until my owners returned. But his wife said to him, "Why do you shackle this high-born youth who was stolen, when he should have been set free and be attended to by servants?" In reality, however, she wanted to see me to indulge her sinful desires, but I was completely unaware of this.

Her husband answered her, "It is not lawful for Egyptians to confiscate property of others without evidence of wrongdoing." This was his judgment concerning the merchant, but as for me, he said that I would have to remain in chains.

(15) After twenty-four days, the Ishmaelites returned. Because they had heard that Jacob my father was mourning for me,

they asked me, "Why did you tell us that you were a slave? We have found out that you are the son of a great man in the land of Canaan. Your father is now dressed in sackcloth and ashes, mourning you."

When I heard this, my spirit was moved and my heart sank within me. I wanted to weep but held back my tears, because I did not want to bring shame upon my brothers. "I know nothing about this," I told them. "I am a slave."

Still, they decided to sell me, lest I be found in their possession. They feared that my father might come and exact a brutal vengeance upon them, for they had heard that Jacob was considered a great man by God and people alike.

The merchant then said to them, "Free me from Potiphar's judgment!"

They therefore came to me and asked, "Say that you were purchased by us for silver, then we shall all be cleared of any wrongdoing."

(16) The woman from Memphis also said to her husband, "Buy the young man, for I hear that he is about to be sold." She therefore sent a eunuch to the Ishmaelites to try to purchase me, but after negotiating with them for a bit, he decided he was unwilling to meet their price and came away. When the eunuch told his mistress that they had set the price too high, she sent a second eunuch with the instructions, "Even if they ask as much as two minas of gold, do not hold back, but buy him and bring him here." The eunuch went and gave them eighty pieces of gold for me but told his mistress that he paid one hundred. Even though I was aware of this, I kept silent, lest the servant be disgraced.

(17) See, then, my children, how many things I endured so as not to bring my brothers to shame. You, therefore, should love one another, overlooking each other's shortcomings in patient endurance. For God takes joy in harmony among siblings, and in the conscious inclination of a pure heart that takes pleasure in goodness.

When my brothers came to Egypt, they found that I had returned their silver to them and did not reproach them, but rather gave them comfort. After the death of Jacob my father, I loved them even more, and anything they wanted I provided for them in abundance. I saw to it that they lacked for nothing; all that I possessed was theirs. Their sons were my sons, and my sons were like their slaves. Their well-being was my well-being; their suffering, my suffering; every sickness they experienced was my sickness; their wishes were my wishes. I did not hold myself in higher esteem than them on account of my reputation and honor, but considered myself as one of the least of them.

(18) If, therefore, my children, you live in accord with the Lord's commandments, he will exalt you and bless you with good things forever. And if someone wants to harm you, continue to do good and pray for him, and the Lord shall deliver you from every evil. You can see, therefore, that because of my humility and long-suffering endurance I was able to take a daughter of the priest of Heliopolis as wife and was also given one hundred talents of gold as dowry, and the Lord has now made them my servants. He also made me very handsome, more distinguished than all the handsome men of Israel, and preserved me into my old age, strong and distinguished, so that I was even like Jacob in every way.

*[Omitted here is chapter 19, a Christian interpolation of a dream of things to come, after which the original text continues.]*

(20) I know that after my death the Egyptians will oppress you, but God will avenge you and bring you into all the blessings promised to your ancestors. Carry my bones along with you, because while you are carrying them there the Lord will be with you in the light, but Beliar will be with the Egyptians in darkness. Take also your mother Aseneth and bury her near Rachel, my mother, at Ephrath.

After Joseph had said these things, he stretched out his feet and fell into a peaceful sleep. All Israel and all Egypt mourned him greatly. During the Exodus from Egypt the Israelites took along the bones of Joseph and buried him in Hebron with his ancestors. He lived to be one hundred and ten years old.

## SUGGESTIONS FOR FURTHER READING:

Collins, John J. *Between Athens and Jerusalem: Jewish Identity in the Hellenistic Diaspora,* pp. 154–62. New York: Crossroad, 1983.

Nickelsburg, George W. E. *Jewish Literature Between the Bible and the Mishnah,* pp. 231–41. Philadelphia: Fortress, 1981.

———. ed. *Studies on the Testament of Joseph.* Missoula, Mont.: Scholars Press, 1975.

Wills, Lawrence M. *The Jewish Novel in the Ancient World,* pp. 163–70. Ithaca, N.Y.: Cornell University Press, 1995.

TWELVE

# TESTAMENT OF JOB

The *Testament of Job,* dated to about the first century B.C.E. or first century C.E., follows the testament form in many respects—there is a deathbed scene of a patriarch, the recounting of his virtue, his moral exhortations, his death and burial, and the lament over his death—but it is much more narrative in its conception than is *Testament of Joseph.* Here the author's goal is to give a complete story of Job and his patient endurance (*hypomone*). Job in the Hebrew Bible may not seem patient—he complains from beginning to end—but he is remembered in *Testament of Job* and in Christian tradition for his piety and perseverance. Somewhat like the biblical Job, the protagonist here also engages in a series of dialogues with different characters: an angel, his wife, Satan, the four interlocutors from the biblical book (now kings), and his three daughters.

In the biblical Book of Job, Job at first refuses to condemn God when Satan takes away his family and possessions. When Satan attacks Job's person, however, the protagonist begins a thirty-five–chapter plaint over God's abandonment. This is what gives the biblical book its center and artistic vision. In *Testament of Job,* in contrast, Job remains steadfast in his devotion to God and never wavers for a moment. In this way he remains a hero of patient endurance throughout. Job is beset with lesions and worms, as in the biblical book, and is also forced to leave his city and live on the dung heap outside of town, which becomes his place of residence for forty-eight years. Further, this more steadfast hero of virtue accepts his life of discipline bravely: "My flesh was full of worms, and if a worm fell off, I would pick it up and return it to the same place saying, 'Remain there in the spot where you were placed until you are instructed by the one who commands you.'" One can see that beyond anything that was in the biblical book, this Job text is advocating an ascetic ethos, a new element in Jewish life in this period that would later be emphasized by Christians but deemphasized in rabbinic Judaism.

Job's actions are part of his religious discipline that will allow him to perceive reality on two levels: on the earthly, where he is the victim of a horrible injustice, and on the heavenly, where his true identity is oriented and where he will ultimately be received. This is an insight that he will try unsuccessfully to communicate to his wife but will finally communicate to his daughters. At the end he bequeaths to them three magical sashes, by which they are able to speak in an angelic tongue. Although this novelistic work also aims to entertain, there is a very pious and even mystical goal; the *Testament of Job* is essentially a novel that affirms this religious insight.

In addition to parallels to the Book of Job (and especially the Greek translation of the biblical book), there are similarities to other biblical traditions and texts of this period. Job's problems begin when he destroys a pagan temple that was erected beside his estate, a rejection that is similar to the legendary accounts of Abraham. A mystical element in *Testament of Job,* the sash that bestows prophetic powers, is similar to that put on by Aseneth during her conversion interlude. Job is depicted as the suffering righteous man who sets his mind on immortality and is vindicated by God, as in *Wisdom of Solomon* 2–5. Similarities have also been seen both to the Therapeutae/Therapeutrides, a communal group of Jews described by Philo in *On the Contemplative Life,* and to later Jewish mysticism. Aside from these specific parallels, *Testament of Job* also has overall similarities to two groups of ancient texts. A general similarity to the Greek novels is seen in the descent of the aristocratic protagonists into lower-class conditions as a sort of hell. A similarity can also be seen to the Christian gospels, in that Job is a persecuted and vindicated righteous person, the benefactor of the poor and suffering, who is tested by Satan. As in the Gospel of Luke, Satan also departs, only to return later. Job also dies, and there is a cult of remembrance established for him similar to that found at the end of the gospels.

## *Testament of Job*

(1) On the day when Job fell ill and wanted to settle his affairs, he called his seven sons and three daughters, whose names were Tersi, Choros, Hyon, Nike, Phoros, Phiphe, Kryon, Hemera, Kassia, and Amaltheia's Horn.[1] He called his ten children and said, "Gather round me, my children, and I will tell you all that happened to me and what the Lord did for me, for I am your father Job, who exhibits great endurance, and you are a chosen and honored race from the seed of Jacob, your mother's father. I am from the sons of Esau, and the brother of Nereus. Your mother is Dinah, with whom I begot you. My first wife died, however, along with ten other children in a tragic death. Listen now, children, and I will tell you all the things that happened to me.

(2) My name was Jobab before the Lord renamed me Job. When I was called Jobab, I used to live very near a venerated idol. As I watched the whole-burnt offerings constantly being offered

1. The three last names correspond to the names given to Job's daughters in the Greek version of the Bible (Job 42:14). The last of them, and some of the other names given here, correspond to Greek mythological figures. Amaltheia's Horn is the Greek cornucopia or horn of plenty.

up to it, I wondered, "Could this be the god who created heaven and earth and the sea and even our very selves? How can I know?"

(3) And one night, as I was sleeping, I heard a loud voice, a voice that spoke from the midst of a bright light, saying, "Jobab, Jobab!"

"Yes," I answered, "here I am!"

"Get up," said the voice, "and I will show you who this is whom you wish to know. The one to whom they bear whole-burnt offerings and to whom they make their libations is not God, but the power of the Devil which leads human nature astray."

When I heard this, I fell down in awe upon my bed and said, "Oh my lord, who has come to save my soul, I beg you, if this is indeed the place of Satan, in which people are deceived, give me the authority and I will go and purge his place so that we no longer make libations to him. And who here could prevent me, since I rule this region?"

(4) From the light came an answer: "You will be able to purge his temple, but I will also show you other things that the Lord commanded me to relate to you."

"Everything he commands his servant," I answered, "I will hear and do."

Again he spoke, "Thus says the Lord: If you try to purge and destroy the place of Satan, he will rise up in anger against you to do battle, although he will not be able to kill you. He will, however, inflict many plagues upon you and strip you of all your possessions, and kill your children. But if you endure, I will make your name renowned for all generations until the close of the age. I will also return your possessions to you twice over, so that you may know that the Lord shows no partiality, bestowing good things on everyone who is obedient. And at the resurrection you will be raised up to become like an athlete who spars and endures many labors but receives the crown. You will then know that the Lord is just and true and strong, imbuing with strength those whom he has chosen."

(5) "And," my children, I replied to him, "I will not back down but will endure to the point of death."

When I had received the angel's seal, my children, and he had departed from me, I arose the next night and, taking with me fifty servants, entered the temple of the idol and razed it to the ground. I then withdrew again into my own house and ordered that the doors be secured. (6) Hear me, children, and marvel, for as soon as I entered my house and secured the doors, I commanded my doormen, "If anyone comes today asking for me, do not inform me, but say, 'He does not have time; he is inside, occupied with an urgent matter.'"

And while I was inside, Satan, disguised as a beggar, knocked at the door and said to the doormaid, "Inform Job that I wish to speak with him."

The doormaid came in and reported this to me, and I told her to say to him that I did not have time now. (7) So Satan departed, put a bag on his shoulders, and returned, saying to the doormaid, "Say to Job, 'Give me a loaf of bread from your own hands for me to eat.'"

But I gave the maid a burnt loaf to give to him and told her to say, "Do not expect to eat any more from my loaves, for I am estranged from you."

Now the doormaid, who did not know that he was Satan, was ashamed to give him a burnt loaf covered with ashes, so she took a good loaf of her own and gave it to him. He took it and, knowing what had happened, said to the maid, "Go back, you wicked slave, and get me the loaf that was given to you!"

Stricken with grief, she began to weep and said, "You are right! I am a wicked slave, because I did not do what my master commanded me." She returned and brought him the burnt loaf and said, "Thus says my master, 'You shall no longer eat from my loaves. I am estranged from you. Just this one loaf I have offered to you, lest I be accused of giving nothing to an enemy who asks for it.'"

When Satan heard this, he sent the maid back to me to say, "Just as this loaf is wholly burnt, so also will I make your body. In one hour I will go away and make you desolate."

"Do what you will," I replied, "Whatever you intend to inflict upon me, I am prepared to endure."

(8) He departed from me and went up to the firmament and requested from the Lord authority over all my possessions. When he received it, he came and took away all my wealth.

(9) Hear me now, and I will recount to you all the things that have happened to me and how many things were stripped from me. I once had 130,000 sheep, from which I set aside 7,000 to be sheared to make clothing for the orphans and widows, the poor, and the weak. I also possessed a pack of eighty dogs to guard my flocks, and two hundred more dogs to guard the house. I also had nine thousand camels, and selected three thousand of them for a special task in all the cities. Loading them with goods, I sent them into the cities and villages and gave orders that the goods be distributed to the poor, the unfortunate, and the widows. I possessed 140,000 asses in my pastures, of which I set aside five hundred and commanded that their offspring be sold and given to the poor and needy.

Everyone from near and far used to come to meet me, and I opened for them the four gates of my house. I gave a standing order to my servants to leave these gates open, since I was concerned that some might come seeking alms, and finding me sitting at the gate, return out of shame with nothing. Now, however, if they saw me sitting at one gate, they could approach through another gate and receive as much as they needed.

(10) There were also in my house thirty tables reserved at all times for strangers, and twelve tables set for the widows. If any stranger came by to beg for alms, he was required to eat first before receiving what he requested. I would not allow him to depart through my gate with an empty stomach. I had also 3,500 yoke of oxen, from which I selected five hundred earmarked for plowing; they could be used in the field of anyone who needed them. I also set aside their produce for the tables of the poor. In addition, I had fifty bakeries, from which I supplied bread to be served on the tables of the poor.

(11) Visitors from afar who witnessed my zeal wanted to assist in aiding the poor. Many others who were penniless and unable to purchase anything came to me with an urgent plea: "We

beg you, since we could also render this service but have no property, have mercy and lend us money to go into the cities and make a profit through trade so that we may also give to the poor. Afterward, we will return to you what you gave us." When I heard this I rejoiced that they could use my money in the service of the poor. Eagerly I accepted their promissory note—no other security did I require—and gave them as much as they asked. Thus they were able to make use of my resources. Often they were successful at trading and gave money to the poor, but sometimes they were robbed and would come to me and say, "We beg of you, be patient with us, and we will find a way to repay you."

Without hesitating I would bring forth their note and read it, and conclude the transaction by canceling their debt, saying, "Since I believed in you on behalf of the poor, I will take nothing from you." As a result, I accepted nothing from those who were indebted to me.

(12) And if ever anyone came to me of a cheerful and generous disposition and said, "I have nothing of my own to give to the poor, nevertheless I would like at least to serve the poor at your table," I would grant it and he would serve and then eat.

When evening came and he was about to leave for his own home, he would receive his payment. If he did not wish to receive his payment, I would require it and say, "I know that you are a worker who expects to receive his pay, so you must take it." Thus I did not allow the man to leave without his wage.

(13) Those who milked the cows also grew weary, since milk flowed down the mountains. They were so covered with milk that they came to resemble hardened butter, and butter was so abundant that it spread over my roads. The herds were forced to sleep in the rocks and crags because so many young were born.[2]

2. The meaning of this passage is not clear, and some conjecture of the intent is used here. It is influenced by the Greek version of Job 29:6.

My servants who were charged with the care of the widows and poor became so exhausted that they began to deride and curse me, saying, "Who will provide us with meats so that we may be filled?"—all because I was so kind.

(14) And I had six psalms that I sang and a ten-stringed lyre. Arising each day after the widows were fed, I would take up the lyre and play for them, as the widows chanted. Through the hymns I turned their minds to God, and they would glorify the Lord. If my female slaves ever began to murmur against me, I would begin to play and sing for them in response. In this way I stopped them from murmuring in contempt.

(15) Each day, after my ministry to the poor, my own children took their meal, entering in to dine with their older brother and three sisters. The sisters were attended by female slaves, while my sons were served by male slaves. I would rise up early in the morning and offer sacrifices on their behalf consisting of three hundred doves, fifty goats' kids, and twelve sheep. I commanded that anything left over after the rites should be considered an unneeded abundance and given to the poor. I said to them, "Take this excess over and above the portion offered on behalf of my children so that you too may pray for them. It is possible that my sons sinned before God, saying contemptuously, 'We are sons of this rich man, and all these goods are ours. Why then should we also serve others?'" Pride is indeed an abomination before the Lord. And so as a precaution I also offered a choice calf on the altar of God saying, "It is possible that my sons conceived evil thoughts in their hearts against God."

(16) As I was doing all these things during the seven years after the angel had disclosed everything to me, Satan, who had now received the authority, at last descended and mercilessly burned up the seven thousand sheep that had been allotted for the clothing of the poor and widows, and the three thousand camels, five hundred asses, and five hundred yoke of oxen. All these things he destroyed on his own, as a result of the power he now had over me. The rest of my herds were taken away from me by my

own countrymen—they whom I had treated so well, but who were now rising up against me and taking away the remainder of my herds! I was informed of the loss of my property, but even then I glorified God and did not blaspheme.

(17) But when the Devil found out what was in my heart, he set a trap for me by disguising himself as the king of Persia. He advanced against my city in an alliance with all the rogues in it and laid before them a bold promise: "This man Jobab has squandered all the good things of the earth, leaving nothing behind. He has distributed everything to the beggars, the blind and lame, and torn down the temple of god, destroying the sacred place for libations. Therefore, I will repay him in accord with what he did to the temple of the great god. Join with me, then, and take for yourself as spoils his livestock and whatever property he owns."

"He has seven sons and three daughters," they replied. "They may flee into some other land and from there in time rally people against us, oppose us as tyrants, and kill us."

"Have no fear," he said to them. "I have destroyed most of his flocks by fire, the rest I have confiscated; now I will destroy his children as well."

(18) After he said this to them, he left and knocked over my house upon my children and killed them. When my countrymen saw that everything he said had come true, they attacked me and drove me away, looting my house of all its belongings. My eyes now saw sitting at my tables and reclining on my couches cheap and worthless men, and I was unable to say a word against them; I was utterly spent, like a woman whose body was weakened from long labor pains. Going through my mind was the battle which was foretold by the Lord through his angel and the victory songs which were sung to me. I became like a person who wants to enter a certain city to see its riches and obtain a portion of its splendor, and when he is on board a ship in mid-ocean and sees the surging waves and violent winds, throws his cargo into the sea and says, "I would rather lose all my possessions and still

enter this city and obtain things more valuable than this ship and its cargo." Just so I now considered my possessions as nothing compared to approaching the city which the angel had described to me.

(19) And when another messenger arrived and informed me of the death of my children, I became violently upset and tore my garment, and asked him, "How then did you survive?" But then I understood what was happening and cried out, "The Lord has given, the Lord has taken away. As it has pleased the Lord, so has it come about. Blessed be the name of the Lord."

(20) When I had thus lost everything I owned, Satan realized that there was nothing that would cause me to show contempt for God. He thus departed and asked the Lord for my body so that he might afflict me with a disease. The Lord delivered me into his hands to deal with my body in any way he wished, but he did not give him power over my soul. So as I was sitting upon my throne, grieving over the death of my children, he came to me and, like some great tempest, knocked over my throne. For three hours I was trapped under my throne, unable to move. He afflicted me with a cruel disease from the top of my head to the bottom of my feet. Greatly troubled and distressed, I left the city and sat upon a dung heap, my body infested with worms. Pus from my body collected and dripped onto the ground. My flesh was full of worms, and if a worm fell off, I would pick it up and return it to the same place, saying, "Remain there in the spot where you were placed until you are instructed by the one who commands you."

(21) For forty-eight years I sat on the dung heap outside of the city, plagued with diseases until, my children, with my own eyes I saw my wife so humbled that she was bearing water as a slave to the house of some nobleman in order to obtain bread to bring to me. Shocked by what I saw, I said, "Oh, the arrogance of the city's magistrates, whom I consider unworthy of my pack of dogs! How can they use my wife as a slave?" But afterward I regained my composure and clarity of mind.

(22) After eleven years, they even forbade her from bringing me bread, barely allowing her to have food for herself. But if she obtained any, she would divide it between herself and me, saying in her grief, "Woe is me! Soon he will not even have bread to eat." She did not even shrink from going into the marketplace and begging bread from the bread sellers to bring me something to eat.

(23) When Satan saw this, he disguised himself as a bread seller, and my wife, thinking he was a man, by chance went to him to beg bread. Satan said to her, "Pay the price and you may take what you want."

"Where would I get the money?" she asked. "Don't you know what horrible things have happened to us? If you have any compassion, show mercy, but if not, you shall see what will happen!"

"If you did not deserve these punishments," he responded, "you would not have received them. But if you do not have the money right now, give me as payment the hair of your head, and I'll give you three loaves. Perhaps you will be able to prolong your life for three days more."

She said to herself, "What value to me is the hair of my head compared to my husband, who is starving?" And so, disdaining her hair, she said, "Go ahead; you may shear it."

Then, with all the townspeople looking on, he took shears and cut off her hair, giving her three loaves. She brought the loaves and gave them to me, but Satan was following along secretly behind her and led her heart astray. (24) As soon as my wife drew near to me, she began to weep, saying to me, "Job, Job, how long will you sit on the dung heap outside the city saying to yourself, 'Only a little longer!' expecting at any moment that you will be saved? I am now homeless and a slave, wandering from place to place. Already those who would ensure your good memory—my sons and daughters, the fruits of the pains and labors of my womb, for whom I toiled in vain—they have all disappeared from the face of the earth. Now you yourself sit here in the filth of worms, passing each night exposed in the open air, while I, wretch that I am, labor strenuously each day and suffer each night just to obtain a loaf of bread to bring you. But now I can no longer even procure that extra loaf to bring—I scarcely receive enough to sustain me, and that I divide between us—and I am consumed all the while with the notion that not only are you afflicted with pains, but starving as well.

"I dared, therefore, to go shamelessly to the marketplace, but to my dismay found that begging from the bread seller was not enough. When the bread seller said, 'Give me money and you'll get your bread,' I told him of our plight. He then told me, 'Woman, if you have no money, pay me with the hair of your head and I'll give you three loaves. Perhaps you will be able to prolong your life three days more.' Then I did something terribly wrong and said to him, 'Go ahead—shear me and keep my hair.' And so he took shears and publicly disgraced me by cutting my hair in the middle of the marketplace with a crowd standing by, watching in amazement. (25) Who would not have asked in disbelief,

Can this be Sitis, the wife of Job?
The woman who once had a door within doors
And fourteen curtains protecting her bedchamber,
So that only those who were deemed especially worthy
Might be admitted into her presence.
Now she trades her hair for bread!

The woman who owned camels laden with good things
That were sent off to other regions to give to the poor—
Now she gives her hair for bread!

Behold, the woman who had seven tables in her home
Reserved for the poor and the stranger!
Now she sells her hair for bread!

See the one who once had a basin for her feet made of silver and
 gold,
But now walks by foot upon the ground.
She must trade her hair for bread!

She is the same woman who once wore fine linen
Embroidered with gold thread—but now she wears rags,
And will trade her hair for bread!

She is the one who had couches made of gold and silver,
But now sells her hair for bread!

"Job, Job! Though many have spoken to you concerning your state, all I ask of you is this: the weariness of my heart overwhelms me—stand up, take these loaves and eat your fill; then make a declaration against the Lord and die. I will then be released from this dismal state we find ourselves in from the pummeling of your body."

(26) I then responded to her, "It is now seventeen years that I have suffered from these plagues. I submit to the worms in my body, and yet I have not been as burdened in my soul by my labors as I have by your plea that I make a declaration against the Lord and die. As for the loss of our children and our wealth—I suffer these misfortunes as much as you do. But would you prefer that we say something against the Lord and become estranged from the greater treasure? Or do you not recall the number of good things we already received? If we were blessed with such good things by the hand of God, should we not endure the bad as well? But let us be patient in all this until the Lord once again shows compassion and has mercy on us. Do you not see the Devil standing behind you and disturbing your reasoning so that he might deceive me as well? He is trying to show you up as one of those stupid women who compromise their husband's integrity."

(27) I then turned to Satan, who was behind my wife, and said, "Step out and show yourself! Can the lion show his strength in a cage? Can a bird take flight while in a basket? Is this not absurd? Come out and fight with me!"

He came out from behind my wife and stood before me weeping and said, "See, Job, I am undone and must yield to you—you who are made of human flesh, while I am spirit! You are afflicted with a disease, but I am the one who is now distressed. I have become like an athlete in a wrestling match who has at first pinned his opponent down. The one on top silences the one on the bottom by filling his mouth with sand and crushing every limb of his body, and yet when the one pinned showed such endurance and did not become distraught, the one on top let out a mighty cry and yielded. So you also, Job, were pinned and struck by plagues, but you broke my hold." So Satan, now thoroughly shamed, departed from me for three years. Now then, my children, you must also be patient in regard to everything that happens to you, for patience is indeed superior to all else.

(28) When I had been afflicted with this plague for twenty years, the kings of the surrounding nations heard what had happened to me. Each came from his own country to visit with me and console me. When they approached me they did not at first recognize me. As they drew nearer, however, they began to cry and weep. Tearing their garments and heaping dust on themselves, they sat down beside me and remained for seven days and nights. None of them spoke to me—not because they were exhibiting patience, but because they had known me when I was much wealthier than they. Indeed, when I had formerly offered them precious stones, they would marvel, and with a clap of their hands say, "When the wealth of us three kings is brought together, it still does not match the value of the precious stones of your kingdom. You are grander than the kings of the east."

When they had first come to the city of Ausitis, they inquired, "Where is Jobab who rules over all of Egypt?"

The people of Ausitis told them, "He is sitting on the dung heap outside the city. For twenty years he has not gone into the city." The kings then asked about my wealth and were told about all the things that had happened to me. (29) When they heard this, they went with the citizens outside the city, but when I was pointed out to them, they refused to believe that it was I.

While they were still debating among themselves, Eliphaz,

king of the Temanites,[3] turned and said, "Are you then Job, our fellow-king?"

Trembling and weeping, I threw dirt upon my head and said, "I am."

(30) When they saw my head trembling so, they fainted and fell to the ground. Their soldiers were disturbed to see the three kings collapsed on the ground as though dead for about three hours. When the kings arose they said to each other, "We do not believe that this is he."

They sat for seven more days and considered my circumstances. Discussing my herds and possessions, they said, "Are we not familiar with all the goods he has distributed to the poor in the cities and surrounding villages, in addition to the goods he gives away in his own home? How then has he fallen to this state of death?"

(31) After seven days deliberating in this way, Eliphaz said to the kings, "Let us draw near to him and question him carefully to see whether it is really he or not." They were about a hundred yards away from me, because of the stench of my body. As a result, they approached me with fragrant spices in their hands while their soldiers accompanied them with censers, fumigating the area around me—only in this way could they approach. After burning incense for three days, they drew near and Eliphaz said to me, "Are you Job, our fellow-king? Are you the one who possessed such great splendor? Are you the one who once shone like the sun by day over all the earth? Are you the one who once shone like the moon and stars by night?"

"I am," I responded.

Then Eliphaz began to wail loudly and cried out in a royal

3. Following other scholars, I replace Elihu with Eliphaz in this section, which fits the sense better and corresponds to the order of speeches in the Greek version of Job.

lament, as the other kings and soldiers wailed also in response. (32) Hear now Eliphaz's lament over the wealth of Job:

What has become of the splendor of his throne?

Are you the one who marshaled seven thousand sheep to clothe the poor?
What has now become of the splendor of your throne?

Are you the one who marshaled the three thousand camels to carry goods to the poor?
What has become of the splendor of your throne?

Are you the one who marshalled the one thousand cattle to plow the fields of the poor?
What has become of the splendor of your throne?

Are you the one who had golden couches, but now sits on a dung heap?
What has become of the splendor of your throne?

Are you the one whose throne was made of precious stones, but now sits in ashes?
What has become of the splendor of your throne?

Who could stand against you when you were in the midst of your children?
You were blooming like a sprout of a fragrant fruit tree.
What has become of the splendor of your throne?

Are you the one who arranged sixty tables just for the poor?
What has become of the splendor of your throne?

Are you the one who once possessed the censers for the songs of meeting, but now sits in putrid vapors?
What has become of the splendor of your throne?

Are you the one who had golden lamps resting on silver lampstands, but now must rely upon the moon for light?
What has become of the splendor of your throne?

Are you the one who once had ointment from the frankincense tree,
but now must sit in pain?
What has become of the splendor of your throne?

Are you the one who made fun of the unrighteous and sinners, but
are now a laughingstock?
What has become of the splendor of your throne?

Are you Job, the one who possessed vast splendor?
What has become of the splendor of your throne?

(33) Eliphaz thus wailed his lament, and his fellow kings joined in response, so that there now arose a loud cry. When he was done I said to them:

Quiet now, and I will show you my throne,
And the glory of its splendor which is with the holy ones.
My throne is in the heavenly realm,
And its glory and its splendor are from the right hand of the father in
heaven.

My throne is eternal,
The whole world shall pass away and its glory shall perish,
And those who cling to it will be present in its destruction.

My throne is in a holy land,
and its glory lies in an unchangeable realm.

The rivers may dry up,
And the roaring waters descend into the depths of the abyss,
But the rivers in the land of my throne will never dry up and
disappear.
They will flow forever.

Earthly kings will pass away, and leaders pass away as well;
Their import and glory will appear as in a mirror.
My kingdom will remain forever,
And the glory and splendor are in the chariots of the father.

(34) I said these things to them in order to silence them, but Eliphaz became enraged and said to his friends, "What good has

it done to come here with our soldiers to console him? Now he accuses us! Let us leave and go back to our own lands. This man sits afflicted in a heap of worms and the smell of dung and then suddenly turns and rises up against us. 'Kingdoms and their rulers are passing away,' he says, 'but mine will last forever'!" Eliphaz, very troubled, turned aside in sorrow and said, "I will go now. We came here to console him, but now he humiliates us in the presence of our troops."

(35) But Bildad restrained him and said, "One should not speak in that manner to a man who is not only in mourning, but afflicted by many plagues as well. Although we are all healthy, were it not for the use of sweet-smelling incenses we would not be strong enough to come near him on account of the stench. And have you forgotten, Eliphaz, that you were ill for two days? Let us then be patient and try to determine what is his true condition. Perhaps he is insane, or perhaps simply heartsick when he recalls his former good fortune. Who would not go out of his mind afflicted with so many plagues? But allow me to approach him and I will find out what is wrong with him."

(36) So Bildad came near me and said, "Are you Job?"

"Yes," I said.

"Is your mind[4] in a stable condition?" he asked.

"My mind is not concerned with earthly things," I replied to him, "since the earth and those who dwell in it are not stable, but my mind is concerned with heavenly things, where there is no instability."

"We know that the earth is unstable," replied Bildad, "since indeed it sometimes changes—at times there is peace, and at other

4. I have used the English word "mind" for the Greek word for "heart," because the latter is often used for the decision-making faculty. There is also an important play on words here: the same root for the stability of Job's mind is used of the stability of the heavens later, creating a notion of a parallel between Job's perception and the heavens. The repetition of the motif of stability here reflects that connection.

times war breaks out—and concerning heaven, we hear that it is stable. But if you are truly in a stable condition, I will ask you a question, and if you answer me in a reasonable way the first time, I'll ask a second question. If your answer shows that you are in a stable condition, it will be clear that you are not out of your mind." (37) So he asked, "In whom do you place your hope?"

"In the living God," I said.

"Who has taken away your possessions," he asked, "and afflicted you with these plagues?"

"God," I responded.

"So," he continued, "if you place your hope in God, why then does he act as an unjust judge, afflicting you with these plagues or taking away your possessions? If he was going to take away, he ought not to have given in the first place. A king would never punish a soldier who had served him well. But at the same time, who has ever plumbed the depths of the Lord and his wisdom only to presume to ascribe injustice to him? Explain this to me, Job. And I ask you this as well: If you are mentally stable and have your wits about you, teach me. Why do we see the sun rising in the east and setting in the west, and yet the next morning we wake to find the same sun rising in the east again. Counsel me in these matters."

"'Counsel me in these matters, if you have your wits about you' indeed!" I replied. (38) "I have my wits about me and my mind is still sharp! Why should I not speak about the great things of the Lord? Could my mouth err concerning my master? May that never happen! Who are we to be meddling in the heavenly realm when we are from the fleshly realm, having a share in earth and ashes? But so that you may know that I still have my wits about me, listen as I ask *you* a question: If food is eaten through the mouth, and water is drunk through the mouth, and both go down the same throat but are separated again when we pass them out, who divides them?"

"I don't know," said Bildad.

To which I said, "If you do not understand bodily functions, how will you understand heavenly things?"[5]

Zophar then responded, "We are not examining things beyond our capabilities but merely wanted to know whether your mind is stable. Indeed, it is clear that you have not lost your senses. What, then, would you have us do? We have brought with us the physicians from our three kingdoms, and if you wish, it is quite possible that they can cure you."

"My therapy and healing are from the Lord," I replied, "who created even the doctors."

(39) But while I was saying these things to them, my wife, Sitis, came in tattered garments, fleeing from the servitude imposed upon her by her overseer; he had forbidden her to leave lest the three kings see her and take her away. But when she came she threw herself at their feet and cried out, "Do you recall, Eliphaz, you and your two friends here, what I was like before and how I dressed? But now, do you see how I come here before you and how I am dressed now?"

They all wailed loudly over her until they were spent, and then they fell silent. Eliphaz tore off his purple robe and wrapped it around my wife. She, however, began to beseech them, "I beg you, command your soldiers to dig through the rubble of the house which fell on my children to recover their bones for a memorial, since we could no longer afford the costs to do that. We would then have something to look at, if only their bones. Am I like a cow, or do I have the womb of a wild beast that my children—ten of them!—could die and I would not provide a proper burial for any of them?"

So the soldiers went off to begin digging, but I would not let them, and said, "Do not labor in vain. You will not find my children. They were taken up into heaven by their creator and king."

5. Cf. John 3:12. Note also Job's technique of countering a test question with another test-question that cannot be answered, and cf. Mark 11:27–33.

They then responded, "Who would not think that you are mad and out of your mind when you say, 'My children have been taken up into heaven'? Tell us the truth!"

(40) "Lift me up," I said, "so that I may stand." They raised me up, supporting my arms on both sides, and once standing I began making my confession to the Lord. After a long prayer I said to them, "Raise your eyes toward the east." When they looked up, they saw my children crowned beside the glory of the heavenly one.

When Sitis, my wife, saw this she fell to the ground in reverence and said, "Now I know that there is a memorial for me with the Lord. I shall arise, therefore, and go back into the city and rest for a while to prepare myself to return to my slave's duties."

She returned to the city and went to the field where the cattle were kept which had been seized by the magistrates whom she now served. She fell asleep there beside the manger and died peacefully. In the evening, when the haughty magistrate who was her master came looking for her and could not find her, he came to the fold of the herds and found her lying on the ground dead. All those present cried when they saw her, wailing loudly over her, and the lamentation could be heard throughout the city. All the people rushed to see what was happening and found her dead, with the beasts standing around her weeping. They carried her out, prepared her body for burial, and laid her in the ruins of the house that collapsed on her children. The poor of the city raised a loud lament saying, "Can this be Sitis, the woman who once had such pride and splendor, but who is now not deemed worthy of a proper burial?" You can find their lament recorded in the "Additional Chapters of Eliphaz."

(41) So Eliphaz and those with him sat beside me for twenty-seven days, arguing and puffing themselves up, until they arose to go back to their own countries. Elihu, however, exacted an oath from them, saying, "Do not depart until I have corrected Job, since you have sat here for so many days putting up with his

boast when he says that he is righteous. I, however, will suffer him no longer. From the beginning I kept up a lament for him, since I remembered his former happiness, but he has so pompously asserted that his own throne is in heaven. Listen to me, then, and I will show you that the portion he hopes to receive does not exist." So Elihu, now possessed by Satan, uttered bold words against me, which are also recorded in the "Additional Chapters of Eliphaz."

(42) When he had finished, the Lord appeared to me in the midst of a whirlwind of clouds, and he censured Elihu and showed me that the one who spoke in him was not man but beast. They heard the voice of the Lord as he spoke to me from the cloud. When the Lord had finished speaking to me, he said to Eliphaz, "You and your two friends have sinned; you did not speak the truth when you spoke against my servant Job. Turn now to him and ask him to offer sacrifices on your behalf so that your sin may be forgiven, for if not for him, I would have destroyed you!"

And so they brought to me what was needed for a sacrifice, and I took it and offered a sacrifice on their behalf. The Lord accepted the sacrifice and forgave their sin. (43) Eliphaz, Bildad, and Zophar realized that the Lord had forgiven their sin but had not considered Elihu worthy, so Eliphaz began to sing a hymn, while the other two and their soldiers sang in response around the altar. Eliphaz sang:

Our sin was wiped out and our trespasses removed.
Elihu, the only evil one, will have no memorial among the living.

His lamp is extinguished and casts no light.
The glory of his lampstand will become for him a condemnation.

For he is from darkness and not light.
The gatekeepers of darkness will inherit his glory and splendor.

His kingdom has passed away, his throne rotted.
The honor of his tent is found in Hades.

For he has loved the beauty of the snake and the scales of the serpent.
Its venom and poison shall be his sustenance.

He did not search out the Lord, nor greatly fear him,
And even those honored of the Lord he angered.

The Lord has forgotten him, the holy ones forsaken him.
But his own rage and anger shall be his tent.

Mercy is not found in his heart, nor peace in his mouth,
But he has the poison of an asp in his tongue.

The Lord is righteous, his judgments true.
He knows no favorites, but looks on all alike.

Now the Lord is come, his holy ones are ready,
The crowns of praise lead the way.

Let the holy ones rejoice, let their hearts exult,
For they have now received the glory they awaited.

Our sins have been removed, our trespasses have been cleansed,
But the evil Elihu has no memorial among the living.

(44) After Eliphaz finished his hymn, with the others in a circle about him, we all arose and entered the city where we now have a house and held a festival to celebrate the favor of the Lord. Once again, I sought to become a benefactor of the poor. All my friends and as many others as knew that I had performed good works came to me. "What do you ask of us now?" they said to me.

And once again remembering the poor to do good works for them, I said, "Let each of you give me one lamb to clothe the naked." Then each of them brought me one lamb and one gold coin. The Lord then blessed all my possessions and doubled my wealth.

(45) So now, my children, I am about to die. See that you do not forget the Lord. Do good deeds for the poor and do not overlook those who are helpless. Do not take for yourselves foreign wives. Now, my children, I shall divide all my possessions among you for each of you to control and possess so that you can do good deeds freely from your share.

(46) His property was brought forth and divided among his seven sons, but he did not give anything to his three daughters. Very upset, they said to him, "Father, sir, are we not also your children? Why did you not give us a share of your property?"

"Do not be troubled," Job said to his daughters, "for I have not forgotten you. I have already given you an inheritance greater than that of your brothers." Job called his daughter named Hemera and said to her, "Take this signet ring, go to the chamber, and bring me the three golden boxes so that I may give you your inheritance." She went away and returned with the boxes. Job opened the boxes and brought forth three multicolored sashes,[6] the appearance of which no one could describe—since they were not from this earth but from heaven. They emitted bright sparks like rays of the sun. He gave a sash to each of his daughters and said, "Tie this around your breast, and it will go well with you all the days of your life."

(47) "Father," his daughter Kassia said to him, "is this the inheritance that you said was greater than those of our brothers? What is so unusual about these sashes? Will these help us to live?"

"Not only will these sashes give you life," said her father, "but they will also conduct you into a better world, and you will live in heaven. Do you not know, my children, the value of these sashes? The Lord considered me worthy to receive them on the day when he showed me mercy and removed from my body the plagues and worms. Calling me forward, he placed before me

6. The similarity to the sashes or girdles of *Marriage of Aseneth* 14 are significant, although the Greek words are different. Here they are *chordai,* which may be strings, cords, sashes, or bands. In *Marriage of Aseneth* they are *zonai,* which are sashes or belts. Women wore them at the waist or below the breasts. Despite the slight difference in physical description, the symbolic import in the two cases is very similar indeed. In addition, the fact that the daughter had to repair to another room to retrieve them is similar as well. Howard Clark Kee provides an alternative translation and explanation: they are net bags that hold magical powers; see "Satan, Magic, and Salvation in the Testament of Job" in the suggested reading. However, the allusion in the next chapter to Job girding himself with the sashes (cf. also 52:1) argues for the present rendering.

these three sashes and said, 'Get up and gird yourself like a man! I shall ask you questions, and you will answer me.'

"I took the sashes and girded myself, and immediately the worms disappeared from my body, as did the plagues. Then by the will of the Lord my body regained its strength as though I had never been sick at all. I even forgot the pains that were in my heart. The Lord miraculously spoke to me and told me the things present and the things to come. So, my children, while you have these sashes you will never be set upon by Satan, nor will he be able to disturb your thoughts; these are protective amulets of the Lord. Rise up now and gird them around you before I die, so that you will be able to perceive those who are coming for my departure, and you can marvel at what God has created."

(48) Then Job's daughter Hemera got up and wrapped the sash around her waist as her father had instructed her. She then received a new heart, and now no longer concerned herself about earthly things. She chanted words in an angelic language and sent on high a hymn to God that was like that of the angels.[7] As she sang these hymns, she allowed "spirit" to be inscribed on her garment.

(49) Then Kassia wrapped the sash around herself and received a new heart and no longer concerned herself about earthly things. Her mouth learned the language of the heavenly rulers and she praised the creation of the heavenly realm. If anyone should now want to know about the creation of heaven, it can be found in the "Hymns of Kassia."

(50) Then the third daughter, Amaltheia's Horn, wrapped a sash around her, and when her heart was changed and she withdrew from earthly matters, her mouth began to speak in the language of those on high. The language she spoke was that of the cherubim, as she praised the master of virtues by exhibiting their glory. The one who wants to discover a trace of the father's glory will find it recorded in the "Prayers of Amaltheia's Horn."

7. At Qumran we also find a hymnic text, *Songs of the Sabbath Sacrifice,* that presumes an identity of the human and angelic voices.

(51) When the daughters had concluded their hymns, with the Lord and the holy angel still present, as was I, Nereus, brother of Job,[8] I sat beside Job on his couch, and I also heard magnificent things, as one sister noted them down for another.[9] I then transcribed a book of notations of most of the hymns sung by the three daughters of my brother, so that they, like the sashes, might also offer protection. These books contain the magnificent words of God.

(52) After three days, while Job had the appearance of being sick on his couch—though he was without pain and suffering; those things could not touch him because of the sign of the sash that was girded around him—he saw those who were coming for his soul. Immediately he got up, took his lyre, and gave it to his daughter Hemera; he also gave a censer to Kassia and a drum to Ameltheia's Horn, so that they might all bless those who had come for his soul. They took the instruments and blessed and glorified God in their special tongue. Then the one who rode in the great chariot came and greeted Job, as the three daughters and Job looked on, although no one else could see him. He took Job's soul and embraced it and flew up and mounted the chariot and set off toward the east. His body, however, wrapped for burial, was carried away to the tomb, with his three daughters leading the way, their sashes tied around their breasts, singing hymns to God.

(53) Then I, Nereus his brother, along with his sons and the poor, the orphans, and all the weak, cried and said,

> Woe to us today,
> for today the strength of the weak ones,
> the light of the blind,
> the father of the orphans is taken away.
>
> The host of strangers,
> the way for the weak,

8. This short section and a section later are in the words of Job's brother Nereus.

9. Or perhaps "interpreted"; cf. 1 Corinthians 13:1, 14:27.

the garment for the naked,
the champion of the widows is taken away.
Who, then, will not weep for the man of God?

Then all together the widows and orphans circled around him, preventing him from being carried into the tomb. But after three days he was laid in the tomb, looking as though he were in a restful slumber. He had received a name renowned in all generations forever. Amen.

### SUGGESTIONS FOR FURTHER READING

Collins, John J. *Between Athens and Jerusalem: Jewish Identity in the Hellenistic Diaspora,* pp. 220–24. New York: Crossroad, 1983.

———. "Structure and Meaning in the Testament of Job." In *Society of Biblical Literature 1974 Seminar Papers,* pp. 1.35–52. Ed. George MacRae. 2 vols. Cambridge: Society of Biblical Literature, 1974.

Kee, Howard Clark. "Satan, Magic, and Salvation in the Testament of Job." In *Society of Biblical Literature 1974 Seminar Papers,* pp. 1.53–76.

Knibb, Michael A., and Pieter van der Horst, eds. *Studies on the Testament of Job.* Cambridge: Cambridge University Press, 1989.

Nickelsburg, George W. E. *Jewish Literature Between the Bible and the Mishnah,* pp. 241–48. Philadelphia: Fortress, 1981.

THIRTEEN

# TESTAMENT OF ABRAHAM

The *Testament of Abraham* will likely be, for most readers, the unexpected discovery of this volume. This challenging and quizzical text defies easy categorization, but it appears to be a humorous or even satirical rereading of the legend of Abraham as an anti-testament. If *Testament of Joseph* and *Testament of Job* display an excess of piety, *Testament of Abraham* is a satire on that genre. A number of things about it argue for this interpretation. Abraham is first described as the most pious man who ever lived, admired by humans and angels alike, but in a series of scenes he reveals himself to be self-centered, vindictive, and even disobedient to God; when he is told it is time to die, he petulantly refuses to go. Further, although this text is called *Testament of Abraham,* the patriarch never manages to do what every other patriarch does: make a last will and testament to his offspring. God tries as hard as divinely possible to convince Abraham to dispose of his property and bless Isaac, but he refuses to do so. What Abraham is actually avoiding, however, is leaving his body behind, and he negotiates for extraordinary experiences while still in this world: seeing the entire world, seeing the judgment of souls, seeing Death as he actually appears to people. In contrast to *Testament of Job,* there is a certain worldly fascination here, as Abraham's religious responsibilities are neglected and his worldly curiosity is given progressively broader rein, somewhat akin to what occurs in Apuleius's

*Golden Ass.* His curiosity eventually catches up with him, however, as Abraham's visions of things that mortals do not usually see overwhelm him, and he slips into the "listlessness of death." But Death here is not proud. He follows Abraham from room to room, discussing heavenly realities, apparently waiting for Abraham to succumb. Also strange is the constant reference to the archangel Michael as "commander-in-chief." Doubtless this is intended humorously, for the words for archangel and commander-in-chief are similar in Greek (*archangelos* and *archistrategos*); the standard title for Michael has been replaced by a military term. Near the end we also see the anachronistic references to the patriarchs as dead and in heaven before their time. In addition to the humor, what also catches the attention of modern readers is the depiction of the tour of heaven and the scene of judgment. These are found in apocalypses, but there is here no sense of the end of time. These apocalyptic motifs, like the testamentary frame, are merely borrowed elements. (Compare the pseudo-apocalyptic vision at the beginning of *Greek Esther,* used there also for literary purposes.)

Despite the outward appearance of a testament, then, there is much here that is novelistic. This text is longer and more narrative than other testaments (the significant exception being *Testament of Job*) and utilizes clever and sometimes even moving dialogue. Further, the narrative is carefully structured in two halves, Abraham's interchanges with Michael and his interchange with Death (adapted from Nickelsburg, *Jewish Literature,* pp. 249–50; compare the tightly balanced two-part structure of *Judith*):

| *Part 1* | *Part 2* |
| --- | --- |
| God commissions Michael:<br>Tell Abraham he will die and should make a testament | God commissions Death:<br>Tell Abraham he will die |

| | |
|---|---|
| Michael goes to Abraham at Mamre | Death goes to Abraham at Mamre |
| Abraham and Michael greet | Abraham and Death greet |
| Abraham hosts Michael | Abraham inhospitable to Death |
| Michael reveals mission | Death reveals mission |
| Abraham asks to see whole world | Abraham asks to see Death's ferocious appearance |
| Abraham asks that sinners die | Death causes servants to die |
| Abraham prays for dead, who are revived | Abraham and Death pray for dead, who are revived |
| Michael returns Abraham to Sarah, Isaac, and servants, who rejoice | Isaac, Sarah, and servants mourn |
| Abraham refuses to make testament | Abraham is suddenly taken |
| Michael returns to heaven | Michael takes soul to heaven |

But within this structure Abraham is also depicted in three separate moods: he is at first righteous and stern, then he learns mercy (both in the section with Michael), and finally he becomes depressed, as his insights bring on a bout of melancholy. Like *Esther,* this novel portrays a rudimentary change of character, something very rare in ancient literature.

Although the *Testament of Abraham* is written in the biblically influenced style typical of much Jewish literature of the period, it plays on that style by repeating titles often (for example, "Michael the commander-in-chief" and "righteous Abraham"), by introducing a large amount of dialogue, but most of all by humor and irony. The beginning of *Testament of Abraham* describes the hosting of an angel similar to the story of Abraham, Sarah, and the three angels at the oaks of Mamre in Genesis 18; the tone, however, could not be more different. The description of the "all-consuming spirit" that Michael must have in order to appear to be eating, not to mention the contagious fits of crying to which the characters are subject, lend an air of humor to the encounter. Finally, the fact that Michael must act as if he has to urinate in order to exit and initiate a conference with God ensures that the angelic visit is not taken too seriously. At times *Testament of Abraham* reminds one of biblical texts such as Job or Jonah, or other ancient texts such as Euripides' *Alcestis* (in that Abraham must argue for the release of souls from Death). It is also somewhat like the Greek and Roman novels that take an archer or even more satirical perspective, such as *Daphnis and Chloe, Satyricon,* or *The Golden Ass.* It also provokes comparisons with modern works as well: Charles Dickens's *A Christmas Carol* or Ingmar Bergman's *The Seventh Seal,* but with a humorous or satirical twist.

The *Testament of Abraham* existed in the ancient world in two main versions, one much longer than the other. It is the longer one, likely written in Egypt in the first or second century C.E., that is translated here. Interestingly, the principal difference is that the shorter version has none of the satirical or humorous aspects of the long version.

## *Testament of Abraham*

(1) Abraham lived the entire measure of his life, nine hundred and ninety-five years, in quietness, gentleness, and righteousness. This righteous man was very hospitable: he pitched his tent at the crossroads of the oak of Mamre, and saintly, most holy, righteous, hospitable Abraham welcomed everyone—rich and poor, kings and rulers, maimed and handicapped, friends and strangers, neighbors and passersby—all on equal terms. But at last that common, inexorable, bitter cup of death and the unforeseen end of life came also to him. Therefore, the sovereign

God summoned his archangel Michael and said to him, "Michael my commander-in-chief, go down to my friend Abraham and inform him about his death so that he may put his affairs and property in order. Indeed, I have blessed him as the stars in heaven and as the sands on the shore; he has an abundance of possessions and has become very wealthy. Yet above all others he has remained to the very end righteous, good, hospitable, and loving. Now archangel Michael, go to my beloved friend Abraham and inform him about his death, but at the same time reassure him that he is about to depart this vain world and leave his body behind to join his true Master and be with those who are good."

(2) So Michael the commander-in-chief departed from the presence of the Lord God and went down to Abraham at the oak of Mamre. There he found him in a field with oxen all yoked for plowing. He was overseeing the sons of Masek and other servants, twelve in all. Michael came toward him, and when Abraham saw him from a distance, coming with the air of a noble soldier, the most holy Abraham arose and met him, since it was his custom to greet and welcome all strangers. The commander-in-chief saluted the righteous Abraham and said, "Greetings, most honored father, righteous soul, true friend of the heavenly God!"

"Greetings, most honored soldier," said Abraham to the commander-in-chief, "radiant as the sun and most noble of all people! You are welcome here. Please grant us the pleasure of your company. From where do you get your youthful vigor? Teach me, your suppliant. Where are you from? From what army? By what road did you come? Show me how to have this beauty."

"Righteous man, I have come from the great city," answered the commander-in-chief. "I have been sent by the great king with orders to arrange for the succession of a true friend of his, because the king has now summoned him."

"Come, good sir," said Abraham, "join me here in my field."

"Certainly," said the commander-in-chief. So they proceeded into the field and sat down to talk.

Abraham said to his servants, the sons of Masek, "Go to the herd and find two tame and gentle horses for this stranger and me to ride."

"No, my lord Abraham," said the commander-in-chief, "let them not fetch us horses, for I abstain from sitting on any four-footed animal. My king—is he not wealthy, owning every possession, with authority over both human beings and beasts? Therefore, I abstain from ever sitting on a four-footed animal. Righteous soul, let us proceed on foot to your house, and enjoy our walk."

"Amen, lord," said Abraham, "So be it."

(3) As they began their walk from the field to Abraham's house, they passed a cypress tree that stood along the path. By the command of God the tree cried out in a human voice, "Holy, holy, holy is the Lord who calls to him those who love him." Abraham supposed that the commander-in-chief had not heard the tree calling and kept this mystery to himself.

When they arrived at the house, they sat down in the courtyard. Isaac, upon seeing the face of the angel, said to Sarah, his mother, "Look, Mother, the man sitting with my father is no member of the human race!" Isaac ran over, fell at the feet of the incorporeal man, and did obeisance to him. The commander-in-chief blessed Isaac and said, "The Lord God will grant to you the promise that he made to your father Abraham and will also answer the noble prayer of your father and mother."

"Isaac, my child," said Abraham, "go and draw water from the well and pour it here in a basin so that we may wash the feet of our guest. He is wearied from a long journey." Isaac ran to the well, drew water in a basin, and brought it to him. Abraham then knelt beside Michael the commander-in-chief and washed his feet. Abraham's heart was moved and he began to cry over the stranger, and when Isaac saw him weeping he began to cry as well. The commander-in-chief, upon seeing them weeping, began to cry with them, and his tears fell into the basin and became precious stones. When Abraham saw what had happened, he was astonished; he secretly took the precious stones and kept the mystery hidden, telling no one.

(4) Abraham said to Isaac his son, "Go, my beloved son, and prepare the dining room. Arrange two couches, one for me and one for this man who is visiting with us today. Prepare for us there also a couch, a lampstand, and a table overflowing with good things. Beautify the room, my child, with spread linen, purple cloths, and silk. Burn all sorts of fragrant incense and fill the room with sweet-smelling plants from our garden. Light seven lamps filled with oil so that we may thoroughly enjoy our meal, for this man who is visiting us today is more noble than kings and magistrates. His countenance is greater than that of any other man." So Isaac arranged everything magnificently. Abraham took Michael and proceeded up to the dining room, where they both sat on the couches, and between them was set a table overflowing with all sorts of delicious foods.

Then the commander-in-chief rose and went outside as if he needed to urinate, but instead ascended to heaven in the twinkling of an eye and stood before God. He said to him, "Lord and Master, let your might know that I cannot bring myself to raise the subject of death with this righteous man. I have never seen upon the earth a man such as him—merciful, hospitable, righteous, honest, pious, abstaining from every evil deed. So you see, Lord, why I cannot raise the subject of death."

God responded, "Return, Michael my commander-in-chief, to my friend Abraham and whatever he asks you to do, do it, and whatever he eats, eat with him. I shall send the holy spirit upon Isaac his son, and place the awareness of death in the mind of Isaac as though in a vision; he will perceive the death of his father in a dream. When Isaac describes his vision, you will interpret it. In that way Abraham will come to know about his own death."

"Lord," replied the commander-in-chief, "all of the heavenly spirits are incorporeal and neither eat nor drink. He has set a table for me with an abundance of all sorts of the goods things that are earthly and perishable. What shall I do, Lord? How shall

I keep him from noticing anything while I am sitting at table with him?"

"Go to him," said the Lord, "and do not be concerned about this. For while you are sitting with him I shall send upon you an all-consuming spirit. It will devour everything from the table that is in your hands and that goes into your mouth. Go and enjoy your meal, but make sure that you interpret well the substance of Isaac's vision so that Abraham may become aware of the sickle of death and the unforeseen end of life and will dispose well of all of his property. Indeed, I have blessed him like the stars of heaven and the sand on the shore."

(5) So Michael the commander-in-chief went down to the house of Abraham and joined him at table, as Isaac served them. When he had finished the meal, Abraham prayed as was his custom, and Michael with him. Then each retired to his bed. Isaac said to his father, "Father, I would also like to sleep with both of you in this room, for I love to listen to the magnificent discourse of this virtuous man."

But Abraham answered, "No, Isaac, my son. Go sleep in your room, lest we impose on him." So Isaac, after receiving a blessing from them, went off to his own room and slept on his bed. God sent the awareness of death into his mind, as though in dreams, and at about the third hour of the night Isaac woke up, got out of his bed, and ran quickly to the room where his father and the archangel were sleeping. When he reached the door he cried out, "Father, Father, get up and open the door! Let me in so that I may hold you and give you one last kiss before they take you from me!"

Abraham arose and opened the door, and Isaac entered and hung upon Abraham's neck, weeping loudly. Abraham was also moved to tears and wept also. When the commander-in-chief saw them weeping, he began to cry along with them. Sarah, who was in her tent, heard them weeping and came running. There she found them, huddled together and crying. Now weeping herself, she said to them, "My lord Abraham, why are you all crying so? Tell me! My lord, did this brother who is visiting with us today bring some news about your kinsman Lot who lives in Sodom? Did he die, and you are mourning because of this?"

But the commander-in-chief, answering for Abraham, responded, "No, Sister Sarah, it has nothing to do with that. Rather, it appears that your son Isaac has had a dream and come running in to us weeping. When we saw him crying, we were also moved to tears."

(6) When Sarah heard the magnificence of the commander-in-chief's voice, she immediately realized that the one speaking thus must be an angel of the Lord. She beckoned to Abraham to step outside the door. "Abraham, my lord," she said to him, "do you not realize who this man is?"

"No," said Abraham, "I do not know."

"Do you recall, my lord, the three heavenly men whom you entertained in our tent at the oak of Mamre, and how we sacrificed the calf and set a table for them? And after all the meat was consumed, the calf got up and happily began to suckle its mother again? Do you not know, my lord Abraham, that they promised Isaac to us as a fruit of my womb, and this man is one of those three?"

"Oh, Sarah," said Abraham, "you are right! Glory and peace from our God and father! And indeed, when I was washing his feet in the basin late last evening I said to myself, 'These are the feet of one of the three men that I washed before!' And later, when his tears fell into the basin, they became precious stones." Abraham then drew the stones out of his bosom and showed them to Sarah. "If you do not believe me, just look."

Falling on her knees, Sarah took them and clasped them to her and said, "Glory to God who has shown us such wonders. Now you know, my lord Abraham, that this is a revelation to us of some miracle, be it good or evil."

(7) So Abraham left Sarah and went back into the room and

said to Isaac, "Now, my beloved son, come and tell me the truth. What were your visions, and why were you suffering so that you came crying to us so upset?"

"My lord," said Isaac, beginning his account, "during the night I saw the sun and the moon above my head, and the sun's rays were in a circle all around me and illuminated me. As I was watching this and wondering what it meant, I saw heaven open and a man descending, full of light and brighter than seven suns. This man, who was himself like the sun, came and took the sun from my head and returned to heaven from where he had come. I was gravely upset because he had taken the sun from me. After a little while, as I was still grieving and in despair, I beheld the same light-bearing man coming out of heaven, and he took away the moon from over my head as well. I wept loudly and asked the man, 'Lord, do not take my glory away from me! Have mercy on me and heed my cry! If you take the sun, at least allow me to keep the moon above me!' And he said, 'Let them be taken up now to the kingdom above, because God wants them there.' So he took them away but left the rays upon me."

"Listen, righteous Abraham," said the commander-in-chief, "the sun that he saw is you, his father, and the moon is his mother Sarah. The light-bearing man descending from heaven is the one sent from God who is about to take your righteous soul. So understand, most honored Abraham, that you are now about to leave this worldly life behind and go away to God."

But Abraham said to the commander-in-chief, "Most marvelous wonder of wonders! Is it you then who is about to take my soul from me?"

The commander-in-chief answered, "I am Michael the commander-in-chief who stands before God. I was sent to you to place in your mind the awareness of death and then to return to God as he commanded."

"And now I know," said Abraham, "that you are an angel of the Lord. You were sent to take back my soul, but I won't go with you. So do whatever he commands."

(8) When the commander-in-chief heard this, he immediately vanished. He went up to heaven and stood before God and recounted everything he had witnessed in the house of Abraham. The commander-in-chief added, "Your friend Abraham also says, 'I won't go with you, so do whatever he commands.' Almighty Master, what do your glory and immortal kingship command now?"

God said to Michael, "Go to my friend Abraham once more and say to him, 'Thus says your God, "Why would I abandon you on earth? I am your God who led you up into the promised land. I blessed you and made your offspring more numerous than the sands of the sea or the stars of heaven. I am the one who opened the womb of Sarah and cured her barrenness, and gave you Isaac as the fruit of her womb in old age. Truly, I say to you, I will indeed bless you and multiply your offspring and give you whatever you ask of me. I am the Lord your God, and besides me there is no other. But as for you, why do you oppose me? Why are you grieving so? Why have you resisted my angel? Do you not know that all those born from Adam and Eve must die? Even kings are not immortal. None of your forefathers escaped the inheritance of death. All of them died, all of them were brought down to Hades, all of them were gathered in with the sickle of death. But I did not send Death to you, I did not allow him to go out to fetch you here, I did not permit the sickle of death to overtake you, I did not allow the nets of Hades to ensnare you. Indeed, it was not my wish that any evil at all should befall you. Rather, I sent my commander-in-chief to you to appeal to your better judgment, so that you would know that it is time to leave the world behind and that you should arrange for the disposition of your household and all your property, and have an opportunity to bless your beloved Isaac. Know also that I have not done these things to cause you grief. Why, then, did you say to my commander-in-chief, 'I won't go with you'? Why did you say this? Do you not know that if I allow Death to come to you, then I would see whether you would come or not?"' "

(9) The commander-in-chief accepted these instructions of the Most High and went down to Abraham. When the righteous man saw him he fell on his face on the ground as though dead, but when the commander-in-chief told him all that he had heard from the Most High, the pious and righteous Abraham got up again, and with many tears fell at the feet of the incorporeal man and implored him, "I beg of you, commander-in-chief of the heavenly powers, since you saw fit to come to me, a sinner and unworthy suppliant, grant me one more favor by interceding with the Most High. Tell him, 'Thus says Abraham, "Lord, Lord, every deed and favor that I have asked of you you have done. You have fulfilled my every wish. Now, Lord, I am not resisting your might, because I know that I am not immortal but will also die. Since, therefore, all things submit to your control, and shiver and tremble before your power, I also am afraid. Yet one more thing I ask of you; Lord and Master, please heed my request. While still in this body I want to see the whole world and all the things that you created by your word, O Master, and when I have seen this I shall quit this life without grieving."'"

The commander-in-chief went away again and stood before the invisible Father. He recounted everything to him and said, "Thus says your friend Abraham: 'I would like to see the entire world before I die.'"

When the Most High heard this, he gave instructions to the commander-in-chief Michael, "Take a cloud of light and the angels who have authority over the angelic chariot and place the righteous Abraham on it. Lift him up into the high reaches of heaven so that he may see the entire world."

(10) So the archangel Michael went down and placed Abraham on the angelic chariot and, lifting him into the high reaches of heaven, placed him with sixty angels upon a cloud. Abraham then embarked on a journey that allowed him to see the entire world as it happened to be on that day. Some men were plowing, others leading wagons. In one place some were keeping their flocks, in another some were frolicking out of doors, dancing

and playing the zither. In yet another place some were wrestling while others were judging, and in another were people weeping and bearing their dead to a tomb. He also saw newlyweds walking in their wedding procession—in a word, he saw everything that was happening in the world, both good and bad. As he proceeded further, Abraham also saw some men holding in their hands sharpened swords. He asked the commander-in-chief, "Who are these?"

"They are thieves," said the commander-in-chief, "who are plotting to commit murder and steal and slay and destroy."

"Lord," said Abraham, "Hear my plea and command that wild beasts come out of the brush and devour them!" And as Abraham said these words, wild beasts came out of the brush and devoured them. And at another place he saw a man and a woman engaged in immoral sexual acts. "Lord," said Abraham, "command that the earth open up and swallow them." Immediately the earth pulled apart and swallowed them up. In another place he saw men breaking into homes and stealing people's property, and Abraham said, "Lord, command that fire come down out of heaven and burn them up." And as he said these words, fire came down from heaven and burned them up.

Immediately a voice also came down from heaven and said to the commander-in-chief, "Michael my commander-in-chief, command the angelic chariot to stop and turn Abraham back, lest he see the entire world. If he sees all of the people who lead lives of sin, he will destroy the whole of creation. For Abraham has not sinned, but neither does he show mercy on those who have. I created the world, however, and do not want to destroy anyone on it. I delay the death of sinners so that they may repent and live. Therefore, conduct Abraham up to the first gate of heaven so that he may see there the judgments and retributions being handed out and repent over the souls of the sinners he has destroyed."

(11) Michael turned the chariot and brought Abraham toward the east, to the first gate of heaven. There Abraham saw two

roads, one narrow and constricted, the other broad and spacious. He saw there two gates, a wide gate for the wide road, and a narrow gate for the narrow road. Outside of these two gates they saw a man seated on a gold-plated throne. The man's countenance was terrifying, like the Master's. They saw many souls being driven by angels, conducted into the wide road. They also saw a small number of souls led by angels through the narrow gate. When the holy and wondrous man sitting on the gold throne saw the small number of souls entering through the narrow gate, and innumerable souls being led through the wide gate, he tore the hair of his head and the beard of his face, and threw himself down from his throne onto the ground, crying and wailing. But when he saw many souls entering through the narrow gate, he got up from the ground and sat again on his throne, rejoicing and in good cheer. Abraham asked the commander-in-chief, "My lord commander-in-chief, who is this wondrous man arrayed in such glory, who at one point cries and laments, but another celebrates and rejoices?"

The commander-in-chief said, "This is the first-formed Adam who sits here in his glory and surveys the entire world, since all people came to be through him. When he sees many souls entering through the narrow gate, he arises and sits on his throne rejoicing and celebrating, because the narrow gate is the gate of the righteous and leads to life, and those who enter through it proceed to Paradise. The first-formed Adam thus rejoices when he sees the souls being saved. But when he sees many souls entering through the wide gate, he tears his hair and throws himself on the ground, mourning and weeping bitterly, because the broad road is for sinners and leads to destruction and eternal punishment. For this reason the first-formed Adam gets up from his throne weeping and mourning for the destruction of sinners. Many are destroyed, but only a few are saved. Out of seven thousand souls there is scarcely found a single soul of an untainted person that will be saved."

(12) As he was speaking, two angels, fiery in appearance, with severe disposition and implacable expression, were driving a myriad of souls, beating them mercilessly with fiery lashes. An angel pulled one soul aside with his hand. They led all the other souls through the broad gate toward destruction. They followed the angels and went inside the wide gate. Between the two gates stood a terrifying throne, as clear as crystal, flashing as though on fire. On it sat a wondrous man, like a son of God, bright as the sun, and before him a table made of solid gold, but which also looked like crystal. On this table there lay a book three cubits thick and six cubits wide. To the right and to the left of it stood two angels holding a scroll, ink, and a pen, and in front of the table sat a shining angel, holding in his hand a balance. To the left of him sat a fiery angel, severe and implacable, who held in his hand a trumpet, from which came forth an all-consuming fire for the testing of sinners. The wondrous man sitting on the throne judged the souls and pronounced sentence. The two angels on the right and left recorded the judgments; the one on the right recorded the righteous deeds; the one on the left, sins. The man in front of the table holding the balance weighed the souls. The fiery angel who held fire in his trumpet tested people's souls with fire. Abraham asked the commander-in-chief, "What are these things we are seeing?"

The commander-in-chief replied, "These things you are seeing, holy Abraham, are judgment and retribution. The angel holding the one soul in his hand has brought it before the judge. The judge has instructed one of the angels serving under him, 'Open this book and find for me the sins of this soul.' When he opened the book, he found that the sins and righteous deeds were equal, and therefore neither handed the soul over to those who inflict punishment nor placed it among those saved. He has set it instead in the middle."

(13) "My lord commander-in-chief," said Abraham, "who is this wondrous judge? And who are these angels who are writing?

Who is the angel who is bright as the sun and holding a balance? Who is the fiery angel who tests with fire?"

"Saintly and righteous Abraham," answered the commander-in-chief, "do you see the terrifying man sitting on the throne? He is the son of the first-formed man, the one named Abel, whom the most evil Cain slew. He sits there to judge all creation and examines the righteous and sinners. For God said, 'I do not judge the world, but every human being is judged by a human being.' For this reason, he gave him authority to judge the world until the day of his great and glorious coming. At that time, most righteous Abraham, there will be perfect judgment and retribution, eternal and immutable, which no one can question. Every human being is descended from the first-formed man, and so judgment is rendered first by his son. At the final coming of God, every action, every creature will be judged by the twelve tribes of Israel. But for the third judgment, every person will be judged by the sovereign God of all. At that point, the final judgment will be rendered, the sentence terrible, which no one can rescind. Thus the judgment and retribution of the world is rendered through these different trials. It is for this reason that a verdict on earth is not established on the basis of one or two witnesses, but 'every matter shall be established by three witnesses.'[1] The two angels on the right and left record the sins and righteous deeds. The one on the right records righteous deeds; the one on the left, sins. The angel bright as the sun, with the balance in his hand is the archangel Dokiel, the just weigher, who weighs the sins and righteous deeds using the right judgment of God. The fiery and severe angel holding fire is the archangel Purouel, who has authority over fire and tests the deeds of people through fire. If the fire burns up a person's deeds, the angel of judgment immediately takes him and carries him to the place of sinners, the poisoned cup of judgment. But if the fire

1. Deuteronomy 19:15.

tests the deed of a person and it does not consume it, that person is judged righteous and the angel of righteousness takes him and carries him to be delivered to the lot of the righteous. Thus, righteous Abraham, all the deeds of every person are tested by fire and the balance."

(14) Then Abraham said to the angel, "My lord commander-in-chief, the soul that the angel was holding in its hand—how was it judged to be in the middle?"

"Listen, righteous Abraham," said the commander-in-chief, "the judge of its sinful and righteous deeds found that they were equal. He therefore could not deliver it over to be condemned nor to be saved until the Judge and God of all comes."

"Then what is lacking for this soul to be saved?" asked Abraham.

The incorporeal one responded, "If it can acquire just one righteous deed more than the number of its sins, it will be saved."

Abraham said to the commander-in-chief, "Come, Michael commander-in-chief, let us pray for this soul, and see whether God will heed us."

"Amen," said the commander-in-chief. "So be it." They then prayed to God on behalf of the soul. God heeded their prayer, and when they arose from their prayer they no longer saw the soul standing there.

"Where is the soul?" asked Abraham.

The commander-in-chief said, "It has been saved by your righteous prayer. The bright angel took it and carried it away to Paradise."

Abraham said, "I glorify the name of the Most High God and his infinite mercy." Abraham then turned to the commander-in-chief and said, "I beg you, archangel, heed my prayer, and intercede once more with the Lord and appeal to his mercy. Let us beg for his mercy for the souls of the sinners whom I, being ill tempered, once asked to be condemned and destroyed, those whom the earth swallowed up and the beasts ripped apart and the fire consumed as a result of my words. Now I realize that I have sinned before God. So, Michael, commander-in-chief of the higher powers, come, let us beseech God earnestly and with many tears to forgive my sin and pardon them."

Immediately the commander-in-chief heeded him and prayed to the Lord God. After they had prayed for a long time, a voice came from heaven and said, "Abraham, Abraham, the Lord has heard your prayer and forgiven your sin. Those whom you thought you had destroyed I have restored out of my great goodness and led them into eternal life. You had punished them with a temporary judgment, and those whom I punish on this earth while they are alive I do not requite in death."

(15) The voice of the Lord also said to the commander-in-chief, "Michael, Michael, my servant, return Abraham to his home, because his end is now near and the unforeseen measure of his life has come to an end. He should arrange for the disposition of his household affairs and anything else he wishes. So take him now and afterward bring him back to me."

So the commander-in-chief turned back his cloud and led the most holy Abraham to his home. Abraham went into his room and sat down on his couch. Sarah his wife came in and embraced the feet of Michael, the incorporeal one, and supplicated him, "I thank you, my lord, for you have brought my lord Abraham back to me. We thought he had been taken from us."

Isaac, his son, came and embraced him. Similarly all his servants gathered in a circle around him and embraced him, glorifying the holy God. The incorporeal one said to Abraham, "Listen, most righteous one, your wife Sarah and beloved son Isaac and all your servants are gathered around you. Make, therefore, whatever arrangements for your affairs that you wish, because the day has come in which you are to leave behind your body and go at once to the Lord."

Abraham asked, "Did the Lord say this or does it come from you?"

"What the Master commanded," said the commander-in-chief, "I have reported to you."

"I won't go with you," said Abraham.

When the commander-in-chief heard these words, he immediately left Abraham and went up to heaven and stood before the Most High God. "Lord Creator of all," he said, "I have heeded your friend Abraham in everything he has said to you and fulfilled all his requests. I have shown him your power and everything on earth and sea that is under heaven. I showed him judgment and retribution from a cloud and chariot. Yet he still says, 'I won't go with you.'"

The Most High God said to the commander-in-chief, "My friend Abraham still says 'I won't go with you'?"

"Yes, thus says your friend Abraham," said the archangel in the presence of the Lord and God, "and I have been reluctant to take him, for from the beginning he has been your friend and has done all the things that please you. There is not a person like him on earth, not even the wondrous Jacob, so I did not take him. Immortal King, tell me what it is I am to do."

(16) Then the Most High said, "Summon Death here to me, who is called the one of abominable visage and merciless demeanor."

So Michael went away and said to Death, "Come, the Master of Creation, the Immortal King calls you."

When Death heard this, he shuddered and trembled, gripped by a profound terror. With great fear he came and stood before the invisible God, shuddering, moaning, and trembling, and awaited the Master's command. The invisible God said to Death, "Come, you whose name is fierce and bitter to the world: hide your savage appearance, put away all of your bitterness; put on instead your youthful beauty and all your glory. Go down to my friend Abraham and bring him here to me. But take care: do not frighten his soul when you bring him here. Rather, convince him with soft words, for he is a true friend."

When Death had heard all this, he went out from the presence of the Most High and clothed himself with radiant garments and made his appearance as bright as the sun and became much more beautiful than any mortal being. Taking the form of an archangel, his face flashing with fire, he went to Abraham.

Righteous Abraham had left his room and was sitting under the trees of Mamre. He rested his chin on his hand as he awaited word from the commander-in-chief. Suddenly, the sweetest fragrance drifted toward Abraham, and a bright ray of light appeared. Abraham turned and saw Death approaching in his full glory and beauty, and thinking that he was the commander-in-chief, he rose to meet him. When Death saw him, he knelt and said, "Greetings, honored Abraham, righteous soul, friend of God Most High, companion of angels!"

Abraham said to Death, "Greetings, sun-like guardian of the law, most glorious and radiant wondrous man, from where has your glory arrived, and who are you?"

"Abraham, most righteous father," Death answered, "I shall tell you the truth. I am the bitter cup of Death."

"No!" said Abraham, "Why, you are the beauty of the world, you are the glory and majesty of the angels and of people, you are the most beautiful of all forms, and yet you say, 'I am the bitter cup of death.' Should you not rather say, 'I am the most beautiful of all good things'?"

"Father," said Death, "I am telling you the truth. The name that God has given me I am telling to you."

"Why have you come here?" asked Abraham.

"I have come here," said Death, "for your righteous soul."

"I understand what you are saying," said Abraham, "but I won't go with you." Death was silent and did not answer.

(17) Abraham arose and went into his house, and Death followed him inside. When Abraham went up to his room, Death went with him, and when Abraham lay down on his couch, Death came and stood at his feet. "Go away," said Abraham, "I want to rest on my couch."

Death responded, "I cannot leave you until I have taken your spirit from you."

Abraham said, "In the name of the immortal God, I say to you, tell me the truth! Are you Death?"

"I am the one who oppresses the world," said Death.

"I ask you," said Abraham, "since you are Death, tell me, do you come to all people in such a pleasing form, in such beauty and glory?"

"No, my lord," said Death, "your righteous deeds, boundless hospitality, and great love for God have placed a crown on my head. I come to the righteous in beauty, serenity, and with kind words, but to sinners I come in decay and corruption, with savagery, great bitterness and a ferocious presence. I come without mercy to sinners who have shown no mercy."

"I beg of you," said Abraham, "heed my request and show me all of your savagery and corruption."

"Most righteous man," Death responded, "you would never be able to behold my savagery."

"Oh yes," said Abraham, "I would be able to look on all your savagery, on account of the name of the living God, because the power of my God in heaven is with me."

So Death took off his youthful appearance, his beauty, his glory, and the sunlike form in which he had clothed himself, and put on instead the garment of oppression. He made his demeanor murky and forbidding, more savage than any wild beast, more foul than any unclean thing. He appeared to Abraham with seven heads of fiery serpents and fourteen faces. One of the faces, full of savagery, blazed more brightly than any fire, one face looked like a craggy precipice, one face was darker than the shadows, one face more terrifying than the viper, one face more ferocious than an asp, one face more fearsome than the lion, one face like a horned serpent or cobra. One face was like a fiery sword, another face wielded a saber, one face flashed like lightning and boomed like thunder. He had one face that foamed like an angry sea, another roiled like a wild river, another was like a terrifying three-headed dragon, and the last was like cups filled with poison. Indeed, he displayed for him all savagery and unbearable bitterness, and all deadly pestilences that bring an untimely death. Seven servants died from the odor of Death and from the great bitterness and ferocity.

Abraham fell into the listlessness of death, and his spirit left him. (18) When the most holy Abraham saw these things, he said to Death, "I beg of you, ruinous Death, hide your savagery and put on once more the beauty and form that you had before." Immediately Death hid his savagery and put on his beauty.

Abraham said to Death, "Why did you kill all my servants? Did God send you to do this?"

"No, my lord," answered Death, "that was not the reason I was sent. I was sent here on account of you."

"Then why have they died?" Abraham asked Death, "if the Lord did not command it?"

"Believe me," said Death, "it is astounding that you were not snatched away along with them. The truth is, if the righteous hand of the Lord were not with you at that moment, you too would have departed this life."

The righteous one said, "I can see now that I have fallen into the listlessness of death, and my spirit has left me. But I ask you, ruinous Death, since the servants have come to an untimely end, let us beg our Lord God to heed our request and bring back to life those who died prematurely as a result of your savage appearance."

"Amen. So be it," said Death.

So Abraham got up and fell with his face upon the ground praying, and Death prayed beside him. God sent the spirit of life on those who had died and brought them back to life. Then the righteous Abraham gave glory to God.

(19) Abraham returned to his room and lay down, while Death came and stood before him. Abraham said to him, "Leave me now. I want to rest, for my spirit is weak."

"I will not leave you alone," said Death, "until I have taken away your soul."

"Who gave you the order to say that?" asked Abraham, with anger in his face and a stern expression. "You have puffed yourself up and said these things on your own accord. I won't go with you until the commander-in-chief Michael comes, then I shall go with him. However, let me say this: if you would like me to go with you, explain to me all of your manifestations, the seven evil serpent-heads. What is the face that is a precipice? What is the sharpened sword? What is the great, turbulent river? What is the storm-tossed sea? Explain to me also the unendurable thunder and terrifying lightning. And what are the fetid cups filled with poison? Explain all these things to me."

"Listen, righteous one," said Death. "For seven ages I destroy the world, and bring everyone—kings and rulers, rich and poor, slave and free—down to Hades. For this reason I am manifested as seven serpent-heads. I showed to you the face of fire because many who are burned by fire die and see death as a fiery face. I showed you the face that is a precipice because many fall from a high tree or cliff and die, and they see death in the form of a high precipice. I showed you the face that is a sword, because many are killed in wars by the sword, and they see death as a sword. I showed you the face that is a great turbulent river because many are caught up in rushing waters and swept away by great streams and are drowned and die, seeing death before their time. I showed you the face that is the wild sea roiling with waves, because in shipwrecks many fall into the great stormy sea and are dragged down into the depths and see death as the sea. I showed you also the unendurable thunder and terrifying lightning because often when people encounter serpents and asps and snakes and cobras, coiled and ready to strike, and are attacked, there is the sound of unendurable thunder and the appearance of terrifying lightning, and they experience death in that manner. I showed you all sorts of wild beasts—venomous snakes such as asps and cobras, prides of lions and leopards, bears and snakes—all in all, I showed you the face of every wild beast, most righteous man, because many are killed by wild animals. Some are killed by serpents, others breathe their last and leave this world after being bitten by an asp, others expire and depart after being bitten by other kinds of venomous snakes. I also showed you the cups filled with dangerous poisons because many die an unforeseen death after drinking potions mixed by others."

(20) "I ask you," said Abraham "is there really such a thing as an unforeseen death? Tell me."

"Indeed, I say to you," said Death, "by the truth of God's word, that there are seventy-two kinds of death, but only one of these comes to the righteous person with a foreseen end. Many, in fact, meet death unexpectedly and are already in their tomb before an hour has passed. Now I have explained to you everything you wanted to know. So I ask you, what will it be? Put away every desire and come with me, for the God of all things has commanded me."

Abraham said to Death, "Leave me now for just a little longer. I want to rest on my couch. A heavy listlessness has come over me. From the moment I beheld you with my eyes, my strength has begun to fail. All of my limbs feel like lead, and my spirit is distressed. Leave me now for a while; I cannot bear to see your form."

The sweat ran down his face like drops of blood. Isaac, his son, came to him and fell upon his chest crying. Sarah, his wife, also came in and embraced Abraham's feet, lamenting loudly. All his servants came in, also crying and wailing. Abraham sank further into the listlessness of death.

Death said to him, "Come, kiss my right hand, and may you receive joy and life and power." But Death was deceiving Abraham, and when Abraham kissed his hand, immediately his soul clung to the hand of Death. At that moment Michael the archangel appeared with a host of angels, and they took their hands and lifted up his venerable soul in a divinely woven linen. For three days after his death they prepared the body of the righteous man with divine aromatic ointments, and they buried him in the promised land at the oak of Mamre. Angels bore his venerable soul up to heaven, singing "holy, holy, holy" to the sovereign God of the universe. They set him down kneeling before the God and Father. After many hymns and doxologies the pure voice of God the Father was heard, saying, "Take my friend Abraham to Paradise, where are found the tents of my righteous and the rooms of my holy ones Isaac and Jacob in his bosom.[2] There is no toil there, nor grief, nor moaning, but peace and joy and eternal life."

## SUGGESTIONS FOR FURTHER READING

Collins, John J. *Between Athens and Jerusalem: Jewish Identity in the Hellenistic Diaspora,* pp. 226–28. New York: Crossroad, 1983.

Nickelsburg, George W. E. *Jewish Literature Between the Bible and the Mishnah,* pp. 248–53. Philadelphia: Fortress, 1981.

———. ed. *Studies on the Testament of Abraham.* Missoula, Mont.: Scholars Press, 1976.

Wills, Lawrence M. *The Jewish Novel in the Ancient World,* pp. 245–56. Ithaca, N.Y.: Cornell University Press, 1995.

2. The use here of the traditional notion of Isaac and Jacob in the bosom of Abraham has created the anachronistic scenario in which this already appears to have been prepared for Abraham *before* he is in heaven.

# INDEX